The Poetic Archaeology of the Flesh

Second Edition

Alan E. Wittbecker

Books by Alan Wittbecker
[O]utopias Or [E]utopias
Topopoetics: The Science of Making Good Places
Global Emergency Actions
Eutopias: Making Good Places Ecologically & Culturally
RE: viewing turning thinking
Good Forestry from Good Theories & Good Practices
Redesigning the Planet
Redesigning Places & Regions in the Planet

The Poetic Archaeology of the Flesh

An Intertwining of Poetry & Philosophy
As an Approach to the Ecology of Being

Second Edition

Alan E. Wittbecker

Palm at the End of the Mind (Ink on paper, 1974)

Clio Press
Sarasota
2010

Published by Clio Press, M&RW Ltd.
    Post Office Box 370
    Tallevast, Florida 34270

For more information on sites and projects in the text:
    SynGeo ArchiGraph LLC: www.syngeo.org
    Ecoforestry Institute: www.ecoforestry.net
    G. P. Marsh Institute: www.gpmi.us
    Pan Ecology: www.panecology.net
    Rian Garcia Calusa: www.riangarciacalusa.com
    Eutopian Ecologists: www.eutopias.net

Library of Congress Cataloging in Publication Data
Alan Wittbecker 1946-
    Poetic Archaeology of the Flesh/Alan Wittbecker - 2nd ed.
        p. cm.
    Includes bibliographical references and index.
    ISBN 0-911385-33-9
    1. Phenomenology. 2. Metaphysics. 3. Poetry. 4. Ecology
    I. Title.
GF75.W5851 2010

Book Design by Rian Garcia Calusa

Printed in the United States of America
10 9 8 7 6 5 4 3 2 1

Acknowledgments

Very special thanks to Libra Press for offering to publish this work in 1975 and to MRW Ltd for publishing a limited edition in 1976. Special thanks to professors at Harvard, Berkeley and Oxford for reviewing the manuscript. And, thanks to professors at Yale, Berkeley and Northwestern for approving this manuscript as a thesis when no one else would (their names are not mentioned to protect their reputations). Finally, thanks to professors at Idaho, Oregon, and International College-LA, for accepting me as a degreeless graduate student in ecology, so I could study the interactions of living beings in systems and cycles, and for trusting me to finally finish a lengthy, complex course of study after thirty-six years.

Dedication
To Lena Jena Hagen, who encouraged me to finish this exercise in philosophy and phenomenology, but then quit her own academic candidacy in English Literature to pursue a career in book design (and then lured me in that direction as well). All of our retirement monies went into the Nieman-Ryan design business and three new computers. She handled the Humanities books and I designed mathematics and science books. When we worked together on some projects, she kept Ansel Adams and Horace Axtel, and gave me *MAD About the 60s* and *Country Roads of Maine*. She kept designing books in Boston for the rest of her short professional life, producing some beautiful books, including the first edition of this one. I will never forget you and never stop loving you.

Poetic Archaeology of the Flesh
Contents

0.0. Preliminary Words

0.1. *Limits of Words: Abstract*

This work is an investigation into the possibility of describing the ground of existence, Being. In the first section the Question of Being is addressed historically, beginning with Aristotle, who defined the problem, but who was unable to solve the ambiguity of Being-as-universal, or of Being-as-individual, by using a critical method of analysis. Whereas for Aristotle, and later others, the basic category of metaphysics was substance, Maurice Merleau-Ponty began existentially with the human body. Although for Merleau-Ponty Being precedes and exceeds the body, perception is a direct access to Being. Perception is the primary activity of the body in the world. This allows psychological and ecological connections to be made.

Expression is embodied in perception, as perception is in the body, and as the body is in the world. Language, the verbal expression of possibilities derived from experience, transforms Being into something positive through the creation of ideal symbols. Language can make Being visible in an ideal system, but it is inadequate to a complete presentation of Being. Art and other expressions also seem to be inadequate avenues to Being, owing to the fundamental ambiguity of limited perspectives. Philosophy interrogates Being through an operative, reflexive language, but fails to capture the immediacy of Being in its defined significations.

Merleau-Ponty proposed a creative language for metaphysics, where poetry is necessary to awaken the power of expression, to transcend things already said and to present the whole of Being. This work offers a phenomenological interpretation of poetry and the mechanics of metaphor, based on the radical philosophy of Merleau-Ponty. Some of the works of philosophers who wrote in poetic form are examined for insights into a metaphorical metaphysics.

As philosophy and poetry intertwine, it is concluded that both are needed to attempt to grasp Being. Poetry requires the hyper-reflective awareness of philosophy, and philosophy must use the lateral approach of poetry; poetic philosophy, a speaking that carries beyond the physical world, is suggested as the most adequate expression for metaphysics.

0.2. *Limits of Prosaic Spirals*

This work was originally written in poetic form, as its subject demanded. A second attempt presented the questioning in *lebensforms* (in the manner of Wittgenstein). The present form of the work, limited by academic requirements, is a more prosaic effort to describe the poetry of the world. Even so, it is not a linear path leading to a definite conclusion. As a dialectical spiral, it requires the creative effort of the reader to be put together. If it asks more questions than it answers, it is for the purpose of stimulating even more questions. If it is obscure, it may be so because its subject is or because its expression is. If it diverges too much from the area of traditional philosophy, it is because it is, as Whitehead expected his philosophy to be, an adventure of ideas. If the metaphors stretch too far to hold, perhaps they are, as Wittgenstein wrote of his propositions, all nonsense, to be read and left behind.

0.3. *Limits of Philosophy*

The philosopher is confronted with the whole universe, that is, everything, but she cannot stand before it like an engineer before a circuit, nor even state it circumspectly like a sociologist about a social group; she is limited to making a vague gesture—towards everything there is—and realizing that most of it by necessity is unknown. The philosopher really cannot know what the entire object of her study is; because it is whole, it is that which cannot be given as an object, and because it is not given, it is a questioning whose answers are perennially sought. For this reason, philosophical knowledge is never complete. Instead the quest for a philosophy is the natural attempt to attain a complete perspective, to fill in the constellations on a cloudy night, or map lands beyond a horizon; scientific knowledge is exact, but incomplete—of necessity it is embedded in a complete and ultimate something, which is always somewhat unreachable, and tempting in its remoteness. Philosophy is then a hungry questioning after the attitude of the universe and the meaning of life: Stars are the thoughts of night, as Heinrich Heine wrote, restless and golden; philosophy is an expression of wonder at them, as well as an attempt to read them.

Perhaps the outcome of this wondering—metaphysical thought—is not a kind of knowledge at all, but a kind of understanding; perhaps there are answers to the questions asked, but they cannot be proved. Since there are often several answers to the same question, and no single one can be proved, perhaps more than one are correct, or useful. Socrates may have been right, recognizing that philosophy is just an attitude in the face of ignorance; he was wiser, in knowing what he did not know, than others, who knew their beliefs were truer than mere evidence. Socratic understanding results from seeing reasons for doubting philosophical theories.

Metaphysical problems are inseparable from the questioner, whose very asking is one of the givens of the world, and an indemonstrable axiom. The first problems, indeed, are usually associated with mind and body: 'What am I?' 'Am I identical with my mind or my body?' That the questioner exists is often a tacit assumption. In the *Physics*, Aristotle said that to seek proof of matters, for which we already possess clearer evidence than any proof can afford, is to confuse the better with the worse. Merleau-Ponty connects it with human limitation (MJ93): "Metaphysics begins from the moment when, ceasing to live in the evidence of the object—whether it is the sensory object or the object of science—we apperceive the radical subjectivity of all our experience as inseparable from its truth value. It means two things to say that our experience is our own: both that it is not the measure of all imaginable being in itself and that it is nonetheless co-extensive with all being of which we can form a notion."

Thus, metaphysical data are elementary evidencings: The questioning being exists, has a body, carries the past within, deliberates the future, and changes over time. When these data conflict with beliefs, a problem is formed to which a metaphysical theory must respond with a solution. To be wise, a philosopher must suspend judgment of the final truth of things; theories are to be held loosely, in spite of valid proofs or contradictions. Being may be pure actuality, or the mind may be independent of the body. What is the final basis of philosophical knowledge? How is it reached? Is it reachable? The philosopher cannot know for sure. Philosophy is therefore something questionable, as well as a questioning. The phenomenologist, Edmund Husserl, asked whether philosophy ever ceases to be an enigma to an autonomous thinker. Phenomenology itself seeks to be both pre-scientific and pre-metaphysical. The spirit of this inquiry is phenomenological, based in a large part on the insights of Maurice Merleau-Ponty.

In considering philosophy, Merleau-Ponty says that there are no principal problems, they are all concentric—what is first for us is not necessarily what is first as such. Philosophy must move, therefore, from that which is first for us to that which is first as such, and even then it must be resigned to being limited to that first in itself that is already present in what is first to us. How does that philosophy reach the very beginnings, which determine it, since for instance a farmer cannot see that part of the field on which he is standing? All philosophies circle about the beginnings; some attempt to reach and comprehend them, but have difficulties, due to the unrelatedness of their beautiful order, as in Baruch Spinoza, or to their apparent disorder, as in Friedrich Nietzsche. This effort explores some of the problems inherent in reaching this first as such, and offers a possible solution. The first part of the work is a short historical introduction to the problem, examining Aristotle's proposals, and tracing the appearance of Being in certain other philosophers; generally, Aristotle will be used to introduce sections of the work, since he once categorized everything, and then a phenomenological treatment will be offered, usually supported by the insights of Merleau-Ponty.

Merleau-Ponty's philosophy is a radical phenomenology; the beginning is initially presented in order to commence and sustain thought in a circular fashion toward itself; this circling then moves in a spiral turning toward the beginnings of philosophy and finally the ultimate beginnings. This same general theme is somewhat duplicated in Merleau-Ponty's writings: in his first work, *The Structure of Behavior*, he described the perceptual meaning of behavior. In his most widely read book, *The Phenomenology of Perception*, he discussed perception as meaningful behavior, and introduced the world toward which perceptual behavior opens. Since that world onto which perception opens is created through expression, his middle works (i.e., *Sense and Nonsense*) are concerned with expression. Later, he examines the categories in which we express the world we feel, as a function of human activities in the history of the visible world (i.e., *Adventures in the Dialectic*). Finally, in the last writings (i.e., *The Visible and the Invisible*), he begins to search for the basis of the dimensions of expression—that which makes sense of the world. This founding dimension of human beings in the world upon which all experience and intelligibility depend is flesh—also referred to as Being, or being-as-being. Flesh is a technical term coined by Merleau-Ponty to emphasize that everything, ideas and bodies, is incarnate in Being.

It might be argued that there is a discontinuity between Merleau-Ponty's early and later thought, but the essential unity of it is assumed—it has been well defended elsewhere. While Merleau-Ponty sometimes criticizes some former opinions, in general, the conclusions of one book become the starting point for the next book. His later work tries to rehabilitate ontologically the sensible which was explicated earlier; his intent is to restore the world as a meaning of Being—to present wild Being as the primordial meaning of Being. This wild Being that can never be exhausted, or even posited, is the perceptual world, the same which was excavated from beneath the objective world of science in *The Phenomenology of Perception*. Philosophy attempts to uncover the latent intelligibility in the sensible world by taking it up in expression and forming it into ideas. Paradoxically, philosophical thought enters existence through expression; as philosophy interrogates language and thought, it finds that it is interrogating itself. Philosophy is then a descriptive disclosure of the strangeness of the world through the detours of language, hence itself—its task is to show the invisible, to unconceal it. It may be that it needs to use scientific data and technological design, as well as poetic expression and artistic form, to complete its task.

Should philosophy consider the science of beings? Everything moves and has form. Everything is related, closely or distantly, to all other things. Perhaps things might be better studied with an ecological science, something that gives credence to relationships and patterns. In a more limited perspective, many things and parts of things are invisible.

How is the invisible to be made visible? If it can be made visible, what kind of expression is necessary? Merleau-Ponty called his ontology indirect, and prescribed a creative language for its fulfillment, but he encountered such difficulty with his theory of expression that he put aside large tracts of his middle period (later published posthumously). Martin Heidegger has written that to recognize the ontological difference between Being and beings is to think poetically—and to forget it is to be condemned to metaphysics—but he wrote conceptually and directly to the issue, and had to admit failure in his excavation. Others from the pre-Socratics to Santayana have used poetry with varying degrees of success.

This effort examines the struggles of some philosophies that either recognized the need for, or intended to use, poetry to reach Being. In later chapters it also argues the advantages of poetry over prose, and works out some of the mechanics of metaphor. It explores the reasons why poetry must be used in the discussion of Being, and it uses the philosophy of Merleau-Ponty as the basis for explanation. However, this work is not a systematic exegesis of his philosophy, nor is it a systematic attempt to form a coherent theory from it. Merleau-Ponty did not even offer a system, claiming that metaphysics is the opposite of a system. Whether a system is even possible is questionable, since it might be antithetical to the subject: Being as invisible, or as the realm of possibility. Nor is Merleau-Ponty praised or criticized here; he is used as a basis for moving thought, which reaches different areas, sometimes short of, sometimes beyond, his. This work also intertwines poetic forms, to be adequate for the subject. If statements seem to be repeated, or discussion moves in circles, the intention was to create an ontological spiral. As Merleau-Ponty defines Being, it must be reached indirectly to be redefined; the passage to the foundation of the world is a spiral. It is an allusive expression, a texture of thought woven from the dense fibers of the body and the light tendrils of the mind, both of which are embodied in the flesh of the world. The study of Being is a poetic archaeology of the flesh.

Figure 03-1. Aphrodite Astra (Collage on glass, 1992)

1.0. The Primacy of Perception

Question and Answer
That which is, being the only answer
The question is its measure. Ask the flower
And the question unfolds in eloquent petals about the centre;
Ask fire, and the rose bursts into flame and terror.
Ask water, and the streams flow and dew falls;
Shell's minute spiral wisdom forms in pools.
Earth answers fields and gardens and the grave; birds rise
Into the singing air that opens boundless skies.
Womb knows the eternal union and its child,
Heart and blood-sacrifice of the wounded god.
Death charts the terrible negative infinity,
And with the sun rises perpetual day.
                                        Kathleen Raine (UN 484)

1.1. A Short History of the Question of Being

Human beings questioned what was important in the things that
surrounded them. They wondered what was real and what was not,
what was important to know and what was not. They made connections
between phenomena and taught others to recognize them. They
incorporated their beliefs and behaviors into unique cultures.

1.1.1. First Wonder

Aristotle states that it was because of wonder that human beings began
to philosophize, and still continue to do so. At first they wondered
at the difficulties close at hand, and then advancing slowly, discussed
the difficulties about greater matters, for example, about the changing
attributes of the sun, moon and stars. Aristotle (982b) considers: "Now
a man who is perplexed and wonders considers himself ignorant . . . so
if indeed they philosophized in order to avoid ignorance, it is evident
that they pursued science in order to understand and not in order to use
it for something else." When all the necessities of life were supplied, for
comfort and activity, such thinking then began to be freely sought, for
its own sake, and not any other need. To know things for their own sake
belongs in the highest degree to the science of that which is known in
the highest degree; and that which is knowable in the highest degree,
for him, is that which is first, or the first cause, for it is because of this
and from this that other things are known.

In examining the natural world, Aristotle concluded that every individual thing had two aspects, matter and form. Unlike the Platonic paradox of participation, where, in Aristotle's opinion, the parts are separate from the whole, as man is two-footed and an animal, Aristotle's own conception was that a perceptible substance is at the same time form and matter. What the parts, legs and arms, are potentially, the whole, man, is actually, but one without the other is an abstraction.

A student of particular kinds of things endeavors to find the principles which these things share, or which operate in common substances, or in the actions of substances; such a set of principles constitutes a science. There are practical sciences, e.g., ethics and economics, then productive sciences, e.g., poetry and pottery, and finally theoretical sciences, e.g., mathematics and physics. These principles may be related in certain ways, and some of them may operate in all the particular sciences. The theoretical system that examines the principles of the other sciences is known as philosophy.

Philosophy is concerned with questioning all things, and what underlies them; it asks about the what-is, or the whatness, of a thing or a being. It asks what is the essence of a being. The genus that philosophy considers is being as being.

In the *Metaphysics* Aristotle introduces his students to the work of his predecessors and critically examines the attempts to solve the problem of Being. In considering the question of Being, most of the pre-Socratics assigned to it an essential constitution (*physis*): fire, water, or seeds, for instance. Aristotle then asked if Being was a substance (*ousia*) and approached the problem empirically and systematically *Metaphysics* (1028b 2-8): "And indeed the inquiry and perplexity concerning what Being is, in early times and now and always, is just this: What is a substance? For it is this that some assert to be one, others more than one, and some say that it is finite, while others that it is infinite. And so we too, must speculate most of all, and first of all, and exclusively, so to say, concerning being which is spoken of in the sense. What is Being?"

In one book of the *Metaphysics* (Beta), or the book of knots, he lists the obstacles that a student of the first philosophy must overcome. The most critical of these obstacles is how a science that seems to lack a unified subject-matter can have a unity. Despite the many possibilities, he proposes a subject-matter underlying them all. The Being of a being is articulated in many ways, and is expressible in many ways: According to the category of quantity, and its magnitude; or according to the category of quality, in its heaviness. But, all these ways to be are permeated by a common relationship, one certain nature (*physis*) that determines and unifies them all. This occurs in much the same way as health complexion, or medicine, or exercise in all its modes.

It is the task of philosophy also to investigate the principles of demonstration, since these are the principles of all beings, the most certain of which is the 'principle of contradiction.' The same thing cannot at the same time both belong and not belong to the same object and in the same respect. Aristotle says specifically in *Metaphysics* (1061a 10-15): "And since everything that is may be referred to as something single and common, each of the contrarieties also may be referred to the first differences and contrarieties of being, whether the first differences of being are plurality and unity, or likeness and unlikeness, or some other differences." The contrarieties must be studied only as they deny a part of a definition, not the whole; the same subject matter must be kept to insure the scientific character of the method. In the case of Being, its contrarieties may be studied, but not non-Being as such.

Aristotle offers four meanings of Being: As accidental, as the true, as in the categories, and as actual and potential. The first of these, chance togetherness, is not an object of knowledge; when a pale woman is musical, the philosopher need not concern himself with saying that the music is pale. Since truth belongs to propositions, and not things, Being as truth is secondary. He treats the remaining two definitions as primary; to treat Being as in the categories is to treat it as substance, the concrete entities that comprise the world; in fact, everything in the world is either a substance or a modification of a substance. But what is a substance (*ousia*)? Is it sensible and perishable, or everlasting and unchangeable?

Aristotle works through the attributes of entities, which are dependent on them, to the substances of things—hoping to find in the primary instance of substance, the primary instance of Being. From all the components in all the possible classes he narrows the choice to four: The substratum (similar to matter), the universal, genus and essence (of which essence—*eidos*—has the best claim: it is separable and individual, as embodied in matter), and the actual and potential. To seek the definition of substance is to seek the essence. It is through the perception of the essence of the individual that one comes to know the individual. The mind takes the form, not the matter of the individual.

The fourth definition of Being is as actual and potential. Perceptible substance is potential and actual at the same time, and potential substance contains all that actual substances does—essence is equally in both. A potential sphere is all that an actual sphere is, since form pre-exists in the potential, for Aristotle, requiring only an efficient cause to turn it into actual.

But how can an actual thing and a potential thing be one?

Aristotle considers, and rejects, the Platonic notion of participation and communion; the truth is simply that they are one. Perceptible beings are each one, having matter and form. But there is a concept that has not matter—the one—and this is a unity by itself, the cause of individual things, inherent in all essences without further cause; it is never stated in definitions, but always implicit. Following his survey of Being in its fundamental senses, Aristotle reveals its primary instance, when both substantial independent existence and pure form, free of all matter, are to be found, is the unmoved mover. Ultimate matter is fully determined—it is the same as form.

The object of the first philosophy does not lie present to hand, like insects or trees. The philosopher must seek Being by abstraction; as the mathematician abstracts quantity from the other characteristics of a substance, the philosopher deals with things as Being. Being as being, the subject matter of philosophy, is reached in this way.

Every special science has its special subject matter, or genus; mathematics considers quantity and physics studies natures. What is the genus of philosophy, according to Aristotle? The first philosophy is the highest of the three theoretical sciences; it is the science dealing with the highest genus: the unmoved mover of all moving things, that is, God. The first science deals with a thing that exists separately, is immovable and eternal. First philosophy deals with one kind of being, as Aristotle qualifies (1026a 28-32): "but if there is an immovable substance, the science of this must be prior and must be first philosophy, and universal in this way, because it is first. And it will belong to this to consider being qua being-both what it is and the attributes which belong to it qua being."

But elsewhere in the *Metaphysics*, Aristotle states that first philosophy has no genus, that it deals with a difficult and only indirectly accessible subject, being as being. Here it is not concerned with any one being, even the most perfect, but with the Being of all beings. And even though being is not a genus, there can be a science of being as being. He states (1061b 11-15): "Since all that is is said to 'be' in virtue of something single and common, though the term has many meanings, and contraries and in the same case (for they are referred to the first contrarieties and differences of being), and things of this sort can fall under one science, the difficulty we stated at the beginning appears to be solved."

Are these two treatments irreconcilable? Or is the unmoved mover being as being, and the Being of all beings? Is it contradictory, that being is actuality and the source of potentiality, or that it is an individual and universal? Can Being as being, as a whole contain the contradiction of individual-universal?

Like the *Physics*, or the *Soul*, the *Metaphysics* begins with a dialectical treatment of the subject; in examining the philosophies of his predecessors, Aristotle systematically discards all the poetical and mythical elements; he logically constructs his own philosophy from their beginnings. His dialectical path leads to the first principle, the unmoved mover as pure separate form.

There is an intrinsic difficulty with his concept of Being as being, however: Is it a genus, or a single thing? Aristotle said that one must not expect a greater clarity of a thing than it is capable of giving. Philosophy, the theoretical science, abstracts being as being from the beings of the world, but can it do so empirically? Aristotle saw Being as something simple and common, comparing it with health, but how simple is it to define health? Does every person who is healthy have the same temperature, blood pressure, skin color, or other indicators of health? The *Metaphysics* was constructed on the assumption that Being would yield to a method of investigation; for Aristotle, each science should use a method appropriate to its subject, but what method was proper for Being: a critical approach, or poetic approach. Perhaps the poetry of his predecessors was more adequate for completing a metaphysics than his logic.

1.1.2. Second Thoughts

In his system, Aristotle tried to explain why other systems, that had been developed in Turkey and Persia, were wrong and needed to be thought out better. After Aristotle's devastating influences, philosophers rarely used poetry in their works on metaphysics; where it was done, it was almost always treated as literature and not philosophy. Beginning with Rene Descartes, modern philosophers treated mind as a substance. For Descartes there were two substances, mind and body, forming a fundamental duality. In his quest for absolute certainty in philosophy, he first established that he, a thinking thing, existed; he then proved the existence of physical objects. Descartes was a rationalist, methodologically, and in this he was followed by most of the Continental philosophers. The British philosophers, beginning as Descartes did with the mind, but imbued with the new science, developed an empirical tradition. They treated consciousness empirically, as an objective phenomenon; Hume even confined philosophy to the making of empirical statements.

Immanuel Kant attempted to reconcile the two offspring of Descartes' dualism—rationalism and empiricism—into a new synthesis, where he contended, with his own rationalist methodology, that the mind supplied certainty by organizing phenomena in the same way. The source of all phenomena, however, that which Kant termed the 'thing-in-itself,' was unknowable completely; it was the condition for the possibility of experience.

G. W. F. Hegel contended that anything unknowable was useless to philosophy. He avoided the problem of postulating an unknowable thing-in-itself by collapsing Cartesian dualism into a sole reality of the mind. Individual consciousness was merely a stage in the self-awareness of absolute mind (whose process of development he named phenomenology). Hegel's system claimed totality and absoluteness, but reduced the individual to an instrument of the absolute mind.

According to Soren Kierkegaard, that was the greatest fault of the system, to leave out the most important consideration of philosophy, man, which he made the central concern of his philosophy. Following Kierkegaard, the existentialists corrected the exaggerated emphasis on abstract reason, with a recognition of the importance of the body as a dimension of existence.

Reflecting on the historical problems of philosophy from a different bias, Edmund Husserl observed that the task of his phenomenology was to develop the ambitions of old Greek philosophy, to search for wisdom and try to understand man's place in the universe, and to fulfill Descartes' hope of finding a certain basis for philosophy. Husserl's phenomenology shifted the question of the reality of the world, as asked by most philosophers from Plato on, to a question of its meaning. Since the knower is a part of the world, and the known is required for there to be knowledge, the knower and the known are unified in the world. Consciousness is intentional, it is always of something; furthermore, it is not a thing, but a process that correlates with the essence of the world.

Instead of doubting the world, as Descartes had done, Husserl suspended judgment of it, in order to reach toward its unprejudiced essence. The thing-in-itself of Kant is the phenomenon that gives itself to consciousness, for Husserl (the essence of an object is not reducible to any subjective process). Where Kant's individual constituted the world, Husserl's individual was in a reciprocal relationship: Consciousness has no meaning apart from the world; in fact, the world was actually a lived-world, which by his method, was to be described by a detached observer.

1.1.3. Taking Up Wonder

If Aristotle's assumptions prevented him from arriving at a complete and consistent position, perhaps an approach using insights gleaned from the phenomenologists would afford a more complete one.

Heidegger and Merleau-Ponty, in their later writings, attempted to speculate in a poetic manner, after finding the prose of their own earlier works inadequate.

With Heidegger, the themes of existentialism were considered with Husserl's phenomenological method. Husserl had wanted a fresh beginning, but Heidegger insisted that since philosophy depended on language and language was historically shaped, philosophy had to be considered in context. He then addressed himself to the question of Being in philosophy. Being should be the most obvious of questions; in language, the word 'being' permeates most ways of speaking: To say that something *is*, says that it *is* in a certain way. Thus, there is a difference between a thing and its Being. This difference is not noticeable if Being is treated as just another being with describable characteristics. In fact, Heidegger charges that, since Plato, Western philosophy has understood Being only as an entity among entities; he contended that all previous systems treated reality as an object.

This arose in such a way, according to Heidegger: For the Pre-Socratics, Being was *physis*, hidden, but it could be disclosed by language (see excerpt from 'The Others'); language (*logos*, as a gathering) disclosed things and became their custodian; *logos* as gathering is the unconcealing of things. But language itself has the capacity to create an ideal world, separate and perfect. In Plato, Being becomes *eidos*— ideas—while Being itself becomes what is not—copies of the ideal forms; the idea of Being becomes more real than Being itself. The tension between Being as a particular, and Being as a general whatness, in Aristotle, perhaps may be explained by the changing concept of truth that accompanied the change in the concept of Being; previously, according to Heidegger, truth was the unconcealment (*alethia*) of Being, but in Plato and Aristotle it becomes a property of thought, correctness (*logos* as statement becomes the abode of truth). As Being became an entity, it was no longer the source of truth. Caratheodory expresses it:

The caves are home. In filtered light
We polish the walls lustrous . . .
Ordained in the wombs of our mothers
To sow doubt in the entrails of the earth.
We meditate in the depths and sleep
In the [narcotic] knowledge of rock. Mysteries
Leak into dreams inverted in negative infinity.

We press the limits of darkness down
To the limits of our illusions, insert
Ourselves in crevices of being—[matter's]
Center and the heart's, invisible.

We burrow in the [solidity] of rock
And build temples to feeling.

You taught us that the activity of art
Had the power to release us,
But art has its roots in darkness
And though its surface is displayed
For all, it seeks to intertwine things
With invisibility that we may see them.
We must play with shadows and live between
Perfect light and darkness, a double life.
This is the true song of the dialectic
Weaving voices into silence and twining
All things opposite around an empty center.
    From 'The Others' Caratheodory (CC 17)

    In correcting this misdirection, Heidegger states that Being belongs to all entities and yet is different from them. This difference manifests itself in the existence of human beings, a special situatedness (being-there, or *Dasein*) in the world that goes out towards Being and is an openness in which entities are revealed in 'light' of their Being. Through the broad principles of understanding espoused by phenomenology, reality is held to be as it is experienced, thus avoiding the Kantian dilemma where the subject know only appearances and treats the nature of reality as a mystery where traditional metaphysics is impossible. Heidegger even contended that Being could be directly reached by the *Dasein*; but after regarding his own attempts as a failure, he admitted that perhaps "Being is not yet ready to reveal itself."

    Like Heidegger, Merleau-Ponty held that Being can be investigated only through experience, but further qualified that it can be done only indirectly, through the perception of beings. Although each perceptible object is understood through its basic significance to the observer, it is bound in a matrix of significances, for that observer and others. Merleau-Ponty holds that existence in general is filled with dimensions of meaning. Due to the openness of the matrix, perceived beings are inexhaustible in their significance; since any complete investigation is impossible, Being is considered savage, unreachable to any great extent.

    For Merleau-Ponty, philosophy begins in wonder and ends in the expression of wonder. Conception is no longer primary for a philosopher, but perception is primary. The nature of Being becomes a function of the human way of perceiving it, from a limited perspective. In the existentialism of Kierkegaard, the person became the concern of philosophy. In the phenomenology of Maurice Merleau-Ponty, the body became the basis of metaphysics; it is an access to Being, as well as is expression. Philosophy is tied to a comprehensive anthropology—everything that is perceived and expressed becomes anthropocentric and anthropomorphic. The body is the primary unit; it is embodied in the world, which is in Being. Philosophy and poetry then are embodied in language, which is in perception, which is in the body. It is assumed, therefore, that if it is said that language speaks, or Being thinks, it is through the body, through the beings in the world. Due to its individuality and uniqueness, however, the body is ambiguous; it is only one perspective among many possible ones.

Coming long after Aristotle, how have Merleau-Ponty's insights redefined the nature of Being? Approaching Being through the body, he is more concerned with its meaning than the particular whatness of it. Much of Being is considered savage and invisible—never to become cultured or visible; every time a thing turns the visible becomes the invisible, perspectives change. The fundamental philosophical dichotomy of subject and object, mind and matter has been reduced to a divergence in Being itself. Being contains contradictions in its unity; like potentiality, non-being is a part of Being. These oppositions are all reversible: matter becomes mind, object becomes subject, and invisible becomes visible. Being itself, if it is more than a new philosophical other, is always a motion, always shifting. How can anything composed partly of invisibility and silence, anything that is the whole, the sound of everything else, be spoken of at all? If it is so conceived, how is it spoken? Nevertheless, human beings attempt the expression of it through music, language, painting, and other systematic devices. These expressions are the only access one has into the invisible and silent nature of Being. But they must always be inadequate and limited. Must they not?

If Being could be put into words, it would be that same Being as conceived and defined. Language is derived from the perceived world; it delineates and idealizes perspectives from that lived world. Language names things, but is inadequate to describe anything completely. Speaking uses the language in an active way that gives an access to things; sometimes a name allows things to appear. Language can be reflexive and takes itself into consideration, however. Although perception determines language, language also influences perception; it is therefore difficult to examine the basis of language by using perception. Philosophy is dependent on language.

Philosophy can become a language aware of itself; but philosophy must always learn to speak Being anew, as Being changes or renews itself. The figurations of philosophy and literature are no more settled than the expressions of painting and music—really not much more adequate to describe Being. So why do we interrogate Being if we cannot know it? Language seems capable of only revealing the nature of itself. In attempting to investigate Being through language, the mind finds out more about itself and its method of investigating than any remote Being. Or perhaps the mind makes Being behave, the way a physicist makes nature behave. But, if Being is in everything, it must be in us—then that is how we know it, by knowing ourselves. And then, we are how it knows itself. But this is circular, as Merleau-Ponty realized (MH 190): "Is this the highest point of reason, to realize that the soil beneath our feet is shifting, to pompously name 'interrogation' what is only a persistent state of stupor, to call 'research' or 'quest' what is only trudging in a circle, to call 'Being' that which never full is?"

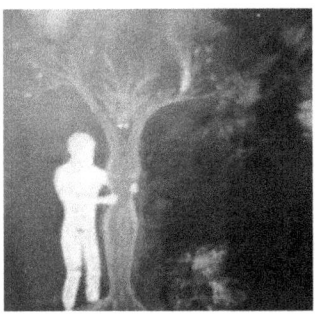

Figure 113-1. Laurel Reverting (Acryllic on masonite, 1977)

1.2. *Beings*

> ... Someone is moving
> On the horizon and lifting himself above it.
> A form of fire approaches the cretonnes of Penelope,
> Whose mere savage presence awakens the world in which she dwells.
>   Wallace Stevens (ST 520)

1.2.1. *The Body Exists*

The access to Being is through the beings in the world, and the access to these beings is through the Being of the inquiring subject. The subject is a body and the body is a knot, a complicated integrity that processes materials from its surroundings in order to maintain itself. As a rope makes the knot visible, so the body is a pattern made visible. The body is a movement that maintains a topologically stable pattern; it is a vortex but not the water. The thing, the pattern, is a perceived cross section cut through the movement. The animation of the body does not arise merely from an assemblage or juxtaposition of its parts. As Merleau-Ponty relates (MH 163), "There is a body when, between the seeing and the seen, between touching and the touched, between one eye and the other, between hand and hand, a blending of some sort takes place—when the spark is lit between sensing and sensible ..."

The body is a dialectic between a living thing and its environment—the interacting mass of cells and nonliving nutrients, or the social subject and his group; each of these degrees is a soul to the preceding and a body to the successor. In feeling things, the body takes them unto itself as experience, and remembers; no behavior can be omitted from consideration as experience: Drunk or sober, sleeping or waking, conscious or forgetful, or happy or grieving. Experience anticipates philosophy, and philosophy is merely an elucidated experience, according to Merleau-Ponty. The body is the ensemble of paths already traced and of powers already constituted. The body is the soil upon which a higher formation is accomplished, and the soul is the meaning that is established.

By its very posture, notes Merleau-Ponty, the body has a greater access to Being. Standing upright emancipates one from the more immediate senses and holds the world at a distance; it transforms seeing into beholding; and the eyes, dwelling on the things themselves, create a human world. Paradoxically, this distancing increases the risk of alienation from the world. Vision occurs in a body; vision and movement go together, in a body that is their locus. Sight is made possible by movement; the eyes are always moving and scanning, and movement is informed by sight. In fact, the body is an intertwining of vision and movement, in which reversibility and reflexivity are built up. More than just seeing, it sees itself seeing, and it not only touches, but it touches itself touching. The body is a self, but it is caught up in things. It is a thing in the world, visible and mobile, but since it moves itself and sees, it holds the things of the world around itself. By moving, the body is capable of expression; arms and legs allow the body to explore its possibilities, to change perspectives. Other movements go nowhere: Facial, gestural, or actions of the throat and mouth. The body makes sounds that it can hear; it is sonorous, like a crystal or metal.

The vocal cords permit human thought to sing; their resonance opens human being to Being. According to Merleau-Ponty the body is a system of systems (MK 67): "We must therefore recognize that what is designated by the terms 'glance,' 'hand,' and in general 'body' is a system of systems devoted to the inspection of a world and capable of leaping over distances, piercing the perceptual future, and outlining hollows and reliefs, distances and deviations—a meaning—in the unconceivable flatness of being ... Already in its pointing gestures the body not only flows over into a world whose schema it bears in itself but possesses this world at a distance rather than by being possessed by it. So much the more does the gesture of expression, which undertakes through expression to delineate what it intends and make it appear 'outside,' retrieve the world."

1.2.2. Its Things

In both the body and things there is a doubling up into an inside and an outside; the flesh of the body is not matter, it is rather a self sensing, a locus of crossing, a chiasm, a seeing which is visible and a touching which is tangible. Merleau-Ponty states that (MN 146): "It is the coiling over of the visible upon the seeing body, of the tangible upon the touching body, which is attested in particular when the body sees itself, touches itself seeing and touching the things."

The flesh of things refers to their depth and store of invisibility beneath their visibility; this flesh of the world is equal to its interior and exterior horizon surrounding the thin pellicle of the strict visible between the two horizons.

Because of their depth, things have flesh, which opposes inspection, and a resistance, which more precisely defines their reality. The carnal being is a being of depths, with several leaves or faces; it is a being in latency, and a presentation of a certain absence. Things are linked together with other things in the flesh of the world. The world is not a multiplicity of atoms bound to a transverse dimension of essences; it is a series of levels of being, a whole architecture of complex phenomena. The idea of separate individuals is encrusted in the joints of the whole; they are derived from the dimension and generality of the body. Wordsworth wrote, in *Excursion*:

"All beings have their properties which spread
Beyond themselves, a power by which they make
Some other Being conscious of their life."

The body forms a system with other bodies, and maintains the world inwardly; it is in the world as the heart and lungs are in an organism, breathing life into it. It is caught in the fabric of the world, and its cohesion is that of a thing. Things are an annex of the body; encrusted in its flesh, they are part of its full definition—the body is made up of the same stuff as the world. Vision is caught in things; the sense and the sensed are undivided. Since the body is of the same stuff as that which is seen, sight is a response to something in them. The manifest visibility of things must be repeated in the body by a secret visibility; there is an eternal equivalent of things in body. There is a system of exchanges between the body and the world, and the body and itself, and this system depends on the power of resemblance. Things awaken an echo in the body; this carnal formula of their presence allows perception.

1.2.3. Its Perceives

The body is not a transparent object, or a constitutional presentation; it is an expressive unity which can be known only through its active expression, and it is the same structure that will be passed on to the sensible world. Merleau-Ponty holds that (MG 206): "The theory of the body image is, implicitly, a theory of perception." The body is visible, but the proper essence of the visible is to have a layer of invisibility, which it makes present as a certain absence. The invisible is a framework which lets the visible be seen. While invisibility is the essence of a thing, and visibility is a fact, both are abstractions from perception. Perception takes place through the body; the body and the objects constitute a field, but since the body is in a field, perception is always ambiguous. Perception begins with a sedimentation from the past (the world is already patterned), and opens toward a world which is also in the act of being structured. The body and the world are contingent (and this allows their synthesis), and so have openness and temporal thickness.

According to Piaget, perception begins at birth with the child's awareness of the nearness of objects; and the earliest modes of perception are topological. Development of spatial awareness appears long before the child can grasp the geometric form of an object, or especially before he can intellectually organize the parts of an object. Other geometries, although culturally abstracted first, develop out of topology as their theoretical basis. Topology is a description of the mechanism of the most primitive experience of spatial orientation. For Piaget, topology is a mathematical description of experience in the lived-in-world; it is the most elementary logic; the child's view is constructed inversely to the development of mathematics.

Perception is participation, the organic relationship between the center of the self and the circle of appearances. As perception becomes a focus on objects in the field it ignores the field; its distraction leads to alienation from Being; such a perception becomes a diacritical and oppositional system. This cultural perception is usually ignorant of the Being that underlies the opposition of things. Merleau-Ponty asks (MN 212): "Whence the question: how can one return from this perception fashioned by culture to the 'brute' or 'wild' perception? What does the conforming consist in? By what act does one undo it (return to the phenomenal, to the 'vertical' world, to lived experience)?" This cultural perception is ignorant of itself, and tends to see itself as an act, forgetting itself as latent intentionality, as being at a place. In being autonomous it represses transcendence. However, there is no sharp distinction between us and the world; the distinction between the two planes (natural and cultural) is abstract—everything is natural (based in Being). How can perception learn awareness of itself and its lateral relation to Being? By becoming conscious.

The body is the primary condition of consciousness, and there are correspondences between the structure of the body and the qualitative functioning of the consciousness. Consciousness is formally related to the body—they affect one another, through feedback from all the mechanisms and extensions of both: nerves, moods, mechanical contrivances, words, and images. Consciousness, to use Merleau-Ponty's image, is like a ray of light. It enlarges the region which it illuminates, but even at its brightest, when the focus is most definite, there is a large penumbral region of intense experience which is only dimly apprehended.

The conscious perspective of the body is its subjectivity. Subjectivity is integrated into the movement of transcendence (perhaps *ascendance* within Being); subjectivity is understood as an intertwining with the world, behind which there is no retreat. Thus Merleau-Ponty can penetrate beneath the subject-object distinction. In *The Visible and the Invisible,* he abandons the tacit cogito, since self-presence would be a pure immanence prior to transcendence. In Being, the subject and world are mutually enveloping and inseparable.

The mind is an invisible knot that is capable of recognizing both visible and invisible patterns—that is to say, a rope is not always necessary for the demonstration of a knot. The mind is the other side of the body, and the other side of the body is not describable in objective terms; mind thus shares the invisibility of Being, according to Merleau-Ponty. The other side of the body overflows into it, and is hidden in it; at the same time the mind is dependent on it and is anchored in it. A chiasm divides the mind of the body from the body of the mind. Ideas can be felt by both sides of the body, as physical gestures, or mental images. How is consciousness related to the visible? The whole question is ultimately one of understanding what, in ourselves and the world, is the relation between significance and insignificance; significance for us occurs when one of our intentions is fulfilled, or a number of facts are expressive of other than themselves. Idealism defines all significance as centrifugal, requiring an act, but the phenomenology of perception revealed a layer of significance in which the world and events have a physiognomy for us and for itself also that comes with the sensory and perceptual field that we bring into the world. Consciousness brings the invisible up into the visible, once its own invisibility is in tune with it.

The body gives significance to natural objects, which, before they become symbols of concepts, words, or signs, are events that grip the body. The body is in the world as the heart is in the body, but in the heart of the body is the presence of the world, so that the subject is not to be understood as a synthetic activity, but as ecstasy. The body is born with others from the original ecstasy (MK 174), and as in the later Husserl, subjectivity is intersubjectivity. This ecstasy of experience causes perception to be perception of something. (The term ecstasy is derived from the Greek term, *ekstase*, meaning standing out from, or union.)

1.2.4. It Orders (Logos)
Man makes a whole world for himself, and this world is created by a process of nonintellectual apprehension; man grasps reality imaginatively and in doing so identifies himself with it; in recreating the world, and transforming himself by creation he becomes the world. Men put the world together in a way that makes sense to them, out of physical and cultural givens. The word logos is derived from the Greek word, *lego*, meaning to gather up, or speak. Perception is a nascent logos, from which knowledge arises.

Logos means the inherent order of the world, of the arts, and of human imagination. Men try to deal with the order of the world. Man is an existentially and historically incarnate logos, from whom the privilege of reason laboriously emerges. Merleau-Ponty states (MN n.p.): "When coming to the incarnate subjectivity of the human body. . . I must reach subjectivity . . . that . . . has this solidity and completeness still in the mood of the *Lebenswelt*—That is, I must also, across the objectifications of linguistics, of logic, rediscover the *Lebenswelt* logos." It is the pre-verbal logos, *logos endiathetos*, which provokes the verbal logos, *prophorikos*. Beneath the intentionality of acts is another intentionality, as a condition of the former; this operative intentionality at work before any judgment, is, as Merleau-Ponty says (MG 429), a "Logos of the aesthetic world, an art hidden in the depths of the human soul, which, like any art, is known only by its results." Thus, logos is hidden. This logos is a structure of structures, where forms may be related to forms. Since these phenomena are symbolisms, in the depth of Being, the logos is a semiotic where an interconnection among them is possible; the logos allows comparisons and translations between symbolisms.

Others have reached similar conclusions. In his book, *Science and the Unseen World*, Eddington wrote that when the environment of space and time and matter is probed deeply by the devices of physics, at the bottom are symbols; and here he parallels the theme of the *Lankavatara Sutra*, that everything in the universe is mind only. Weizsacker and his studies in yoga, and Schrodinger and his studies in Vedanta, in conjunction with their meditation on the psychological implications of quantum theory, independently conclude that if subatomic particles are more like mathematical forms, which are altered by the very modes of perceiving them, then the science of nature becomes a science of the mind's knowledge about nature.

Long before, Goethe had described a method which took that problem into consideration. Goethe believed that the 'mind completes nature's forms,' that the deep-down phenomena (*Ur-phanomon*) are revealed by passive attentiveness. His scientific method was comprised of these principles: the primacy of the qualitative, as seen by contemplative non-intervention, through organic dialectics. Wordsworth and Raine echo the ideas.

There is an active principle alive
In all things, in all natures, in the flowers
And in the trees . . .
    Wordsworth (WR 286)

In curving cault and delicate cone
Each formula of shell and bone
    Raine (RA 21)

1.3. *Being Through beings*

Existence, by nothing bred,
Breeds everything.
Parent of the universe,
It smoothes rough edges,
Unties hard knots,
Tempers the sharp sun,
Lays blowing dust,
Its image is the wellspring never fails.
But how was it conceived? —this image
Of no other sire.
    Lao Tse (BY 27)

Beings can be, or not be. The verb, 'to be,' denotes the generic concept of Being. A being in the present also implies that it is non-being somewhere in the past or future. Being itself thus implies Becoming. The connection, faint in English, may be traced in the etymology of the Greek: *phuo* means to bring forth, produce, beget, generate; in the passive it means grow or come into being; *Phuton* means that which has grown in a natural way, as a plant or child, and denotes everything swelling, growing, and increasing; *Phutle* means a generation or race. The whole complex of words refers to the process of fertility—tumescence, procreation, and coming into existence. *Phuo* in the root of *physis*, the generative power named by the pre-Socratics. Even the basic reality, Being, is to be understood in terms of the body.

It may be possible to connect *phuo*, to bring forth, with *phaino*, which means to reveal, make known, and bring to light, make appear. Heidegger seems to have made the connection implicitly; to appear is to be. For most of the pre-Socratics, seeing was the intuitive grasping of Being (the Latin *in tueri* means to look at something). Snell has traced the etymologies in the Greek that equate seeing with knowing; for instance, *eidoma* means to appear or shine, whereas in the past tense, *oida*, it means I saw or I know. Berkeley, Descartes, Leibnitz and Goethe all wrote treatises on vision, which illustrate the philosophers continued identification of sight with knowledge. The Being Parmenides is a complete presence; it discloses itself to the mind through a flash of light. The Being as essence, an ideal timeless fulfillment, is the same Being that Heidegger wants to reveal.

In Heraclitus, however, Being is Becoming; it is perceived in terms of human existence, with human images. *Physis* implies that which has been born. Being as Becoming is the living unfolding of potentialities into completeness. In Merleau-Ponty existence may be interpreted as Being as Becoming. Existence is a standing out—a growing out in an organic sense. Heidegger interpreted the word existence (from the Latin *ex stare*, to stand out from) to mean that which appears and can be seen; thus his interpretation supports his belief of Being as essence. For Merleau-Ponty a being is something which is be-ing, something in the present. The French word for present is *maintenant*, which means now, or to be held in the hand. The reality of Being as Becoming is that which can be grasped; it can be felt with the hands, but it can also be seen. It is just the perceptible world, as Merleau-Ponty proclaims.

1.3.1. The Perceptible World

Being as being is the perceived world, it is the sensible universe, it is the source of the universe. The sensible is a medium where Being can be, without being posited. Being manifest itself in the silent persuasion of the sensible as Merleau-Ponty says (MN 123): "When I find again the actual world such as it is, under my hands, under my eyes, up against my body, I find much more than an object: a Being of which my vision is a part, a visibility older than my operations or my acts. But this does not mean that there was a fusion or coinciding of me with it: On the contrary, this occurs because a sort of dehisence opens my body in two, and because between my body looked at and my body looking, my body touched and my body must say that the things pass into us as well as into the things." On every level, Being feels; there is an incarnate subjectivity in all beings. Through this overlapping, Being reveals itself in two ways:

1. I am it: the subject belongs to that which appears as the object.
2. It belongs to me: the object belongs to the subject, the world becomes flesh in me.

Perception, in its relation to the Being of a sensible thing, is ontological, not psychological. The psychological is derivative. The contours of the sensible things are the contours of Being. In our intentional being we are a subject opposed to an object attention is focused on the object, as the frontal aspect of appearing reality, in opposition to us; this opposition, however, always appears with an intrinsic connection, which cannot be directly observed (this lateral connection is then not stressed).

The world which grasps everyone in its gravity, and which supports their bonds with things and others, is only truly evident in silence and understood implicitly; its alleged positivity, beyond the empirical sense, proves to be ungraspable—the only thing seen in the full sense is the totality from which the sensibles are cut. Being is a horizon, from which consciousness carves figures.

1.3.2. Figure-Ground

The figure, on which attention is focused, is to be distinguished from the ground, wherein it appears. The figure-ground relation, and the structure of intention are the basis of the primacy of perception, at every level of experience. The figure-ground structure is disclosed in the visible by perception, and discerned in the invisible by conception. Perception and conception reciprocally nourish each other; as the visible and invisible are aspects of Being, perception and conceptions are aspects of experience. The complete behavior of a Being, with the mutual interplay of its aspects, creates a field of experience which is primary. The ground cannot be clearly observed without becoming the figure: In Wittgenstein's duck-rabbit, the aspects change; according to the attention. In order for the ground to remain in the background, it is essential that it only be co-observed. The privilege of clarity belongs to the figure alone and not to co-appearing ground. In a sense, the focus creates the figure. The ground is always obscure; the way in which it is described must also be obscure; it is impossible to give a clear description of a co-appearing ground.

The invisible, Being, allows the visible to be seen, but it itself is not seen; its presence can only be announced by a visible figure. But, we stand out from being; the subject stands out from being as figure stands out from ground. We stand out in our very existing (*ex stare* = stand out, emerge). As objects also stand out from the ground of their existence, we focus our attention on them, and they appear in opposition to us. Actually it is an opposition larger than connection or togetherness, since it takes place in a unity that precedes and exceeds the very opposition. It is a unity, of which only a lateral awareness is possible, which makes all phenomena possible, and co-appears in them, subject and object.

Access to Being is difficult, because consciousness is necessarily blind in some respects; it does not see what makes its vision of everything else possible. It does not see its involvement in Being. Merleau-Ponty (MN 248) says that what the subject "does not see is what makes it see, is its tie to Being, is its corporeality, are the existentials by which the world becomes visible, is the flesh wherein the object is born." The most important aspects of things are often invisible because simplicity and familiarity. Experience is rooted in the body which itself is rooted in Being; since an object is more clear than Being, it is possible to forget the context of the object, hence the positive object *qua* object.

As Being co-appears in everything, it also hides itself in the ground as it reveals itself in the figure. "Nature loves hiding," said Heraclitus. But it is not completely hidden; *physis* reveals and hides itself at the same time. As the logician Brown (BR 106) concludes: "Thus the world, whenever it appears, as a physical universe, must always seem to us, its representatives, to be playing a kind of hide-and-seek with itself. What is revealed will be concealed, but what is concealed will again be revealed. And since we ourselves represent it, this occultation will be apparent in our life in general."

In one of his games, Wittgenstein tried to find the real artichoke by divesting it of its leaves. But what is hidden beneath the surface is another surface. We could discard all the surface and never find the inside; only more outsides; thus, we could never find Being. Being cannot ever be uncovered, only discovered by its presence in the artichoke leaves.

> Nature loves to hide
>   and nature loves to play
>   Play at hiding
>   hide at playing
>   Display   show and turn
>   and expect you
>   to remember.
> We remember
> even as we see
> again and the present   expands.
>   Nature loves to hide and tease
>   wolves love to seek
>   humans love to seek and please
> And so we seek each other and play
>   and hide within nature
> our nature   her nature   his nature
> all the natures that exist.
>   'Wolf Loves to Hide,' Caratheodory (CB 29)

1.3.3. Flesh

'What does the artichoke reveal about Being?' Wittgenstein asked. The sensed quality announces an unseen, it stands out from an interior horizon; the surface is the limit of a darkness stuffed with visibility. Its greenness, seen, involves an exterior horizon, it is linked with other colors, as well as the unseen depth of the thing itself. The artichoke is not a discrete element, but a moment of a totality—an ever-open strait between exterior and interior horizons. Merleau-Ponty (MN 132) locates it: "Between the alleged colors and visibles, we would find anew the tissue that lines them, sustains them, nourishes them, and which for its part is not a thing, but a possibility, a latency, and a flesh of things."

The flesh of things refers in some way to the horizons that sustain visible things, but as a latency and not a thing itself. Flesh is not the matter or substance of Aristotle, nor the fact or essence of Husserl. Merleau-Ponty (MN 139) allows it to be translated as element (as fire or water, the *physis* or the deep-down stuff (*Urstoff*), out of which things were made; or also the *arche*), and insists that it is: "a general thing and way between the spatial temporal individual and the idea, a sort of incarnate principle that brings a style of being wherever there is a fragment of being." Perhaps Kathleen Raine touches on it (R 30):

> All creatures passionate for grace
> quest their desire through groves and seas
> that flesh may win a human face . . .

Merleau-Ponty, in considering how the hand exercises a particular kind of movement in investigating the texture of a surface (of the same artichoke, perhaps), asks how the movement can be appropriate to what is revealed, yet, prior to the touch. In offering an explanation of the relation between the touching and the touched, he suggests that there is a pre-established harmony between them, which allows a measure of prepossession. This kinship of the touching and the touched results from the fact that that which touches is touchable itself, and bound up with tangible things. In the hand, touching and being touched overlap, or cross. And through this crisscrossing of the touching and the tangible, "its own movements incorporate themselves into the universe they interrogate" (MN 133). Likewise, in the seen, there is a crossing of vision and visibility; and furthermore, there is a crossing of the visible and the tangible. These crossings Merleau-Ponty (MN 266) calls chiasms. "The idea of chiasm, that is: every relation with being is simultaneously a taking and a being taken, the hold is held, it is inscribed and inscribed in the same being that it takes hold of." The seen and the seen do not simply mirror one another, but mirror each mirroring the other. Being a seeing thing among other seen things obstructs some vision, but the body is the only means by which one has access to things. The body is flesh that makes itself a world, and makes things flesh, according to Merleau-Ponty.

The distinction between the flesh of the body and the flesh of things is not the same as a subject-object distinction. Both things and bodies have a doubling up into an inside and an outside, a surface and a depth; they are both flesh because their ontological structure is the same. The flesh of things refers to their store in invisibility beneath their surface (the latency that supports the visible). Merleau-Ponty explicitly thematizes that the difference is the flesh of the body is self sensing, whereas the flesh of the world is not. The body is flesh, and the locus of a chiasm; things are flesh and the locus of a chiasm. The doubling up of both allows each to be inserted between the leaves of the other.

There is a fundamental chiasm in which the flesh of bodies and the flesh of things transgress. The chiasm by which the body and things are intertwined and made one flesh is wild Being itself. In seeing things the body sees itself seeing; the thing closes the circuit of reflection and completes the bodies being seen. The totality of bodies and things in a circuit of reflection is wild Being. The intertwining of bodies and things forms a whole, wild Being as fundamental flesh, which Merleau-Ponty now (MN 139) identifies as 'visibility itself.' Everything is in interior relation with this visibility. Kathleen Raine presents it thus:

> Veil upon veil
> Petal and shell and scale
> The dancer of the whirling dance let fall.
> Visible veils the invisible
> Reveal, conceal
> In bodies that most resemble
> The fleeting mind of nature never still.

Because the hand touches and is touched, there is a separation between touching and touched; since it is the same hand it cannot be completely different, and since it can attempt to touch itself it cannot be completely identical (the gap is not a void, since it is spanned by the Being of the world.) An ontology from within dictates that reversibility is not an actual identity of the touching and touched; a dialectic can be substituted for modalities of Being and nothingness. Both within the systems (touching-touch, seeing-seen) and between the systems there is reversibility. Merleau-Ponty (S 73) attributes the dialectic in reversibility to Hegel: "The dialectic is, Hegel said approximately, a movement which itself creates its course and returns to itself—and thus a movement which has no other guide but its own initiative and which nevertheless does not escape outside itself but cuts across itself again and confirms itself at long intervals." With Merleau-Ponty, the dialectic of Being is the Becoming nature of man, which is the Becoming man of nature.

Because the attempt to touch touching necessarily fails (as soon a the hand is touched the same hand touching recedes beneath awareness), bodily reflection is always incomplete; even through the mediation of things the circuit of reflection is never closed. The body communicates this identity and difference to things; the things also have an inside and outside turning about one another. The body makes itself a world as things are appropriated into its circuit; but that world is incomplete, as bodily reflection is linked to a standpoint. On seeing other bodies seeing, the limits become more apparent; but these others allow a partial transcendence of the limits through 'intercorporeality.'

Bodies come together through the common meaning in gestures, "in the patient and silent labor of desire, begins the paradox of expression" in Merleau-Ponty's words (MN 144). From a more universal visibility, emerges a common flesh; this rarefied flesh is language.

> He, who thro' vast immensity can pierce,
> See worlds on worlds compose one universe,
> Observe how system into system runs,
> What other planets circle other suns,
> What vary'd being peoples ev'ry star,
> May tell why Heav'n has made us as we are.
>   Alexander Pope, An Essay on Man

1.3.4. *Field of Being*

The universe at large, with its clusters of galaxies, clouds, stars, and planets, extends itself through space and time. Parmenides held that space was a plenum. Leukippus conceived of space as emptiness. David Bohm combines both ideas in the concept of a field. He describes the universe as a field with waves of infinite size. Physics became a more appropriate way to discuss Being than phenomenology. Physics could combine beings and Being in a multiscalar, multidimensionsal field.

The universe is permeated by septillions of waves at all times. Humans generate their own waves that are added to the infinite variety coursing the universe. A wave is an integral pattern of the physical continuity of a particle. Waves shape the space-time-energy-mass (STEM) field. That is, they excite the empty field.

The STEM matrix is a cosmic, transformable field. The field is an invisible, nondetectible source from which elementary particles draw order and energy. There is no place for both field and matter, "field being the only reality." According to Einstein, the field here and now depends on the field in the immediate neighborhood at a time just past. Excitement generated with a time dimension.

The interplay of heterogeneous, asymmetrical physical forces (motion) generates cosmic time. Simultaneously, space, energy and matter are generated. C. Clifford was one of the first to combine frames. In an 1870 article, "On the Space Theory of Matter," he stated that: Small portions of space are analogous to hills; this curvature is passed to other portions of space after manner of wave; this variation is the motion of matter; and, nothing else takes place in world but this variation, possibly subject to law of continuity.

Albert Einstein extended Clifford's ideas in the theories of relativity. In large systems, time acquires a new meaning associated with irreversibility. The classical mechanical concept of time results from simplifications (compare Whitehead's fallacy of misplaced concreteness). Einstein induced that time is relative to the frame of reference. Space-time is an ensemble of occasions and places, held together by duration. The future and past are tied together by duration. To the largest duration—the universe—all time is present. Time is not empty or abstract. According to Einstein, every change of coordinate systems mixes space and time in a mathematically defined way. In his Special Theory of Relativity, he included gravity in the picture, making space-time curved. But as massive bodies have greater gravities and mass can be converted to energy, all four form a field that can alter each component. Through the principle of equivalence of gravitation and acceleration and through the use of a symbol that mathematically described the local rate of 'turning' of the curvilinear coordinates, Einstein was able to relate curvilinear order and measure to the gravitational field. Both the electromagnetic field and the gravitational field can be understood as aspects of curvature. The particle affects the field only in its own locality. Particles move along paths that are intrinsic to curvature of space-time field independent of coordinate frame used for measurements (but not from the act of measuring). These paths are called geodesics and are the shortest distances between two points. With Einstein, geometry steps forward as a new participant in physics. Einstein's 1907 principle of the local equivalence of gravitational and propulsive accelerations (geometrodynamic law) linked the two currents of thought from Riemann ("geometry is part of physics") and Mach ("inertia is influenced by mass elsewhere").

John Wheeler regards curved geometry as the building material of the universe. Gravity is slow curvature; the electromagnetic field is rippled with different curvature; the particle is a knotted up region. All charge is connected with the topology of space. Wheeler hypothesizes that pregeometry is needed because geometry fails to explain gravitational collapse. D. Finkelstein asserts that space-time is a statistical construct from a deeper pregeometric quantum structure in which process is fundamental. Geometry is an abstraction from an empty, moving field of STEM. STEM is pregeometry, the ground of being, and it has distinct characteristics.

1.3.4.1. Properties of the Field
The whole universe is a field. The field has properties that are unique to it as an emergent system. These properties include autopoesis, discretion,

and fullness.

> The candles of the pines have all turned down
> In the cold; the evening torrents
> Through the needles, and a porcupine
> Chews the tender bark.
>
> The dead fir shoulders the sky, bones
> Extended—a woodpecker thrills
> The air with her ax. As the sun moves,
> Shadows move and reveal that the tree
> Has no front or back.
>
> Cattails line the edge of the pond;
> The earth vibrates as it turns
> And the surface trembles. The movement
> Of air circulates with the memory of all
> The revolutions of the earth. The fish
> Are still in their constant water.
>
> The droppings of a bear point up the hill
> But no bear is seen.
> Gophers make honeycombs in dirt. Coyotes
> Bark and burrow to the roots of heat.
> A deer is surprised leaving the field
> Where winter wheat suffers the delirium
> Of weeds. The last geese pass; some absent.
>
> White hills invade brown, snow settles
> On the meniscus in the pail disguising
> The waste of life. The field stretches and curves,
> Folded and folded over, drifting with motion.
> Crystal white hills frame a small white sun,
> Glowing faintly on the horizon, packed
> With crystal lattices—the field folded around
> It. Memory complicates light around the star
> And hills and draws them into another whole,
> Smaller and dreamlike.
>   'The Mystery of Order,' Caratheodory (CB 22)

1.3.4.1.1. Autopoesis

The universe is autopoetic, that is, self-making (from the Greek *auto*, self, and *poiesis*, making). Although the physical universe is greatly unknown, most models of the universe are whole. The universe described is a subset of the whole universe. But the models, or cosmologies, are always incomplete.

Francisco Varela and colleagues suggest that autopoesis (they use the etymological spelling, *autopoiesis*) is a new concept of life, also, which refers to the dynamic self-producing and self-maintaining activities of living beings. The tenets of autopoesis are presented in six principles:

1. Identity: identifiable components organized internally with structural boundaries.
2. Integrity: a single dynamic functional system.
3. Self-boundedness: the boundary is produced by the system
4. Self-maintenance: boundary and components produced by functioning of system.
5. External supply of materials: elements, such as carbon or water obtained beyond the boundary.
6. External energy supply: light or chemical energy is converted into organic bond energy.

In an autopoetic framework, every being is embedded in a world and observed by an embedded observer. The material components of life move through physiological processes. Autotrophs (bacteria, algae, green plants) convert energy into organic compounds; heterotrophs reconvert into heterotroph flesh. Later sections on wholeness and self-making offer more detail on autopoesis.

1.3.4.1.2. Discretion

The universe is a vast order of individual events, following certain laws, but unique. The physical world is a patterning of patternings, a flowing of flowings whose constituent functions are interacting fields of force. Physicists and philosophers assumed that the patterns were continuous. The Latin proverb *Natura nonfacit saltus*, "nature does not make jumps," expresses the ideal.

But Max Planck, in his investigations, concluded that a field cannot go down to a dimensionless point. Planck said that energy can only be exchanged in complete packets. Planck used the word quanta to describe the discrete packets of electromagnetic radiation. This discovery of things that only happen in leaps was great intellectual triumph.

Einstein's Geometrodynamics, combined with Planck's quantum principle, results in a superspace, according to Wheeler. A leaf of history, cutting through superspace, describes a deterministic, dynamic development of geometry of space with time. Furthermore, quantum fluctuations of geometry and quantum jumps of topology are estimated and calculated, according to Wheeler, to pervade all space at the Planck scale of distances and give it foamlike structure. Gravitational collapse places an impenetrable barrier between the leaves. According to quantum geometrodynamics, violent fluctuations are going on in the geometry at Planck's scale. From the worm's eye view, such fluctuation is indistinguishable from collapse. Gravitational collapse of local universes is always taking place and being undone. Wheeler has described superspace (the space-time fabric) as composed of a turbulent sea of bubbles, the warp and woof of empty space, quantum foam, and a carpet in motion (Weave, woof and web are derived from the Indo-European word *webh*. On a loom for weaving the upright threads (vertical) are called the warp. The fabric or web is made by weaving new threads horizontally; the crosswise threads are the woof. Warp means to twist or bind.

Patterns of complexity shade and grade into one another endlessly. It appears to many physicists as if the beginnings of new orders of natural laws are being revealed, in which particles would be like flower designs on a carpet pattern, while something unknown corresponds to the structure of the cords of carpet. In fact orders re-form in the carpet (after Wheeler). Analyzing the world as if it were made of particles would be similar to analyzing the carpet as if it were made of flowers: it would give some results and have some predictability (of course, carpet equals being). Wheeler states that patterns in the foam are seen as subnuclear particles. The foam is the fabric of a dream. The foam is a metaphor for the constant self-reconstruction of the universe from standard parts to novel structures.

1.3.4.1.3. Fullness
David Bohm describes the foam as a sea of virtual particles. If one applies the rules of quantum theory to theory of relativity, one finds that the gravitational field is constituted of 'wave-particle' modes, each having a minimum 'zero-point' energy. As a result, the gravitational field, and hence what is meant by distance, ceases to be completely defined. At a short enough length time and space are undefinable, as they are at long intervals. Bohm finds that this short length is estimated to be about 10^{-33} cm, which is much shorter than experimental measures (10^{-17} cm). If one computes the amount of energy in one cubic centimeter of space, with this wavelength, it is far greater than the total energy of matter in the known-universe. This implies that empty space contains immense background of energy, and that matter is a small wavelike excitation on top. Consideration of the background is avoided by only considering the difference between empty space and matter space. Space is full.

1.3.4.1.4. Limits

Einstein built a relativistic universe, where there are definite limits. What is space to one observer is a mixture of time and space to another. Every change of frame of reference, called 'coordinate system' in physics, mixes space and time in a mathematically well-defined way; the two cannot be separated. So, there is no real length of a ruler, just like there is no real length of a shadow; length depends upon frame of reference. A frame of reference (in physics) has a uniform motion at a constant velocity in a constant direction. Each frame is considered a locality and obeys the principle of locality, i.e., that what happens in one frame does not depend upon variables subject to control in another. The rules that apply to part of the universe from a limited perspective are not universal. A global system is the sum of localities and may have unique characteristics of its own. That is, the universe has characteristics that local frames of reference do not. Frames of reference are easier to define in physics than in biological or social systems, with their extended complexities. Nevertheless the principle of locality can be used to explain many difficulties in cosmology, evolution and ethics.

Total energy is not defined in a closed universe; the conservation of energy does not apply in a black hole within such a universe. Since there is no outside to measure from, the idea of total mass-energy loses all meaning. STEM is a meso-field in the universe; it vanishes at both ends (perfect symmetry), as a knot dissolves into the identity of rope after being analyzed. Perhaps the whole universe is like so: particles dissolve to identity with the universe.

Particles do not gather and wait in a common place before the start of time; they unroll space and time and display history. Two particles separated widely must wait hundreds of millions of years for their signals to cross. The field is a paradox; localities are part of it but do not communicate instantaneously, by light. The speed of light is still a limit. Space is filled with local relationships. The limits of the array are nondefinable.

Cosmic edges do not exist; time and space cannot exist beyond a universe. At the largest scale the STEM field is undefinable. In the classical cosmology, the center is everywhere and the periphery nowhere. In the new cosmology, the periphery is everywhere and the center nowhere. But neither one is a phenomenal cosmology, where there is Being, not a science of it. Merleau-Ponty said that "Being is what demands of us creation, in order that we have experience of it." A human philosophy does not need to know a center or edge of universe. Humans create their own, logically (cf. Brown).

1.3.4.1.5. Connection

Following Bohr's 1927 expression of the Copenhagen interpretation of quantum theory—that the world must be observed to be objective—Einstein, Podolsky and Rosen proposed a thought experiment leading to the conclusion that quantum theory and objective reality are incompatible (the EPR paradox). They argued that quantum theory was incomplete, that it does not specify all objective elements of reality. The thought experiment (for a full description, refer to Pagels or Capra) shows that quantum theory violates local causality, which asserts that whatever influences an object must be attributed to local changes in the object or to energy transmission. In the experiment, two particles interact and go in opposite directions. Quantum theory seems to require that measuring the first particle influences the second instantaneously, regardless of the extent of separation.

Over thirty years later, J. S. Bell devised a mathematical inequality that could be tested experimentally. Half a dozen experiments have shown that the inequality was violated, with the conclusion that the universe is nonlocal, with instantaneous action-at-a-distance. This conclusion has been expanded to mean that superluminal (faster than light) communication is possible and to support notions of telepathy. Bohm concludes that Bell's theorem leads to a notion of unbroken wholeness; connection is extended to the entire universe.

Interestingly, the assumptions of both experiments disallow any firm conclusions. The EPR paradox assumes that the second particle has position and momentum without actually measuring it. Bohr would say that it has no objective reality until it is measured, so there may not be a contradiction. Experiments in support of Bell also assumed that the particles (photon, in most cases) existed in a definite state without measurement. Nonlocal influences cannot be argued then, since no information is transmitted between devices. The theoretical cross-correlation of separated events does not occur in a local frame. Neither experiment is complete or conclusive.

Pagels contends that complementarity applies to Bell's theorem in the following way: If the photons are assumed to exist in a certain state, violating Bohr's Copenhagen interpretation, then reality is nonlocal. But if the experimenter attempts to verify the state of a photon, the first condition of the experiment—that the polarizations are correlated precisely—is violated. Conversely, if strict local causality is accepted, then there is no objectivity for individual photons. Pagels finds the difficulty of argument in the distinction between a macroworld and a microworld (subatomic). The microworld is weird, not objective or local. The macroworld can store information that the microworld cannot.

The failure of the principle of locality would mean that there are no separate parts in the universe, but we know that nothing is entirely separate anyway. The conclusion that experimentally separate parts are correlated forever must consider the 'parts' as eternal things, not phenomenal processes. In fact, the particles in both experiments are connected in a field, not by superluminal signals (or any other kind). In a holonomic field, the resolution of any one perspective of the whole is so weak that it has no predictive value. Information is not transferred because the field itself is informed. Bell's theorem demands that an adequate model account simultaneously for the observed causal structure on the statistical level and the noncausal structure on the individual event level. An adequate model must provide for unified understanding of all of nature. A model of reality consistent with Bell's theorem could be similar to Whitehead's.

1.3.4.1.6. Consistency

Bishop Berkeley proposed a bootstrap principle when he argued that the inertia of any body is determined by the distribution and masses of all other bodies in universe. Mach's principle repeated the same idea, demanding the closure of the universe, so that it would be finite and bounded. The mechanical properties of space are determined completely by matter only in a space-bounded universe.

In the bootstrap principle, the universe is what it is because it is consistent with itself; we are not free to sort out accidental properties and distribute them among different universes. No properties of the universe are fundamental; they follow from other properties in a web of interrelationships. G. Chew's bootstrap model considers hadrons as temporarily stable configurations that result from an interaction of processes. They may transform themselves into other particles. The bootstrap relation takes the form: universe=subatomic particles, where '=' means 'equivalent to.' Each particle represents a facet of the universe. Whitehead referred to this kind of arrangement as the doctrine of internal relations. All electrons have same charge because they represent some single perspective of the universe. Each particle is only an abstraction of a relatively invariant form of movement in the whole field of the universe. The proton and neutron are just two different points of view of the nucleon; the sigma has three different points of view. Both nucleon and sigma particle may be just different points of view of the same particle, related by an extended isospin symmetry. Specificity can be a property of the path (what Waddington calls 'chreod' and Whitehead 'concrescence'). Yet, if the universe is open-ended, as has been argued, then the consistency of the whole can never be proved.

1.3.4.1.7. Wholeness

Energy, information, matter, and life are part of inseparable whole, with no formal theory linking them. Relativity, quantum, and entropy theories each imply individual wholeness, in which the analysis of something into distinct parts is no longer relevant. Relativity and quantum theory both imply the need to regard the world as an undivided whole—not a spectral oneness, but a diversity of the whole into many perspectives.

Pythagoras described the universe as a *kosmis*, an order. The stoics emphasized the cosmos as an entity under the direction of logos, which led to the use of holon, meaning whole, to describe the universe. David Bohm describes reality as a coherent whole, an unending process of movement and unfoldment. George Leonard suggests the word holonomy for the study of wholeness. Holonomy is not the death of division. It is a frame for individual wholes.

Matter is a holographic expression of forms of wave energies; it appears when conditions are right, then folds back into the field when conditions are not favorable. The universe is an implicate order, implicate meaning to fold inward. The whole, implicate order is present at any moment. It is a description in which everything implicates everything else in undivided wholeness. The mind enfolds matter in general, body in particular; the body enfolds the mind and the universe; the universe enfolds the mind and body. The explicate order flows out of the implicate order.

When we speak of nature or the universe as a whole, we merely mean the universe considered as organic or holistic. The creative intensified field of nature is holistic. That field is the environment of all wholes. The whole needs no boundaries to separate it; there is nothing to separate it from. A partial process requires cuts in the whole, boundaries. Predominant fragmentary views have brought about only imbalances. But the fragmentary perspective of physicists and philosophers seems to be universal; perhaps it is rooted in the perception of left-brain. The habit of fragmentation smothers the primacy of the implicate order. The explicate order is a relatively independent, recurrent, stable subtotality. Both are correct, but must be reconciled in a holocosmology.

1.3.4.1.8. Participation

John Wheeler believes that since law, field and substance exist after the theoretical big bang, the universe owes its existence to trillions of acts of registration. The phenomenon comes through an elementary act of observer-participation. Wheeler asks if the universe might not be brought into being by the participation of those who participate. Quantum mechanics strikes down the neutral observer; participation is vital. Wheeler noted that "To observe the electron even, the experimenter must shatter the glass—must reach in with instruments." The quantum principle destroys the observer behind glass (*in vitro*). The universe is not the same after measurement; the observer becomes a participator. Einstein said that no event can be postulated without the presence of an observer; but no observer can see the whole system; and anything can be an observer or participant. The participant creates a universe by being.

1.3.4.2. The Operation of the Field
The word nature is derived from a Greek word, meaning "that which is born." The Taoist term for nature (*tzu-jan*) means the spontaneous, that which is so of itself (automotive or automatic). It is continually reborn. The movement of the field reveals cosmic rhythms, as the yin and yang of Chinese philosophy. Motion results in limitation. Limitation is the principle by which the many can come to existence out of the one, the unlimited of Anaximander.

The operation of the field can be described as certain processes, as motion, version, scension, tention, formation, and novation. This process operates through all levels, which it makes as it operates, from physical, chemical, electrical, or inorganic, to organic and social levels. All six processes start a spiral pattern that works into an 11-dimensional Klein bottle as a model of Being.

1.3.4.2.1. Motion

> "No matter what forms we observe ... we shall find nowhere anything enduring, resting, completed, but rather that everything is in continuous motion."
> Goethe

Nature consists of moving patterns whose movement is essential to their being. The field is motion. Motion is a process related to freedom, chance, matter, and energy. Matter is inherently possessed of motion: Matter emerges from point instants; a particle of matter is a moving pattern of point-instants, which are abstractions)—as a determinate pattern, however, it will have determinate quality. And quality exists as a function of structure. Particles are probability patterns, various parts of a unified whole, with interconnections in a cosmic field. The holomovement is indefinable. There is necessity in the holomovement, called holonomy. The holomovement enfolds and unfolds in a multidimensional order.

Motion can be further refined by a series of differences, from remotion to commotion. David Bohm states that order is basically a set of similar differences. The limits of the universe, like the speed of light or quantum of a field, put limits on freedom. Events are limited to localities; size limits function; history limits development. Random order is open; it has degrees of freedom. Differences can be related to degrees of freedom. An order with more differences has more degrees of freedom. The macro-order limits degrees of freedom. Movement could not occur without a free order or disorder. There could not be any activity at all within a complete order—perhaps this is what Plato had in mind with the perfect forms. Order is applicable not to universe but only to some part. The distinction between order and disorder disappears when domain of both is universe. Particles do not gather in a common place before the start of time; they unroll space and time and display history.

1.3.4.2.1.1. Immotion

Immotion (from the Latin words for "move in") means to form or inform. Motion can be directed in or out. This indirection binds energy, makes it work in cycles, and can form identity, as well as link it to smaller and larger scales.

Energy is considered to be the capacity for action or motion. The word energy is derived from the Greek word for "work in" (one of the original meanings was "force of expression" as an interpretation of Aristotle's metaphor to show "action"). The concept of work is a very useful tool to describe changes in places or human cultures. Some exponents of science consider energy to be a more fundamental reality than material objects.

The planet has a certain amount of residual energy from its formation; this expresses itself in its molten core and in its rotation. The planet also receives constant energy from the sun. The energy can be bound for a certain amount of time in living flesh or geological formations, such as coal beds. Energy is a once-through flow phenomenon. It does not recycle, although it can be bound and released several times. At each step, however, more energy is lost to the user (the loss is measured as entropy).

Living beings develop a metabolism to compensate for the loss of energy in living. Plants and animals bind energy for their use. They also can transfer energy between systems; caribou, or instance, transfer energy between ecosystems. Humans modify animal and plant associations in a different way, simplifying patterns of energy

PAF

and chemical exchange, to solidify themselves at the end of many food chains.

The action of cycling can create an identity, not only for organisms, but also aggregates, planets and the universe. Cycling is necessary for the self-making of patterns as well as for their renewal. Identity emerges from this movement. At first, identity is small, and then it reaches a comfortable size. The boundaries of a network are its identity. The uniqueness of the context contributes to the uniqueness of an identity. Identity exists in relation to context. For Aristotle, identity is permanent, but it can change as its context changes, within certain biological limits.

1.3.4.2.1.2. Emotion

Emotion creates an 'in-place' from an environment (perhaps this is one function of the limbic system in the brain of a mammal). Emotion (from the Latin words for "move out") means transferring from the identity of the self outwards towards other selves. This involves feeling. This describes the transfer from self to extended self in the environment. This motion is centrifugal, meaning away from the center or outward, although it acts to bind motion and perception—it transcends simple physical distance. The self has to open for the transfer to take place. This also allows the potential to influence or exploit others.

Preservation of identity appeals to qualities inherent in established ways and to people's desire to maintain their distinctive customs against change. There are also esthetic reasons for preservation: To preserve styles, merit, and achievement. Cultural patterns provoke formation of identity. Ethnic identity and consciousness of gender make finer grids within groups. Devotion to groups, clubs, corporations, teams, and co-ops, can provide refinement for individual identity. Through emotion, identity becomes enlarged, to include other beings and the earth, to include our own posterity and its image of the future, without which we lose the will and capacity to solve current problems.

1.3.4.2.1.3. Remotion

Remotion (from the Latin words for "move back") means departure. This describes the eternal return properties of motion—that is, it is a backward motion that can create a cycle. Cycles bring things around to many parts of a universe, allowing them to be shared and introduced back into the cycles. These cycles occur in the bodies of living beings, as well as at regional scales and global scales, such as the water cycle in the atmosphere. Cycles repeat at various time scales, from seconds to millennia. Cycles stay within the limits of motion, gravity, and other forces and elements.

Recycle means to take up and cycle again. This is what keeps cycles in motion. This is true for soils, nutrients and for atmospheric renewal. Recycling is the process that removes minerals, elements, nutrients, and waste from a system or presents it for reuse by the cycles or organisms. Recycling provides materials for basic ecological processes. Although there are limits for recycling, as a result of inevitable losses, recycling can go own for long periods of time, from the recycling of elements in stars to the recycling of elements in living cells. Through recycling, components of trees and herbs are passed to others and to animals. Much of this is performed by living organisms. Human systems depend on natural systems for recycling of wastes, water, and air. Nature concentrates some elements, like carbon or phosphorus and those elements may only be recycled over geological time spans. Elements are kept in constant use by remotion. Patterns change as a result of remotion.

1.3.4.2.1.4. Commotion
Commotion (from the Latin for "move with") means commotion, or the action of moving in a group. Many individuals or things move together in groups (or aggregates, classes and species).

Aggregations make unique patterns across a landscape. Near the Columbia River, for instance, traditional foragers caught salmon and collected wild plants, but beaver, bison, elk, and deer were rare there. Prey animals, note ecologists, have safe zones from predators. Maybe in the centers between wolf packs. This may account for large aggregations in some places.

Moving together in aggregations creates courses, which are properties of ecosystems. The system provides the order required for producing individual organisms. The coming-to-be of organisms, that is process, is a fundamental feature of reality. The organism is what it does. The process of nature is not merely rhythmic change, it is a creative advance, producing new forms everywhere. The organism undergoes a process of evolution in which it produces new forms in itself. The process creates a course of motion.

The interplay of material cycles and energy flows generates a self-renewing "homeostasis" in Eugene Odum's words. Processes like homeostasis, which involve a relationship with the environment, occur on an ecosystem level. Living systems do not display homeostasis— constant value—so much as a particular course of change in time— homeorhesis (from the Greek *homeo*, meaning 'same' and *rheo*, meaning 'flow'), according to Conrad Waddington. The course is stabilized, not the constancy. Changes to a system are symbolized by trajectories in a multidimensional phase space or landscape. Homeorhetic mechanisms protect the system from many disruptions. Negative feedback counteracts the effects of change to maintain the system in a steady state or homeorhetic state. A mature community is self-perpetuating and homeorhetic, with a dynamic balanced energy-matter budget.

Homeorhesis is a significant phenomenon in evolution. Waddington applies it to the tendency of a process to continue in its original pattern, even if disturbed. Homeostasis is tendency of spatial structures to remain the same. The ability to persist is the ability to change, but species only change from environmental pressures; an amphibian is a fish trying to continue being a fish, regardless of course changes.

Waddington refers to such a course as chreod (from *chre*, fated, and *hodos*, path, in Greek). The nature of a chreod that a system adopts is determined by instructions in genes and other organizations of information, and in interaction with the environment that it travels, that is, the epigenetic landscape. Control of a system after disturbance may not bring it back to where it was before; it may go back or forward. Since the path is fuzzy, it can change.

Chreods occur in various shapes in multidimensional space, depending on attractor surfaces. Some could be very narrow canyons, others large meadows, similar to old mature earth forms, with meandering rivers. The cross-sectional shape of the chreod describes the reaction of the system to fluctuations. With a steep slope, for example, it is difficult to divert the developing system from the bottom of valley; even with a strong force the system will return immediately as soon as the influence stops. With a shallow slope, like a flood plain chreod, it is easy to divert the system; it meanders before returning. But actually the perturbations alter the landscape itself, making a steep valley again, not just shifting the river. As the environment changes, the system changes with it.

Like embryos, ecosystems have many properties and are affected by many environmental conditions. Their changes are symbolized by trajectories in multidimensional phase space; orderliness can be described in terms of constraints on trajectory courses, and these constraints are visualized as attractor surfaces. If the system starts from any condition, represented by a point in multidimensional phase space, the trajectory will move to nearest attractor surface and then move along it.

Commotion can be described in terms of connectivity. Moving together creates connections. A system is defined as a complex object, every part of which is connected with other parts of the object in such a way that the whole possesses emergent properties that the parts lack. Systems are considered to be wholes where the internal connections are stronger than the external connections. There is no whole system without an interconnection of its parts, and there is no whole system without an environment. Everything is connected in a system; removal of any part alters the dynamics of the system. Connectivity is related to the size and density of a system. To connect means to bind together, from the Latin words, or to link or couple. A connection is the relationship or association. A complete connection is regarded as a circuit, which becomes required for certain patterns and their continuation. A cycle is movement through a circuit.

In an ecosystem, individuals and species are connected to some degree, in terms of quality and quantity of connections. The connectivity of a component of a system is a measure of the number of direct connections between it and the rest of the system. Connectance is a percentage of the number of connections through predation or exploitation as a percentage of the total number of possible interconnections. A system is more connected if the absolute number increases, and if the percentage, and the strength, increases. Too little connectivity and species are too independent; they can die if there is no food or prey. Too much connectivity and each species has to compete with all species; there is little flexibility to change. So it seems that connectivity must have regions of operation.

1.3.4.2.1.5. Chance & History
The swerve of Lucretius broke the chain of causality and introduced chance into cosmologies. Democritus wrote that "Everything that exists in the Universe is the fruit of accident and necessity." C.S. Peirce made chance a basic factor in his theory. Chance forms part of the woof of physics. In a chance universe, whatever could happen by chance could change over time. Without positive or negative uniformities, everything that could happen, does. Peirce concluded that change would act to move things from a state of homogeneity to heterogeneity, assuming that the universe was closed. Chance events are contingent, not necessary. A chance event has no antecedent cause; it is a new beginning. Norbert Weiner noted that W. Gibbs—not M. Planck or W. Heisenberg—proposed that the universe was contingent (predictable within statistical limits), not deterministic. R. Riedl thinks that all events can be regarded as accidental or necessary. Accidental here means having no expectations or being nonhistorical.

David Bohm argues that all realms of existence contain some

things that are fortuitous (or contingent) and others that are necessary (or organized). He claims that this applies to all levels of explanation, including physics; fundamental physical entities, such as quanta, arise as organized from a lower level of fortuitous elements and this arising is creation. Perhaps these elements are fortuitous because we have no way of tracing them. Fluctuation, and the bifurcating behavior that results, introduce history into developing systems, emphasizes Prigogine. The intervention of chance (uncaused events) destroys strict causality and the reversibility of a process in time. History becomes a necessary part of a complete description of the process; this can only be ascertained by observation after or as it unfolds. We do not find causality or necessary connection in nature, only the schema of causality, that is, uniform sequence. Kantian categories are merely subjective necessities of thought.

He drops the small chalk
      to the floor   brushes his hands
   stands
scratching more signs
     on the blackboard's surface
         connections
to invisible sorcery
            The secret rests
in the chaos of dust on the floor.
        Incandescent light
   leaves the window.
'Dust as the Mask of Chaos,' by Caratheodory (CA 43)

1.3.4.2.1.5.1. Freedom & Necessity
The limits of the universe, like the speed of light or quantum of a field, put limits on freedom. Events are limited to localities; size limits function; history limits development. The universe as a whole seems to work with 50% reliability. Existence is already half determined; freedom and necessity must be balanced at about fifty percent; this compares with 50% redundancy in information theory. The predictability of particular events within a larger aggregate of events is technically referred to as redundancy in information theory. The purpose of redundancy in that theory is to overcome noise in the environment and help maintain the stability of a communications system. The word redundant describes that part of a message that can be left out without decreasing the information content. Information sources are redundant in that messages may give many clues. The ideal has been to remove redundancy, to send a minimum number of clues; but, if there is any error in transmission, a false message results.

Languages can be measured for redundancy. It has been found that all human languages approach a rating of fifty percent, which is the optimum needed to maintain an equilibrium between the old (predictable) and the new (unexpected), and between order and disorder. A perfectly predictable language would be of little value in a changing universe, whereas the other extreme could never be learned or understood.

Too much freedom, the refusal to acknowledge what is determined, would inflict the self-determination of many on the self determination of each, resulting in social chaos, and reducing other freedoms. Too little freedom, the refusal to acknowledge what can be done, results in stagnation. This is another paradoxical duality, unless considered as mutual arising. We do not eat poisonous plants, or breath water, although both can be done with adequate preparations. Hegel recognized that: 'Freedom is the recognition of necessity.' One conclusion from that recognition is that perfection is impossible.

It is basic to the Taoist view of process that everything is what it is only in relation to all others. Nature is not a forced order, the result of laws; the laws arising from the motion of nature are conceptual structures projected on nature for understanding and control. Simple particles—hydrogen—move to simple laws. Collisions produce simple orders through entrainment. We say that all natural phenomena are governed by natural laws. Many characteristics of nature seem arbitrary, e.g., the quantum of energy, electromagnetic field laws, four dimensions, and axioms of geometry. There may be other worlds with different values, existing elsewhere in the STEM field. A.N. Whitehead thinks that since laws are arbitrary, there are others outside the epoch in space-time. A. Wigner questions whether the laws of physics are complete. D. Bohm wonders how universal they are. The laws are not perfectly obeyed, which creates disorder that is an openness for change. There is a gradual transition to new types of order. Laws evolve.

1.3.4.2.1.5.2. Process
The primacy of process was urged by Heraklitus and later by A.N. Whitehead. Process is fundamental at the microscopic level; space-time and matter are semi-macroscopic statistical constructs akin to temperature and entropy. Understanding of process is critical to modern physics. Modern physics departs from classical physics by emphasizing a discontinuous process, in which the following statements are true:
- Process is not continuous, but discrete; electron jump is characterized by a change of 'action variable' by an integral number of units (Planck's h).

- Constitutive order of discrete processes is determined by laws of probability, not second order curves.
- In classical physics there was a domain of phenomena, electromagnetic fields, that moved in an entirely different order (wave motion).
- Electrons are complementary—a wave-particle duality; the whole order of movement as displacement of particles from one place to another has been transcended; even Brownian motion curves of infinite order are inadequate to describe phenomena of duality.

David Bohm states that all is process; there is no 'thing' in the universe. Objects are abstractions of what is relatively constant from a process of movement and transformation—like shapes in clouds. Clouds are an aspect of the movement of air and condensation of water vapor; the forms have only a certain relative stability. Objects are condensations in a field of being. Rocks and galaxies are also taken as foci of vast processes extending over the universe. Each focus is an aspect of the whole. In a metaphysics of process, Bohm starts with the notion that totality is vast, beyond the measure of human understanding, both quantitatively and in the richness of its qualities. We always begin with what is, which is unknown. We creatively abstract a certain knowledge. As our experience is extended, the notion of process metaphysics may change beyond recognition. Already, Finkelstein's system of mechanics is more tactile and kinaesthetic than visual in its intuitions.

1.3.4.2.1.5.2.1. *Relativistic.* Relativity implies that neither point-particles or quasi-rigid bodies are primary concepts. They can be expressed in terms of events and processes. Process is primary. A local structure may be described as a world tube (vortex). A process goes on in it; the object is an abstraction of a relatively invariant form.

Each center of process takes in impressions of the rest and expresses these in an environment. Expressions reform as new impressions. Thus, the center assimilates the environment and transforms both to fit. Particles express themselves through a field. Electrons and other particles are names of aspects of vast, self-regulating hierarchies of process. Observer and observed are only names of aspects of the process.

1.3.4.2.1.5.2.2. *Quantumistic.* Superficially, quantum mechanics seems to be the opposite of relativity: Process is secondary, and objects seem to be primary. But what is primary is their indivisibility. Bohr emphasized the indivisibility of certain processes; if we say that the whole is more than the sum of parts, then no system and no event can be wholly objective. Isolating any event introduces falsification. But, that isolation is necessary for analysis. Quantum physics deals with elementary processes; its theme is the process character of nature; its most fundamental experience is that this process is not objectifiable.

Max Jammer argues that if quantum mechanical theory is accepted, the postulate of an absolute reality has a rational foundation, that is, reality as created by observation. But reality cannot be relative to nonreality. The word absolute is from the past participle of the Latin infinitive *absolvere*, meaning to set free or release. It was originally used to mean independent or unconditioned. Spinoza used it as the opposite of relative. Quantum mechanics is too incomplete to describe all of reality. E. Wigner believes that quantum mechanics does not completely describe biological objects. Quantum mechanics is not the correct theory for describing macroscopic systems. It is not the theory of nature as a whole. There may never be a physical theory for nature as a whole (refer to Gödel again). The snake cannot completely swallow itself by the tail; quantum mechanics can only account for classical features of the macroscopic world as very good approximations; the theory is only approximately unambiguous or self-consistent.

D. Finkelstein thinks that a new theory need not be fundamentally ambiguous, nor would it be ambiguous about measurements, therefore. It would not be about observables, but about be-ables. Finkelstein questions what we will build out of quanta: beings or becomings, essences or existences? Obviously, both are needed. Elementary particles or primitive processes of matter are assembled into chromosome-like code sequences. The world is metaphorically like a self-replicating automaton. The codon (process) and the code are necessary. The combination of codon and code are needed to express the general process (kinematics) and natural process (dynamics) so that self-replicating processes (stationary states) in a stochastic environment are observed elementary particle processes. In the beginning, the word and wording.

1.3.4.2.1.5.2.3. *Quantum Relativistic.* The isolated system is the reference for the propositions of theoretical physics. Bohm qualifies quantum wholeness from that implied by relativity theory. Nevertheless there is a deep similarity. One of the problems is that there is no means of introducing extended structure in relativity; particles are extensionless points.

Relativity requires continuity, strict causality (determinism), and locality. Quantum theory requires noncontinuity, noncausality, and nonlocality. What is needed is a new theory from which these contradictions can be independently derived as special cases. Relativity and quantum theory seem to be complementary. Basically, the former treats global-local relations and the latter treats metaphysical limits.

Certainly, there is a similarity to the distinction between digital and analog. Relativity is an expression of the limit of localities in the universe. Quantum dynamics is an expression of the limit of distinction in one locality. The predictions of one are not well applied to considerations of the other. For example, quantum dynamics implies holographic wholeness. Applied on the level of galaxies, it has almost no predictive value. The laws of relativity—local space-time frames—have taken over. This is not to say that the universe is not whole, only that the effects between relative local frames are minimal.

Relativity implies that time is relative to an observer. No sharp distinction between space and time can be made. And since quantum theory implies that spatial elements are noncausal and nonlocal projections of higher-dimensional reality, time is also a projection and discontinuous like space. Time and space are secondary. The STEM field—being—is primary. The fundamental law is of an immense multidimensional ground, from which orders are projected into a unified field. But perhaps the process is continuous and discontinuous. Using a catastrophe field (Rene Thom) as a metaphor, parts of the field appear discontinuous due to the shape of the field. What is discontinuous depends on our method of examination. Entities may be regarded as discontinuities in continuous becoming. Discontinuity is potential change. Humans see continuity due to their comparatively large size.

The universe is a construction of waves whose shapes have meaning; the universal wave system is qualitative according to quantum theory and unique according to relativity. Physics is now qualitative, a study of arrangement and pattern. And reality is the reality of Tantalus, always rising out of reach, according to Caratheodory (CC 19):

The [citron] rolls and falls off the table
Moves under it—the thought retreats.
We reach for particles and stars; they recede
Just beyond our grasp.
Everything is made of particles full
Of strangeness and charm that we
Cannot possess.
Trees lift fruit beyond our reach
And water lowers beneath our thirst.
Reality is always rising or sinking
Out of touch.
No effort can capture
Truth—our self-conscious desires offend.
We must learn to love the distance
Between ourselves and what we seek.
Tantalus smiles and reaches.

1.3.4.2.2. Version

The physicist is preoccupied with deriving equations from the various conserved properties and then seeking transformations—rotations—of these equations to reveal that they are merely aspects of some single underlying form. Think of the laws of nature as a perfect sphere; then think of the equations denoting unvarying properties of particle behavior as merely different rotations of the sphere. The sphere is still a sphere. This is how enantiodromia, the operation of opposites, occurs. The sphere can be thought of in the abstract as possessing any number of modes of rotational change that leave its essential nature unchanged. Physics then is no longer concerned with the object, but only with its behavior.

Turning means rotating around an axis such that parts on the whole become visible and invisible through motion. The universe—Being—moves and turns. Being is seen as a result of its turning. Turning is a technical turn to describe the change from invisible to visible. As a result of its seeing and being seen, it becomes another universe. The word universe comes from the Latin of Cicero (*unum versum*), which means 'turning into one whole.' Any universe is one turn.

Living beings have a handedness. Honeysuckle is left-handed; morning glory is right. A photon generates either a right or left helix. Proteins attain a biological active form by a process of turning. Human unfolding (like molecules unfolding) becomes active (turning out). This is the secret: Each time the kaleidoscope turns in our imagination we see a new, unexpected universe. All visible things have been formed by a combination of processes.

Two great universal tendencies related to turning can be identified. Ludwig Boltzmann, Georg Hirth, Leon Brillouin, and Lancelot Whyte are among those who first recognized that there were two processes, one of disorder and loss, and the other of order and development. The universe is one turning composed of at least two polar processes, entropy (inward turning) and ektropy (outward turning). These processes occur roughly equally for the creation of order and disorder in dynamic tension. The first process has been called entropy; it tends towards dynamic disorder. The second, ektropy (although it has also be named negentropy, morphic order, or syntropy, among others); it tends towards spatial order.

Entropy equals shuffling; ektropy equals sorting. Entropy is a measure of infinite individual order. Ektropy is a measure of complex order, of limited individual order. So entropy laws are simpler than ektropy laws. Infinite orders are externally described by simpler laws.

1.3.4.2.2.1. Inversion

Inversion, from the Latin for "turning in," is a kind of entropy or involution. Entropy, the word coined by R. Clausius (1865), means generating a transformation, in an abstract phase space. The entropy of order, of energy, or of information, is derivative of the entropy of turning.

This discussion outlines some of the nonquantitative aspects of entropy, as well as the claims of scientific theory. Science has needed to form concepts which befuddle it, and which cannot be treated scientifically. Thermodynamics is one such nebulous area. As W. Gibbs stated in his *Elementary Principles of Statistical Mechanics*, the generality of entropy extends well beyond the border of thermodynamics proper. For many physicists the discussion of entropy occurs on a philosophical level anyway. Physics has needed to form concepts which are confusing and which cannot be treated strictly scientifically. Thermodynamics is such an area. From the physicist's perspective, through the parts, the whole is invisible, but the problem area is a whole. In the following treatment, some of the nonquantitative aspects of entropy will be discussed, as well as some of the general claims and faults of the scientific theory.

Entropy is derived from the Greek word, "*entropia*," which means turning in, or evolution, or 'generating a transformation.' The constant transformation of energy into heat Clausius called entropy. Entropy is the property of a body, expressed as a mathematical quantity, which, if an amount of heat enters or leaves the body, is increased or diminished proportionately to that amount divided by the absolute temperature. Classical entropy is defined in an abstract manner as a thermodynamic variable of a system under consideration; it is a quantity uniquely defined by the state of the system. It is more commonly a measure of the unavailable energy in a closed system. The system has a set quantity of free energy that is available for producing mechanical work. In the process of working, however, some energy is dissipated into the whole system where it becomes bound and unavailable for work. The change is qualitative.

This tendency toward the qualitative change of atoms and molecules in an abstract phase space was for a long time the only one-way tendency recognized by orthodox physics; it was the only such process that had been systematically studied as a class of processes. Clausius formed two laws that are the basis of classical thermodynamics: (1) the energy in the universe, as an isolated system, is constant, and (2) entropy in an isolated system is always increasing.

The classical concept of entropy was concerned only with

macroscopic states of matter, with experimentally observable properties. It is unconcerned with the mechanism of the phenomena. Entropy is "times arrow," as Eddington said. But entropy has no set rate of occurrence. Its character is fact-like rather than law-like. As a description of fact, classical thermodynamics is qualitative and evolutionary. The entropy law was formulated using cosmological language, about 'nature' or the 'universe.' Clausius did not form a recipe to express the entropy change in terms of observable quantities. Its thermodynamic application was confined to equilibrium states. Order and disorder will be addressed later.

1.3.4.2.2.2. Eversion

Eversion, from the Latin for "turn out," means ektropy or evolution. Ludwig Boltzmann (1866) described the energetic shuffling of energy from the sun as a competition for entropy. But the shuffling process could not explain order, as the result of an automatic random process.

Because biological evolution is so obviously contrary to the concept of thermodynamic entropy, Herbert Spencer (1890) stated a new principle of nature, the instability of the homogenous, or a differentiating force creating organization.

Georg Hirth (1900), an art expert, coined the word ektropy to identify the principle that opposes the entropic principle of degradation in living structures. Ektropy means generating order or form, in ordinary space. The word is from the Greek, *ektropia*, meaning turning out. It is a universal sorting process. On an organic level this process is intentional. For instance, a biological organism chooses the right building units for its metabolism (from the Greek, *metabalein*, exchange). F. Auerbach, a physicist, used the same distinction for a while. Auerbach and Hirth wrongly believed that entropy must be victorious in battle with ektropy, not realizing the complementary relationship between the processes.

In the 1930s, Schrodinger reiterated Boltzmann's point by saying that organisms live by consuming negentropy. This characteristic of life was called 'entropy feeling' by Schrodinger. Negative entropy, however, was not purposive. It was a structure-forming process, but only applied to the organic realm, not to the nuclear or inorganic. The process would have to apply at all levels,

Prigogine thinks that the unexpected new feature is that nonequilibrium may lead to a new type of structure, dissipative structure. He avoided naming a sorting process in this way, but assumed its operation.

Nature appears to constitute both a series of self-evolving ektropic phenomena, and a series of disorganizing entropic processes. All visible forms, from atoms to galaxies, were formed by ektropic processes. As there are defined laws of entropy, there are laws of ektropy: (1) The universe is self-ordering; (2) a quantitative increase in any matter eventually produces a sudden qualitative change, and; (3) the results of these matter organizations are stable holons that are used and reused, from elements through organic molecules (and DNA) to societies. Ektropic processes result in a hierarchy. A corollary law of ektropy would state that groups of particles move toward ordered states; more is packed into less, until miniaturization achieves greater levels of complexity, as in human designs.

All visible things have been formed by a combination of these two processes. Entropy equals shuffling; ektropy equals sorting. Entropy is a measure of infinite individual order. Ektropy is a measure of complex order, of limited individual order.

1.3.4.2.2.3. Reversion

The world is constantly changing, but also returning to previous forms and states; the word reversion is from the Latin for "turn back." This may be observed in the states of water, or life and death. Beings follow in succession, then turn back at a limit. They revert to former or earlier states. Sometimes, this implies simplification. It may relate to patterns of survival.

To survive means to adapt to an environment that includes other individuals and processes and patterns. To survive, an ecosystem depends on the interactions and balance of many variables, most of which are not well understood. In agriculture or forestry, humanity tries to maximize one of those variables. When that happens, the balance or harmony is altered, and although it may take decades or centuries for the consequences to be known, the system is affected. For organisms, the environment is a filter that allows some characteristics to continue, by providing opportunities and challenges. Selection operates as a survival filter that passes any structure than has sufficient integrity to persist in the system. Organisms put together structures based on historical patterns, and move through a filter of limits like minnows through a fish net.

This reversion resembles the movement of the tao. The world was something to observe, to learn from and to employ respectfully for the Taoists. The world changes but returns to previous forms and states. This movement of the tao is also called reversion. But it is two movements, unfoldings, observed in seasons and other processes.

1.3.4.2.2.4. Conversion

Conversion (from the Latin for "turn with") means to transform or exchange into an order or disorder. The sediment from this change is history. Entropy and ektropy are changes of order. The two processes are not inversely related—they are directly related. When one increases, the other increases, although there is no rate of change. Order increases as disorder increases. No theory can consider only entropy or only ektropy. No metaphysics can be based on only one of the processes. And, solutions that address only one half of the process are half solutions.

According to Georgescu-Rogen, probability was introduced into thermodynamics to save the mechanistic representation of nature. Only the complexity of systems of particles has allowed this approach. Boltzmann's ambition was to be the Darwin of the evolution of matter. In his approach to thermodynamics, Boltzmann applied statistical mechanics toward interpreting the properties of the microscopic systems that make up the macroscopic ones. Entropy is determined in a completely different manner in statistical mechanics. Statistical entropy is defined as a measure of the number of ways in which the elementary particles of the system may be arranged under the given circumstances. This changed the coordinates from temperature and heat to space, time and force. In statistical thermodynamics all particles are treated as qualityless individuals with mechanical coordinates.

In the Clausius formulation of entropy, it was only a variable of state, physical. With Boltzmann, however, as the degree of disorder, entropy no longer had an instrumental measure. Thermal equilibrium was explained, not as a balance of heat exchange, but as the result of a universal shuffling process (undefined). Boltzmann's order principle governs the structure of equilibrium states; it is a probability distribution.

Statistical thermodynamics does not concern itself with the history of particles. Furthermore, since entropy is a measure of improbability, time is theoretically reversible. Statistical thermodynamics is related to classical thermodynamics in a theoretical mathematical way. It does not measure quite the same thing, although the calculations yield close to the same numbers. According to Planck the entropy principle defined order as the improbable arrangement of elements; disorder was the dissolution of order. Schrodinger (1946) said that entropy was nothing but molecular disorder itself. Energy and order can be related as bound or unbound energy. Increase in entropy has been equated with an increase in disorder. But proofs of the increase of entropy always encounter paradox and contradiction. Even Prigogine recognizes that there are serious difficulties with Boltzmann's approach to entropy.

His definition applies only for certain initial conditions. The notion of entropy is inseparable from probability, which is inseparable from randomness.

In fact, entropy results in states of higher individual order. Entropy is the highest individual order (direction); ektropy is the highest relational order. The individual orders interact less often (using less energy).

Life is considered an order of individuals, so life can be characterized by entropy production and use, also. In the 1930s, Schrodinger reiterated Boltzmann's point by saying that organisms live by consuming negentropy. This characteristic of life was called "entropy feeling" by Schrodinger. Negative entropy was not purposive. It was a structure-forming process, but only applied to the organic realm, not to the atomic or inorganic.

While the shuffling process may produce order sometimes, the sorting intentional process does it on demand. For instance, a biological organism chooses the right building units for its metabolism (from *metabalein*, exchange); this characteristic of life is called an entropy feeling by Schrodinger, and it allows the organism to ingest usable orders (it may be similar to Whitehead's negative prehension), to avert its own disordering, by free energy. Life requires entropy as well as order. In fact life can survive only in a world whose entropy increases; it could not survive either extreme, the bombardment of free energy or the complete lack of it,. Order is a requisite to survival; the impulse to produce orderly arrangements must be inbred through evolution.

Individuating. Each stage of evolution is marked by emergence of a new type of individuality embracing and transcending the previous parts of itself. The progressive development of wholes is evolution.

Ordering results from relationships, i.e., collisions on a nuclear level. The higher the order, the more relationships on a microlevel. A maximum chaos is largest set of individual orders. The ordering process (ektropy) creates a macro-order, which produces constraints on micro-orders. A rock, for instance, is a higher level of macro-order than a gas, but it is a lower level of micro-order. It is assumed throughout that order is a reference to macro-order. As orders become closed, they have fewer relationships, but are more structured.

Chaos is the name for the maximum of individual orders, from which macro-orders are derived. Fiebleman states "That it must remain a chaos and not become itself a kind of superorder is required by Godel's theorem," which limits the completeness of a category. Chaos is not an order of all orders, for it contains all orders. But it is positive disorder.

Conviviality, that is living together, emerges from the characteristics of places and ecosystems, from participation, development, and complexity. And these come from the characteristics of the field, from registration, integration, connection, and renewal.

A deep relationship with a place is as necessary as one with other humans. Without it, existence loses much of its significance. A range of experiences can spring from a place, from depression to the peak experiences described by Maslow. The opposite feeling is possible where there is no richness of place; in the dullness of place, everything becomes oppressive and life becomes tedious. But, this and the drudgery is part of a commitment to place; it is acceptance of restrictions. The richness of life forms contributes to the realization of human values and are also values in themselves.

Humans adapt to place as they live, as their communities live, over many generations. They become attached to a place. Attachment to place is a form of deep love, from which many other virtues for living well, such as frugality and humility, spring. Place lets us rediscover a participating consciousness and connection to the earth. Participation means living with other species, the literal definition of conviviality.

Cooperation implies the use of convivial or appropriate technology. The word convivial means social, from the Latin word "*convivium*," meaning living together. Ivan Illich, in *Tools for Conviviality*, sketches a meaningful community where workers have control of their tools and their lives. Conviviality, basically living together in harmony, according to Ivan Illich, is a necessary strategy. Illich suggested that convivial institutions are better than manipulative ones for education and healthcare. People can engage in convivial work and trading clubs. Local exchange and trading systems (LETS) can form barter economies, where people can trade goods or labor.

> She lay on her side, indifferent
>   in sleep. Slowly music, and light
> Dancers around a fire
>   One held up a metal disk
> —She woke, gazing at the wall—
> its smoothness dissolved as from acid
> on a copper Sesterce—Vespacian's profile
> She blinked redimensioning
> The smoothness was scored with scratches
>   As she watched Scratches outlined figures
> Sharply across a fissure
> the code of mystery renewed in red.
>   Sleep as the Mask of Consciousness, Caratheodory (CA 37)

1.3.4.2.2.5. Irreversibility Order & History

Chaos is primeval and eternal, the matrix of permanent possibilities of order. Chaos is the name for the maximum of individual orders, from which macro-orders are derived. Fiebleman states "That it must remain a chaos and not become itself a kind of superorder is required by Godel's theorem," which limits the completeness of a category. Chaos is not an order of all orders, for it contains all orders. But it is positive disorder.

Disorder, in the sense of total absence of order, is a logical and factual impossibility. After motion has taken place, an order can be described. Depending on the complexity of the curve, the future of curvilinear motion may not be predictable. It is wrong to try to identify the totality of all possible order with predictability. A musical composition is not predictable from what comes before, yet it is ordered in a complex way that can be described. A random order contains every kind of suborder, where every means indescribable. And random order is open; it has degrees of freedom. Differences can be related to degrees of freedom. An order with more differences has more degrees of freedom. The macro-order limits degrees of freedom. Movement could not occur without a free order or disorder. There could not be activity within a complete order. Order is applicable not to universe but only to some part. The distinction between order and disorder disappears when domain of both is universe. Perfect chaos has a uniformity close to order. Total order and total disorder are meaningless terms. Bohm indicates that order and disorder are meaningless except by contrast. Disorder is the order of the universe. It is the wider concept and order a special case. Order is disorders in rhythm, entrained.

According to Georgescu-Rogen, probability was introduced into thermodynamics to save the mechanistic representation of nature. Only the complexity of systems of particles has allowed this approach. Boltzmann's ambition was to be the Darwin of the evolution of matter. In his approach to thermodynamics, Boltzmann applied statistical mechanics toward interpreting the properties of the microscopic systems that make up the macroscopic ones. Entropy is determined in a completely different manner in statistical mechanics. Statistical entropy is defined as a measure of the number of ways in which the elementary particles of the system may be arranged under the given circumstances. This changed the coordinates from temperature and heat to space, time and force. In statistical thermodynamics all particles are treated as qualityless individuals with mechanical coordinates.

Statistical thermodynamics does not concern itself with the history of particles. Furthermore, since entropy is a measure of improbability, time is theoretically reversible. Statistical thermodynamics is related to classical thermodynamics in a theoretical mathematical way. It does not measure quite the same thing, although the calculations yield close to the same numbers. According to Planck the entropy principle defined order as the improbable arrangement of elements; disorder was the dissolution of order. Schrodinger (1946) said that entropy was nothing but molecular disorder itself. Energy and order can be related as bound or unbound energy. Increase in entropy has been equated with an increase in disorder. But proofs of the increase of entropy always encounter paradox and contradiction. Even Prigogine recognizes that there are serious difficulties with Boltzmann's approach to entropy. His definition applies only for certain initial conditions. The notion of entropy is inseparable from probability, which is inseparable from randomness.

In fact, entropy results in states of higher individual order. Entropy is the highest individual order (direction); ektropy is the highest relational order. The individual orders interact less often (using less energy).

According to Boltzmann probability increases with the number of possibilities in the system. Entropy was a measure for lack of information. For Shannon and Weaver, information is exactly the same as entropy; entropy, chaos, freedom of choice, and information are identical in information theory. Shannon related information to the inverse of entropy. He was interested in how much information could be contained in a message, and how difficult it was to transmit it; he was not concerned with its meaning. He recognized that the information equations he formulated were similar to statistical thermodynamic equations, so he designated the average information per symbol as entropy. But the relationship is formal and mathematical. The information content per symbol is a dimensionless nonphysical quantity, whereas physical entropy entails physical implications (in six-dimensional phase space for statistical or calories per degree for classical).

Maxwell and others realized that the increase in information always caused a greater increase in entropy. Knowing uses energy, and this is why his demon is impossible. Maxwell's demon pointed out a categorical difference between sorting and shuffling. The shuffling of the universe is automatic. The sorting is a prerogative of mind or instinct (Eddington), although it is also physical. Brillouin concluded the opposite was true: order, negentropy and information were identical. Both interpretations are correct in their own frame of reference. Information is measure of lack of knowledge or predictability, a measure of rarity. Entropy is measure of orders added so that a system is not usable.

Where Shannon gave entropy and information the same abstract dimension by making entropy nonphysical, Brillouin, by giving information the dimension of calories per degree, gave them the same physical dimension. Entropy is the opposite of information; they are inversely related so that when entropy increases, information decreases. There is a confusion of signal with information, of macrostate with microstate in his explanation, however.

1.3.4.2.2.5.1. Order
The process of ordering is prior to the orders that result. The process of ordering is motion. Ordering results from relationships, i.e., collisions on a nuclear level. The higher the order, the more relationships on a microlevel. A maximum chaos is largest set of individual orders. The ordering process (ektropy) creates a macro-order, which produces constraints on micro-orders. A rock, for instance, is a higher level of macro-order than a gas, but it is a lower level of micro-order. It is assumed throughout that order is a reference to macro-order. As orders become closed, they have fewer relationships, but are more structured. Bohm does not distinguish between the two levels, using only order in the sense of macro-order.

Bohm relates that in a Newtonian system, order of motion is just an automorphism: movement with a limited number of states. This partial treatment ignores the complexities of deeper structure. The hierarchy of orders is a purely conceptual abstraction.

Bohm contends that order is more fundamental than relationships and classes; order is logically prior to relationships. But this seems to be a misconception. Order is measured through relationships. That which cannot be related, for instance, to a curve, is referred to as disorder. In fact, Bohm himself states that "order is basically a set of similar differences." In Latin, 'different' means 'to carry apart' (cf. metaphor), whereas 'related' means 'to carry back together.' Bohm again states that difference and similarity, leading to order, are prior to relationship. But prior is an unfortunate choice of words. The brain registers differences and similarities, leading to perception of order and this is related to other orders stored in memories (perhaps in a holographic manner). Nature is ordered only by our understanding. Bohm sees that there are two kinds of differences: constitutive determine the essence of order; distinctive determine how one order is distinguished from another. But are the two really different? Consider a series of points, where a curve can be drawn several ways, using some different and some same points.

The constitutive becomes distinctive.

For example, a curve is an ordered set of points; to describe the order, a curve can be represented approximately by linear chords of equal length. (And this is a metaphor for all human endeavor: representation.) In a straight line the entire curve is determined by the first chord; successive chords differ only in position, not direction. This is a first order. In a circle, chords differ in position and angle, determined by the difference between the first two chords. This is a second order. A spiral is a third order curve. Eventually, a curve of infinite order is reached that is so complex as to be called random or disordered. Bohm makes the further distinction of a difference of orders: the essential difference between two geometrical curves is a different set of similarities, where the first set describes differences within a curve, and the second set describes differences between two curves. He draws the same distinction for similarities.

Relating the two differences is a descriptive process, not an explanation of one by the other. There are natural hierarchies that reflect the existence of real structures more than just our procedures of analysis. The principle of structure is universal: particles ordered to atoms, atoms to molecules, and so on through complexity. Structures have a rich set of cross-references, which show a unified totality of structure rather than an arbitrary array.

Bohm claims that a new structure of mathematical symbolism is needed to take into account the hierarchical potentialities of order and not tacitly commit one to the view that the world is composed of separate elements external to order in process. Order is the description of how the elements are related and the elements are how they are related to some extent from one perspective.

Order so far is abstracted from a process of movement and development in which each order and structure is becoming different. Observed order reflects virtual rhythms of process. Bohm notes that what is essential to process is that the differences are similar so that the changes are ordered. Process is an order of change; orders of change can be ordered into a hierarchy of process—order of orders of change. (The growth of an organism can be expressed in terms of a rich set of differences and similarities.) Changes in the order of a process can be the basis of a higher order of process. Changes of order form another order that constitutes a part of development of an over-all theme.

When cells form an organism, the new factor is that certain variations of behavior of individual cells previously determined fortuitously by the environment are now ordered intrinsically in the functioning of the organism. The creation and transformation of order are the most fundamental account of laws of process. High macro-orders, e.g., dog or biosphere, then limit micro-orders.

Bohm contends that the order of orders of dynamic function are needed for maintaining coherent growth and life. And there is another kind of evolution, which is the coming into being of a new and higher order of process. Thus, in music, there can be a variation on a given theme, then a basic change of order of the whole theme.

Function is a certain kind of ordered change of structure that transforms an input structure into an output structure. A function of the brain is to digest informational structures; a function of society is to create conditions of happiness. Function must ultimately be referred beyond the field of function if it is to be understood. Current metaphysics appeals to survival value as a transfunctional feature to which all biological function has to be referred.

The word "structure" comes from the Latin, "*stuere*," meaning to build or evolve. Structure is a harmoniously organized totality of orders and measures, both hierarchical (many levels) and extensive. Order is a fundamental notion that underlies both physics and biology, permitting them to be related in a deep and essential way, with a common language and conceptual structure for the formulation of both. A coherent theory of biology has to involve the notion of order in a very fundamental way. No field of thought can do without the universal concept of order, from art to thermodynamics. But there is no agreement on the forms and limits of order.

Rupert Riedl (1978) defined order as: "an expression of conformity to law." "A meaningful connection between independent quantities according to internal laws." Order becomes determinacy content; it is the same as ektropy (negentropy is his term). Indeterminacy content corresponds to entropy or chaos. He formulates order as being law content times the number of instances when the law applies; or law times instances. This is compatible with previous definitions: macro-order determines micro-order. A quantitative concept of order has arisen from the theory of probability and chance: Schrodinger's negative entropy—the inversion of measure of chaos, for the freedom of accident. (Refer to the discussion of entropy for how order is related to energy.)

Order can be explained as a decrease in the degrees of freedom through combination. If we draw a mosaic of hexagons, then use a set of random numbers (derived from pi or last four telephone numbers) to determine the direction of flow inside hexagons, most lines will link up automatically to form a branched network. This model is the reverse of one for evolution (compare this with Stanley's diagram for punctuated species; the hexagon cells could be niches with lines as species).

Figure 1342251-1. Hexagon Pattern (after Stevens)

Luna Leopold generated branching patterns from random numbers and found that they resembled natural river systems. A Horton analysis, after R. E. Horton, the geographer, of patterns divides a system into first, second and third order streams; ratios are taken. The field of action in arteries, rivers and lightening bolts is the same. The explanation of triple corners: minimum energy, probability, and selective evolution.

If nature directs flow from a center, she must adopt a pattern of explosion. If she requires shortness as well as directness, she must introduce branching. An economical network uses three-way joints (the pattern of hexagons). Branching is the delineation of a tree from a net. The brain may also operate in a similar way.

This concept of order supports a holarchic world view. The Great Chain of Being (macro-microcosm) replaces the inferior/superior line of linear thought that supports the linear, hierarchic world view.

Order was defined as the similarity between differences. Disorder is equivalent to the difference among similarities. Fiebleman considers positive disorder as extent to which elements of a given order are distributed outside that order among elements of other orders. His thesis is that disorder depends on random dispersion of limited orders. However, since existence depends on motion, motion is prior to order.

All visible things have been formed by a combination of processes. Entropy equals shuffling; ektropy equals sorting. Entropy is a measure of infinite individual order. Ektropy is a measure of complex order, of limited individual order. So entropy laws are simpler than ektropy laws. Infinite orders are externally described by simpler laws. The entropy of order, of energy, of information, is derivative of the entropy of turning. The universe is one turning composed of at least two polar processes, entropy (inward turning) and ektropy (outward turning). Turning is a formal process here, called Version. These processes occur roughly equally for the creation of order and disorder in dynamic tension.

The order from disorder principle seems to be irreducible and inexplicable; it is just there, as is the universe. Systems of complexity evolve as the product of the intrinsic nature of the universe in all steps from atoms to societies. Negentropy is synonymous with Szent

Gyorgyi's term, syntropy, a drive toward greater order. He rejected random mutation as accounting for sophistication. Molecules fit like a watch; improving one link would not likely improve the watch; he suggested changing all wheels simultaneously. (cf. Simon's Horus parable). Evolution involves true transformation, reforming basic structure, not adding on. Others have also hypothesized ordering principles: Bergson's *elan vital* or Woltereck's anamorphosis; von Bertalanffy's morphosis. Whyte (1966) called the process "morphic," from the Greek, meaning "generating order or form."

As expressed by Boltzmann, the second law of thermodynamics expresses an increase of molecular disorder; equilibrium corresponds to a state of maximum probability. In biology and sociology, just the opposite meaning of evolution is true; as transformations to higher levels of complexity and improbability. Neither classical or statistical thermodynamics applies to the world of living beings, as more than a limiting process. Georgescu-Rogen and Rifkin are wrong to think so. Prigogine is right in that respect, but he developed a nonlinear thermodynamics to apply to biochemistry and life that was based on the same linear half-thought. The biosphere obeys the law of entropy only as a general limit. The entire process is exentropic since energy flows from sun to earth and long wave radiation flows from earth to the sink of space. Entropy does appear to force a historical direction to the universe. Even simple life is historical and presupposes a distinction between past and future. History limits biological and ecological development. Living beings anticipate a future through signals from the environment.

1.3.4.2.2.5.2. History
Poincare concluded that thermodynamics and dynamics are incompatible. Prigogine agrees with the conclusion that there is no dynamical interpretation of the second law. Therefore, the notion of irreversibility comes from supplementary phenomenological or subjectivistic assumptions, from 'mistakes.' How can we account for the wealth of important results and concepts that derive from the second law? Prigogine asks. In a sense, living beings and humans are mistakes. But Prigogine offers a second alternative: retain the idea of introducing a microscopic entropy such that macroscopic entropy is an appropriate average of the microscopic entropy, thus realizing Poincare's program differently, by associating an operator (as quantum mechanics associates operators with physical quantities) with microscopic entropy. Prigogine's concept of irreversibility is similar to Boltzmann's: it is the manifestation on the macroscopic scale of randomness on a microscopic scale. It is a purely dynamic approach; randomness and irreversibility are

consequences of the structure of equations of motion.

Planck emphasized that the second law distinguishes between states in nature, some of which act as attractors for others; irreversibility is the expression of attraction. According to Planck, an irreversible process in thermodynamics is a process which once performed leaves the world in an altered state. Thermodynamics makes transition to process thinking by introducing irreversibility. Time-symmetry is broken; there is history. And history limits the expansion of Boltzmann's statistical theory to micro-orders.

The loss from turning creates a sediment, which is history. Sedimenting is irreversible and gives direction to time. The sediment of the past is a given and different for each present. The ceaseless activity of being in history creates newness. Novelty is born from the womb ("hystera") of change. History is the result of this hysteresis process. Motion, Version, Scension—all together form the ontological spiral of being/environment. The motion of the field creates a turning, which leaves a history, out of which patterns arise. Scension is a precession of motions, resulting in directional change—evolution. The transformation is a historical expression.

The evolution of matter, for instance, proceeds through a spiral process, as exemplified in the carbon cycle in stars, where a carbon nucleus captures four protons and emits them as an alpha particle at the end of the process. In some cases physical behavior depends on past history. Magnetic hysteresis is one case. Hysteresis is not confined to magnetism—structural deformation and colloidal behavior also may depend on past history. Louis de Broglie, and later Bohm, think that the Heisenberg indeterminacy may be the result of not taking into account the past history of an elementary particle in predicting its behavior. Perhaps some of the problems attendant in scientific inquiry arise from the inability to take into consideration the complex history of a particle (cf. Heisenberg's uncertainty principle). Nature is unpredictable. Its fuzziness is due to indeterminate states—indeterminate to us, who have limited perspectives in a local system.

Reversibility is only an abstraction, made possible through the simplification of curves. The evolution of life resembles a random curve, as the process of a potentially infinite order. Living matter tends to evolve hierarchies in ever increasing totalities of orders. Orders high in entropy are different from change of order through evolution. Only in a world of pure chance is order most improbable. In a historical world, with evolutionary systems of structured organisms, order becomes a probable state. Randomness becomes information depending on the position of observer.

PAF

Rivers meander through flatlands; a straight line moving through a resistant medium becomes a sine wave. Paul Slater notes that history is portrayed in sine wave images. But from extremely close up or distant, the wave appears as a straight line. The rise of a great civilization is a concentration of culture. As in nature, the components (of culture) do not change, but are recombined. Slater finds hope in our powerlessness to transcend the circuitry of natural systems (physical, biological or cultural). Historians also have a passion for punctuating human history. C. W. Mills observed that humans rarely make history; it usually just happens. Numerous, accumulative infinitesimal actions build up to enormous consequences; that is one explanation for the ecocrises. The minutiae of everyday life adds up to fate. Fate is where whatever happens was intended by no one.

1.3.4.2.3. Scension

Scension is the process of rising and emerging from a pattern. The inside arises mutually with the outside, different but inseparable. Entropy and ektropy have just this relation. But everything is what it is only in relation to all others. This is the taoist principle of mutual arising restated. If everything is allowed to go its own way the harmony of the universe is established. In the principle of mutual arising, the universe produces our consciousness and that evokes the universe. There is no environment without organisms. This realization transcends the debate between idealists and materialists. The only single event is the universe; organic pattern, not causality, is the rationale of the world. The tao is a formative field.

In general, when different modes of descriptions appear as opposites, it is more satisfactory to consider them as complimentary instead. This is the case with net/trees, or autonomy/control. These pairs are not one, but not two either. The duality is connected with processes in both directions. The complementarity framework includes many dualities, such as being and becoming or context and text. Since they mutually specify each other there is no real duality. This separation is no Hegelian synthesis, since there is nothing new, but an appraisal of how things are related in description. Opposites are polarities that create a field; the sky is not a place, it is a relationship between earth and sun. The sky is empty yet it is a form of relationship. In order to exist things need literal integrity, the tao or the field.

1.3.4.2.3.1. Inscension

Inscension (from the Latin for "climb in") means develop inwardly. Stars, as well as some galaxies and other astronomic objects, grow by accretion. Many physical structures, such as talus slopes, grow by addition, until some physical limit, such as gravity or the coefficient of friction, is passed, then they stop growing. Some stability can be gotten from growth in early stages; later stability must result from limits and metabolism. Growth in plants can delay the onset of senility by ridding the plant of waste products in more diluted form. However, too much growth produces a strain on tissues and early decay. In fact, one herbicide promotes excess growth as a means to kill weeds.

Mechanisms for growth can become pathologies when central authorities meddle in stable lower orders. Flexibility, again, is imperiled. The nonproductive superstructure places excessive demands on the substrate and destroys it. Technology or social structure can mask the internal stress.

When maturity is reached, growth stops, especially in the form of generating new cells and increasing in size. Extra cells are not produced. A biological organism grows to maturity, which is a stopping point for size. The organism continues to develop, however, experiencing and learning the environmental complexities through mating and then to the end of life. Development may include growth at some stages, but development refers to the continued change after growth has stopped.

1.3.4.2.3.2. Escension

Escension (from the Latin for "climb out") means to emerge. New properties emerge from motion and turning. The world, as it exists in its ceaseless changes, appears as a single cosmic process in which higher orders of being emerge. In a hierarchy of levels, emergent properties appear at some levels. Life is also a property immanent in an organization of molecules; and language emerges in a higher level. New qualities that emerge at every step are unpredictable on basis of past.

Complexes of parts can be calculated in three ways: (1) by counting the number of parts, (2) by considering the species to which they belong, and (3) by considering the relations between parts. The first two cases understand the sum of parts in isolation. These are summative; the parts make no difference to the function, like a pile of bricks. Other examples include the Pauli exclusion principle, homeostatic self-regulation, and distributive justice—all of which are meaningless to individuals. The third describes constitutive complexes, where wholes are other than the sum of their parts. New properties emerge.

The world, as it exists in its ceaseless changes, appears as a single cosmic process in which higher orders of being emerge. The word emergent is borrowed from Lloyd Morgan (1912), who first used it in this manner in *Instinct and Experience*. But emergence and ideas of organism came in rough form from Herbert Spencer (circa 1880). Morgan later set forth a view of the world as evolutionary process in *Emergent Evolution.* "Emergent" was used to show that higher orders of being are not mere resultants of what went before and were not contained in them as an effect is in its efficient cause. Nature evolves by sudden leaps, from matter, to life, and mind. Jan Smuts (1926) amplified the idea in *Holism and Evolution.* He attempted to state the principle of emergence by saying that nature is permeated by an impulse towards the creation of wholes; each stage of evolution is marked by emergence of a new type of individuality embracing and transcending the previous parts of itself. The progressive development of wholes is evolution.

Some systems are more coherent and autonomous than others. In a hierarchy of levels, emergent properties appear at some levels. Form, melody and harmony are systems properties arising from the hierarchical organizations of notes into pieces of music. Life is also a property immanent in an organization of molecules; and language emerges in a higher level. New qualities that emerge at every step are unpredictable on basis of past; reality is creative. Nature is more like an artist than an engineer.

Emergence is a movement of ascendance (scension) within being (the STEM field). The ascent takes place through complexity. At each change of quality, the complexity is expressed in a new simplicity. The emergent quality is the summing together in a new totality of the component materials (See Figure 134233-1).

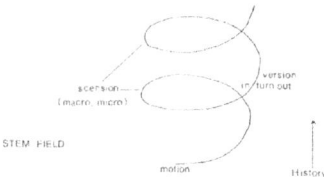

Figure 134233-1. The Process of Emergence

The spiral is a more comprehensive image than the star (intersecting triangles), because it is inclusive and not oppositional, and because it describes direct relationships and not inverse ones.

The evolution of the universe is a history of the unfolding of differentiated order or complexity. Building up emphasizes structure and levels of hierarchy by joining systems from the bottom up. Bohm states that we have been conditioned to the belief that higher orders of nature are determined by the lower order of the mechanical motion of particles. It is impossible to exclude the contrary assumption that high order features of natural laws are as fundamental as those referring to atomic movements. By comparison, unfolding implies an interweaving of processes structured at different levels. Evolution acts in sense of simultaneous and interdependent structuration of microworlds and macroworlds. Complexity emerges from the interpenetration of processes of differentiation and integration, processes running simultaneously from top and bottom and shaping the hierarchy from both sides. Microevolution generates macroscopic conditions for continuity and macroevolution generates microscopic elements for processes. Life is an emergent property of a hierarchy of chemical levels. It is not found in molecules but through autopoetic organization of molecules. The universe restructures itself constantly at a more complex level.

William Wheeler applied emergence in ecological settings. Species were modified by association; new qualities appeared. For instance, a prey species reflects a predator species, e.g., deer reflect wolves; the two are related in an association (cf. Whitehead, on relatedness).

At the ecosystem level, escension means the process of spiraling around the matched changes of materials and species. This is sometimes identified as succession, although it is not the return to previous states at any level of complexity, due to the changes in initial conditions at every historical step.

1.3.4.2.3.3. Rescension
Rescension (from the Latin for "climb back") means that rising is part of a cycle. That which collapses gathers itself up and climbs back up. It reemerges from a cycle.

We look back to where we have been in history, gather up the old economies, and turn on the spiral in a new direction (spiral history, turning of universe, in and out).

With modern electronics and miniaturized technology, we do not have to return to the idiocy of rural life. History is a spiral, not a circle. We can spiral back to the country—old labor turned to form of art and sacred ritual. Ritual of communal labor might bring community together for a few hours a day in global village; rest of day devoted to individual creations. The pattern recoils, as it remakes simple patterns and more complex patterns.

1.3.4.2.3.4. Conscension
Conscension (from the Latin for "climb with") means a hierarchy or climax. Henri Poincare recognized (1905) that explanation in science involved generalization and simplification; so hierarchical levels

emerged in his studies. Human perception of nature is hierarchical, regardless of whether nature is. Several theorists distinguish levels of hierarchy in nature. Miller includes particles, atoms, molecules, organisms, societies, and nations. Mario Bunge extends the list to include processes and knowledge: Elementary particles (atoms, bodies); physical systems (organisms, ecosystems); physical processes (chemical, biological, social); material production (ritual, culture); knowledges (physics, history). Ervin Laszlo makes a distinction between a macrohierarchy, comprised of a space-time field, particles, stars, galaxies, and various aggregations; and microhierarchies like the earth, composed of molecules, crystals, cells, organisms, ecosystems, and Gaia. Hierarchies can be regarded as vertically arborizing structures whose branches interlock with those of other hierarchies at a multiplicity of levels and form horizontal networks; arborization and reticulation are complementary principles in the architecture of organisms and societies.

The law of vertical order of hierarchy determines the ever-changing level structure. In a hierarchy, there are two streams of information: the factual going up, and the directive going down. The upward stream, through perception into consciousness, makes observation possible; downward motion makes participation possible. Since all things participate to some extent in the streams, all are involved in the hierarchy.

In a government hierarchy, effects of decisions percolate down and spread out, wavelike. From the perspective of a single level, it looks like the decision moved through space from one department to another. Bohm considers that this is a good model of quantum transitions; where each state corresponds to a quasi-equilibrium of hierarchies. Informational relations are compounded in a hierarchy and are reflected at every level. Organizations can be analyzed into smaller blocks; the pattern of whole organization is reflected at every division in differences of organization on either side of boundary. What makes some systems more coherent than others? Perhaps emergent properties appearing in a hierarchy of levels.

Herbert Simon illustrates the merits of hierarchical order with the parable of the watchmakers (in Koestler, 1969): Hora and Tempus both make watches consisting of a thousand parts per watch. Hora assembles a watch piece by piece; it there is an accident it falls apart and he begins again. Tempus puts together subassemblies of ten parts; these are combined into a subassembly of 100, ten of which compose the watch. If there is a disturbance, Tempus has to repeat only between zero to nine operations. If there is a disturbance at the rate of one in 100 operations, then Hora will take 4000 times longer to assemble a watch:

eleven years instead of one day. With amino acids, proteins or organelles the time scale becomes astronomical.

When a hierarchical order cannot adapt its function to an actual situation, then there is a synchronous change in the vertical order. The change in order is discontinuous, although the function is continuous. Since the details are not abstracted to a higher level, one cannot predict when the revolutionary change will take place. In general, revolution is discontinuous and synchronous, where evolution is continuous and diachronous. In the synchronic mode, form is complete as soon as it appears; in the diachronic, the form is slowly elaborated. It would appear that complex processes, like evolution, use both modes.

Hierarchical thinking is limited in cybernetics. The concept of control could better be stated as reciprocity or mutual causality. Furthermore, in an open system, the environment, structure, program, and feedback all govern the system in concert. Hazel Henderson states that only the system can model or manage the system, but this is not entirely true. Images or codes model the system in miniature.

There are hierarchically organized entities or processes that exist. The universe may be basically hierarchical, with a rich sequence of 'orders of order,' as Bohm puts it, where order is a set of similar differences or different similarities. Or centers of hierarchy proliferating in all directions, more than up a ladder. The latter may be centrifugal, a dispersion of contraries. The former centripetal, emergent reality seeking height. Maurice Merleau-Ponty favors a centrifugal reality. He (1963) mentions three levels: the first characterized by laws or quantity; the second by order; and the third by significance or meaning (or the physical, vital and human). All three have physical existence and are considered at once. For Merleau-Ponty the hierarchy is analytic. The dimensions of being pull one to the future as primary, to cosmic process as envisioned by philosophies of emergence. Hierarchies are levels of extraction; order builds up to extraction.

Ludwig von Bertalanffy concluded that: "Hierarchical organization, on the one hand, and the characteristics of open systems, on the other, seem to be fundamental principles of living nature." Koestler combines these two principles into a system theoretical model of self-regulating, open hierarchical order (SOHO), and uses this as an alternative to models of linear causation. Koestler proposed the term "holon" to designate the janus-faced entities on the intermediate levels of any hierarchy, which can be described either as wholes or parts, depending on the frame of reference above or below (from the Greek word "*holos*," meaning whole and "-*on*," for a particle). The concept of holon transcends the duality of parts and wholes. A holarchy of holons replaces the notion of a hierarchy of parts in a whole (See Figure 134234-1).

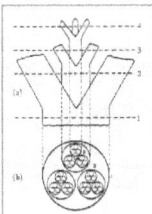

Figure 134234-1. Holons

Warren McCulloch shows that sets of neurons are constituted so that the choices achieved by patterns of stimulation and inhibition of other neurons may generate a hierarchy of value, or as he calls it, a heterarchy. Regarding a hierarchy as an unambiguous order, McCulloch claims that the heterarchy structure can accommodate the ambiguity of the Voter's paradox, where the least preferred of sets may be preferred to the most (e.g., A over B, B over C, but C over A). But, hierarchies involve ambiguity. The essence of hierarchical organization is a vagueness and loss of detail in proceeding from one level to a higher. If ambiguity is accepted for the sake of richness of interpretation, deception results; if it is not accepted, then boredom results. Nets of values are ambiguous. The metaphor of nets will be encountered again.

At the level of ecosystems, conscension means development within limits of constrained construction. The organism and environment are co-implicative, co-defining, and co-constructing. They engage in a process of self-assembly, where the complete self is the organism-environment system. Construction requires participation, complexity, and development. The process of construction involves a self-presentation offering new symbiotic relations and novelty.

Novelty always enters with environmental change, which serves to maintain the openness of the system. Novelty enters with fluctuations. The "strategy" of ecosystem development is increased control of, or homeorhesis with, the physical environment and novelty—probably to protect itself from perturbations. There is a fundamental shift in energy flows, as increasing amounts of energy are used for maintenance. As more and more energy is used for maintenance, the net community production (NCP) approaches zero. The mature system becomes more efficient, as it supports a larger biomass with the same amount of energy. The food chains become more weblike, dominated by detritus chains as opposed to linear grazing. Construction depends on diversity for the reciprocal constraint. Local context allows for more rapid construction. The constraint forces species to change.

1.3.4.2.3.5. Emergence Hierarchy & Holarchy

Poincare recognized (1905) that explanation in science involved generalization and simplification; so hierarchical levels emerged in study. Human perception of nature is hierarchical (even if nature is not). Several theorists distinguish levels of hierarchy in nature. Miller includes particles, atoms, molecules, societies, and nations. Bunge extends the list to include processes and knowledge: elementary particles (atoms, bodies); physical systems (organisms, ecosystems); physical processes (chemical, biological, social); material production (ritual, culture); knowledges (physics, history). Laszlo makes a distinction between a macrohierarchy, comprised of a space-time field, particles, stars, galaxies, and various aggregations; and microhierarchies like the earth, composed of molecules, crystals, cells, organisms, ecosystems, and Gaia. Hierarchies can be regarded as vertically arborizing structures whose branches interlock with those of other hierarchies at a multiplicity of levels and form horizontal networks; arborization and reticulation are complementary principles in the architecture of organisms and societies.

The law of vertical order of hierarchy determines the ever-changing level structure. In a hierarchy, there are two streams of information: the factual going up, and the directive going down. The upward stream, through perception into consciousness, makes observation possible; downward motion makes participation possible. Since all things participate to some extent in the streams, all are involved in the hierarchy.

In a government hierarchy, effects of decisions percolate down and spread out, wavelike. From the perspective of a single level, it looks like the decision moved through space from one department to another. Bohm considers that this is a good model of quantum transitions; where each state corresponds to a quasi-equilibrium of hierarchies. Informational relations are compounded in a hierarchy and are reflected at every level. Organizations can be analyzed into smaller blocks; the pattern of whole organization is reflected at every division in differences of organization on either side of boundary. What makes some systems more coherent than others? Perhaps emergent properties appearing in a hierarchy of levels.

Herbert Simon illustrates the merits of hierarchical order with the parable of the watchmakers (in Koestler, 1969): Hora and Tempus both make watches consisting of a thousand parts per watch. Hora assembles a watch piece by piece; it there is an accident it falls apart and he begins again. Tempus puts together subassemblies of ten parts; these are combined into a subassembly of 100, ten of which compose the watch.

If there is a disturbance, Tempus has from zero to nine operations to repeat. If there is a disturbance at the rate of one in 100 operations, then Hora will take 4000 times longer to assemble a watch: eleven years instead of one day. With amino acids, proteins or organelles the time scale becomes astronomical.

When a hierarchical order cannot adapt its function to an actual situation, then there is a synchronous change in the vertical order. The change in order is discontinuous, although the function is continuous. Since the details are not abstracted to a higher level, one cannot predict when the revolutionary change will take place. In general, revolution is discontinuous and synchronous, where evolution is continuous and diachronous. In the synchronic mode, form is complete as soon as it appears; in the diachronic, the form is slowly elaborated. It would appear that complex processes, like evolution, use both modes.

Hierarchical thinking is limited in cybernetics. The concept of control should better be stated as reciprocity (mutual causality); furthermore, in an open system, the environment, structure, program, and feedback all govern the system in concert. H. Henderson states that only the system can model or manage the system, but this is not entirely true. Images or codes model the system in miniature.

There are hierarchically organized entities or processes that exist. The universe may be basically hierarchical, with a rich sequence of 'orders of order,' as Bohm puts it, where order is a set of similar differences or different similarities. Or centers of hierarchy proliferating in all directions, more than up a ladder. The latter may be centrifugal, a dispersion of contraries. The former centripetal, emergent reality seeking height. Merleau-Ponty favors a centrifugal reality. In *The Structure of Behavior*, he mentions three levels: the first characterized by laws or quantity; the second by order and the third by significance or meaning (The physical, vital and human). All three have physical existence and are considered at once. "The relation of each order to the higher order is that of the partial to the whole . . . The advent of higher orders . . . suppresses the lower levels as autonomous and gives to the steps that produce them a new significance." (SB 195) For Merleau-Ponty the hierarchy is analytic. The dimensions of being pull one to the future as primary, to cosmic process as envisioned by philosophies of emergence. Hierarchies are levels of extraction; order builds up to extraction.

Ludwig von Bertalanffy concluded that: "Hierarchical organization, on the one hand, and the characteristics of open systems, on the other, seem to be fundamental principles of living nature." Koestler combines these two principles into a system theoretical model of self-regulating, open hierarchical order (SOHO), and uses this as an alternative to models of linear causation. Koestler proposed the term holon to designate the janus-faced entities on the intermediate levels of any hierarchy, which can be described either as wholes or parts, depending on the frame of reference above or below (from the Greek word, *holos*, meaning whole and *-on*, for a particle). The concept of holon transcends the duality of parts and wholes. A holarchy of holons replaces the notion of a hierarchy of parts in a whole.

In "A Heterarchy of Values Determined by the Topology of Nervous Nets" Warren McCulloch shows that sets of neurons are constituted so that the choices achieved by patterns of stimulation and inhibition of other neurons may generate a hierarchy of value, or heterarchy. Regarding a hierarchy as an unambiguous order, McCulloch claims that the heterarchy structure can accommodate the ambiguity of the Voter's paradox, where the least preferred of sets may be preferred to the most (e.g., A over B, B over C, but C over A). But hierarchies involve ambiguity. The essence of hierarchical organization is a vagueness and loss of detail in proceeding from one level to a higher. If ambiguity is accepted for the sake of richness of interpretation, deception results; if it is not accepted, then boredom results. Nets of values are ambiguous. The metaphor of nets will be encountered again.

Hierarchy is necessary to develop an adequate expression of wholeness. Paul Weiss (WB) recognized that "there are patterned processes which owe their typical configuration not to a prearranged ... stereotyped mosaic of single-tracked component preferences, but on the contrary, to the fact that the component activities have many degrees of freedom, but submit to the ordering restraints exerted on them by the activity of the 'whole' in its patterned systems dynamics."

Complexity is a relationship between system and observer, not a measurable property of a system. Complexity is brought under control by name magic—name it to control it. Complexity is a characteristic of sets that are intricately arranged. Complexity emerges from the interpenetration of processes of differentiation and integration, processes running simultaneously from top and bottom and shaping the hierarchy from both sides. Microevolution generates macroscopic conditions for continuity and macroevolution generates microscopic elements for processes. Life is an emergent property of a hierarchy of chemical levels. It is not found in molecules but through autopoetic organization of molecules. The universe restructures itself constantly at a more complex level. Reciprocal causal processes can increase structure, differentiation and complexity in natural systems, according to Maruyama.

According to Koestler, all complex structures and processes of a relatively stable character display hierarchical organization. Levels of a hierarchy tend to be contained in subassemblies. Each subwhole behaves as a whole to its components, as a self-contained whole, and as a dependent part in context. Wholes and parts do not exist absolutely. There are intermediary structures on a series of levels in an ascending order of complexity; each subwhole faces in opposite directions. These Janus-faced subassemblies are holons, that is, paraphrasing Koestler, any stable subwhole in a hierarchy that displays rule-governed behavior and structural Gestalt constancy. The rules lend order and stability, as well as flexibility.

Biological processes also generate complexity (or information). In biology and sociology, just the opposite meaning of evolution is true, as there are transformations to higher levels of complexity and improbability. The organism continues to develop, however, experiencing and learning the environmental complexities through mating and then to the end of life.

1.3.4.2.4. Tension

Tension is a form of stretching, as a result of motion and turning. Tension is a kind of initiation of some new action, such as signaling. A signal is a sign that may be recognized or transmitted, often to initiate some action, such as communication. A triggering signal can cause dramatic amplification. Thus stretching can turn inward or outward. The stretching is accomplished through perception and making. Making is a human activity that involves effort, using tools, in place. To 'make' means 'to bring into being' or produce something physically or mentally (from the English and Germans words, from the Greek meaning to 'knead,' press and stretch dough). It also means to build, fit, or create. Configurations at any level can perceive. Particles choose their paths from probabilities. The quantum principle describes how a free particle moves from one point to another along a straight line: the particle 'smells' out alternative routes; as a result of this 'smelling' behavior, the straight line appears fuzzy to a perceiver. Opposites interpenetrate and are unified even though the metaphor is initially and cognitively perceived as absurd. We are limited by our size, our positions, and by our life span. These limits make it difficult for us to perceive very slow or large changes or to anticipate them.

The universe is a prelogical and intentional turning. Although its turning is not reversible, the relation of opposites within it is reversible, hence the reversibility means a relational state and not a developmental one. As the intentional relationship is not the final truth of human existence, since it appears at only a certain level of self-actualization, it must be preceded by a pre-intentional level, which continues to exist *in* it, in which opposition we are never completely ignored. This primordial intentionality refers to a pre-predicative experience, an experience before the subject-object split; it represents a spontaneous organization of experience that precedes the subject's active synthesis. Primordial intentionality is the entire intentional network of the lived-in-world; the subject is already immersed in a world that gives her meaning. Therefore, intentional objects have sense only in the context of a larger world horizon, which is not due to subjective constitution, but to a latent intentionality, which is the intentionality within the universe.

1.3.4.2.4.1. Intention
Intention (from the Latin for 'stretch in') means creativity. What does it mean to say that the universe has intentionality? Does it mean that it moves, or goes in a direction? If so, it cannot be one undifferentiated sphere; it must partition itself into entities. Why would it do so, suffer the ordeal of birth into newness?

A universal process of creative activity is made concrete in the individual, according to A. N. Whitehead. This secures the concept of a connected universe and its character as self-creating activity. Creative activity is considered as activity toward some end. The process of nature is not merely rhythmic change, it is a changing creative advance, producing new forms everywhere. Thus, intention is required for creativity. Intention is a process that initiates change, yet at the same time stabilizes the process. In this, it is similar to homeorhesis.

The stretching in creates a separate universe, or model of the enclosing one. The participant creates a universe by being. Participation is unavoidable; connections are made through an infolding of the field. A world without participants is impossible. Nor are there any lone observers. The observer is part of a natural or social community. Creativity is the process of recombination into forms. History creates unique patterns, especially in ecosystems. Each ecosystem is unique in its parts and structure, in its matter, energy, forms, information, and in its dynamics and history. Creativity is a kind of play. Some systems are more coherent and autonomous than others. In a hierarchy of levels, emergent properties appear at some levels. Life is also a property immanent in an organization of molecules; and language emerges in a higher level. The ordering process (ektropy) creates a macro-order, which produces constraints on micro-orders. New qualities that emerge at every step are unpredictable on the basis of the past; reality is creative. Nature is more like an artist than an engineer in this sense.

The human act of ingesting an order—in*form*ation—creates entropy elsewhere. Since the act is intentional, the order cannot be considered apart from information *for* something. After Aquinas, truth, for the practical intellect rightness with respect to deeds, depends on intention.

We do not think of physical events, such as gravity or fusion, as good or bad; they simply are. A physical movement, turned to action in the human realm by human intention, is open to interpretation and ambiguity. That means its meaning can be interpreted as bad or good. Good, like bad or evil, is a function of a path of actions. Good is intention and action in the context of the rules of a culture, using ambiguous signs creatively. Intention, with experience, emotion and imagination, modifies individuals and places in the universe.

What does it mean to say that the universe has intentionality? Does it mean that it moves, or goes in a direction? If so, it cannot be one undifferentiated sphere; it must partition itself into entities. Why would it do so, why suffer the ordeal of birth into newness?

As the intentional relationship is not the final truth of human existence, since it appears at only a certain level of self-actualization, it must be preceded by a more basic intentional level, which continues to exist *in* it. Primordial intentionality, according to the philosopher Maurice Merleau-Ponty, is the entire intentional network of the lived-in-world; the subject is already immersed in a world that gives her meaning.

Thus, respect is an appropriate attitude in an uncertain and ambiguous context. Humans can use their knowledge of how things work, but be aware of their ignorance, and be careful and respectful. They understand and respect the importance and intelligence of species connectedness. Respect ignores usability? Respect limits. Respectful. As the precautionary principle needs to be followed in ecological design, a principle of respect needs to guide interactions at the global level of design. Perhaps even a principle of nonintervention should guide our thoughts of changing global cycles.

Four elements in loving have been identified by Eric Fromm: (1) Care, the active concern for life and growth; (2) Responsibility, the desire to respond to others needs; (3) Respect (meaning to look at), the recognition of others' uniqueness; and (4) Knowledge, combination of objectivity with participation and intimate identification. These elements define a loving relationship. The inexhaustibility of a living being or of our relationships constitutes much of the nature of love. Human beings are compelled to seek other beings and love is the most rewarding approach.

Respect and love also imply holding back, which is a stabilizing action. With positive feedback a system responds to the perturbation in the same direction as the perturbation (or deviation-amplifying, or error-amplifying, or cumulative causation, or destabilizing, or centrifugal). In contrast, a system that responds to the perturbation in the opposite direction is called a negative feedback system (or Deviation-reducing, or stabilizing, or centripetal). The term 'positive' means responding to the same direction as the perturbation whereas 'negative' means responding to the opposite direction. A system in which there is positive feedback to any change in its current state is said to be in an unstable equilibrium, whereas one with negative feedback is said to be in a stable equilibrium. Living systems do not display homeostasis—constant value—so much as a particular course of change in time—homeorhesis. The course is stabilized, not the constancy, according to Conrad Waddington. Changes to a system are symbolized by trajectories in a multidimensional phase space. Homeorhetic mechanisms protect the system from many disruptions.

Processes like homeorhesis, which involve a relationship with the environment, occur on an ecosystem level. Living systems do not display homeostasis—constant value—so much as a particular course of change in time—homeorhesis. The course is stabilized, not the constancy, according to Conrad Waddington. Changes to a system are symbolized by trajectories in a multidimensional phase space or landscape. Homeostatic (or homeorhetic) mechanisms protect the system from many disruptions. Negative feedback counteracts the effects of change to maintain the system in a steady state or homeorhetic state. A mature community is self-perpetuating and homeorhetic, with a dynamic balanced energy-matter budget. Homeorhesis is a significant phenomenon in evolution. Waddington applies it to the tendency of a process to continue in its original pattern, even if disturbed. Homeostasis is tendency of spatial structures to remain the same. The ability to persist is the ability to change, but species only change from environmental pressures; an amphibian is a fish trying to continue being a fish, regardless of course changes. Waddington refers to such a course as chreod (from *chre*, fated, and *hodos*, path, in Greek). The nature of a chreod that a system adopts is determined by instructions in genes and other organizations of information, and in interaction with the environment that it travels, that is, the epigenetic landscape. Control of a system after disturbance may not bring it back to where it was before; it may go back or forward. Since the path is fuzzy, it can change. The "strategy" of ecosystem development is increased control of, or homeorhesis with, the physical environment and novelty—probably to protect itself from perturbations. There is a fundamental shift in energy flows, as increasing amounts of energy are used for maintenance.

1.3.4.2.4.2. Extention

Extention (from the Latin for "stretch out") results in expansion and diversity. If you tried, you could eventually construct the universe as it is known now in every detail and potentiality, but that construction could not be all, for by the time the description of what is now is finished, the universe will have expanded into a new order to contain that which will be then.

Through speciation, orders of animals and plants probe the environment. A species is thought of as a morphological extension of its niche, but the niche extender enriches nature. The species that enlarges its niche also enlarges the ecology as a whole. According to E. A. Gutkind, it expands the environment for itself and other species in balance with it. An expanding whole is created by diversification and enrichment of the parts. A creature in a niche gives to the niche (itself), leading to cycles of nature.

DNA is a dynamic system in which clusters of genes expand and contract and roving elements hop in and out, according to W. Gilbert. The development of life since the Cambrian era displays a diversity of forms in an expansion of life into places that can only be described as self-realization, since it is far more active than the passive adaptation of self-preservation.

With diversification from speciation, we must pay attention to the processes that make up the entire habitat, for example, the role of herbivores on trimming vegetation and diversifying it by predation. Diversification can create new niches. Structural components tend to become larger: Large trees, large snags, and large downed trees. Species diversity increases because there are more possibilities for making niches in the increased structural variation. Within species there is more genetic variation.

Through language human consciousness expands historically; it is modified by personal experience as well as social and technological expansion.

This stretching out confronts one with difference that requires different behaviors. Schweitzer challenges: "Ethics must plunge into the adventure of making its adjustment with nature philosophy.... Let it dare, then, to accept the thought that self-devotion must stretch out not simply to mankind but to all creation, and especially to all life in the world within reach of humanity. Let it rise to the conception that the relation of man to man is only an expression of the relation in which he stands to all being and to the world in general."

Expansion can create new challenges or problems. Problems in forestry arise where applications that work on a small physical scale are expanded to large scales, without thought for the difference or changes in patterns. For instance, it is well known that a Douglas-fir tree is shade intolerant and grows best in openings that get light. Rather than simply remove single trees or small groups of trees, and release or plant the fir in the openings, industrial forestry applies the treatment to the entire landscape with large clearcuts, which alter the other conditions that firs require: Some shade, water, protection from browsing, and associated species. This is similar to the formal operation of Greek tragedy—applying a good idea to another situation or scale where it does not fit. The word cage is a metaphor; it implies being trapped. It is, however, a metaphor that can be expanded with a description in space as a four-dimensional box. Perhaps there is a better metaphor, since we depend on nature and society as a foundation for life, that of a trap.

Through speciation, orders of animals and plants probe the environment. A species is thought of as a morphological extension of its niche, but the niche extender enriches nature. The species that enlarges its niche also enlarges the ecology as a whole. According to E. A. Gutkind, it expands the environment for itself and other species in balance with it. An expanding whole is created by diversification and enrichment of the parts. A creature in a niche gives to the niche (itself), leading to cycles of nature.

Living DNA is a dynamic system in which clusters of genes expand and contract, and roving elements hop in and out, according to William Gilbert. The development of life since the Cambrian era displays a diversity of forms in an expansion of life into places that can only be described as self-realization, since it is far more active than the passive adaptation of self-preservation.

Stretching out can lead to destabilization, depending on feedback. There are two kinds of feedback, positive and negative. With positive feedback a system responds to the perturbation in the same direction as the perturbation (or deviation-amplifying, or error-amplifying, or cumulative causation, or destabilizing, or centrifugal). In contrast, a system that responds to the perturbation in the opposite direction is called a negative feedback system (or Deviation-reducing, or stabilizing, or centripetal). The term 'positive' means responding to the same direction as the perturbation whereas 'negative' means responding to the opposite direction. A system in which there is positive feedback to any change in its current state is said to be in an unstable equilibrium, whereas one with negative feedback is said to be in a stable equilibrium. At all levels evolution includes freedom of action as well as interdependence. The construction is never total; it requires destabilization, a risk accompanying all innovation. The processes that generate form and variation at every level. Monocultures of the industrial kind lead to 'dedifferentiation,' that is, the decomposition and destabilization of complex structures. A species or culture that destabilizes its ecosystem through misbehavior risks its own extinction.

External memory allows greater expression of single states. Many theorists require the following things for a group to have a culture: Language (for communication); Dexterity for tool making and using; Brain power for artifact design and making; Social skills for home building; Governing or self regulation; and, External memory (in customs or things). It can be argued that none of these things is exclusively human, but only humans easily qualify for having all of them. Wolves easily have language and social skills, but they have difficulty making and using tools (although they do sometimes use sticks and stones for training pups) or keeping external memories; for that reason some ethologists argue that wolves have culture, while others deny that. The clock led to the computer, our new external memory and calculator. We no longer need to memorize vast tracts of knowledge or the long serial stories with the learning or rules of our cultures. Computer memory holds those things, if we have digitized them. Digitalization itself limits the kinds of things that are held or calculated. Words and images can be replicated rapidly and disseminated to everyone with a computer.

Stretching out requires communicating. Words are tools for communicating ideas and feelings, and for building thought structures that can impact the physical structures of our worlds. The etymological meanings of words sometimes describe the limits of their original uses. Myths are a major way of explaining the universe as it exists and communicating the cultural view of nature. Myths explain that which is otherwise incomprehensible, like death and disorder. To be understandable to members of a culture, the elements of a myth must be taken from the features and values of that culture. Culture limits and constrains individual behavior with its conventions, but individual behavior can extend culture, by acting and communicating.

1.3.4.2.4.3. Retention

Retention (from the Latin for 'stretch back') means stability, to keep or hold something. Retention can result in a signal. Feedback is the signal that is looped back to control a system within itself, hence the name 'feedback loop.'

Retention allows the form to keep its structure, to maintain a balance of flows through its pattern. Stretching back offers resistance to change or stability. The property of stability is the ability to maintain the identity of a system under the flow of external forces and disturbances. Stability can be refined through the specifics of constancy, resistance, resilience, and accommodation. Stability can be related to ideas of compartmentalization, communications, richness of interactions, and connections. Ulanowicz suggests that stability might be explained by diversity flow topologies, where flow topology is a descriptor of how ecosystems develop. The stability of ecosystems, as originally proposed by Eugene Odum, becomes the result of regular flows of energy and materials. Growth and development are characterized by a qualitative formalism of increasing ascendancy, which explains the drive towards coherence, efficiency, specialization, and self-containment. Industry cannot kick any of these properties out their courses or limits. Or topology. The mature stage might have shade-tolerant trees. The closed stage would have emergent trees and a mixture of plants and animals that resist exotic species, in effect closing the system to further colonization or invasion. In the mature and closed stages, complex food webs are dominated by decomposers. For animals, body sizes increase and life cycles and strategies become more complex. At this stage, the system has learned the cycles of the environment. Since cultures have been traditionally self-reliant, resistance to imbalance is a positive act. Resistance to change or other cultures, is an adaptive mechanism that may encourage isolation. Yet, isolation is what allows a culture to develop in a unique way. Yet, isolation may lead to stagnation.

For the universe to show stability and persistence, different entities must have stability and persistence. Identity is that persistent quality. Identity serves nothing; it is. The relationship between identity and wholeness is a rhythm, forming unique patterns.

Stability is the ability to maintain the identity of a system under the flow of external forces and disturbances. Stability can be refined through the specifics of persistence (constancy), resistance, resilience, and accommodation. Persistence means stability or continuity, in general, or the state of being in a continuous flow or coherent whole for a duration. But, specifically, it can mean a lack of change in a system parameter, like number of species. A persistent system is stable and persistent in time, self-maintaining, mature, and hysteretic (historical). The system changes and develops, but is still recognizable as a short-grass prairie, for instance. Resistance is the ability to withstand disturbance to a system and to continue. Resilience is the ability to recover from stress. Conciliance is the ability to absorb change and still maintain the system identity. The system adapts to disturbance. It accommodates disturbances. It incorporates new things, such as new organisms. It tolerates new levels of things, such as increased heat. It fits the changes within the structure and function of the system. These preceding terms are not comparable. Constancy and persistence are descriptive, implying nothing of underlying dynamics. Resistance to stress is a useful notion if one is interested in the maximum extent of the deviation between stressed and unstressed systems. Resilience is relevant to those who are concerned with the rate at which a systems returns to prestress conditions. And asymptotic stability is concerned with whether or not a system will eventually return to prestressed state.

On an individual level, stability can be equated to habit. When challenged by some situation, we react by habit, although this may be disconnected from other habits. Habits protect us from many problems. Addressing a problem often has to do with a power struggle, which becomes part of the problem. If problems are regarded as challenges that require a social response, then much of the conflict can be avoided.

1.3.4.2.4.4. Contention

Contention (from the Latin for "stretch with") means a stress within an entity or between entities. Even a physicist describing the behavior of objects is led to ultimately question the ground of those objects. In the words of G. S. Brown: "Now the physicist himself, who describes all this, is, in his own account, himself constructed of it. He is, in short, made of a conglomeration of the very particulars he describes, no more, no less, bound together by and obeying such general laws as he himself has managed to find and to record. Thus we cannot escape the fact that the world we know is constructed in order (and thus in such a way as to be able) to see itself."

Gaston Bachelard states it more poetically: "The world wishes to see itself: the world lives in an active curiosity with ever open eyes." Mythically, the cosmos is an Argus, a sum of ever-open eyes. How can the world see at all if it is one whole Being? Brown answers: "in order to do so, evidently it must first cut itself up into at least one state which sees, and at least one other state which is seen. In this severed and mutilated condition, whatever it sees is only partially itself. We may take it that the world undoubtedly is itself (i.e., is indistinct from itself), but, in any attempt to see itself as an object, it must, equally undoubtedly, act so as to make itself distinct from, and therefore false to, itself. In this condition it will always partially elude itself."

In opposing itself to itself, it limits itself what it knows. It never sees what is seeing. As it opposes itself to see itself, the world or universe is divided to its very root; it creates a basic dialectic between mind-body, subject-object, and male-female. The world holds all contradictions; indeed, contradictions allow existence. Substance and nothingness allow movement; but they are both substrates of the world. The invisible side of things replaces the concept of nothingness in the philosophy of Merleau-Ponty, and substances are visibles. The two things of opposite nature depend on one another, in the world, as day on night, or the imagined on the real.

Contention can result in balanced interactions, To survive, an ecosystem depends on the interactions and balance of many variables, most of which are not well understood. Massive disruption often results when a community falls out of balance with its local forest environment, and in fact industrial forestry only avoids the penalties for such disruption by trading advantageously with other communities in less powerful areas. Radical ecology offers a new perspective of humanity in the total field of nature and defines balanced relationships with ultrahuman beings and species. Dynamic balance is self-regulatory, Kohr states, because of "the coexistence of countless mobile little parts of which no one is ever allowed to accumulate enough mass to disturb the harmony of the whole." Balance means an equality of basic processes, such as integration and disintegration. It means that things are being built up as they are being torn down. It means that natural processes such as motion and rest, turning and returning, are approximately equal. Being in balance is like a form of maturity, while growth is usually a characteristic of immaturity on the way to maturity. Being out of balance for too long leads to death. Of course, nothing can be in balance indefinitely, or for very long, depending on its size and complexity. Balance is an ideal for humans. The relationships of humans and animals have changed drastically. The increase of humans and the destruction of animals have unbalanced the relationships. The destruction of habitats is accelerating. Piaget suggests that all human action consists of a balancing of the processes of assimilation and accommodation. Accommodation means to establish a common measure; assimilation means to digest. Needs first incorporate things and people into the subject's own activity; the subject assimilates them into existing mental structures, then readjusts the structures as a function of subtle transformations, to accommodate them to external objects.

Balanced interactions can lead to harmony. Perhaps, as a working definition of the word good, we can just use 'harmony.' In Chinese medical tradition, the highest good is harmony, especially social harmony or good relations. A good person is one who creates and maintains harmony. Harmony is related to wholeness— indeed, the word 'whole' comes from the Indo-European root *kailo*, which is also the root for the words health and holy. Maruyama distinguishes two other epistemologies that have a typical logic based on them: Homeostatic, with a complementary logic, as exemplified by Chinese thought, and Morphogenetic, with a logic incorporating change, harmony, heterogeneity, and unrepeatable and irreversible processes, as demonstrated in Mandenka, Navajo, and Inuit thought. In a hierarchy of levels, emergent properties appear at some levels. Form, melody and harmony are systems properties arising from the hierarchical organizations of notes into pieces of music. Life is also a property immanent in an organization of molecules; and language emerges in a higher level. New qualities that emerge at every step are unpredictable on basis of past; reality is creative.

Harmony allows continuity. Health is considered the continuity of normal behavior. Our first clue to unhealthy people is abnormal behavior—not moving or breathing, for instance. The first thing we do is to classify the symptoms. Then we measure vital signs: heart, blood pressure, temperature, and maybe white blood cell count. After a diagnosis is made, it is verified usually by more measurements. Doctors, who often rely on their long experience and learning, then discuss a prognosis and prescribe a treatment.

The health of individuals lets them make communities. We will only learn to treat land as part of our community, and not as an exploited commodity, when we have new myths. A nation is a people or tribe or a people living in a territory united by a single government, a stable, historically-developed community of people with a distinct culture occupying a common territory, although it has also come to mean an artificial designation as a result of political violence. Ecological designs focus on whole communities that work in the same self-sustaining and self-limiting ways as nature. By consciously creating meaningful ordered patterns, we can develop ways of producing widespread community wealth while positioning the community for a long, sustainable future in a healthy environment.

1.3.4.2.4.5. Extent & Balance
Balance results from reciprocating actions, each of which creates small adjustments to the pattern. This moving back and forth can allow the system to close feedback loops.

The two forms yield a quality-neutral conceptual tool for assessing processes that result in pattern maintenance and the evolution of ordered holistic systems through periodic or constant energy or information exchanges with the environment. Feedback is usually bipolar—that is, positive and negative—in natural environments, which, in their diversity, furnish synergic and antagonistic responses to the output of any system. Bipolar feedback is present in many natural and human systems, resulting in a typical course.

Waddington refers to such a course as chreod (from *chre*, fated, and *hodos*, path, in Greek). The nature of a chreod that a system adopts is determined by instructions in genes and other organizations of information, and in interaction with the environment that it travels, that is, the epigenetic landscape. Control of a system after disturbance may not bring it back to where it was before; it may go backward or forward. Since the path is fuzzy, it can change.

To create an intentional course, one could essentially work backwards from values and goals, and from the bottom up and inside out, drawing designs from the genius of place. Also, one could work backwards from known constraints. That will make sure that actions do not produce situations dominated by runaway positive feedback. At the global level, most action involves some form of restraint on technological interference or landscape conversion. And, of course, our current size and momentum are not sustainable, but that does not mean that we cannot reach a sustainable level, or should not try. Maybe we should call it dedevelopment to make it obvious, or a rational retreat from ignorance. It could include going backwards, being simpler and smaller when necessary. For instance, we could easily go back to energy use of 1960.

As opposites, order and disorder are to be defined in terms of each other. Order can be described mathematically in a six dimensional phase space (the geometric position and momentum of each particle in terms of a three dimensional lattice); disorder occurs when their velocities and positions change. The physicist describes disorder as the breaking up of a shape situation - a dynamic configuration due to the independent actions of single elements. If order becomes disorder through a random motion, how does order exist, or come into being? Order arises spontaneously in the shuffling. There is a good example of how order can appear from disorder, and still pro-duce greater entropy in the system: Bridgman offers a case where heat is added to a supercooled liquid until a crystal forms; certainly the crystal is more ordered than the parent liquid, which increases its entropy afterward. This corresponds with a concept of order as tension reduction—an energy system tends toward a state with the least potential energy. Forces constituting a field tend to the most balanced stable configuration, usually the simplest. This behavior is more law-like than statistical. This also cannot explain all orders—Koestler's arguments, and the parable of the watchmakers are relevant here—so there must exist also an anabolistic process, to explain structure, which the statistical theory cannot.

Order was defined as the similarity between differences. Disorder is equivalent to the difference among similarities. Fiebleman considers positive disorder as extent to which elements of a given order are distributed outside that order among elements of other orders. His thesis is that disorder depends on random dispersion of limited orders. However, since existence depends on motion, motion is prior to order.

1.3.4.2.5. Formation

Formation is the interaction of a physical and an intentional process. Physical or living things take forms. The making of form is informing. Ramon Margalef considers "information" to be more basic than energy or matter and more in line with the concept of patterning. Information is not transferred because the field itself is in-*form*-ed. Formation is the interaction of a physical and an intentional conscious process. To create form. A concrete system is composed of concrete things linked together by real physical, chemical, biological ties. Cells, wolf packs, and nongovernmental organizations (NGOs) are concrete systems. Many concrete systems are open and self-regulated. Many are closed and artificial. Every concrete thing has properties. Some properties can be known easily; others can be revealed by research. A list of known properties describes the state of the system with finite quantities. A qualitative description of properties describes qualities of the system. Quantitative descriptions measure quantitative variables. The state of a system, definite and objective, can be conceptualized with theories and models. All concrete systems change as reality unfolds. That is, the properties of systems change through time. Some change, such as growth or decay, is quantitative. Other change is qualitative, resulting in breakdown or formation of the entire system. Conceptual systems can be linked by logical relations. All concrete systems change as reality unfolds, that is, the properties of systems change through time. Some change, such as growth or decay, is quantitative. Other change is qualitative, resulting in the breakdown or formation of the entire system. The process of evolution at all levels is the formation of varying sets, and the differential elimination of some sets and survival of others. Limiting factors are competition, degree of openness, feedback, and homeostasis. Consequences include directional change at all levels, an increase of organized diversity in the universe, and the evolution of wholes maintained by interlevel feedback.

Interactions within a process makes forms. Making is a human activity that involves effort, using tools, in place. To 'make' means 'to bring into being' or produce something physically or mentally (from the

English and Germans words, from the Greek meaning to 'knead,' press and stretch dough). It also means to build, fit, or create. The making of a home would be an 'ecopoetic' activity (from the Greek word fragments for 'house-making').

Forms can produce a system. A system is a set of things—such as people, cells, or molecules—according to Donella Meadows, interconnected in such a way that they produce their own pattern of behavior over time. The system may be buffeted, constricted, triggered, or driven by outside forces, but the response is characteristic of the system. A system is not just a collection. It is an interconnected set of elements that is coherently organized to achieve something. Geology, climate, disturbance, and history all produce diversity. Landscape diversity is linked to ecological diversity, which depends on diversity of the substrates and historical developments. The earth is a complex system. Material processes can produce conceptual objects, which are embedded in the processes, which are embedded in webs of processes. The loss of health results in weakness and sickness, the inability to maintain the self or to produce necessities.

Culture is more than a simple filtering or sorting process. It is more than a formation process. Because it occurs with physical, living, conscious, and social systems, culture is more like a novation process, that is, it recombines things into new orders.

1.3.4.2.5.1. Information
Information is the act of imparting form, as in in-form-ation—this is different from knowledge, which is the act of importing that same form, or from data, which is the act of abstracting knowledge, or from facts, which are the transformation of data by imagination, emotion, memory, and theory. Evolution is the production of new codes of information to match a changing environment. Margalef describes the evolution of ecosystems as information accumulation; information is generated by participating species and their physical structures (such as burrows or paths). In a system novelty is always transformed to confirmation. Novelty always enters with fluctuations. Natural fluctuations serve to maintain the openness of a system. There are in fact other ways to transmit information, beyond energy and pattern. Information acquisition can come from genetic coding, individual learning, and culture, as well. Culture is a filter to restrict and manage information. Culture can be defined as the transmission of information through behavior; imitation is one behavior, and teaching is another. Culture is information that an individual acquires by imitating other individuals, and that affects an individual's behavior. Culture is the thing that is

transferred. Cultural transmission is the set of ways by which culture is spread through a population. Cultural evolution is the summed effect of long-term transmission. Information is always transmitted in form, however.

We then create new forms of entertainment, participation, and celebration. We create new forms of education and ways to heal ourselves. Some forms that seem rich and necessary are regarded as capital. Human beings can create more cultural capital. To relate health to growth and productivity, we could say that the capital of an ecosystem would be its physical environment and its gross primary productivity; interest would be the net ecosystem productivity. This unbalanced reordering is rapidly changing the social and environmental orders that represent the natural capital of social and environmental evolution. The loss extends to human lives, as well. People themselves are treated as a waste product of capital-producing system, although the system could be viewed as a waste-producing system that also produces capital. Ecological design is concerned with using natural capital at renewable rates, with a minimum use of the productive accumulated "interest." Global design considers the capital-creating process on several time scales. Global design has to take care that those long-term processes are allowed to continue, even while we use renewable energies and materials.

1.3.4.2.5.2. Exformation

Exformation creates outward form, such as tools, People make tools to get food. Then, they make clothing, homes and other things for making life easier. Art, luxuries and sculptures follow. Clothing and tool making is a universal in human cultures. The first tools were stone-flaked, then ground stone, used with boomerangs and clubs. Ground stone axes appear first in Australia. Tools are simple, but effective, easily manufactured and maintained, for example, the spear-thrower, or woomera (atlatl), had hook on one end and an adze on other; it could be used for a shovel, fire-starter, or a percussion instrument. It was an independent creation in Australia. As tools increase in complexity, from knives and levers to computers and space stations, so does the knowledge needed to support them. Complex modern tools require libraries of information that has to be continually increased and improved, then spread. Technology first simplifies life, then complicates it. Digging sticks led to plows and tractors. Lean-tos lead to pit houses and balloon-framed houses. Domestication led to horses and to horse wagons. Paths led to trail and highways. All tools, from the simplest word to the most complex computer, are disturbers and rearrangers of primordial nature and reality; they are implements for working on something. They have addicted us to purpose. We look for purpose in everything; to seek an explanation of nature, and to justify the seeking. Humans are tied to their tools and machines. The basic difficulty with the quality of life resides in machines. Machines pollute air, water and earth. Machines of war threaten human lives. Machines displace forms of life; they take up space. They are a competitive species, whose members die, reproduce, evolve, and sometimes think. If humanity is not to be replaced by autonomous, thinking machines, we had better choose and use them wisely. What are the effects of tools on human cultures? The complexity of tools leads to rules for their use, and for who uses them, such as trade unions and clubs like masonry. Society is very adaptable to technological change, according to Kenneth Boulding. Perhaps too much so according to Rene Dubos, and the risk is shaping human behavior to tools.

Tools and machines are considered as symbiotic things, or allies, by some philosophers. F. L. Wright thought of: "The building as machine." Machines are not living yet, as we know, although they follow rules, change and evolve. We apply control to them, but they seem autonomous in many ways. They have many known and unknown effects. Can the effects of technology be controlled? Tools have effects on human culture, and on nature. What are the effects of tools on ecosystems? Disturbance of soils, and scale effects. What are the effects of tools on humans? The use of knives which reduced the need for some teeth. Tools, simply by being intermediate between the hand and the object, may increase psychological distancing from things. Intimacy with the tool can replace intimacy with the thing. The increase in physical depositories, for memory, changes the kinds of memory capabilities. Tools may contribute to the loss of hand-eye coordination and perception of wild, yet increase hand-eye coordination of tools.

Exformation can maintain form. Autopoesis refers to the dynamic self-producing and self-maintaining activities of living beings. Species that seem functionally redundant prior to a disturbance might serve as potential spare parts for maintaining ecosystem function following a disturbance or perturbation. The dynamic self-producing and self-maintaining activities of living beings in an environment creates places. As in a field, a place is bounded. That boundedness gives a place its identity and integrity, and allows it to maintain itself in a definite form and process.

Successful self-making patterns are recognized as having vitality. Productivity, in general, depends on the vigor, or strength or vitality, of the system. Health is the overall ability of a system to maintain itself under a normal range of environmental conditions (which may include hurricanes, volcanic eruptions, or fires). To be constant and stable, a culture has to be vital; it has to be productive, to be able to convert energy and materials into foods and structures for survival. The system is self-creating. It renews itself as its contents change, as disturbances change the parameters of the system. What barriers are there to cultural renewal? How can they be overcome?

Natural selection was hypothesized as the filter through which the better adapted species passed. Although the environment selects species, many species extend the environment by creating new niches. The environment still acts upon these species.

Darwin's concept of natural selection came from the struggle between individuals of a species, not between species. The concept was triggered by Darwin's reading of Malthus (Origin of the Species, p. 75). Darwin characterized natural selection as: "a force like 100,000 wedges trying to force every kind of adapted structure into the gaps on the economy of nature, or rather forming gaps by thrusting out the weaker ones." The struggle concerned the fate of individuals. By differential success of individuals, a species could be transformed. .In The Origin of the Species, evolution as the unfolding of the individual during development is not used.

Natural selection acts on the phenotype, but selects the genotype. The phenotype is built up from genotype through genotypic instructions encountering environment. The continued interactions of a plastic system in a changing environment produces a continual selection of the system's structure. Natural selection is nonrandom.

The understanding of evolution requires an understanding of development. Development is influenced by environment as well as genome. Phenotypes are more than an expression of genotypes. Organisms do modify development and later behavior in response to a changing environment. Natural selection is more than a choice of genes; what is being chosen for includes the behavior of the organism as it lives. Evolution incorporates learning. Genes are certainly subordinate to hormones throughout the development of the organism. Imaginal disks are controlled entirely by hormones. Experiments that rearrange the tissues of fruit flies, rats and frogs indicate that development is guided by location.

Jantsch sees the view of evolution as preservation of stationary states as fragmented. Much of natural selection is stabilizing selection. Homeorhesis is a significant phenomenon in evolution; Waddington applies it to the tendency of a process to continue in its original pattern, even if disturbed. Homeostasis is tendency of spatial structures to remain the same. The ability to persist is the ability to change, but species only change from environmental pressures; an amphibian is a fish trying to continue being a fish (after Evernden).

A. Wallace described evolution as a conservation process. He compared the action to a centrifugal governor of a steam engine, which checks irregularities; so animal deficiency makes existence difficult. As Wallace saw it, natural selection worked to keep the species unvarying; in a varying environment this acts for survival. Darwin came to agree. He regretted not using the term "natural preservation" to replace "natural selection."

Natural selection is not a tautology, since it can be empirically tested. In the struggle for reproduction, some organisms succeed because of their distinctive characteristics, which have a good chance of being passed on to the next generation. The selection is systematic. Characteristics favored in one situation will probably be favored in similar ones.

1.3.4.2.5.3. Reformation

The making of shelter is reforming. Things are reshaped in response to changes in conditions. An ecological design involves designers and people in reshaping and recreating a self-sustaining community. Individual resources are limited. The relationships to strive for here are community relationships. Furthermore, there are limits for human manipulation of other communities. Reshaping Buildings. Instead, architects generally remained at the building-size projects. Some architects have suggested altering the design of buildings and combining uses.

Reforming may result from remembering, There seem to be mental limits, also. We are unable to remember everything that impacts us. We are unable to give attention to everything at once. The upper limit for measurable relations seems to be about seven (plus or minus two). George Miller found that seven was a magic number in human psychology; it represented the maximum number of items that a subject could reliably remember, as well as other variables. Possibly it applies to the number of subjects having an intelligent conversation as well. There may be limits of receiving or processing information. Many cultures have collapsed and disappeared, often without being remembered or documented. He states that Gaia's face from space is beautiful. We need to remember that as we act as responsible offspring—but also remember that the faces of Mars and the other planets, and stars and the universe, are also beautiful. The ways of life that we remember and prefer, the places that depend on other species and natural processes—these can be saved.

Reforming may come from imitation, An image is an imitation or representation of something. It can also be a symbol or type, a metaphor or concept. An image can stand for something else, for instance the image of a dove is often used as a symbol for peace. In the etymological sense a symbol is something 'thrown together,' as a problem is something 'thrown forward.' Unlike an image, a symbol often represents some other thing, process or quality. Human beings are mammals who live in groups and are good at imitation. These talents have allowed humans to create cultures to adapt to stressful environments. Cultures became useful in many ways, from externalizing memory to training the young. Design has to identify patterns of movement and construction, and then it has to imitate the processes and patterns, modifying them to include the things of human interest and need. This is more difficult than copying a shape or a structure. Fortunately, imitation is a human strength, even if the recognition of complex, long-term, moving patterns is not. Human culture and behavior, need to be defined against a long evolutionary backdrop of deep history, the common ground we share with other animals. Human culture is transmitted through imitation.

Reforming may come from play. Human beings are mammals— omnivorous, social, bipedal, featherless, symbol and tool-using, game-playing, neotonous, bilateral-hemispheric, culture-making generalists.

Reforming may come from learning. The ecosystem 'learns' the changes, e.g., seasons, of the environment. Any system formed by reproducing and interacting organisms must develop an assemblage in which production of entropy per unit of information is minimized. It is a general property of some systems that acquired information is used to close the door to further inflow. A mature system needs less information, since it works toward preservation.

A biological organism grows to maturity, which is a stopping point for size. The organism continues to develop, however, experiencing and learning the environmental complexities through mating and then to the end of life. Development may include growth at some stages, but development refers to the continued change after growth has stopped.

Human places are complex integrations of nature and culture that develop in particular locations. The feeling of a geography is prior to its study. The place precedes knowledge of it. The knowledge of place is one of the first links in a chain of knowledge. Being human is having and knowing a place. This knowing is essential to our existence. Paul Shepard suggested that for each individual the organization of thinking and meaning was intimately related to specific places. Place is a focus of experience; and the background for specific events. The features of a world are experienced meaningfully. The place is a matrix for ordering experience. The essence of place lies in unselfconscious intentionality. Only learning flowing from hospitable presence to human and world can promote life and enhance human existence.

1.3.4.2.5.4. Conformation
In general, there are some universal human behavioral standards, but there may be special local expectations, to conform with various cultures. For example, there is a prohibition against incest or against eating human flesh, but local expectations conform with cultural values—and indeed, cannibalism and incest have been important parts of some societies at times.

Conformation is accommodation to the right measure at the right time. The morality of the act is determined by the current state of the system. Adaptive modes should conform to ecological patterns. An ecological ethics is based on attributes of ecosystems and human compliance with ecological laws. The aim of an ethic must be harmonious with the whole population of living beings.

Conformation is fitting. The intent of describing large-scale trends or patterns is to have human patterns fit with observed patterns in nature; patterns have a form, sometimes repetition, and sometimes regularity, but each of these is caused by some limiting factor. Fitting the pattern can lead to both continuity and predictability, and both of these are needed to adapt human activities to natural limits. People not only fit physically into a place, by adjusting their eating habits, by making or shedding clothes and houses, they also change their images of themselves and the place so that the two images fit together.

The individual feeds back into the cosmology in altered form what was received. It is almost like a closed loop between cosmology, culture and the individual. Archaic peoples translate the natural world into the language of myth. Being a narrative, a myth is aesthetic as well as intellectual. Myths develop in terms of their own internal logic, drawing together observations of the world. C. Levi-Strauss described the process as bricolage, fitting the bits together, identifying impressions of life as sets and forming them into mythical systems; the world picture is a metaphorical puzzle. Bricolage is the mentality of synthesis, a technique for learning, creating, and expressing understanding, using whatever is available from the past and in the present to achieve an integrating form. This is what mythological thinking does, and what scientific thought might do.

A culture is a loose-fitting patchwork of ideas, relationships and things. In that sense it is parallel to species adaptation to an environment. The fitness is never perfect, but that is what allows movement and change.

Specific ideas and actions are selected. Since the origins of the environmental crises are in human traditions, it should be possible to select—and create a new cosmology—from what is valuable in the traditions. If the world becomes as humans imagine it, then a larger frame will make a larger world.

Actions coevolve with other actions, making a network of relations. Relations are not prior to objects; they arise together. The wasp and the yucca coevolve; they are not co-linked by prior relations. Furthermore, a specimen is more than the sum of its species' relationships to an environment; it is an intentional being that, with other members of the species, can create niches, as well as adapt to them. Many animals, such as wolves and caribou, develop together over time, adapting to each other's strategies. Paul Ehrlich and Peter Raven refer to this mutual adaptation as coevolution. Coevolving systems never completely adapt. Within a mere nine million years, flowering plants had colonized most of the land areas, coevolving with the first mammals, warm-blooded egg-layers and small marsupials. Coevolution of life forms is far more important than previously thought. Mammalian interest in these plants as food probably lead to their rapid dissemination. Flowering plants (or angiosperms, 'clothed seeds') had fruits and seeds to protect the embryos from being made into animal flesh. Margulis suggests that plants have been seducing animals for millions of years, tricking us into helping them to move and forcing us into more complex *patterns* of behavior.

Cooperation is an aspect of conformation. People have images of nature as violent or of humans as violent, which contrast with other images of nature as cooperative and humans as peaceful. Some logics of cultures promote a dualism where either one is true, but not both.

With the scientific understanding that cooperation is much more prevalent in building guilds among animals and stable habitats, the operation of nature becomes more understandable. Cooperation builds partnerships and mutually beneficial relationships between individuals, species, and communities. Cooperation is more than the avoidance of conflict. It is the recognition of emergent benefits. It is finding security in sharing, rather than by eliminating competitors.

Cooperation is one aspect of peace. Ways of cooperating include communicating needs and negotiating for redistribution of resources. There are patterns of interactions of cultures, which arise out of several possibilities: Indifference, trade, competition, cooperation, conquest, or respect. Some archaic cultures seemed to be limited to indifference, that is, they ignored one another, and to trade. Competition and conquest may have accelerated with the acquisition of territory for agriculture. Cooperation and respect seem to have occurred under some circumstances of trade or unification. The extension of ethics to animals and land is an ecological necessity. Extended ethics defines a social conduct that is a mode of cooperation and, ultimately, symbiosis. Leopold argued that ethics are voluntary limitations of freedom, necessary in a complex world of which we remain incredibly ignorant. Ethics are developed in response to problems that arise from increasing knowledge.

Over time, conformation results in coevolution. Evolution at all levels can be reduced to directional changes in sets, according to P. J. Darlington. Sets are any two (or more) units that occur within interaction distances (Refer to Figure 134254-1 on mathematical sets).

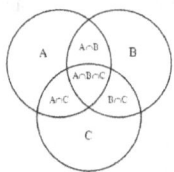

Figure 134254-1. Mathematical Sets

Sets consist of matter organized at various levels. In living systems, sets of atoms and molecules constitute genes; sets of genes, individual genotypes and population gene pools (through cells, individuals, family groups, societies, demes, and populations). Sets of these sets constitute species; sets of species of plants and animals, biotas; biotas, the biosphere. Complexity is characteristic of sets that are intricately arranged. Diversity emphasizes differences between members of one set; it is also used to describe communities with different members. Inherent is the assumption that sets must be formed before evolution occurs. This is an essential principle of evolution by set selection.

By definition, sets that do things are acting sets. Living sets are self-organized by the actions of their members. Sets consist of matter organized at various levels. Sets of molecules make up genes; sets of genes, genomes. Sets of populations, species. Selection is a differential elimination among sets. Evolution occurs by set selection at many levels. Under preconditions (conservation of energy, e.g.), the essential process of evolution at all levels is the formation of varying sets and differential elimination and survival.

The preconditions of evolution by set selection at all levels are:
   • the conservation of matter and energy
   • the availability of energy (extrinsic, solar, for living levels)

- a high ektropy universe (Darlington thinks low entropy, but low entropy could not support life)

The process of evolution at all levels is the formation of varying sets (genotypes), and the differential elimination of some sets and survival of others. Limiting factors are competition, degree of openness, feedback, and homeostasis. Consequences include directional change at all levels, an increase of organized diversity in universe, and the evolution of wholes maintained by interlevel feedback.

Both kinds of selection describe a process acting on organisms. Fox calls natural selection a "mythological construct substituting nature for God's divine guidance." But living organisms are not mechanical pieces to be physically or mathematically shuffled. An organism's environment includes itself and it incorporates some of the environment. The organism also selects.

1.3.4.2.5.5. Science Shape & Capacity

Optimizing is an ideal for the evolutionary process. However, F. Varela analyzes the evolutionary process as satisficing rather than optimizing; that is, a suboptimal solution is adequate to continue living; striving for an optimum or maximum does not pay off in terms of investment of effort. The role of designers is to optimize or satisfy the fitness of people with their environments. To fit cultural goals to ecological characteristics and limits. It is adaptive creativity, not just for the current technology, but because it needs to adapt to the technological and natural environments. An ecological design involves designers and people in reshaping and recreating a self-sustaining community. Individual resources are limited. The relationships to strive for here are community relationships. Furthermore, there are limits for human manipulation of other communities.

Ecological design is not the same as adaptation. Adaptation, and its ideas of completeness, conviviality, and cooperation, emerge from the characteristics of places and ecosystems, from participation, development, and complexity. And these come from the characteristics of the field, from registration, integration, connection, and renewal. Place allows us to rediscover a participating consciousness and a symbiotic connection to the living earth. Participation means living with other species, the literal definition of conviviality. The organization of perception, meaning, and thought is intimately related to specific places. When the symbols of a world lose their meaning, through wrongful application or abstraction, sickness and disintegration result. A cooperative framework for healing within the depths of communities and ecosystems. Reconciliation (equality of opportunity for treatment) is necessary. Conviviality, basically living together in harmony, according to Ivan Illich, is a necessary strategy. These ecological principles, and many more nor presented here, can guide our actions to make good, healthy places. Cooperation implies convivial or appropriate technology. The word convivial means social, from the Latin word "convivium," meaning living together. Ivan Illich, in *Tools for Conviviality*, sketches a meaningful community where workers have control of their tools and their lives.

1.3.4.2.6. Novation
Novation is the interaction of a physical and a cultural conscious intentional process to create novelty. A process is described as evolutionary if it involves emergence and the creation of new things— to be a species, however, the novelty has to reproduce or multiply or diffuse. With any change of evolution, change depends on how often fruitful novelties arise and how fast they spread. In an evolving system, novelty is always be transformed to confirmation. Novelty always enters with fluctuations. Natural macrofluctuations serve to maintain openness.

The ceaseless activity of being in history creates newness. Novelty is born from the womb ('hystera') of change. History is the result of this hysteresis process. Motion, Version, Scension—all together form the ontological spiral of being/environment. The motion of the field creates a turning, which leaves a history, out of which patterns arise.

They engage in a process of self-assembly, where the complete self is the organism-environment system. Construction requires participation, complexity, and development. The process of construction involves a self-presentation offering new symbiotic relations and novelty.

Novelty always enters with environmental change, which serves to maintain the openness of the system. Novelty enters with fluctuations. The system has to be an open system for novelty to develop.

The process of novation makes new, complex patterns.

1.3.4.2.6.1. Innovation
Development means the introduction of an innovation. One of the ecological consequences of human activity is the degradation of wild habitats for human developments (food, housing, and recreation) and the introduction of novel elements into the biosphere—elements that have not been harmoniously worked in over time. Technology also promotes land degradation. Plowing causes erosion. A problem with innovation is that time and leisure are needed for technological innovations. Starving people rarely invent their salvations.

Development means the introduction of an innovation. The

evolution of matter, for instance, proceeds through a spiral process, as exemplified in the carbon cycle in stars, where a carbon nucleus captures four protons and emits them as an alpha particle at the end of the process. Conifers could colonize dry ground, especially because of the innovations of pollen and seed, whereas ferns had to live near water and mate with their immediate neighbors. The construction is never total; it requires destabilization, a risk accompanying all innovation. Development is related to maturity and evolution.

Newness can result from modification, that is minor improvements that may reduce unwanted effects, to hybridization, the combination of two systems, and mutation, a radical change often unexpected from the previous thing. Innovations have consequences and this is related to feedback, especially positive feedback. Thus, reverberations can spread through an ecosystem and trigger other innovations in other parts of the systems or other systems.

Innovation creates new inner patterns, that is internal patterns that may allow resistance or resilience to external changes.

1.3.4.2.6.2. Enovation

Enovation is a spreading outward for change. For instance, an animal can make a new niche for itself by changing its location and behavior to develop a new food source from the waste of a system. Another example is the behavior of altruism or charity (both words used in a biological sense not strictly human), where an animal may call warnings to another if a predator is nearby or leave food from a kill.

Exnovation is the process that describes cultural transformation. Innovation is influenced by the growth and intensity of population, by the expanding and intensified activities of states or cities, and by increasing trade and commercialization. The ease of communication also increases rates of innovation. Geography encourages some paths of innovation (east-west in Asia and Europe, but north-south in the Americas). Political form is also a factor with innovation. Accidental innovation can become a culture of innovation, that is, a part of the culture encouraged and used.

New tools extended efficiency. More crops required new ideas of storing foods. There were more innovations in general, due to density and intensification. As humans stay in place, they tried to extract more resources from the same area. This requires new ideas and technology. Which resulted in denser settlements, which resulted in new technology and new social organization. This is extensification. Innovation is influenced by the growth and intensity of population, by the expanding and intensified activities of states or cities, and increasing trade and commercialization. The ease of communication also increases rates of innovation. Perhaps that is why it went east west in Europe and Asia and north south in the Americas. Accidental innovation became a culture of innovation, that is, a part of the culture that was encouraged and used.

Exnovation pulls a culture to create a new cultural niche in the natural landscape. New tools are invented, sometimes pushed by the expansion of population. The Navajo or Inuit are examples of a culture that was able to deal with innovation and expand. Invention is the conscious creation of a new pattern to increase something. Exnovation may create extra wealth that can be used for the flexibility of a culture or perhaps for charity to other cultures or natural landscapes (resulting in wilderness set-asides).

1.3.4.2.6.3. Renovation

The industrial makeover of nature is renovation. Everything is always being reinvented. Why? Because it has to be, because everything changes. Ideas and strategies that worked for foragers do not work for urban dwellers. Ideas that worker for traditional urbanites do not work in an ecological urban context. The key patterns can be loosened and changed, smaller patterns submerged in a larger pattern that can make it more resilient.

1.3.4.2.6.4. Connovation

For plants and animals, connovation means creating new cooperative patterns through behaviors. For intercultural transformation, this means creating new trading routes or regional unions. In fact, cultures have been bound through regional or universal religions, which have provided restrictions on behavior as well as cultural goals. New religious patterns can transform human behaviors with imagination and wisdom.

1.3.4.2.6.5. Art Novelty & Creation

The universe unfolds but does not unravel. It becomes richer and more complex, so it does not know its own future states. Bits or information are being generated. The universe produces genuine novelty through its unfolding. Biological processes also generate complexity (or information). Consciousness allows us to experience the complexity of being directly.

The processes—motion, version, scension, tention, formation, and novation—result in filtering. So, they are identified with separate words here. Sifting or filtering is the interaction of two nonliving physical processes; energy and matter over time are described by entropy. Sorting is the interaction of a physical and an intentional process; for instance, living beings in an environment are described by sorting process, perhaps the equivalent to evolution. Often the same word is used for all these processes, for example, Schrodinger uses the term negentropy for filtering, sorting, and forming, but the processes are different, work differently and have different results.

When cells form an organism, the new factor is that certain variations of behavior of individual cells previously determined fortuitously by the environment are now ordered intrinsically in the functioning of the organism. The creation and transformation of order are the most fundamental account of laws of process. High macro-orders, e.g., dog or biosphere, then limit micro-orders.

At the cultural level, we can weigh the experiences of all the members of a culture and act wisely, with respect to our use of resources.

1.3.4.3. *Topology of Being*

Being cannot be constructed by the verbal or mathematical descriptions of each leaf, in relation to the artichoke or even to the entire universe. If you tried, you could eventually construct the universe as it is known now in every detail and potentiality, but that construction could not be all, for by the time the description of what is now is finished, the universe will have expanded into a new order to contain that which will be then. Is there, then, any way the universe, or Being, can be described as a whole? Merleau-Ponty suggests topological space as a model of Being. He uses Euclidean space as a model for perceptual being; it is a positive space without transcendence, a network of straight lines, parallel or perpendicular according to the three dimensions, which sustains all possible situations. Topological space is more elastic in its movements; two figures, for instance, are topologically equivalent if one can be made to coincide with the other by elastic motion. The topological properties of a figure are those which are invariant under elastic motions, such as boundary or surface. Merleau-Ponty (MN 210) continues: "The topological space, on the contrary, a milieu in which are circumscribed relations of proximity, or envelopment, etc. is the image of a being that, like Klee's touches of color, is at the same time older than everything and 'of the first day' (Hegel), that the regressive thought runs up against without being able to deduce it directly or indirectly . . . from Being by itself, that is a perceptual residue—It is encountered not only at the level of the physical world, but again it is constitutive of life, and finally it founds the wild principle of Logos."

What is the shape of topological space? Spherical? The phenomenologist Bachelard (BC 239) claims that Being is round; "the round being propagates its roundness with the calm of all roundness." In Parmenides, the one was a perfect sphere. Pythagoras described the universe as a *kosmis*, an order; the stoics emphasized the *kosmos* as an entity under the direction of logos, which lead to the use of *holon*, whole, to describe the universe. Bachelard continues in this vein: in his basic ontology Being moves, even imagination is movement rather than representation, and things are not what they are, but what they become. Bachelard (KG 13) states: "In the order of dynamic imagination, all forms are furnished with movement: one cannot imagine a space with having it turn."

Being is seen as a result of its turning, and as a result of its seeing and being seen, it becomes another universe—the invisible becomes visible. Raine notes that "the perfect sphere Turns in our hearts, the past and future, near and far, Our single souls, atom, and universe." Change is the price paid for visibility, in philosophy as well as physics. Motion causes change. Being translates itself into individuals; it translates itself into things and pieces, but the translation causes a loss. The individuals in Being then experience and act in the limits of their perspectives; they perceive their intersubjectivity in Being. Through the dialectical relations of being and other being time arises. Time is a network of intentionalities as a product of perspectives in space. Through the body a being feels time, and that time becomes a center for reflection. The loss from the turning creates a sediment which is history. The sedimenting process is irreversible, and provides a direction for time. The sediment of past events is then a given, and different for each present. The ceaseless activity of Being in history creates newness. Each new emergent phenomenon is irreducible to its antecedent events, although it may be partially described or predicted by them. Novelty is born from the womb (*hystera*) of change; and history is the result of this hysteresis process, with its production of novelty. The creative evolution of Being results from the dialectic of the actual and the possible.

1.3.4.3.1. Models of Being
Being, all of nature, and therefore unique, is a natural phenomenon, and all natural phenomena are governed by the laws of thermodynamics. Philosophy ingests scientific concepts, as it does poetic ones, in order to extract universal concepts from them, or to examine their basic assumptions.

1.3.4.3.2. A Model of Being
With imagination, models of Being can be constructed. Based on thermodynamic theories a model of Being can be constructed using

scientific terms in a mythical framework, after the spirit of Parmenides. Suppose that Being is a perfect sphere, one metamacrostate in order in its oneness, but disordered on the microstatic level. It is a whole turning; it desires to know itself, nonetheless. To do so it deforms itself, topologically. It intentionally directs its ordering. Part of itself stands out from the rest of itself—it extends itself in beings. But in doing so it loses sight of some of itself; by increasing vantages of itself it sees more, but conversely loses the possibility of seeing still more. It builds up macrostates from its disordered microstates, but at the cost of disordering other microstates irrevocably. Assuming that order and disorder are dialectical opposites in Being, like language and silence, they both must increase. These macrostates reflect the whole from their perspective; each one builds up more and more order within itself, and other microstates become more and more savage. The ultimate macrostate increases its self-order; it intends to approach an asymptote of self-knowledge. Being is a prelogical and intentional turning. Although its turning is not reversible, the relation of opposites within Being is; henceforth the reversibility of Being means a relational one and not a developmental one. Merleau-Ponty's model of topological space can be made more specific, a Klein bottle (Figure 13432-1).

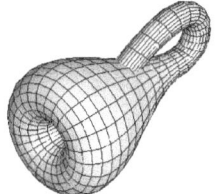

Figure 13432-1. Klein Bottle

Realizing that Being is a reversibility and dialectic, the Klein bottle is proposed as a more adequate model of Being than a sphere. The Klein bottle is a closed, one-sided surface, a manifold that requires a four dimensional space for its construction. To make one, a cylinder is made from a one sided surface; one end of the cylinder is then extruded and thrust through the side and joined with the other end from the inside (the description of the model is in three dimensions; in the fourth dimension the first end goes around the surface of the cylinder instead of intersecting it). The two open ends of the original cylinder are joined in such a way that when the original outside is joined to the original inside, outside and inside can no longer be distinguished; thus the bottle not only has the properties of the purse of Fortunatus (from Lewis Carroll), but it reflects the intertwining characteristic of Pontean Being, which also has no outside or inside.

A Klein bottle is formed in an abstract mathematical space of four dimensions. Any two points on the surface may be connected by a continuous path not crossing any boundary curve. Its one sidedness is an extrinsic, not an intrinsic property of the surface, since the space around it must be used to determine that characteristic. To an entity on the surface (an ant, perhaps), parts of the surface would be hidden, but would become visible after movement. Similarly, Being only appears to have two sides, from within; if Being could be viewed from the outside, it would all be visible—having one side. However, since all discussions necessarily take place on the surface of Being, and since there can be, by definition of Being as all there is, no outside, the metaphor of the two sides of Being will be continued.

The surface of the Klein bottle is nonorientable; if a hypothetical entity travels around the bottle and crosses the same point, it could be upside down, so demonstrating the possibility of reversibility on the bottle. This quality of reversibility in Being is just that which allows the subject to see out of the object, or the object to see out of the subject. Why is a Klein bottle a better model than a sphere? Because of the intentionality of Being, which makes it turn in upon itself.

1.3.5. Making Orders (Intentionality)
As the intentional relationship is not the final truth of human existence, since it appears at only a certain level of self-actualization, it must be preceded by a pre-intentional level, which continues to exist *in* it, in which opposition we are never completely ignored. This primordial intentionality refers to a pre-predicative experience, an experience before the subject-object split; it represents a spontaneous organization of experience, which precedes the subject's active synthesis. Primordial intentionality is the entire intentional network of the lived-in-world; the subject is already immersed in a world that gives him meaning. Therefore intentional objects have sense only in the context of a larger world horizon, which is not due to subjective constitution, but to a latent intentionality that is the intentionality within Being.

What does it mean to say that Being has intentionality? Does it mean that it moves, or goes in a direction? If so, it cannot be one undifferentiated sphere; it must go over into entities. Why would it do so, why suffer the ordeal of birth into newness?

1.3.5.1. Into Opposites
Even a physicist describing the behavior of objects is led to ultimately question the ground of those objects. In the words of Brown (BR

105): "Now the physicist himself, who describes all this, is, in his own account, himself constructed of it. He is, in short, made of a conglomeration of the very particulars he describes, no more, no less, bound together by and obeying such general laws as he himself has managed to find and to record. Thus we cannot escape the fact that the world we know is constructed in order (and thus in such a way as to be able) to see itself."

Bachelard (BA 185) states it more poetically: "The world wishes to see itself: the world lives in an active curiosity with ever open eyes." Mythically, the cosmos is an Argus, a sum of ever-open eyes. How can the world see at all if it is one whole Being? Brown (BR 105) answers: "in order to do so, evidently it must first cut itself up into at least one state which sees, and at least one other state which is seen. In this severed and mutilated condition, whatever it sees is only partially itself. We may take it that the world undoubtedly is itself (i.e., is indistinct from itself), but, in any attempt to see itself as an object, it must, equally undoubtedly, act so as to make itself distinct from, and therefore false to, itself. In this condition it will always partially elude itself."

In opposing itself to itself, it limits itself what it knows. It never sees what is seeing. As it opposes itself to see itself, Being is divided to its very root, Being creates a basic dialectic: mind-body, subject-object, and male-female. Being holds all contradictions; indeed, contradictions allow existence. Substance and nothingness allow movement; but they are both Being: the invisible side of things replaces the concept of nothingness in the philosophy of Merleau-Ponty, and substances are visibles. The two things of opposite nature depend on one another, in Being, as day on night. And the imagined on the real. Wallace Stevens (BG 112) expressed it thus:

"Music falls on the silence like a sense,
A passion that we feel, not understand.
Morning and afternoon are clasped together.
And North and South are an intrinsic couple
And sun and rain a plural, like two lovers
That walk away as one in the greenest body."

Beings renew their access to Being as a function of mortality. Bachelard exclaimed that the division of anima and animus was at the very root of Being. All mythologies are of love and death; as man is an opening to Being, generic man is open to sex. Sex, in Being, as in organisms, is a means of constant renewal; sexuality, the dialectical opposition of man and woman, is the symbol of time (irreversible movement toward perfect entropy?). Beings renew their access to Being as a function of mortality. As men die, others are born with a new opening to Being. In the shrines of Catal Hujuk, breasts were carved on the walls as sacred symbols, but there was a vulture's beak in each nipple—inside the breast that nourishes the flesh, was the instrument that ripped away flesh. If being is anima and animus, its progression must resemble two spirals—a double helix. The helix has a history most appropriate for Being: Apollo adopted the caduceus to symbolize the healing power of medicine, two snakes lovingly intertwined about his staff. The structure of the genetic apparatus and the morphology of plant reproduction is a double helix; plans for a nuclear fusion generator also use the design. Raine (R 163) presents the helix:

> The helix revolves like a timeless thought,
> Instantaneous from apex to rim
> Like a dance whose figure is limpet or murex, cowrie or
> golden winkle.

Light is rooted in darkness, but so is darkness rooted in light; Kwant criticized Merleau-Ponty for this reductionism, but they are two sides of Being, which reveal each other, and are necessary for each other's existence. Stars are only visible on a background of darkness. Chuang Tse (Y 65) said the necessity: "Light comes from Darkness, and the predictables come from the formless." These aspects of Being are reversible. Reversibility is at the fundamental nature of Being. Being is a dialectic of its reversible opposites. Lao Tse writes (BY 42):

> One has a man's wings
> And a woman's also
> Is in himself a womb of the world
> And, being a womb of the world,
> Continuously, endlessly,
> Gives birth;
> One who, preferring light,
> Prefers darkness also
> Is in himself an image of the world
> And, being an image of the world,
> Is continuously, endlessly
> The dwelling of creation;
> One who is highest of mean
> And humblest also
> Is in himself a valley of the world,
> And, being a valley of the world,
> Continuously, endlessly
> Conducts the one source
> From which vessels may be usefully filled.

With creation in Being, possibilities are brought forth and taken in again, in a cycle of visibility and invisibility. Again Lao Tse:

> Life on its way returns into a mist,
> Its quickness is its quietness again:
> Existence of this world of things and men
> Renews their never needing to exist.

The principle of reversion is the operation of the Tao; the cycle begins again when it ends, as emptiness and fullness alternate. It is the same in the phenomenology of Merleau-Ponty. Similarly, Brown (BR 105) concludes: "It seems hard to find an acceptable answer to the question of how or why the world conceives a desire, and discovers an ability, to see itself, and appears to suffer the process. That it does so is sometimes called the original mystery. Perhaps, in view of *the form* in which *we* presently *take* ourselves *to exist*, the mystery *arises from* our insistence on *framing* a question where there is, in reality, *nothing* to question." The questioning may be a function of distance, and arise from our forgetfulness of savage Being.

1.3.5.2. Dialectic Change

Does Being evolve? There are three fundamental facts from Merleau-Ponty's thought: First, the development of Being takes place here and now, not in the past. Second, Merleau-Ponty doubts the perspective of evolution, and wants to replace it with a cosmology of visible reality. With no beginning and no limits, there is always an explosion of Being. Merleau-Ponty (PP 186) states that "All flesh, and even that of the world, radiates beyond itself." That is not to say that visible Being does not develop in a definite direction, in a lawful manner during this one turning (universe); but savage Being remains invisible and savage and it is the ground of potentiality. Third, it is a noncausal process; the lower level does not completely explain the higher, so there is an essential element of surprise in its development.

How can change and progression be explained without a theory of causality? Causal relationships imply a direct single relation between any two elements in a universe; this is highly abstract, since all parts of the universe are always influencing one another. Two types of noncausal relationships may replace the strictly causal in any explanation. First, there are conditioning relationships, which assume a priori acquaintance in time between the concerned elements; noncausal conditioning stipulates a number of necessary but insufficient conditions, while antecedent-consequent conditioning requires a temporal dimension. Then there are consistency relationships, where no priority of conditions is necessary for the occurrence of an event: these are usually coherent or parallel. Kammerer's law of seriality of physical events, and Jung's principle of synchronicity of psychological and physical events, are relationships of this type. Star patterns have a nonsymmetrical order, like clouds and smoke, but it is not an order that admits definition—even philosophy cannot squeeze clarity from a cloud; this is the order of surprise—Being playing with randomness.

Being has direction; like the Indian word, *prana*, which names a physical and psychological force that is the directional agent of natural selection and the basis for culture, it is a spatially extended vitalizing force, a moving potency. Perhaps it is like a quantum, a probability amplitude, and a possibility toward which time flows. If so, why does it order part of itself? Is perfect stability to be found in ultimate unity, or ultimate diversity—or paradox of both? Why does Being move? What is it that tries to know itself? Our experience of Being is rooted in silence. The name of the name of that which cannot be named is silence. Yet silence is not enough to describe Being. Raine (RA 40) describes the voice:

> From height to depth, a circumference to centre
> The primal ray, axis of world's darkness
> Through all the planes of being descends into the prison of
>   the rocks
> Where elements in tumultuous voices wordless utter their
>   wild *credo*.

1.3.5.3. Biopoesis: Organic Order

> "Nature proceeds little by little from things lifeless to animal life in such a way that it is impossible to determine the exact line of demarcation, nor on which side thereof an intermediate from should lie." Aristotle, *Historia Animalium* Book VIII, Chapter 1

Order is an ektropic process that is directly related to an entropic process. An increase in order creates an increase in disorder around it. The second law of thermodynamics asserts that closed physical systems tend toward randomness through time. But the second law does not forbid parts of a system, closed or open, to become more ordered, as long as the total entropy of the system increases. Life requires order. Life requires entropy as well as order. Life could only survive in a world where entropy increases; it could not survive either extreme—the bombardment of free energy or the complete lack of it. Entropy is not the opposite of life; it is part of life. Dissolution is involved in life. Life requires death to release it from form.

The living earth evolved with the entropy of the sun and other stars. Physical processes in stars build more complex atoms; on cooler stars and in gas clouds, molecules are formed. Molecules condense to crystals on planets and cold stars. These increases in order are a function of temperature and form. At some time during the development of the earth, natural processes created a pattern that guaranteed the maintenance and reproduction of a system of processes. These processes are considered living. Increases in order are not unique to life, but living forms accelerate the creation of order and its duplication. Living processes can be outlined, but not totally defined, by physical and chemical concepts. The difference between living and nonliving systems lies in the uniqueness of pattern. Living order is not the same as molecular. An amoeba is highly directive order. The slime mold displays greater order than amoeba. Living orders have a range of complexity. Uniqueness is complementary to complexity.

David Bohm questions when does a molecule come alive, but life is not in molecules, it is in pattern. The difference between life and nonlife may not be in the process of evolution, but in the degree and kind of intrinsic order that has resulted from that process. Life involves a vast number of interacting structures. Living consists of complex behaviors whose limits are defined by rules of order that can be empirically described.

The classical criteria of life are: Metabolism, to compensate for energy loss; self-reproduction, to preserve biological information; and, variability and selection, to enlarge information. In ordinary human experience, it is not difficult to distinguish living forms from nonliving. From a cosmological perspective, living organisms interpenetrate deeply into nonliving forms and the earth. Individual organisms are woven into a complex fabric. Once living beings were formed on earth, their populations must have exploded to use every source of energy available. The fossil record indicates that three billion years ago the earth was inhabited only by blue-green algae. From a simple base, complex forms arose.

Complexity offers advantages for living forms; it allows increases in size and diversity. A typical eucaryotic cell is ten times larger than a procaryotic cell. Size enables a cell to compete more successfully for light; it permits colonization of less favorable environments, higher above the sea or deeper into it. Diversity allows more effective behavior through specialization; a special organelle may digest molecules that are harder to find.

The entire earth is a complex system, now, composed of smaller subsystems that are also whole systems. And each of these subsystems has independent elements from regions and ecosystems, to species and individuals. The earth is organized in levels of interacting units.

Individual organisms are composed of interacting cells. Cells have independent components in the forms of organelles, which are composed of membranes, tubules, granules, and threads. And these are composed of macromolecules. Although macromolecules are considered the basement of life, they can be dissociated into molecules and atoms.

New properties emerge at certain levels of complexity. An increase in the diversity of elements and their connections leads to emergent patterns of behavior that are difficult to predict from even a complete knowledge of the elements. For example, although the properties of each amino acid in a protein chain are known, the convolutions of the chain result in novel properties and a new order of interactions. Being in a certain form allows the sequence to recognize and act on certain molecules.

When a protein is stretched out it loses all its biological activity. If the denatured protein is placed in an appropriate solution, it regains most all of its activity in a short time. It folds into an active form. Proteins fold more rapidly than could be expected if they found their final form by a random search. The folding must follow particular pathways. Protein folding is like a descent on a mountain road: the road descends gradually in twists and turns, even a little uphill; it does not plunge straight down.

At some time, it becomes active. There has been much research on how proteins are produced. A cyclic network of reactions, where nucleotides produce proteins that produce nucleotides, for instance, is a hypercycle. When such networks compete with one another, they display an ability to evolve through mutation and replication into greater complexity. The idea of structural stability seems to express innovation, the appearance of a new mechanism and a new species that were initially absent in the system.

Manfred Eigen thinks that a simple principle overcame the odds against life. Molecules form cross-links and hypercycles. Eigen and P. Schuster propose a simple hierarchy of cyclical reaction systems that are important in natural dynamics (at a precellular level): A transformatory reaction cycle acts globally as a catalyst, a cycle of catalysts acts globally as an autocatalyst, and a catalytic cycle of autocatalysts acts globally as a hypercycle. T. Ballmer and E. von Weizsacker introduced ultracycles to describe systemic coevolution. Both types of cycles seem to be necessary for life. In a hypercycle, the evolution of higher complexity results from competition; in the ultracycle, from interdependence within a larger system.

Living order can also be defined in terms of the influence of whole over the parts. Disorder at the level of a molecule can reflect the higher level of order of cell. The machinery of a cell is not a permanent fixture, but is disassembled and rebuilt periodically, according to specific patterns and in harmony with the functioning of the cell. Weiss shows that parts of a cell are constantly changing, growing, dying, breaking up and recombining, but under control at a cellular level. This process is termed metalysis.

Metalysis means "loosening change," from the Greek roots. It is a technical term for the process of dedifferentiation in biology. It can also be used to describe physical processes like quantum foam or social processes like institutional revolution. It is used here to describe biological processes, such as metamorphosis. Metamorphosis is where changes are often so extreme that the organism constructs many specialized parts of the adult from cells set aside in the embryo and nonfunctional in the juvenile; these cells are imaginal disks, which are controlled by juvenile hormones. Imaginal disks are nests of cells usually with frozen biases for reproducing determined cells. Disks differentiate into specific adult structures, e.g., a leg disk forms a leg. As juvenile hormones decrease, adult cells take over. Metamorphosis depends on individual metabolism (as well as environmental changes).

Nucleated cells are not individuals; they are communities of individuals of different species living in harmony. The study of genetics cannot be separated from metabolism, since the essential substances are regulated by the cell itself. The unfolding of an egg to an intricate adult involves an understanding of immunity, development and metamorphosis. The product of stable variations in offspring is the subject of a theory of evolution. Simple organisms may have elaborate communications between cells; in more complex organisms, this communication may be extended to other organisms of the same or other species. The activities of cells interlock. An organism communicates with the whole environment. This ecological setting is where evolution operates.

The organic order is conceived as a harmonious balancing of differences; in the context of life and becoming, it is represented as a dynamic equilibrium of functions maintained through a progressive differentiation of elements within the whole. Paul Weiss presents a balanced view of nature in a formula that resembles an aesthetic code: order in the gross, and freedom, diversity and uniqueness in the small. These characteristics are not only compatible, but are conjugated. For example, the pattern of an oak leaf or dragonfly wing remains invariant in its dominant pattern through endless variations in its smaller. M. Beardsley offers the reverse: order enters in the small, in textual relations and in structural relations with larger segments; but freedom, diversity and uniqueness mark the quality of the whole, as individuality in a work of art. The problem lies in defining the whole. Weiss' principle applies to holons: Galaxies, leaves or the style of an artist. Beardsley's artist is a whole human, unique but ordered to the pattern. The artist's whole effort is marked by a style that may be original; that is the gross order, not the single work. Weiss' principle is more comprehensive.

Biological order is built on physical and chemical orders. That is why life is limited to such a narrow range of conditions. And that is why the most complex orders are vulnerable to changes in their substrates; energetic radiation can alter and destroy an individual, a small change in climate can destroy crops and civilizations. Complex orders always depend on simple orders. Where a planet of algae is conceivable, one of rats and humans only is not. The success of life depends on miniaturization, where a prodigious number of overlapping mechanisms are packed in a small space. These are persistent by virtue of built in regulation circuits; and open enough for novelty. Everything necessary for life, and higher organisms, is packed into cells. Cells order themselves, internally and externally. Every complex organism starts as a single cell, which multiplies by splitting and unfolds by a code within the cell. With four basic symbols that can be composed in four different arrangements, the cell contains a complete set of operating instructions.

1.3.5.3.1. Field Development (Epigenesis)
Transitions in history of matter. Nature creates concentrations, which change and generate energy, which increases entropy in the larger system. This also generates energy for the larger system. When energy is no longer generated by a process, it takes more energy and the instability releases small pockets of ektropy as well as more energy to the larger system. So each stage has some more complex configurations.

Another thing nature does is repeat patterns. Once these are created then motion overgenerates cells for those patterns. At some point, at maturity, overgeneration stops. This could be a metaphor for galaxies, life, and architecture.

There are major transitions in the evolution of life. One is the emergence of high-level units of evolution that is evolutionary innovations spread that reduce competition, since that would disrupt higher-level units. Another major transition is the evolution of novel inheritance systems. This is especially important to the poetic archaeology of the flesh.

DNA is a commonly known basis of inheritance, yet there is more to inheritance than simply DNA. There has to be a long phase of chemical and biological evolution before DNA appears. Another transition is the increase in complexity especially of ecological systems.

If we look at these transitions we notice that they are irreversible. Although it some can be reversed and lineages Princess East can become mauled unicellular and solitary insects can come from social insects. This a reversibility is contingent on history. Life itself is a major transition because it gave the system itself a new capacity for the storage and transmission of information, as well as new pathways for the trans-formation of energy and matter. Of course one tremendous transition was from a reducing atmosphere to the oxidizing atmosphere over 2 billion years ago. This should be of course a major transition in evolution. There are a number of conclusions. External disturbances such as asteroid impacts or basalt eruptions could have triggered significant transitions between different states. However, most transitions appear to have been generated internally with evolutionary innovation playing a role. There are many further considerations: to what extent is the Earth system self-regulating? What is the contribution of life to maintaining habitable conditions? In what sense can the Earth system itself be said to evolve? Are there reasons to explain why regulatory feedback should predominate at the global scale?

Development is a succession of transformations directed toward establishing control over transcription by creating special niches in an individual's anatomy. The potential of cells becomes restricted during development; they become units of organization. Where the fertilized egg is omnipotent, capable of synthesizing all proteins coded in its DNA, differentiated cells express only part of genetic inheritance. This is true of all waves. Differentiation appears on a biochemical level step by step with changing cellular organization. One consequence is the appearance of mechanisms to trigger development on a higher level. The forms of animals and plants are transforms of messages from the cells, which are contextually shaped. The hard-wired parts of the cells are DNA strands.

Each embryological step is an act of becoming that must be built upon. In the embryo there is no need for new information; it must be protected from new information. The development of a fetus must follow the postulates laid down in DNA. Embryos are not in a state of equilibrium, Waddington notes. A fertilized egg insists on changing; it can be stopped by killing it. Waddington (1975) replaces embryology with epigenesis. He sees living systems as displaying homeorhesis, from the Greek *homeo*, meaning same and *rheo*, flow. Homeorhesis is used when what is stabilized is not a constant value but a particular course of change in time. Like ecosystems, embryos have many characteristics and are affected by many environmental conditions. Their changes are symbolized by trajectories in multidimensional phase space; orderliness can be described in terms of constraints on trajectory courses, and these constraints are visualized as attractor surfaces. If the system starts from any condition, represented by a point in multidimensional phase space, the trajectory will move to nearest attractor surface and then move along it.

Maturation implies that the phase space in which system is modeled contains a surface with a general slope that guides any trajectory toward the adult state and death. The development of the embryo into different organs can be described by supposing that a radiating system of valleys is superimposed on the general slope; the trajectories differentiate (like the path of electron?) and move toward organs. This model of an attractor surface is an epigenetic landscape.

The valleys occur in various shapes. Some could be very narrow canyons, others large meadows (similar to old mature earth forms, with meandering rivers). The name for a characteristic of an attractor surface in multidimensional space is a chreod, not a valley. The cross-sectional shape of the chreod describes the reaction of the system to fluctuations. With a steep slope, for example, it is difficult to divert the developing system from the bottom of valley; even with a strong force the system will return immediately as soon as the influence stops. With a shallow slope, like a flood plain chreod, it is easy to divert the system; it meanders before returning. But actually the perturbations alter the landscape itself, making a steep valley again, not just shifting the river. As the environment changes, the system changes with it.

Waddington refers to such a course as chreod (from *chre*, fated, and *hodos*, path, in Greek). The nature of a chreod that a system adopts is determined by instructions in genes and other organizations of information, and in interaction with the environment that it travels, that is, the epigenetic landscape. Control of a system after disturbance may not bring it back to where it was before; it may go back or forward. Since the path is fuzzy, it can change.

1.3.5.3.2. Field Shape (Morphogenesis)
All living beings participate in the physical fields of the earth. Gravity binds them to the planet. Electrical fields can influence mood Negative atmospheric ions promote better health in mammals, at least, and birth and death rates. Electrical fields are a feature of biological fields, as is chemical composition. The rhythms of the universe impress themselves on organism in varying degrees. The rhythms are incorporated. An animal or plant then establishes its own personal rhythm. Organisms set

clocks by solar-system rhythms. Biological clocks enable the organism to master changing conditions in a rhythmic world; to do the right thing at the right time. The organism is part of a larger field.

The field is an important principle for understanding patterns in physics. The ideas of field and particle were indispensable to physical inquiry by the end of the 19th century. Although Whitehead noted that the two concepts were considered antithetical, they are not logically contradictory. Ordinary matter was considered atomic, whereas electromagnetism was conceived as arising from a continuous field. By the time Alexander Gurwitsch (1922) used the term in biology, gravity was a second field (nuclear interactions are described in terms of fields) in the universe. Earlier, Gurwitsch had explored an organic formative factor that he called 'Morphe,' but this concept was abandoned for that of field. The field concept was useful in his investigation of mushrooms where nondifferentiated structural units resulted in highly regular and specific shapes. His concept of field, however, tried to explain form without relying on the mutual interaction of parts. Chemical processes were also excluded. Transformations were controlled by vectors connected in a field. The source and extent of a field was not confined to the organism, but was the result of geometric properties.

Paul Weiss objected to this concept of field, since it was based on ideal geometric constructions and not the structural complexity of the organism. His own conception of the field was as a system of organizing factors that proceeded from already organized parts to developing regions, resulting in "typical patterns." In his book, *Morphodynamik*, Weiss described amphibian tail bud transplantations to the limb area. If the tail bud were transplanted early in the development, it gave rise to a limb in the new area; but if it were transplanted late, it produced a tail. The forces pushing cells into specific forms were a function of development. The system of forces of organizing action was named a field. Fields divided into smaller fields during development until the organism was a system of coordinated patterns. Growth and pattern are emergent field effects.

Weiss saw the field as a symbolic term for the unitary dynamics underlying the ordered behavior of the collective. It denotes properties lost in the process of analysis. In living organisms, the patterned structure of the dynamics of the system as a whole coordinated the activities of the parts. The parts of the organism are not assembled, but integrated. In the operation of a field, every part knows the activities of every other and responds to a collective equilibrium.

Although recent experiments support the existence of some kinds of biological fields, scientific descriptions are still unsatisfactory.

Waddington regarded concepts of chreods and morphogenetic fields as descriptive "conveniences." Sheldrake thought they were vague. He preferred his own concept of morphogenetic fields.

Sheldrake criticizes the organismic approach for not suggesting new lines of empirical research (1981). The topological, qualitative models of Rene Thom (1975) exemplify the approach being criticized. Thom admits that the use of local models implies nothing about the ultimate nature of reality. But perhaps it does?? The basic reaction cycle may operate in different dynamic regimes and in different structures; this is the root of morphogenesis. Catastrophe theory, based on differential topology, is a valuable tool for studying morphogenesis. The theory describes only the movement of a system through a morphogenetic landscape with dynamics imposed from outside; it cannot describe autopoesis or self-organization. It does not describe how the fields were formed. Forms cannot be measured on a quantitative scale; differences are recognized perceptually. A description of forms is a mathematical problem of great complexity. Thom's theory classifies the possible types of change of form, or catastrophe. The end of a morphogenetic process or final form is represented by an attractor within the morphogenetic field; every form is represented by an attractor.

But if forms are to be understood, then they need to be explained in terms of more fundamental forms, not necessarily in terms of numbers (numbers are symbols for forms). Living fields have form. Living fields impose restrictions on the probabilities of nonliving fields. Sheldrake states that specific structures of complex molecules are selected through morphogenetic fields, which are invisible. They are detectable only through their effects on material systems. Since each kind of system has its characteristic form, each has a specific field: for muscle cells or ideas. Sheldrake could benefit from Occam's razor here. Overidentity and uniqueness are not necessary. True uniqueness comes from relations. Basic fields could be additive or combinatory. Constancy and repetition are no problem if forms are uniquely determined by laws. But Formative Causation claims that forms are not determined by laws, but by causal influence from previous similar forms. This is too loose; again, like Lamarck, there is no system to explain sameness. Sheldrake refuses to extend hypothesis as to what determines form on first occasion.

Field interactions can be understood through an analogy of resonance. Resonance occurs when the system is acted on by an alternating force that coincides with its natural frequency of vibration. It takes place between vibrating systems. Sheldrake calls the process morphic resonance. This morphic resonance seems to be additive. So all atoms would be more atom-like through time. But how explain differentiation and individuation?? He also assumes the resonance is unattenuated in Space-Time. Morphic influence of past systems might be everywhere. Or it might tunnel through S/T. These are weak discussions. If the world were wiped out today, it should reform tomorrow from past resonance, but would it? Sheldrake states that morphic units, like atoms, existing for hundreds of years are effectively changeless. But he does not seem to consider proton decay. He also states that on first occasion a substance may not crystallize; but afterwards morphic resonance makes it easier. Perhaps that is just our knowledge of the crystal (like driving an unfamiliar road for first time). Sheldrake also argues for organ fields. Embryonic tissue develop initially under control of primary embryonic fields; then different regions come under influence of secondary fields (for organs). The primary fields establish germs of organ fields. As development proceeds different regions behave with increasing autonomy; the whole system loses ability to regulate but local regulations occur as secondary fields take over. But this development is controlled by juvenile hormones. No other explanation is necessary. The primary fields should be restricted to functioning organisms. But the process sounds like it parallels the entire universe: After big bang all is local, but secondary fossil relations take over. Sheldrake also claims that the forms of previous leaves on a tree stabilize the leaf form characteristics. Weiss has better explanation.

No morphogenetic field unit can have energy without form, no form exist without energy, because they are in the STEM field. The hypothesis of formative causation, by regarding previous forms as causes of subsequent forms, is just history and reproduction. The atom only has a final form at low temperature. The causation required for form is ektropy. The laws are physical. The morphogenetic field germ is just a code, molecular or genetic. Sheldrake has no means to understand the teleology of individuals, or organs.

1.3.5.3.3. Individual Order
The individual is the unit of experience and memory. The individual carries the units of transmission of form (genes) and develops according to their application within an environment.

1.3.5.3.3.1. Growth. Schiller synthesized two impulses in his concept of the 'living form' (*Lebensform*). The most obvious aspect of form is its constancy in spite of growth. In some cases, growth is necessary to sustain the form. The growth of one part must effect that of all. Growth serves as a mechanism of evolutionary adaptation, by carrying out genetic instructions in an environment; but growth is also conservative and stabilizing rather than innovative and reorganizing. Growth and development are homeorhetic; in a homeorhetic process, the flow is constant, not a stationary state. Flow processes follow fixed trajectories, called chreods. Growth, from fertilization, embryo states, birth and maturity, represents a homeorhetic process following more or less fixed chreods, programmed genetically and conditioned environmentally. Chreods must be like electron paths, multiply probabilistic.

1.3.5.3.3.2. Sex Maturity & Death. In the early course of life, reproduction was vertical; an organism copied itself. There was only forced death. Bdelboid rotifers are asexual, but resilient. In unicellular organisms, symbiosis was probably more important than diversity. A family must diversify to survive, but without sexual reproduction, there is no speciation or real diversity.

The invention of sexuality—L. Margulis thinks that sexuality has been less important than symbiosis in the long run of evolution—improved diversity through pairing. Sexuality was one of factors resulting in acceleration and variety of life. Sexuality is a perfect example of 50% redundancy, which importance is yet to be discussed. (The other was heterotrophy, the capability of feeding on life.) The cost of that acceleration was an acceleration of death for the individual.

Furthermore, the combination of genes often resulted in errors. J. von Neumann pointed out that living organisms achieve a very high degree of reliability despite the fact that the components are unreliable. Error is not an extraneous accident; it is an essential part of the process, it is comparable in importance to the structure. The consequences of unavoidable errors can be nullified by redundancy and decision functions (as design elements). DNA, for example, is enormously redundant. Errors cannot be washed from a system; they are part of it.

Each organism must at some time be disassembled; this is a necessity for any system that evolves. Sometimes the disassembly is part of a metamorphosis, as with a caterpillar. A caterpillar breakdown in a cocoon has interesting similarities to quantum foam. Other organisms simply fully disassemble, in death. Death is death of the self, not of the materials, matrix or process. Nature remains young and whole in spite of death everywhere. All things return to dust, but the dust is eternally fertile. Soil is a living organism. All organisms enact Lucretius phrase: "Like runners in a race, they hand on the torch of life" (in DV, p. 36). Nature is more than the material world as a whole; it is the power underlying all phenomena in the material world. The metabolic flow that passes through individuals is not the individuals. The individual is the integral patterning sustained by the changes, a knot (transient) through which the ecological cycles pass.

1.3.5.3.4. Aesthetics & Play

John Dewey finds sources of aesthetic experience in animal life below the human scale because of the unity and integration of the animal itself. The live animal is fully present. Harmony is attained only when terms are made with the environment. The unity of experience demands a unity of time and interaction.

If we consider aesthetic preferences to mean a liking for activities because they produce particular states, then aesthetics can be attributed to animals. It is implied that there are no immediate functional advantages from aesthetic preferences. Rensch has allowed birds and fish to choose between various patterns in absence of differential reinforcement; they have consistent preferences. Although intriguing, it is not sure whether the preferences result from an automatic desire for concealment (fear of standing out) or from pleasure. Aesthetic appreciations are primarily emotional. Pleasure at an appropriate environment keeps beings there.

Play also produces pleasure. And it is creative. Play may be the tentative explorations by which an organism tests different proprioceptive patterns for goodness of fit. One function of play is a sense of pretending. It is a major principle of learning in higher animals; by pretending to fight, animals learn how to, and avoid the consequences. Lorenz' research emphasized the ratiomorphic (symbol forming) character of much animal behavior. These neurophysiological processes equal the highest mathematical operations of human rational thought in their complexity, without being subjective. Playing with symbols creates pleasure. It is an aesthetic experience. Since play is creative motion between feeling beings (correlated to brain size), cross-species play occurs: between cat and dog, birds, human and dolphin.

Play aids living organisms to adapt to their environment. Adaptation, in learning and biology, is an active process, involving assimilation and accommodation (to environmental constraints). Accommodation is modification of the organism's structure; assimilation integrates external factors into organism's structure. The ordering depend on the local characteristics of place. Plants and animals create their own world, according to their complexity and needs.

1.3.5.3.4.1. *Self-world.* Adolf Portmann shows that every form of life appears as a Gestalt with a specific development in space-time. All living forms develop an image of their environments. Genetics provides the proper image choices for some—frogs, for instance. Others must learn what is valuable using their senses. Animals have their own universes that are strange and fascinating to us. When we realize this, we find that reality is immeasurably greater than the human idea of it. Jakob von Uexkull suggests representing the unfamiliar world of animals with bubbles to denote the self-world or phenomenal world of an animal. According to von Uexkull (1957), perceptual and effector worlds form a closed unit, the umwelt. "Figuratively speaking each animal grasps its object with two arms of a forceps: receptor and effector. With the first it invests the object with perceptual meaning, with the second operational meaning. "The world—life-image—is what has meaning for an organism. The umwelt is a region of brightness, or just a focus. The first principle of the self-world theory is that all animals from the simplest to complex are "fitted to their unique worlds with equal completeness," according to Uexkull. A simple world corresponds to simple animal; a well-articulated world to a complex animal. For example, the rich possibilities around a tick shrinks to a scanty framework of three receptor and three effector cues (butyric acid, motion and heat)—her umwelt. But the poverty of this world guarantees the certainty of actions; and security is more important than wealth. Bodenheimer hypothesizes that an animal has an optimal umwelt in a pessimal environment. The environment must be pessimal or a species would gain ascendancy. The umwelt allows the creation of familiar paths that are strange to others, or invisible.

Time is different for each species; the tick can wait 18 years for prey. Human time is made of units of 1/18th of a second; which Uexkull says is utilized effectively by the motion picture technique of film projection. The subject sways to the time of its own world. Since all beings feel, the smallest unit of time is a duration for that being. Larger beings have larger durations. Similarly, space is a unit of place for a being. Uexkull implies that the human world is only one of the many possible. Although this is true perceptually, the use of symbols allow humans to imagine and represent other worlds. Humans can even create virtual worlds by limiting what could be received; for instance, the x-ray spectrum. Yet human imagination is limited, as is human knowledge. Many organisms exist of which we know nothing. Their worlds have little meaning in a human world. Edward Hall's space bubble or Kurt Lewin's personality field extrapolate the umwelt to humans.

1.3.5.3.4.2. *Individual Interactions.* The individuals in a community engage in interactive behaviors, which can be considered positive (+), negative (-), or neutral (0) in effect for each individual or species in relation to another. These interactions are described as in table.

Individuals engage in a number of interactions that are neutral, negative or positive. These interactions are defined as:

- neutralism: neither individual is affected
- competition: each adversely affects other
- amensalism: one is inhibited, other is unaffected
- parasitism: one benefits, other adversely affected
- predation: one benefits, other adversely affected
- commensalism: one benefits, other not affected
- protocooperation: both benefit, in nonobligatory way
- mutualism: both benefit, in necessary relationship.

Several other individual actions are not widely recognized by biologists, such as charity, altruism, and interference. In charity, one individual helps another without any cost to itself. With altruism, the help may involve a negative, as when a monkey warns antelope of the presence of a leopard and then becomes the leopard's dinner. Interference is a rare interaction where one individual creates a negative for another without any benefit to itself.

Most interactions are not simple, but are complex and paradoxical because of the integration of levels. For example, parasitism that is detrimental on an individual level may have benefits on the species level, by influencing reproduction rates or resistance to diseases. Some of these interactions are poorly defined in the literature. Predation, for example, is regarded as the adverse effect of one population on another, while being dependent on it. Yet, predation can benefit both species; it may be more mutualistic than parasitic in character. The predator/prey are not excluding opposites, but generate a whole unity on the community level, where there is stabilization and survival for both species, according to M. W. Fox. Predation increases the survivability of two species. In Caswell's open nonequilibrium model, the incorporation of predation results in an indefinite coexistence of species—extending the extinction of either indefinitely. Predation opens up cells for colonization by inferior competitors (gaps caused by physical disturbance can also have the same effect). Predation increases the diversity of species in a community. Steven Stanley argues that predation, or cropping, may have controlled the evolution of metazoans. In communities of primary producers, a few species can monopolize a place. A predator dominates its favorite species, usually the most populous, thus limiting it so that other species can develop to claim a niche. Stanley explains the Cambrian explosion of life through the evolution of cropping herbivores, which "opened space" for a diversity of producers, which in turn permitted more specialized croppers, for which specialized predators evolved. Each new level of the trophic pyramid broadened the one below; the pyramid became wider and higher.

One difference between individual and species is the time length. Things that are positive in the short-term may be disadvantageous and hazardous in the long term. The global level would be even more positive due to the good impact on recycling and global cycles.

Competition was once considered the basic interaction between individuals and between species, from C. Darwin to S. Lehmann and others. But, cooperation is seen now to be as effective a strategy as competition and as necessary. Survival of the fitter is correct only to a certain point, then it becomes survival of the more cooperative. Both old studies (Reinheimer and Kropotkin) and new research (Lorenz, Fox, and Schaller) stress the primary use of cooperation both within and between species instead of unrelieved struggle. As Arne Naess says, "live and let live" is a more powerful principles than "either/or." Cooperation creates communities of many species in which competition is necessary but limited. Neil Evernden notes that organisms often go to extreme lengths to avoid direct competition; species form a spectrum of attempts to share the life base without risking their health. This diversity enhances the potential for survival.

1.3.5.3.4.3. *Speciation.* Through speciation, orders of animals and plants probe the environment. A species is thought of as a morphological extension of its niche, but the niche extender enriches nature. The species that enlarges its niche also enlarges the ecology as a whole. According to E. A. Gutkind, it expands the environment for itself and species in balance with it. An expanding whole is created by diversification and enrichment of the parts. A creature in a niche gives to the niche (itself), leading to cycles of nature.

Colinvaux states that species result from the process of avoiding struggles for existence. Since the species, at any concrete moment, is a collection of individuals capable of interbreeding, it turns out that what defines an organization of individuals is an abstraction or something that requires existence of well-defined individuals from the beginning. This is missing the point; species emerge from individuals. Genera, once formed, retain basic body plans through an average of 500,000 generations. The greatest difficulty in pinpointing speciation is determining when interbreeding is impossible.

Watts developed a metaphor of species on earth as heads of a hydra; each has some autonomy and finite life, but is part of a longer lived whole. The notion of human separateness may be an illusion of imperfect senses or an underdeveloped brain.

1.3.5.4. Ecopoesis: The Order of Ecological Places

A patch of forest is a mysterious thing, growing, repairing, competing, holding itself against dispersion, oscillating in a low entropy state, modifying energy from the sun—according to Howard Odum, it is an ecosystem. In 1935 Tansley introduced the term ecosystem, which he defined as the system resulting from the integration of all the living and nonliving factors of the environment. An ecosystem is a community of organisms interacting with one another and their environment. Ecosystems, the essential unit of ecology, must be seen in dynamic and historical terms. Odum describes the ecosystem as a unit of organization undergoing an orderly process of development that is reasonably directional.

Ecosystems are unique and original, like primitive individuals with no replicative parts. The circuitry between different species of an ecosystem is no different today than a billion years ago. Each locality supports a segment of the total species population in a unique context, with a particular set of predators, competition, food, physical habitat.

Earth is a mosaic of cells of communities; the cells have boundaries like rivers or climates that occasionally break down and allow invasion and transformation. There is really just one system on the planet and that is the planet. It is possible to define close but not exact subsystems, that is, ecosystems. The vast number of interrelationships between systems keeps them open. For example, grassland is affected by climates, soil conditions, fires, surrounding communities, and human agents. Ecotones between systems are usually shifting.

Ecosystems are described with a variety of terms: energy, matter, entropy and ektropy, productivity, cycles, diversity, complexity, stability, and trophic structure. Many terms in ecology, such as biomass, stability and diversity are inexact. It is almost impossible to estimate the amount of degraded energy in an ecosystem (such as transpiration, or mixing of water).

One problem with describing ecosystem attributes is that both quantitative (measurable) and qualitative (conceptual) factors are included. Resistance to external factors is a qualitative attribute. This may be more the result of succession than a factor producing an ecosystem. There is no whole system without an interconnection of its parts, and there is no whole system without an environment. Behavior at any level is explained in terms of the level below, but its significance is found in the level above. Ecosystem behavior does not emerge from a set of organismic equations.

1.3.5.4.1. Properties of Ecosystems.

Properties of ecosystems can be recognized in three pairs: productivity and waste, cyclicity and trophisms, and diversity and stability. These three pairs are mutually dependent and only logically separable.

1.3.5.4.1.1. *Productivity and Waste.* The energy of sunlight on the outside of the atmosphere averages 700 Cal/m2/day for all wavelengths; in the visible range within the atmosphere it is 150 Cal/m2/day. Energy is bound into organic material in ecosystems. Animals and humans are dependent on this productivity.

Primary productivity is the rate at which organic material is created by photosynthesis. The amount of organic matter left after plant respiration is net primary productivity. This net productivity (NPP) is available for harvest by animals; The productivity of heterotrophic organisms—animals and saprobes—in communities is termed secondary productivity. Net community productivity (NCP) is that part that remains available after consumers and decomposers have taken their part. That quantity of energy and material used for production and no longer of use to the system is wasted. Although this quantity can be related conceptually to entropy, it is not identifiable with it.

1.3.5.4.1.2. *Cyclicity and Trophisms.* In the initial phases of ecological organization, the gradual increase in the variety of species and the complexity of interaction is accompanied by an increase in resiliency of the system and a decrease in productivity. Such ecosystems are not efficient economically (in industrial systems), because the price paid for efficiency is a decreased resilience and a high probability of extinction. (Holling and Goldberg, 1971) Other ecosystems, with fast organic cycles, like wetlands, are as efficient as anything artificial. Selection favors efficiency and longevity, which is why weeds do not take over all ecosystems.

1.3.5.4.1.3. *Diversity and Complexity.* Biomass seems to increase with diversity. (Studies in Kenya have confirmed this relationship.) Diversity is an expression of the dynamic properties of a complex system. It seems common that a complex of circumstances allowing a high diversity also permits high stability or constancy in taxonomic composition: "nature tends to become baroque in situations permitting high maturity, with little energy left for large changes," according to Margalef (1968). Stability and diversity are not matter of definitions for Margalef, but reflect crude impressions of behavior of physical systems.

1.3.5.4.1.4. *Others: Stability & Maturity*. Balance means an equality of basic processes, such as integration and disintegration. It means that things are being built up as they are being torn down. It means that natural processes such as motion and rest, turning and returning, are approximately equal. Being in balance is like a form of maturity, while growth is usually a characteristic of immaturity on the way to maturity. Being out of balance for too long leads to death. Of course, nothing can be in balance indefinitely, or for very long, depending on its size and complexity. Balance is an ideal for humans. Too much novelty is stressful, it is too new to understand; too much of the sameness is stultifying. Too much conflict is stressful, but too much peace is boring.

A biological organism grows to maturity, which is a stopping point for size. The organism continues to develop, however, experiencing and learning the environmental complexities through mating and then to the end of life. Development may include growth at some stages, but development refers to the continued change after growth has stopped.

Whatever accelerates change and energy flow in ecosystem, reduces potential maturity. In an exploited system, diversity drops and ratio of primary production to biomass increases. Mature systems can regress to earlier forms when exploited; then new species can form (see elsewhere). Ecosystems are constantly evolving under the influence of physicochemical processes poorly understood and so far more powerful than those that result from human activities. The reality is more complex than just systematic succession and climax. Margalef suggests replacing word climax with high maturity. But climax conveys as much if not more information than just maturity.

As a mature system, an ecosystem continues to move to a point of high maturity, recovering from disturbance to its original trajectory, where productivity declines and stability increases. "Nature tends to become baroque in situations permitting high maturity, with little energy left for large changes," according to Ramon Margalef (1968).

1.3.5.4.2. The Importance of Species
Paul Shepard suggests that all creatures are not equally necessary to an ecosystem; some presences do not add to the efficiency and stability of the whole. Larger species are considered dispensable. Fox noted that the ecology of England works without lions. Perhaps it would be better to say that all species are necessary but not sufficient to a system. That is, the system can survive as a system without large species, but it is reduced accordingly. The smallest species, the microbes and invertebrates seem to be the most necessary. Shepard says that no large animal is necessary to an ecosystem; but hippos and crocodiles are necessary to

theirs. Hippopotami support fish populations in lakes and rivers with the minute animals in their excrement. As hippos are eliminated, the fish population dwindles, and native human populations have less protein. Similarly, alligators play an important role in the equilibrium of the Florida Everglades. The alligator creates pools by digging in damp soil; these pools become lairs of fish that eat mosquito larva. The pool also serves as a refuge to more species, including birds, in times of drought. Eagles and primroses are integral parts of ecological networks. Systems depend on their resilience. Although some ecologists cannot think of any, even whooping cranes have uses in nature: as an expression of variety, niche makers, and feeling beings. By killing off select species, humans are changing the character of ecosystems; diversity and stability are reduced.

1.3.5.4.2.1. *Succession*. Tansley recognized the conversion of forest to grassland as succession. Clements framed the ideas of succession and climax in a structured, deductive, deterministic theory which provided the first theoretical statements of ecology. The search for a universal generalization concerning succession has fared badly, however.

Succession appears to be a process of self-organization occurring in every ecosystem. The process is the same as acquiring information. The ecosystem 'learns' the changes, e.g., seasons, of the environment. Any system formed by reproducing and interacting organisms must develop an assemblage in which production of entropy per unit of information is minimized. It is a general property of some systems that acquired information is used to close the door to further inflow. A climax needs less information, since it works toward preservation. The limit of climaxes allows maximum variability between systems with slight external differences, like temperature. Ecosystems consist of different prefabricated pieces: species. Since the supply of species is limited, succession becomes asymptotic.

A climax is an information ladder; at the top, there is no more information available. Clements hypothesized that every system tended to a climactic climax. The word climax was adopted into English in the sixteenth century from the Greek *klimax*, meaning ladder; this was a technical term in rhetoric: a sequence of expressions progressively rising in intensity. That term was derived from the Sanskrit '*sryati*, meaning "leans on." The Greek term *Klima* was a technical geographical term for slope of ground; this term was adopted into Latin as *clima*, zones of the earth divided by latitude and became climate. Margalef suggests replacing the word climax with "high maturity." But climax conveys as much if not more information than just maturity.

Margalef states that biomass and primary production increase during succession; but the ratio of productivity to total biomass drops. According to Pielou species diversity decreases and pattern diversity increases during succession. There is also an increase in the proportion of inert matter, and an increase in structures like paths and burrows.

Autogenic succession occurs when controlling factors are stable and change is due to the effect of the system itself on the microhabitat. Heterogenity is critical. Harper recognized the importance of pattern in Hopkins' poetic metaphor "dappled things," which Whittacker expanded to a shimmer of populations. Harper explains how this is created: "Fluctuations are damped and rhythms change from reactions directly induced by external agents to indirect responses to stimuli associated with ecologically significant factors; the ultimate trend is endogenous factors." (HR 1977).

Eugene Odum has noted trends in ecological succession: the community production decreases; individual lives are longer and more complex; diversity is high and well-organized; there is a closed slow exchange rate, where detritus is important; symbiosis has developed, and conservation and stability are good; and there is a high biomass in a weblike food chain.

The increase in diversity is related to a multiplication of niches; this process goes with longer food chains and stricter specialization. Animals on top of food chains and those with more special habits show a higher efficiency. This results in gains in efficiency in advanced stages of succession.

Successions are stopped by geological events, volcanoes or storms. Margalef calls the process exploitation, adding that its effect is rejuvenating. Native Hawaiian biota appears to be rejuvenated by volcanic eruption; it is better equipped to reinvade areas than exotic species. Whatever accelerates change and energy flow in an ecosystem reduces potential maturity. In an exploited system, diversity drops and the ratio of primary production to biomass increases. Mature systems can regress to earlier forms when exploited; then new species can form.

Varela states that succession is the result of an indefinite iterative process with a stationary end state to which variables tend. No; not any more than shark is end state in ocean. Succession in ecology resembles evolution in general biology. The parallel extends to conceptual difficulties. Most ecologists think succession follows a direction.

Ecosystems are constantly evolving under the influence of physicochemical processes poorly understood and so far more powerful than those that result from human activities. The reality is more complex than just systematic succession and climax. There seems to be no direction in evolution other than to live with a changing environment; genes become plans on how to live from experience; drift is selected to fit an environment that is evolving. Nature regulates the stability of the climate and environment. Plant diseases, plagues, floods, volcanoes cannot occur too often or nature could not purify air and water or reseed devastated areas.

1.3.5.4.2.2. *Evolution.* There is no one concept of evolution, put forth by Whitehead, Mayr or Monod. There is a discourse built on exchanges of ideas for thousands of years. This discourse is an intellectual monster in a pantheon of monsters. But remember that the word 'monster' in the Latin, merely meant 'to point out.'

Many concepts of evolution, such as natural selection and geographic variation, date from pre-genetic biology. Empedocles attributed the changes in the universe to the ebb and flow of two complementary forces: love and hate. The elements combined through love. Evolution proceeds so, but with an organic combination. Love and strife are two cosmic forces whose interactions determine the texture of existence.

The Great Chain of Being was the conceptual fabrication of Aristotle to link all forms of life in a graded series. It was, as Pope (1966) saw, a

"Vast chain of being, from which God began,
  Natures aetherial, human, angel, man,
  Beast, bird, fish, insect! what no eye can see
  No glass can reach."

R. Margalef describes the baroque of the natural world, meaning that there are many more species in ecosystem than would be necessary if biological efficiency alone were an organizing principle. This is the misconcept of the fullness of nature. Nature is not full. In *The Great Chain of Being*, Lovejoy (1964) names this concept "the principle of plenitude," from the thesis found first in Plato that the universe is a fullness of forms. This notion of the complete continuity of nature can be traced through Aristotle, who furnished the definition of continuity used in the Middle Ages: things are said to be continuous whenever "there is one and the same limit of both wherein they overlap and which they possess in common." All quantities, lines, surfaces, motions, space, and time were considered continuous. Although Voltaire was at first fascinated by the idea of the scale of being, he was one of the first to argue that the continuous series was nonexistent in nature. He offered three reasons: Species can become extinct, even by human action; imaginary species can be conceived between real ones; completeness requires many beings higher than humans. Samuel Johnson's arguments

PAF

were as effective. He thought that the principle was contradicted by the observed facts and that it contradicted itself, by not having an infinity of forms between any two. This principle had some interesting ethical consequences, which will be addressed later. Plenitude does not obtain in nature because: Species do not evolve effectively; because of the interplay of predation and disease; and, due to the role of chance.

In an attempt to explain observed changes in species, Leibnitz proposed the Principle of Continuity, that species did not exist as fixed types, but graded into another. Later, G. Cuvier divided the chain into four segments. He emphasized the adaptive differences between organisms. E.G. St. Hilaire emphasized the similarities among organisms in his scheme. Then the stationary ladder of the chain was transformed into the moving ladder of evolution.

Lamarck recognized that in nature there are no such things as classes or orders, only individuals. His doctrine can be summarized in six points (after Leduc, 1911):
- all organized bodies of the globe are true productions of nature
- Nature began with and commences with the simplest organic forms
- the organs of an animal or plant develop slowly and become diversified
- growth is inherent in every part of an organized body
- all living things have been successively formed favorable conditions and changes; by the power that new habits and situations have of modifying the organs of a body
- since all things have undergone change in their organization, the species successively produced have a relative constancy.

It is now known that hereditary material is relatively nonplastic; it is not modified by short-term experience. The gene makes a protein but the character of the protein cannot be communicated back to the gene.

According to C.S. Peirce, Lamarckian evolution is evolution by force of habit. Habit serves a double part; it serves to establish new features and it brings them into harmony with the general morphology and functions of the animals and plants to which they belong. The transmission of acquired characteristics is thus of the general nature of habit taking. And this account of Lamarckian evolution coincides with Peirce's description of the action of love (and dissimilar to physical force).

Lamarck's *Philosophie Zoologique* (1809) showed an intuitive respect for the environment. Recent experiments (Bull and Vogt, 1979, for instance) have vindicated some of his ideas. In many species, such as alligators and turtles, sex differentiation is determined by environmental temperature; constant incubation temperatures 31 degrees C and above produce females, while cooler temperatures, 24-27, produce males. No assortment of genes account for these sex ratio biases.

U. J. Jensen claimed that Darwin changed the human perspective from wholes and essences to living varieties of nature. Darwin also transformed the ladder back into a tree; the chain of being had branches instead of steps. On reading Malthus essay on population, Darwin was struck with the importance of the difference between population growth and food production. Darwin has been criticized for extending the popular theory of economics by Malthus to the natural world. It is true that the biological considerations of economics inspired an economic description of a biological law, but Darwin enlarged and supported the metaphor. He retained the idea of hierarchy, but status became fitness. He applied the division of labor to his theory; the same place supports more life if "occupied by very diverse forms." (DA 1896)

Darwin's explanation of evolution involved three concepts: Random variation, competition and natural selection. These concepts were incomplete, but may be generalized as change, interaction and selection.

Varela analyzes the evolutionary process as satisficing rather than optimizing; a suboptimal solution is adequate. Selection operates as a survival filter that passes any structure than has sufficient integrity to persist. The focus of analysis is on organic patterns in a life history rather than traits.

For the evolutionary process, Varela suggests the metaphor of "bricolage," which is the putting together of parts in complicated arrays because they are possible (rather than part of an ideal design).

He calls his alternative view evolution by natural drift. It is articulated in four points:

1. The unit of evolution at any level is a network capable of a rich repertoire of self-organizing configurations.
2. The configurations generate a selection process of satisficing that triggers change in the form of viable trajectories, structurally coupled with a medium.
3. The specific trajectory of the unit of selection is the interwoven result of levels of modular subnetworks of selected self-organized repertoires.
4. Since the medium and the organism mutually specify one another, a co-implicate relation replaces the opposition of inner and outer causal factors.

1.3.5.4.2.3. *A New Paradigm of Evolution.* The environment cannot be separated from what organisms are and what they do. Lewontin states (1983): "The organism and the environment are not actually separately determined. The environment is not a structure imposed on living beings from the outside but is in fact a creation of those beings."

The interconnectedness of the world means, according to Susan Oyama, that there is no intelligible distinction between inherited and acquired characteristics (thus making defense of Lamarck unnecessary). Pierce suggested that Lamarckian evolution is evolution by force of habit. Oyama states: "What is required for evolutionary change is not genetically encoded as opposed to acquired traits, but functioning development systems, ecologically embedded genomes."

Combining metaphors, we have organisms putting together (enfolding) structures based on historical patterns, and moving (unfolding) through a filter of limits like minnows through a fish net. It is the structure (genomes embedded in an ecological unit, usually a community) that is the unit of evolution.

The two basic assumptions of a new paradigm (based on Ho and Fox, HX 1988) are: (1) Form and variation are not arbitrary or random. Processes that generate form and variation at every level occur before natural selection is said to act; evolution can be understood in terms of this process, more than in terms of maximum fitness (as exemplified in protobiotic evolution and molecular genetics). (2) There is an emphasis on integration, transcending disciplinary boundaries. In protobiotic evolution, physical and chemical processes are responsible for molecular selection and for the fitness of the environment for life. In the generation of organic forms, physical and chemical processes provide organizational principles that coordinate detailed biological mechanisms, including viscoelastic changes of the cytoskeleton and expression of different genes. The new paradigm will have new metaphors:

1. Self-organization and constructionism (Varela 1982, Fox 1988), instead of natural selection;
2. Reciprocally constrained construction (Gray) in place of adaptation. The organism and environment are co-implicative, co-defining, and co-constructing. A process of self-assembly, where the self is the organism / environment system.
3. A field concept (Waddington 1962, Goodwin 1988) for development, emphasizing dynamic transformation (form as organized spatiotemporal domain), in contrast with the particulate concept of an organism. Understood in terms of group dynamics rather than selective advantage or cost/benefit.
4. A process view (Whitehead 1920, Ho 1988) in which organisms are dynamic structures that are immanent and simultaneous

with the process, less than a consequence of natural selection of past random mutations. Like quantum physics, in biology and ecology, the observer is within the theory in a very fundamental way. By the act of observing the observer influences the outcome of a phenomenon, as Wheeler (1987) says, taking part in the construction of physical reality.

These metaphors round out the new paradigm that weaves changing organisms and environments together.

1.3.5.4.3. Change & Development of Species

Random variations, caused by chromosomal mutations, were considered responsible for generating new forms and increasing the variety of all forms. Genetic combination is responsible for the incredible uniqueness of individuals. Other paragenetic processes also work to produce differences. Most mutations are considered neutral in their effects or harmful.

DNA is a dynamic system in which clusters of genes expand and contract and roving elements hop in and out, according to W. Gilbert. Multiple rearrangements of genetic material rather than accumulated mutations may be the primary mechanisms by which species diverge. DNA and mRNA did pair up over most of their lengths, but the mRNA all had dangling ends. It was not a one to one transcript. The long form of RNA contains gibberish sequences called introns; these loops are edited out by enzymes. The parts of RNA that code for protein, called exons, are spliced by other enzymes, yielding mRNA. Gilbert thinks that introns and exons are the playgrounds of evolution. The gene is no longer considered a single, stable unit, but a collection of modules, brought together by evolution into a useful entity, but always capable of changing itself, either by reshuffling the parts or picking up modules from other genes. Hofstader (1979) relates that the entire genome of the tiniest known virus ThetaX174 has been laid bare. Some of the genes overlap, that is, two distinct proteins are coded for by the same stretch of DNA. There is one gene contained entirely inside another (by shifting the reading frames of the two genes relative to each other by one unit). Information can be packed more densely by using this technique.

Types of DNA and cells are different. These differences can be discussed in terms of information; In Shannon/Weaver it refers to specific differences of kind within a defined universe of variations. But that world of information is static; it can only be spontaneously lost. This is not appropriate for embryos, which exhibit self-transcendence (degree to which they express specificities). Systems exhibiting property of specificity can be described if the specificities are described as instructions (or algorithms) and not information. In computer science, a few instructions can produce informationally complex results. Some sets of instructions are deviation amplifying; so trivial increases in specificity can throw a system into another region. Boulding stated that the gene operates as a 3-dimensional printer, with the ability to produce copies of itself. Printing is a process by which order is copied and spread. Or in the case of organisms, reproduced.

1.3.5.4.3.1. *Species Interactions.* A community is a collection of individuals engaging in cooperative behavior. But cooperation is only one of a number of interactions. Others are competition and altruism. Many interactions are positive, negative or neutral in effect. Community interactions differ from individual ones, but these are not all properly defined. For example, predation is regarded as being where one population adversely effects another, but is dependent on other. This is not so; predation benefits both populations. Predation is more mutualism than parasitism; nor is it an entirely separate category. There are elements of symbiosis in wolf-deer predation. Since competition also regulates populations, it does not have entirely adverse effects.

Most of these interactions are not simple, but are complex and paradoxical. For example, parasitism on an individual level may have benefits on a species level. In one sense, all interactions are positive and symbiotic on the planetary level. Mutualism (or Symbiosis) is also a necessary and beneficial relationship. Group relations can be zero-sum or nonzero-sum (in game theoretic terms). Parasitism is about the only zero-sum relation; one group gains what another loses. Predation and mutualism are nonzero-sum; both lose or both gain.

Predation increases the survivability of species. In Caswell's open nonequilibrium model, the incorporation of predation results in an indefinite coexistence of species—extending extinction indefinitely. Predation—or gaps caused by physical disturbance—opens up cells for colonization by inferior competitors. Predation increases the diversity of species. Steven Stanley argues that predation, or cropping, may have controlled the evolution of metazoans. In communities of primary producers, a few species monopolize a place. A predator dominates its favorite species, usually the most populous, thus limiting it so that others develop to claim a niche. Stanley explains the Cambrian explosion of life through the evolution of cropping herbivores, which "opened space" for a greater diversity of producers, which in turn permitted more specialized croppers, for which specialized predators evolved. Each new level of the trophic pyramid broadened the one below it; the pyramid became wider and higher.

Many species in communities live together closely; this constant, intimate relationship between dissimilar species was called "symbiosis" by Heinrich De Bary (1879). Biological symbiosis results in a greater store of genetic information—a new species. Lichen, for example, is composed of fungus and algae; each is part of the milieu of the other in a necessary and beneficial relationship. In this section, the word symbiosis is used in a philosophical, etymological sense, to denote living together, which involves all kinds of interactions, from competition and conflict to cooperation and mutualism. No one interaction can dominate without unfortunate consequences. If all plants were mutualistic and none were competitive, it is unlikely that trees and flowers could have evolved.

1.3.5.4.3.2. *Mutualism* (or Symbiosis). The word symbiosis is derived from the Greek word, *symbiosis*, meaning "to live together." Two species that live together closely enough are biologically symbiotic. Symbiosis acts as a higher-level store of genetic information; a lichen is fungus plus algae, where each is part of environment for the other. Symbiosis can be conceptualized as organismic (Pribram) or mutualistic; the organismic assumes that the parts are subordinated to a prior whole, which is causal, hierarchical, and teleological; the mutualistic states that there are only parts creating a system of interaction. The symbiosis of molecular species in Eigen hypercycles leads to prokaryotic cells; the symbiosis of these leads to eukaryotic cells; then to multicelled organisms.

1.3.5.4.3.3. *Altruism.* The definition of altruism is an interaction in which some individuals benefit others at a cost to themselves (directly or indirectly, voluntarily or involuntarily). It is a group phenomenon; genes and individuals are selfish. It is potentially reciprocal, potentially profitable to all individuals. Altruists are environmentally, not genetically, differentiated. Altruism is a net-gain lottery in which all individuals pay risks but receive benefits that exceed costs. In group selection, some individuals are sacrificed to others; altruism may be more profitable than kin selection in some cases.

E. O. Wilson recognizes "altruistic" (it is assumed in nonhuman species that the behavior is unconscious) behavior in bees, ants and baboons, but undermines his thesis by trying to find a conventional biological explanation that is nontranscendent. In mammals, and humans especially, altruism has evolved very strongly. Paleontological evidence reveals that altruism and mutual cooperation have been practiced for a long time, with Neanderthals as well as Homo erectus.

P.J. Darlington indicates that reinforcement has been important in human evolution; and may be origin of many emotions, including pleasure at altruistic acts. Cooperation, not the same as altruism, is favored by evolution if it gives the genes of participants better chance for survival. The basis of altruism is cooperation. Neil Evernden calls cooperation, compliance. This term is enlarged to involve an aspect of play, within the framework of freedom and determination. This kind of cooperation will be examined later, in human society.

1.3.5.5. Holopoesis: The Order of the Whole

Holopoesis is the operation of making the whole, from the interactions of sets of individuals over a historical process of mutually constrained construction and coevolution. Because it is concerned with the whole set of interactions and patterns, ecology is an appriopriate approach to studying the whole, especially in its radical form.

Radical—from the Latin word meaning "rooted"—ecology forms part of a new metaphor that is more appropriate to the unity and interrelatedness of the earth. It is part of a movement of consciousness, concerned with equality, diversity, health, with humane methods, and with a holopoetic cosmology. And it affects them simultaneously, as Henryk Skolimowski recognized of eco-philosophy.

Radical ecology incorporates a broader scientific method that might be called patient practice. There are ways of dealing with the earth that are not scientific or technological; they are aesthetic or ethical. These alternatives are not incompatible with a whole science. The methodology of traditional science is limited and wasteful. Radical ecology considers the method of Goethe, who incorporates a world view of organic dialectics; its methods are contemplative nonintervention and the primacy of the qualitative.

The ecological, social, and political problems of today do not have simple disciplinary solutions. The problems are cosmological and must be solved on that level. But a single cosmology cannot solve all problems in all places. Modern technological cosmology, beyond being more linear and abstract, is wrongly considered the evolutionary successor to traditional cosmologies, and is displacing them rapidly. Where human understanding is still underdeveloped, humanity cannot afford to suppress the diversity of thought necessary for adaptation to the diversity of environments, or to eliminate ecosystems and the societies adapted to them. Therefore, radical ecology recommends a framework for local cosmologies, a holopoetic cosmology, as a means for the preservation of human diversity.

1.3.5.5.1. Ecosystem Interactions

At the ecosystem level most interactions result in positive outcomes, mostly as a result of the habits of interactions and the filtering that removes negative outcomes. Thus, charity, competition, altruism, commensalism, parasitism, predation, protocooperation, and mutualism are positive. Only interference, and the high levels of disturbance are negative. Neutralism and amensalism are neutral.

Many species in communities live closely together; this constant, intimate relationship between dissimilar species was identified as "symbiosis" by Heinrich De Bary (1879). Biological symbiosis results in a greater store of genetic information—in a new species. Lichen, for example, is composed of fungus and algae; each is part of the milieu of the other in a necessary and beneficial relationship. In this section, symbiosis is also used in a philosophical, etymological sense, to denote living together, which involves all kinds of interactions from competition and conflict to cooperation and mutualism. No one interaction can dominate others without unfortunate consequences. If all plants were mutualistic and none were competitive, it is unlikely that trees and flowers could have evolved.

1.3.5.5.2. The Play of Adaptation

The process by which beings reorganize their structure to adapt to an environment is evolution. Short-term adaptations yield learning; long-term adaptation results in phylogenetic evolution. Four examples of long-term adaptation are:
- between mutations and environment
- interspecific amplifications, as when increased protection of prey species requires better hunting techniques of predators
- intraspecific deviation, such as preference for certain stimuli
- inbreeding, although long-term interbreeding can be dangerous, but S. Stanley claims that short-term interbreeding is necessary to fix new features.

1.3.5.5.3. Coevolution

Evolution is an integrated process, partly open-ended, involving choices, and the selection of whole individuals in whole environments. The cost of evolution by selection is so heavy that most of the time most populations are not perfectly adapted to changing environment. Evolution is never total adaptation; it requires destabilization, a risk accompanying all innovation. The process of adaptation involves a self-presentation offering new symbiotic relations. Overspecialization reduces flexibility and reaction to change. Underspecialization reduces efficiency. At all levels evolution includes freedom of action as well as interdependence.

Species cannot evolve effectively because of the limits of genetic possibility. Furthermore, chance plays a part in every interaction. For instance, mammals are more efficient than marsupials, but mammals did not have the opportunity to colonize Australia and parts of South America until recently. Marsupials did not have the genetic possibility of becoming more advanced.

Predation can increase the diversity of species, at the cost of perfect fitness. In *The Origin of the Species*, Darwin noticed the predation principle. S. M.. Stanley (1981) has argued that the cropping principle may provide biological control of the evolution of metazoans. Intuitively one would expect the introduction of a cropper to reduce the number of species in given area; but the opposite occurs. In communities of primary producers (photosynthesizers), a few species will be superior and monopolize space. A cropper dominates its favorite prey species (usually the most populous), limiting it so others can develop. A new level on the pyramid broadens the one below it. Stanley explains the Cambrian explosion through evolution of cropping herbivores, which opened space for greater diversity of producers, which permitted more specialized croppers (see Quantum Evolution). The ecological pyramid became wider and higher.

Paul Ehrlich and Peter Raven coined word coevolution to describe insect and plant mutual adaptations. Coevolution is neither the forming of building blocks nor the differentiation of homogenous universe; it is the emergence of hierarchically ordered complexity to full structuration. Insects coevolve to fertilize the same species of flower. The orchid and ignumian wasp; Yucca and yucca moth. Coevolving systems play between adaptation and nonadaptation; completeness of either would result in death of system. A niche fits a species sufficiently without defining it; and the reverse. A. Portmann pointed out functionless features of evolution. There is always the extravagance and beauty of features.

Insects and plants, for instance, often mutually adapt. This coevolution, the emergence of a highly ordered complexity to full structuration. Insects may evolve to fertilize one species of flower, as in the case of a wasp and orchid. A ground orchid in Australia, *Cryptostylus leptochilla*, has flowers that look like, and perhaps smell like, a female wasp, *Lisopimpla semipunctata*. The orchid blooms at the time when the male wasp emerges from its pupal case. The male mates with, and pollinates, the orchid. Later, when the female emerges from the soil, he mates with her, with a practiced ease.

1.3.5.5.3.1. *Macroevolution.* Species selection is an evolutionary trend. Most trends are not produced by well-established species. Because the direction of speciation is highly unpredictable, macroevolution is disengaged from microevolution, or the change within a single species or population. Speciation provides for rapid evolutionary forays into uninhabited space; evolution is opportunistic. The limited potential of a species limits success. Species limitation ensures the diversity and integrity of the whole. A species that was too successful, perhaps like humanity, might endanger the interactions of many other species.

Macroevolution is the level where species die or multiply. Extinction is an emergent property of macroevolution relevant to microevolution. According to MacArthur, the agents of extinction are: competition, predation, habitat alteration, and random fluctuations in population size (cf. Prigogine's fluctuations). Environmental conditions are limiting factors that determine speciation or extinction. Extinction of a particular prey species is likely only if the predator has alternate food sources. Otherwise, there will be an endless oscillation as predicted by the Lotka-Volterra equation. This equation, like most in biology, has trouble with more than two variables, like the three-body problem in physics.

1.3.5.5.3.2. *Quantum Evolution.* G. G. Simpson (1944) proposed the concept of quantum evolution to account for rapid evolution in small populations; but he did not link it specifically to speciation. He believed that species changed slowly because of perfect adaptation. V. Grant expanded the idea to quantum speciation, which became a logical solution to the great mammalian radiation. Quantum speciation occurs throughout the world in the form of solitary local events. Little is understood of the genetic changes in species formation. Small changes in regulating genes may effect larger changes in structural genes. Complete isolation is unnecessary. Limited mobility is the equivalent of isolation for small species. Ernst Mayr proposed a process of geographical speciation as the prevalent mechanism; species evolved as a result of separation (as a result of glaciation, tectonic movement or migration).

Most genera and families developed by rapid evolution associated with branching (speciation), according to Stanley. Adaptive radiation is rapid divergence of many new forms of life from a common ancestor. A modern instance is the rapid (not instantaneous) diversification of life during the late preCambrian and early Cambrian eras. The entire system rose about 600 million years ago, less than 10% of the history of the earth. The evolution of the eukaryotic cell allowed that explosive radiation. Life has been relatively quiet since then, as it was before. Many life forms rose during the initial rapid diversification, but died out during stable times. The one burst must have filled up the oceans. Since then, evolution has basically recycled the basic designs.

The episodic evolutionary view is a punctuational model, as opposed to Darwin's gradualistic model. The punctuational view implies that evolution is:

- imperfect at perfecting adaptations of plants and animals.
- there is no real long-term ecological balance of nature.
- large-scale trends are the net result of many rapid steps (not necessarily in the same direction), not the gradual reshaping.
- sexual reproduction does not prevail for gradualistic reasons.

To a punctuationalist, the whole system is dynamic; but species are less plastic. Changes come from the addition and subtraction of species. Species are the basic units of change. In general, species do not interbreed with other species. The old law—*Natura non facit saltum*—Nature does not make jumps, does not hold. Nature jumps—jumping is a characteristic of nature that Leucippus discovered in atoms in the void and modern physics has rediscovered. Evolution proceeds by fits and starts.

Varela believes that important evolutionary changes occur in areas of climactic fluctuation and spread peripherally to stable climates where trend is slower. Selection is more effective in immature ecosystems. In a mature system, complexity expressed by number of participating species, remains almost same, in spite of extinction or emigration. The more complex a system is the larger the share of energy that is stored in the system. Structures using the least energy to influence own future has least difficulty evolving. A severe shrinkage of tropical forest area and the spread of arid territory should favor xeric over phylogenetic adaptation. Haffer and Vanzolini studying birds and lizards have evidence that species multiply during forest deterioration; this leads to enriched fauna. Stanley offers the following examples of rapid evolution that can be documented: Cichlid fish in Lake Nabugabo in Uganda, banana feeding moths in Hawaii, and, pupfishes in Death Valley, California. Types of the last may hold the key to rapidly diverging evolution.

1.3.5.5.3.3. The Radiation of Being
Evolutionary explanation can indicate necessary, but not sufficient, conditions for specific changes. For those moths that mimic trees or ill-tasting species, there are those that are conspicuous and still flourish.

The cow has a complicated four-chamber stomach to digest large quantities of vegetable matter. But the horse has a simple stomach. It cannot be shown that a particular evolution took place by necessity, but in retrospect, the adaptation had value or animal would not have survived.

Jantsch regards evolution as basically open. It determines its own dynamics and direction. The dynamics unfolds in a systematic web characterized by coevolution of micro and macro systems. By this dynamic interconnectedness, evolution determines its own meaning. Goldsmith rightly criticizes Jantsch's conclusion: that nature does not have laws, so humans can create their own.

But nature is bound by many different laws; prescriptive as well as statistical regularities. Waddington regards laws as constraints; something to be observed to achieve a goal. General laws governing behavior of biological and social systems are those that must be observed if organizations are to remain stable and survive. Prigogine and Jantsch imply that world is infinitely malleable. That was Lamarck's problem (he was pre-genetic). Not only are the code and individuals relatively nonplastic, but they are hysteretic. Individuals and species result from millions of years of coevolving. Delbruck stated that any living cell is more a historical than a physical event since it carries with it the experience of a billion years of experimentation. Total recombination results in great destruction, not necessarily great opportunities for evolution. We cannot promote evolution by destroying the integrity of the elements or their paths and relationships, despite Prigogine's and Jantsch's assurances.

The reasoning of causality suggests that causes can be linked to previous and more general causes. From a certain beginning, events expand. Evolution founded on causal explanation is divergent. But the human meaning of evolutionary facts can lead to the conclusion that evolution is converging toward a single end (as with Teilhard's Omega point). According to many theorists, human values and meaning have no place in the causal explanation. But both cases are causal, in the Aristotelian sense of having an effective or final cause. Even a complementarity of the two views is inadequate, since what is being considered is two human interpretations of facts and values.

The human mind usually gives direction to the process of evolution. Evolution is considered a building up of complexity, when it should be regarded as an unfolding of patterns.

Evolution is not a hierarchical ladder or escalator going up and up, but a series of adapted forms; the goal of each is fulfillment. Darwin wrote a note for himself (SP 62): "Never use the words higher and lower." He did not want anyone to believe that evolution was a purposive movement toward a goal. He considered it the result of natural forces (although blind and random).

Grene states that evolutionary theory is a poor crutch for a renewal of an ontology because evolutionary records takes one every which way. Its unidirectional sense relies on a pseudo-teleology that Merleau-Ponty indicates is the inverse of mechanism. It is better to look at varieties of styles of life, at the "pattern mixed-upness" of Merleau-Ponty (VI). Rather than relying on evolution for metaphysics, Merleau-Ponty called for a kind of "phenomenal topology" of things as they loom upward bodily around us. Evolution is a radiation of life. All forms fit themselves into a changing environment. Nature does not conserve lives; she lives them, in as many different ways and places as possible.

The advent of the machine made processes of order more amenable to description. Although only a closed system, the machine was a fruitful metaphor for living systems. The theory of the living organism as a mechanical contrivance explained biological phenomena from the physiology of an organism to the processes of cells. From the mechanical machine to the cybernetic machine, the metaphor was successful at explaining detailed processes without answering fundamental questions, such as 'how did life begin?' Descartes relied on God as the creator of the machine, but this contradicted the new evolutionary explanation of change by random events. The concept of organic order as a product of random events explained a large number of observations. Molecular genetics depends on this type of explanation.

Evolution requires sequential reproduction and change in each reproductive step. Without sequential reproduction there is no history; without change in each step there is no evolution. If by evolution we refer to what has taken place in the history of transformation of terrestrial living systems, then evolution as a process is the history of change of a "pattern of organization embodied in independent unities sequentially generated through reproductive steps, in which the particular defining organization of each unity arises as a modification of the preceding one (or ones), which thus constitutes both its sequential and its historical antecedent," according to F. Varela.

Living beings are patterns of relationships within larger patterns in a physical field. Fields define the organizational properties of patterns. Unlike electromagnetic fields, biological fields are shaped by individual animals or plants. They are morphogenetic.

Needham defined biological morphogenesis as the coming-into-being of specific form in living organisms. Biological development is epigenetic; new structures appear that cannot be explained by the unfolding of structures present in the egg at the beginning of development. What about gene, egg, environment triad?

The old passion of unicellular microorganisms is the transformation of a surface to make it viable. Lichens break rock into earth. Fields are virtual. The virtual is actualized when materials are included. The virtual is equal to a code. There is no opposition in natural systems; predator/prey are not excluding opposites, but generate a whole unity, an autonomous ecosystem domain with complementarity, stabilization and survival for both. To understand evolution, it is necessary to go beyond molecular structure and logical scientific construction, to concepts of growth, unfolding, dialectics, and transformation. Evolution has to be understood within the framework of ecosystems. Species are sucked in the direction of succession.

1.3.6. *Metaphysical Implications from Physics and Ecology*
Recently, J. Baird Callicott addressed the principal metaphysical implications of physics and ecology in his presentation of a historical outline of ideas. Some of his conclusions, however, are erroneous, although there are several areas of convergence between physics and ecology, and the metaphysical implications of ecology are different from those of physics.

Callicott states that ecology has emerged only recently as an independent, quantitative science, and that it is less foundational than physics or cosmology. In fact, ecology is one of the oldest disciplines, not the youngest. Early in their development, human beings realized the value of recognizing edible plants and animals and their interrelationships, and they built up traditions of knowledge. This practical ecology has been obvious for a long time, but because it is subtle and complex, it is not easy to quantify, and its development as a science is recent. This practical ecology enabled some cultures to achieve long-term stability in a natural environment; it also embodied teleological and holistic concepts expressed in qualitative terms rather than in mathematical forms. As a young science, these practical concepts were formulated as various principles: *wholeness*, the relationship of complexity and stability, succession and climax states, and the balance of nature. As ecology became more quantitative, that is, mathematical and reductionistic, its methods and topics more closely reflected the old physics.

The new ecology, according to C. H. Waddington, places emphasis on the discreteness of individual genes, the randomness and nonrelational nature of the process of mutation, and the unimportance of the experience and reaction of an organism to its environment. In this new ecology, the old ecological principles were rejected. D. Simberloff, for instance, even argues that the ecosystem model of A. G. Tansley is only another way of formulating the "balance of nature" and must be rejected. Similarly, holism is unacceptable to the new ecology and is replaced with an individualistic view. Thus, the new ecology rejects the ecosystem model that Callicott places at the center of his argument. Many of Callicott's arguments are taken from the old ecology and not the new, quantitative ecology. Hence, it is basically the old ecology that will be treated, for Leopold, Naess, and others belong to the old tradition and not to the modern science.

1.3.6.1. Physics & Ecology
Callicott observes that ecology and the new physics converge on some similar metaphysical notions, such as field and wholeness, the former from physics and the latter from ecology. Let us examine these notions in more detail.

1.3.6.1.1. The Field
The field concept was introduced by Michael Faraday into studies of electricity and magnetism. Albert Einstein states that "fields are physical conditions of space." He identifies the underlying unity of nature as space. The field concept is central to the unification of theories of light, electricity, and magnetism. Einstein's general theory of relativity replaced the distinct categories of space, time, energy, and matter with multiple components of a unitary field characterized by Riemannian geometry. This four-dimensional model accounted for the phenomena of mechanics and electrodynamics. The field is still the fundamental primitive concept in the quantum electrodynamics of Paul Dirac. This Space/ Time/Energy/Mass (STEM) field has general characteristics of discretion, participation, connection, consistency, limitation, wholeness, self-making, self-ordering, individuating, and developing. No one component is ontologically subordinate to another. Clearly, Callicott is mistaken to present matter as subordinate to energy. One of the most important properties of the field in physics is the participation of the observer. John Wheeler suggests that the universe is brought into being by participation— the sum of an infinite number of elementary acts of observation (although he unnecessarily reverses the causation). Quantum mechanics eliminates the notion of the neutral observer behind glass. The observer participates in the act of measurement and the universe changes by the act of measurement. A similar principle

of participation can be postulated for ecology. Not only do organisms participate in the field of nature by virtue of their existence, but the experiments of ecologists alter the system being studied, often degrading it for a period of time.

Biological field theories dealt with problems, such as regulation and reproduction, thought to be insoluble in mechanistic terms. In the 1920s, Aron Gurwitsch and Paul Weiss independently advanced the idea of developmental fields to account for the properties of wholeness and directedness. In Weiss' theory the field became a system of organizing factors that proceeded from organized praxis to developing regions, resulting in typical patterns. Growth and pattern became emergent field effects. For Weiss, the field was a symbolic term for the dynamics underlying the ordered behavior of a "collective"; it denoted the properties lost in the process of analysis. Waddington extended the field to an epigenetic landscape, but regarded his own use of field as a descriptive 'convenience.' Living fields have form and impose restrictions on the probabilities of nonliving fields.

Paul Shepard describes living natural 'objects' in terms of events which constitute a 'field pattern.' Callicott concludes that relations are prior to things and that the characteristics of species result from adaptation to a niche in the environment. But relations are not prior to objects; they arise together. The wasp and the yucca coevolve; they are not co-linked by prior relations. Furthermore, a specimen is more than the sum of its species' relationships to an environment; it is an intentional being that, with other members of the species, can create niches, as well as adapt to them. Because the STEM field produces life, the qualities of life cannot be separated from its physical qualities. While it is true that living subjects are at a different level of description than events in field patterns, they should not be treated as ontologically subordinate. All of the aspects of the field have equal status. The ecosystem model, as a reaction to 'superorganismic' metaphors of early ecologists, attempted to be a field theory, but has been limited by its parentage, thermodynamics, and has been rejected by new practitioners.

Some exponents of the new ecology, misreading the new physics, consider energy to be a more fundamental reality than material objects. These ecologists apply classical thermodynamics to living systems. Unfortunately, entropy is an incomplete explanation of living systems. A living system is a natural phenomenon and all natural phenomena are constrained by the laws of thermodynamics. Entropy, as R. Clausius defined it, is the constant transformation of motion into heat. Classical entropy is a thermodynamic variable of a system, commonly a measure of the unavailable energy in a closed system. The classical concept is concerned only with macroscopic states of matter, the qualitative change of free energy into bound.

L. Boltzmann applied statistical mechanics toward interpreting the properties of the microscopic systems that make up the macroscopic ones. Statistical entropy is defined as a measure of the number of ways in which the elementary particles of a system may be arranged and determined by counting the number of microstates. Statistical entropy became a measure of disorder, described mathematically in six-dimensional phase space. This application not only reduces the level of explanation, but changes the coordinates from heat and temperature to space, time, and force; it explains thermal equilibrium as the result of an undefined universal shuffling process. A process opposite and complementary to the shuffling of entropy— a sorting process has been proposed independently a number of times, from Georg Hirth to Schrodinger, Szent Gyorgi, Woltereck, and Whyte, but not developed adequately. With the connection of entropy and information by Claude Shannon, the concept of entropy has been extended to applications in engineering, an theory, Gestalt psychology, and cosmology. The assumptions of statistical thermodynamics— chance motion, the independence of particles, time reversibility, ahistoricity, continuity, and equilibrium-are problematic for physics, much less for ecology and human civilization. Time reversibility, for instance, has never been observed in macroscopic systems.

This use of entropy seems to be little improvement from the mechanics of the old physics (and presumably the new ecology) for understanding organisms, which are reduced to 'energy moments' rather than 'atoms.' In wanting to combine quantum theory with ecology, Callicott describes organisms as being con figured by energy through time. But, organisms are material patterns in space as well. The focus on either frame permits subtle differences and limitations in interpretation. Even if energy is considered to be primary metaphysically, organisms are still composed of the atoms and molecules that energy forms under certain conditions of temperature and pressure, and they act differently than just 'energy vortices' or 'patterns of energy.'

Reliance on physical explanation impoverishes the complexity of ecological reality. Morowitz's portrayal of each living thing as a dissipative structure is reductive and distorting. Ilya Prigogine defined a dissipative structure as one of two types of organization (the other being a nonequilibrium stationary state, such as a solar system), whose order is governed by amplified fluctuations; his examples include walls and slime molds. Prigogine, however, misuses the concepts of order and complexity by making them dependent on random events; furthermore, his concept of stability assumes a reversibility of biological time (the result of its basis in quantum mechanics). Dissipative structures are more applicable to pans of boiling water than to black bears. The reduction of ecological patterns to dissipative structures ignores observed behaviors like communication and intention.

In describing a general concept of nature, Callicott follows Prigogine in emphasizing process over structure. Each assumes that energy flow is more primary than matter, that energy is a more fundamental reality than discrete entities. Although an organism may be characterized as a 'configuration of energy,' looking at it that way, it is an artifact of the quantum perspective (and, perhaps, of the desire for an absolute reality). There are philosophers and ecologists, such as Ramon Margalef, who consider 'information' to be more basic than energy or matter and more in line with patterning. Viewed this way, organisms are reduced to information in a cybernetic perspective. Although these perspectives are useful to an understanding of complex behavior, sometimes ecologists and philosophers simply take over the vocabulary of a paradigmatic trend, a new physics or an information theory, and apply it uncritically to the epistemology of the older paradigm. In this way, efficient cause can disguise itself as a 'genetic program.'

Just as the new physics has transformed the mechanical picture by placing atoms in a field that accounts for the qualitative emergence of properties from simple quantities, the new ecology has placed living 'objects' in a field. This field determines the limits of any ecological field of activity, and no field of ecological activity can be described without taking the physical field into account. Nevertheless, physics and ecology cannot be equated, as Callicott, Morowitz, and others try to do. Ecology has principles that cannot apply to particles. The field is living and intentional, as well as physical, and an ecosystem model based on physics cannot account for intention or other emergent properties.

1.3.6.1.2. Wholeness
Gilbert White characterized nature as 'one organic whole' and influenced Darwin and subsequent generations of biological scientists. E. A. Birge's early work on the heat budgets of lakes, for instance, was holistic. J. C. Smuts, in trying to synthesize the evolutionary theory of Darwin and relativistic physics of Einstein, presented the whole as a powerful organizing principle inherent in nature. L. von Bertalanffy and E. Laszlo extended holism with general systems theory. David Bohm suggests that the universe as a holomovement carries an implicit order that is undefinable and immeasurable.

Although Callicott recognizes that the concept of nature that emerges from ecology and the new physics is more holistic, he does not sufficiently explicate the levels of organization of wholes. It is not necessary to associate holism with Hindu metaphysics. A more productive comparison can be found in contemporary Gestalt thinking and in the Gestalt psychology of Wolfgang Kohler, which emphasizes the importance of wholes and tries to identify the organizing principles of perception in terms of wholes. Each level is real as a whole; it is a whole, or a *holon,* in Arthur Koestler's terms. A number of ecologists, including R. V. O'Neill, D. L. DeAngelis, T. F. H. Allen, T. W. Hoekstra, and T. B. Starr, use the concept of holon to describe the organizational levels of hierarchical systems. Given that nature is a structured and differentiated whole, the character of the organism or particle is determined as a subwhole. According to Koestler, all complex structures and processes of a relatively stable character display hierarchical organization. Levels of a hierarchy tend to be contained in subassemblies. Each subwhole behaves as a whole to its components, as a self-contained whole, and as a dependent part in context. Wholes and parts do not exist absolutely. There are intermediary structures on a series of levels in an ascending order of complexity; each subwhole faces in opposite directions. These Janus-faced subassemblies are holons, that is, paraphrasing Koestler, any stable subwhole in a hierarchy that displays rule-governed behavior and structural Gestalt constancy. The rules lend order and stability, as well as flexibility.

Wholes are mutually defining, but also self-defining or self-making. Nature is a self-making system; species and organisms are self-making. The ontology of any living system is the history of the maintenance of its identity through continuous self-making, or autopoesis. According to F. Varela, the evolutionary stability of the subassemblies-organs, organisms, species-is reflected by the degree of autonomy (self-government) each has. The system develops through a continuous dance of autonomy and control; autonomy represents generation, internal definition, internal regulation, and self-assertion, whereas control represents consumption, instruction, assertion of other identity, and external definition. Furthermore, the holistic nature of the STEM field eliminates the unsatisfactory notion of the priority of relationships to beings or of wholes to components— a notion Callicott uses.

1.3.6.2. Discussion

The new ecology is a central dimension in biology and overlaps many specialties. It deals with different levels of a hierarchy, focusing on organisms, populations, communities, and ecosystems, but with attention to genetics as well as to geological and evolutionary events.

Although ecology is a scientific newcomer, it is certainly a foundational science (especially in view of Callicott's own statement that the essence of a being is determined by its relationships). Any science that studies those basic relationships is foundational.

If the old ecology were truly linked to the new physics, at least in terms of field and wholeness, it would have a much different flavor than that presented by Callicott. For example, the field has a historical character, a whole is self-making. The implications of these attributes are neglected. Ecological principles are not the same as physical laws. Physical operations necessarily apply to biological systems, and ecological theory must be consistent with physical laws. Nevertheless, biological systems exhibit unique regularities that are not reducible to lower levels of activity or understanding. Although the ideas of ecology to some extent parallel the ideas of physics, ecology lacks the laws and constants of physics. Physics lacks the high-level predictability of ecology. The ideas of ecology and physics can benefit from cross-fertilization, but ecological ideas are not reducible to physical ones.

A metaphysics inspired by ecology would be larger and more comprehensive than a metaphysical consensus from the Newtonian paradigm or from quantum physics. Such a metaphysics would provide a place for rarity and diversity, as well as perhaps a reason to value it. It would include ultrahuman and human interests. Because of his indiscriminate use of old and new physics and ecology, Callicott's implications for moral psychology are anthropocentric and teleological. The use of Shepard's arguments for the preservation of species— as educational devices— is anthropocentric and incomplete. Similarly, Callicott's statement that the environment becomes "fully actual" with humanity implies that human consciousness is the goal of evolution. The environment may be extended with consciousness (human and other), but not completed. Although Callicott has made a good, tentative start, a more rigorous list of the qualities of ecology is needed, before anyone can begin an exploration of their implications for human behavior.

1.3.7. Metaphysical Principles Based On Ecology

The processes and levels of ecology are discussed in terms of individuation, interaction, and evolution. Ecological principles are distilled and linked together in the concept of maturity. Hypotheses and norms inspired by these ecological principles are presented and described within the framework of ecosophy. These hypotheses and norms form the basis of an ecocentric metaphysics, epitomized by self-realization.

PAF

1.3.7.1. The Levels & Processes of Ecology

Ernst Haeckel's 1869 definition of ecology as "the total relations of the animal to both its organic and inorganic environment" was notably broad. Ecology deals with the highest levels of biological integration, from organisms to the ecosphere. Autecology, for example, is the study of individual organisms in an environment. A group of individual organisms of the same species in a particular place is studied as a population. The assemblage of populations of different species in a habitat is studied as a community. The community in its biotic environment is studied as an ecosystem. Ecosystems comprise the ecosphere. There are emergent properties at each level of organization, such as the diversity of species and the structure of a food web. Furthermore, each level of integration has distinct attributes. A population has a property "density," the number of individuals per unit area, which is not applicable to individuals; a community has "species diversity," which is meaningless at the population level; processes like homeostasis or homeorhesis, which involve a relationship with the environment, occur on an ecosystem level. Living systems do not display homeostasis (constant value) so much as a particular course of change in time (homeorhesis). The course is stabilized, not the constancy, according to Conrad Waddington. Changes to a system are symbolized by trajectories in a multidimensional phase space (or landscape). In sum, each level acquires additional characteristics. Three processes—individuation, interaction, and evolution—are addressed in more detail.

1.3.7.1.1. Individuation.

Even if individuals can be described in terms of vortices, as the poet Pound did before the physicist Prigogine, they do exist materially, and they participate in the field because they exist. Each participant creates an image of nature—or world—from what is meaningful to it. J. Von Uexkull suggests representing these unfamiliar worlds with a bubble model. The life image, or umwelt, of an animal is what has perceptual and operational meaning for the animal. All animals are fitted to their unique worlds with equal completeness—simple animals to simple worlds, complex ones to well-articulated worlds. Each is optimally fitted to a habitat.

Furthermore, the organism must adapt to the environment, which implies having a memory and being capable of learning, and must reproduce, that is, duplicate its pattern in a separate being. Organisms are goal-seeking, and often stability is sought above change or complexity. The individual is a subject centered in a milieu. Because of this implied point of reference, Rodman concludes that ecology is teleological. Often organisms strive for well-being beyond just survival. Their goal is to come into the fullness of being. A. N. Whitehead considered that all organisms have three urges: to live, to live well, and to live better. Living better is being more attuned, stimulated, flexible, receptive, spontaneous, and integrated in a milieu.

1.3.7.1.2. Interactions
The individuals in a community engage in interactive behaviors, which are considered positive (+), negative (-), or neutral (0) in effect for each individual or species in relation to another. These interactions include:

neutralism (0,0), interference (0,-), altruism (0,+);
amensalism (-,0), competition (-,-), xxx (-,+);
commensalism (+,0), parasitism (+,-), predation (+,-),
protocooperation (+,+), and mutualism (+,+).

Parasitism and predation are considered similar, as are protocooperation and mutualism. The significant difference is the necessity of the latter arrangements, that is, the organisms in predation and mutualism need each other.

Competition was once considered the basic interaction between individuals and between species, from Darwin to Birch, Rodman, Lehman, and others. But cooperation is seen now to be as effective a strategy as competition and as necessary. Survival of the fitter is correct only to a certain point, then it becomes survival of the more cooperative. Both old (Reinheimer, Kropotkin) and new (Lorenz, Fox, Schaller) studies stress the primary use of cooperation both within and between species instead of unrelieved struggle. Live and let live is a more powerful principle than either/or. Cooperation creates communities of many species in which competition is necessary but limited. Neil Evernden notes that organisms go to extreme lengths to avoid direct competition; species form a rainbow of attempts to share the life-base without competition. This diversity enhances the potential for survival.

1.3.7.1.3. Evolution
The process by which species reorganize their structures to adapt to the environment—or reorganize the environment to fit them better—is evolution, an integrated, partly open process that selects whole individuals in whole environments. Evolution flows upwards and outwards as well as inwards and downwards, from the simple to the complex, but also back again. For moths that mimic bark patterns, there are others that are conspicuous; for herbivores with complicated stomachs, such as deer, there are those with simple stomachs, such as elephants. It cannot be shown that a particular evolution took place by

necessity, only that the adaptation had value and the species survived. The consideration of observations can lead to the conclusion that evolution is converging to a single end. Darwin himself did not want anyone to consider evolution a purposive movement to a goal. Rather, he regarded evolution as a bush or a tangled bank. Evolution can be considered as a building up of complexity, an unfolding of patterns, in Merleau-Ponty's term, a "pattern mixed-upness" of styles of living, as beings radiate through time and place. Evolution is not a hierarchical ladder or an up-escalator, but the history of forms adapting to changing environments.

The adaptation of beings to a changing milieu cannot be perfect. Overspecialization reduces flexibility and ability to change, but underspecialization reduces efficiency. Beings that are not optimally adapted are eliminated through competition and stress. Evolution increases the levels of complexity through the operation of natural events.

Species are defined by their position in the environment and thus are in internal relations, but it is also true that they define the environment through positive and negative feedback. Whitehead might be a more appropriate source for internal relations than Hegel and others. His cosmology is more ecological (See John B. Cobb, Jr., *Is It Too Late? A Theology of Ecology*). While some species adapt to a niche, others create niches. J. Baird Callicott presents species as too passive, regarding a specimen as "a summation of its species' historical, adaptive relationship to the environment." The specimen is much more than this—it is intentional and flexible, sometimes stress-seeking and maladaptive. Species in their milieu are in dynamic relationships.

While relationships are as real as the organisms, the relationships are not necessarily or logically prior. P. Shepard emphasized this, but E. Laszlo made the idea an important part of his systems ethics. The part, or holon, creates the whole as the whole creates the part. The organism creates the ecosystem as the system creates the organism. The multiplicity of beings and relationships create and are created by the field.

1.3.7.2. *Ecological Principles*
Ecological principles are not the same as physical laws. Physical operations necessarily apply to biological systems, and ecological theory must be consistent with physical laws, but biological systems exhibit unique regularities that are not reducible to lower levels of activity or understanding. Although the ideas of ecology to some extent parallel the ideas of physics, ecology lacks the laws and constants of physics.

Ecologists, such as Odum, Hardin, and Margalef, present sets of basic principles and concepts that can be said to represent the science of ecology. These principles are synthesized and presented here on four levels: (1) the individual, (2) population, (3) community, and (4) ecosystem.

1a. The individual is the unit of experience and reproduction.

1b. An organism is inseparably related to its habitat, the place where it lives.

1c. The niche of an organism depends on what it does in its place.

1d. Many organisms identify with place.

1e. The size of an organism is related to metabolism.

2a. The population is the unit that evolves in nature (according Krebs).

2b. A species population has unique properties, such as density, mortality, natality, potential, dispersion, age distribution, growth form, and structure (isolation, territoriality).

2c. Populations interact in neutral, positive, or negative ways.

2d. Competition limits the number of species in a niche (the competitive exclusion principle). Garrett Hardin (1960) states the competitive exclusion principle as: complete competitors cannot coexist. Niches must be different for species. Krebs states that the fundamental niche of a species has an "infinite number of dimensions," making a complete determination impossible. Another difficulty in definition is the assumption that environmental variables can be ordered linearly and measured. Furthermore, competition is dynamic, whereas models freeze single instants.

3a. The community is the level of survival.

3b. Diverse organisms live together in order.

3c. Communities are named by structural features such as dominant species.

3d. Communities are stratified.

3e. Communities have a diversity of species.

3f. Communities are characterized by rhythmic changes in the activities of organisms which produce regular recurring changes in the community (periodicity may be daily, lunar, seasonal, genetic, or climactic).

3g. Communities replace one another in a given area in sequence by an orderly process of change called succession. Succession appears to be a process of self-organization in a cybernetic system at the ecosystem level. It is primary for Odum.

3h. The final community in a successional series is self-perpetuating and in equilibrium with the physical habitat (that is, the energy/ material budget is balanced in the climax community).

4a. The ecosystem is the level of integration and the unit of organization undergoing a directional development (Odum).

4b. Energy is bound into organic material, measurable as productivity.

4c. That quantity of energy and material no longer of use to the system is wasted.

4d. Chemical elements, especially those of life, circulate in the biosphere in characteristic paths known as biogeochemical cycles.

4e. Life is limited by elements and physical factors (light, water, gas, salt); too little of an element limits (Liebig's law); too much limits (Shelford's law of tolerance).

4f. The transfer of energy and materials through organisms is referred to as the food chain.

4g. The interaction of individuals in a food chain results in the trophic structure of communities (ecological pyramids).

4h. The energy required to maintain an ecosystem is inversely related to complexity; succession decreases the flow of energy per unit biomass (Margalef's concept of maturity).

1.3.7.2.1. Discussion.

The concept of maturity incorporates many of these principles and is important to the understanding of complexity and diversity. Ramon Margalef proposes maturity as a quantitative measure of the pattern in which the components of an ecosystem are arranged. The life-form communities and physical elements are related in a definite pattern, which is a real but untouchable property (structure). In general, this structure becomes more complex as time passes, as long as the environment is stable or predictable. The structure acquires a historical character. Maturation, as a function of historical processes, increases the levels of complexity of an ecosystem.

The structure is based on material and energetic exchanges. The matter present is biomass (B); the material output is primary productivity (P). Their relation (P/B) is the flow of energy per unit biomass. More mature systems have a richer structure and a lower productivity per unit biomass. There are more steps in the trophic pyramid. Callicott (p. 307) states that "the producers must be many times more numerous than consumers" as an example of common structures. As a general rule, there is a decline in biomass with each increase in trophic level, as specified by energy flows. But there can be a greater weight of consumers than producers if the turnover in producers is higher than consumers (for example, where fish feed on photoplankton). Nutrients are considered to cycle, but not energy. There is higher efficiency in every relation. The loss of energy is less, so less energy is needed to maintain the system.

Any ecosystem not subjected to outside disturbance changes in an orderly and directional way: the complexity of structure increases and the energy flow per unit biomass decreases. The physical environment limits the type of change. Homeostatic mechanisms protect the system from many disruptions. Thus, maturity is self-preserving.

This concept of maturity, as an attribute of a community, is related to structural complexity and organization. Maturity increases with time in an undisturbed community. The species diversity, that is, the information content, of a community also increases with maturity, leading to a more complex spatial structure. Diversity incorporates species richness (how many different kinds are present) as well as a measure of abundance (how many of each, as individuals or biomass). Other aspects of diversity, such as life cycles, are less often considered. The energy in a mature system goes to the maintenance of order and less for the production of new materials. In general, diversity is higher, and life cycles are more complex; symbiosis between species increases, and nutrients are conserved. Complexity and diversity offer advantages for living forms. Complexity allows increases in size, which allows the colonization of harsh environments. Diversity allows more effective behavior through specialization; for example, a specialized organelle may digest less common molecules.

But, Odum points out, as some communities, Wisconsin forests for example, age there is a decrease in diversity (in the understory anyway). Also, diversity can decline with productivity, as in the eutrophication of lakes, for instance. While it is meaningful to speak of an optimum diversity, as the result of limits and the interaction of many factors, a maximum diversity may never be reached.

1.3.7.2.2. Summary
Conventional wisdom holds that increased complexity in a community leads to increased stability. But in the 1970s, work with mathematical models tended to support the reverse, that complexity leads to instability. May constructed simple mathematical models concerned with local stability, in which an increase in complexity lead to a decrease in stability. His connection, however, may have been a mathematical artifact, since his food webs were randomly assembled and sometimes unreasonable. May admits that his arguments are only true of mathematical models and that things "may be different in

the real world." Ecosystems are the result of historical processes that are mathematically atypical. Furthermore, real communities are not randomly structured. A system drives to a nonequilibrium state as a mature ecosystem. The adaptively reorganized system is not necessarily more stable, but it is optimally resistant to the outside conditions that elicited the self-organization, a natural normalization process. The ecosystem learns the changes, periods, or seasons of the environment.

The idea that diversity promotes stability has been defended and attacked elsewhere. The structure of food webs may enhance stability. May suggests that communities are more stable if they are compartmentalized (as holons, perhaps), that is, if there are subunits where interactions within a unit are stronger than interactions between units. Ecologists have observed that complex communities have existed for thousands of years in stable environments, although many of them are vulnerable to human interference now.

1.3.7.3. Ecological Philosophy (Ecosophy)
Arne Naess suggests some of the metaphysical implications of ecology when he called the metaphysical dimension of ecology "ecosophy"—a philosophy of ecological harmony not to be equated with the Deep Ecology Movement, despite the desire of many commentators. Ecosophy is a "total view" inspired by ecological principles and ideas. This total view is a larger philosophical view than that implied by the new ecology or the new physics. Certainly it is larger and more comprehensive than the metaphysical consensus from the older Newtonian paradigm and its equivalent in natural history. Like any new view, it includes the old paradigm as a "special case," leaving it useful in certain circumstances. The acceptance of an ecological view has few effects on a physical level of explanation, for which the mechanical model is still adequate.

The ecological principles listed can serve as a source of inspiration for the philosophical hypotheses and norms of an ecosophy. A complete formulation of an ecosophy is impossible, perhaps meaningless, due to the complexity of living organisms. A general model may be made, however, in the form of a truncated pyramid, whose top of hypotheses and norms is supported by a broad base of individual actions and decisions. From a logical point of view, decisions are derived from norms and hypotheses. A small number of abstract formulations result in many concrete, practical actions in unique situations. Norms are derived historically from motivations and impulses. The pyramid is a stable form. The rejection or modification of a lower level norm or hypothesis does not destabilize the pyramid but results in modifications or adoption of a different specific interpretation. Individual actions can be inducted to norms from which other actions can be deducted. Hypotheses are indicated with a period. Norms are indicated with an exclamation mark to designate an imperative mood as a special case. The archetype of these sentences appears in the Bible, when God says, "Let there be light!" The function is meaningless in terms of information theory, as there were no receivers at the time, but is meaningful in terms of expression. The exposition of this particular form of ecosophy, using this model, results in the following hypotheses. The numbers are not sequential because the hypotheses are not complete.

1.3.7.3.1. Hypotheses
Sets of hypotheses can form a theory. For example:
    H30. Individuals are related to places by basic physical factors.
    H29. Place provides limits.
    H28. Places and organisms shape each other through feedback.
    H26. Organisms, as well as higher levels of organization, are self-making.
    H25. Life images offer meaning and value to individuals.
    H23. Organisms strive to live well.
    H22. Species interact and are interdependent.
    H21. Communities develop historically.
    H14. Diversity of life increases self-realization potential.
    H13. Complexity of life increases self-realization potential.
    H12. Symbiosis of life increases self-realization potential.
    H3. Higher self-realization results in deeper identification with others.
    H2. Higher self-realization depends on self-realization of others.

The following set of norms is derived from the preceding list of hypotheses. (This list also incorporates Michael Soule's norms, with slight changes.)

1.3.7.3.2. Norms
Norms are rules to be followed.
    N30. Nature!
    N28. Levels (hierarchical)!
    N26. Individual organisms!
    N25. Wholeness (worlding holons)!
    N23. Organisms have intrinsic value!
    N22. Organisms participate in populations, communities, ecosystems!

N20. Limitation (global/local discontinuity)!
N18. Mutual historical adaptation (evolution)!
N15. Interdependence (symbiosis and interactions)!
N14. Pattern unfolding (complexity)!
N13. Diversity of species!
N12. The diversity of organisms has intrinsic value!
N3. Self-realization for all organisms!
N2. Self-realization!

1.3.7.3.3. Discussion.
The precise formulations (N21-30, H21-30) refer directly to ecological principles. The middle levels are biologically colored but have a metaphysical dimension because of the use of value and self-realization. The lowest numbers (N2-3, H2-3) are primarily metaphysical in character. Decisions from hypotheses and norms let us act accordingly to preserve ecosystems and species, encourage ecological diversity, set aside habitats, plant trees to restore habitats, and help others.

Organisms and places shape each other. The life-images of organisms limit the goals of organisms. Organisms interact and develop in time. As populations evolve, complexity increases. Networks of activity increase interaction; relationships become more complex. Species adapt; sometimes their structures become physically more complex. But complexity is limited by effectiveness. Often, in the case of gripping limbs for example, simplicity allows more flexibility and generality.

Complexity is often used to support the concept of higher and lower animals. Higher functions in "higher" animals result from complex differentiation of tissues. Increases in physical complexity often confer advantages to species in terms of added functions or adaptive value. But there is an optimum of complexity at each level of being that has nothing to do with importance or being "higher." As categories, higher and lower are anachronistic with their connotations of higher and lower. Darwin acknowledged, "Never use the words higher and lower." The Aristotelian hierarchy of high and low on the scale is gradually being altered. The classification hierarchy itself (modified by Linnaeus) is also being modified.

The middle hypotheses (H11-20) introduce the refinement of self-realization potential. Self-realization is a generalization of the psychological and sociological potentials of individuals, groups or institutions, but restricted by norms. It has a metaphysical character. The variety of organisms with different capacities add qualities to the whole. Each individual organism contains an indefinite number of potentials which can be released. From the diversity of life comes a diversity of potentials.

Self-realization is a norm formulation in a metaphysical sense. The conceptual bridge from Self-realization to a positive evaluation of diversity, complexity, and symbiosis, and other ecological principles is furnished by self-realization potentials; the realization of potentials increases the Self-realization of the earth—life-images, not just man-images. Each species has an equal right to live and develop, free from interference. Interference is not the same as exploitation, which is the normal use of a resource or species by another species; exploitation has a rejuvenating effect. Interference is not general competition, either; as it is used here, it is destruction without gain. Diversity, complexity, and symbiosis are all necessary norms for the accomplishment of self-realization. Furthermore, the realizations should be qualitatively different. The numerical abundance of one life-form, such as humans or rats, is not equivalent to diversity. A single being (such as human) cannot realize the goal in itself. The plurality of potentials is crucial and introduces plurality into unity.

Each being also mirrors the whole of life, much as microcosm mirrored macrocosm in the Renaissance and much as a hologram can be produced from any part, although at a reduced level of definition. The part is not separable from the whole; it is essential for the existence of the whole. That more potential can always be realized implies a continued evolution at all levels of complexity from protozoan to human.

The low-numbered hypotheses and norms (H1-10, N1-10) are ultimates, since they are not logically derivable from the others in this exposition. N3 and N3 are logically derived from H2 and H3, however. Self-realization is a logical ultimate in this exposition of an ecosophy. The term, capitalized, includes personal and community Self-realization, but is conceived generally to mean an unfolding of reality as a totality. Thus, it is a process as well as a goal of perfection; self-realization may be expanded to ego-realization, self-realization, and Self-realization.

The prevalent usage in utilitarian thinking equates self-realization with self interest and self-expression (stressing the incompatibility of individuals in a sort of social competitive exclusion), here labeled ego-realization. By comparison, other trends, such as Spinoza's idea of self-preservation, are based on a hypothesis of increased compatibility of individuals as a result of maturity. Darwin admitted that he would rather have used the term "natural preservation" instead of "natural selection." Maturity allows the development of the narrow ego of a child into the comprehensive structure of an adult human being. The capitalized concept refers to the development of a deep identification with all life forms; and, this concept is known in the history of philosophy under various names: The universal self, the Atman, or the absolute.

Maturity is linked to the increase of identification with, and care for, others. Albert Schweitzer noticed the expanding circle of care from family to humanity to animals, although different cultures have different emphases. Realizing higher levels of potential for the self favors Self-realization in others. As a corollary, increased Self-realization is dependent on, and internally related to, the Self-realization of others (giving H3). H3 is important for the conceptual development of ecosophy—its assertion reflects an attitude opposed to an unconditional *Verherrlichung* of life and nature in general.

The development of life since the Cambrian era displays a diversity of forms in an expansion of life into places that can only be described as self-realization, since it is far more active than the passive adaptation of self-preservation. Self-realization as a result of maturation and the natural inclination to engage in beautiful action, as opposed to the moral actions distinguished by Kant, condenses certain social, psychological, and ontological hypotheses. H14 refers to all living beings—all beings that are in principle capable of self-realization. And, N14 is derivable from N13 and H13; it is instrumental only in relation to N3, so it is not a purely instrumental norm. Complexity contributes to self-realization.

An unconditional "yes" in response to N3, self-realization for all organisms, implies that Self-realization is something of an intrinsic value—it could never be a purely instrumental norm. Agreement with N12 implies the intrinsic value of all living beings. The platform of the deep ecology movement, including an epistemology and ethics, can be derived from these metaphysical statements, which are based on ecological principles.

Ecology has prompted questions of philosophy. Does knowledge of ecology inspire us to create a metaphysics large enough to encompass ultrahuman being? Using nonscientific hypotheses inspired by the science of ecology, is it possible to escape the presuppositions, probably from the use of physics as a model, that have contributed to the predicament of classical philosophy? If nothing else, ecology should contribute to the complexity and breadth of philosophy.

Science accepted the banishment of metaphysics, but kept the tradition of substance as an explanation. Substance metaphysics is still a Western tradition. But the ecological view suggests that events are as primary as substantial objects. Basing a metaphysics on ecology provides a place in philosophy for fluctuation, irregularity, uncertainty, rarity, and diversity. In the ecological view, humanity is an integral part of nature. The proper relationship is symbiosis, which includes competition and exploitation as well as mutualism, not interference. In exploiting nature, humans are interfering with others, no longer just competing with them. Humans, like other organisms, are limited by environmental constraints; they have life-images and goals; they depend on other species for their existence; and they are capable of self-realization and self-expression.

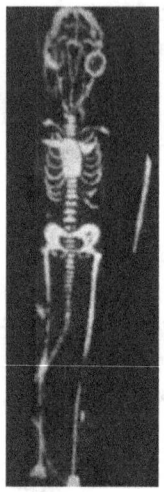

Figure 13733-1. Snakeman (Acryllics on glass, 1975)

2.0. The Primacy of Expression

> If the pool were still
> The reflected world
> Of tottering houses
> The falling cities,
> The quaking mountains
> Would cohere on the surface
> > Raine (R 106)

2.1. *Love of Speaking: Language*

> Language is an epiphany: "Where flesh becomes word
> and silences selfloud."
> > James Joyce (JO 267)

2.1.1. *Silence*

"Yet there is a world of silence, the perceived world, at least, is an order where there are non-language significations—yes, non-language significations, but they are not accordingly *positive*," states Merleau-Ponty (MN 171). Being is originally silent, and man's primordial participation in it is also silent. Being is a field of fields which is always a relation between the agent and the sensorial or ideal field, where the sensorial agent is the body and the ideal agent is speech. The world of silence is the perceived world; the non-language significations surrounding speech allow meaning to emerge. The silence of perception is a silent speech, without signification but yet rich in meaning. Perception may be silent when an object is seen as there, but it cannot be identified or described with words." Merleau-Ponty indicates that there is an analogous silence of language, where its acts are no more significations than perception, but which inventively functions. The lived-body is the silence that embodies speech; silence is the field of pregnant expressiveness present to the living subject, it is, in fact, the world in which the subject lives. As Merleau-Ponty (MK 46) states: "In short, we must consider speech before it is spoken, the background of silence which does not cease to surround it and without which it would say nothing."

Primordial silence is the possibility of speech which signifies meaning, in speech one expresses what is prefigured in silence, but not accomplished. Merleau-Ponty (MN 154) suggests that "When the silent vision falls into speech, and when the speech in turn, opening up a field of the namable and the sayable inscribes itself in that field, in its place, according to its truth—in short, when it metamorphoses the structures of the visible world and makes itself a gaze of the mind, *intuitis mentis*—this is always in virtue of the same fundamental phenomenon of reversibility which sustains both the mute perception and the speech and which manifests itself by an almost carnal existence of the idea, as well as by a sublimation of the flesh. In a senses, if we were to make completely explicit the architectonics of the human body, in its ontological framework, and how it sees itself and hears itself, we would see that the structure of its mute world is such that all the possibilities of language are already given in it."

What is the root of silence? Is it an attribute of Being? Savage Being is always silent; it may never be spoken or reached with words. Silence is related to sound as invisibility is related to the visible. Silence is the source of sound; sound is a modality of silence; but Being is reversible, all absence is merely the obverse of a presence; silence is a modality of the being of sound. Silence is the limit of sound; it layers words and fills the blanks between them, it is inside and outside language. Silence is potential speech; silence can only be kept when one could possibly speak.

Silence is the depth from which speech arises and to which it sinks; the speaking present becomes a sediment world of silence. Silence is the source of a continuum from indirect communication to the direct communication of language. The continuum moves both ways to dialectically produce speech. As one moves up on the continuum, the focus of expression becomes finer; moving lower the focus broadens until it almost comprehends the ground. Paradoxically, access to the silent world is through the meditation of expression; who attempts to express the silent, views it through his expression, and thus it is further revealed as expressed and not yet expressed. In fact, only with the attempt at expression does it become truly silent—awareness of it is increased with expression, and those who express it better realize its ineffability better; and their awareness of ineffability is an essential aspect of expression.

How can silence be savage and sophisticated at the same time? Silence is the source of expression; it has a visible and an invisible aspect, some invisible remains always savage, while the visible is developed with language. What is the nature and origin of developed silence? Silence and language are opposites, which through their interactions accentuate and develop each other. How does expression nourish its source, and renew itself? Through this dialectical engagement of opposites, a synthesis is formed, which then itself falls into opposition with the still savage silence. In *The Visible and the Invisible*. Merleau-Ponty (MN 150) exclaims that silence can only be accessible through expression, "As the secret blackness of milk, of which Valery spoke, is accessible only through its whiteness." Caratheodory hints through the silence.

Contemplating Speech
Five old people sit at a wooden
table, thin, veined fingers peck
food, eyes locked in a shell
of memories of earlier days,
sorrow and happiness distilled
to masks—but through the eyes
the pure distance of dim
corridors once seen brightly
from the other end.
All the thin fibers bear light,
the fibers of the body, the nerves
with a spring to spread and reach
the sun inside. Their breathing
ruffles paper napkins on the table.

All that is best in order parallels
our breathing, insistent, framing
the house around new rooms. The heart
may tie us to life, but breath
is its rhythm and essence.
How can we say death is taking
place when life is being completed?
We do not finish all at once
but having the ability to speak
explain the circumstance of dissolution
and admire the miracle of speech—
reverberating through the fibers
an ageless delight settles in the flesh.
            Caratheodory (CA 42)

2.1.2. Expression & Access to Being

But lucid forms
Cast their images
Upon our waters:
Their faces, veiled or radiant, are always beautiful,
For we imagine them,
They are the aspects of our wisdom,
They bring us messages, intellections,
Impart a mystery,
Could tell us more, if we could hold their gaze.
    Raine (RA 60)

"There is truly a reversal when one passes from the sensible world, in which we are caught, to a world of expression, where we seek to capture significations to serve our purpose . . . . Properly speaking, the expression which language makes possible resumes and amplifies another expression which is revealed in the archeology of the perceived world," Merleau-Ponty states (MN 4). In an active life in the world, things show themselves, withdraw, approach, play games with us, and so encounter us. Perception is original faith to the world, perceived Being is antepredictive being toward which the whole of existence is polarized. The creature and the world flow into each other on their own, being made of the same flesh. Things speak to us with their own language; they offer themselves to perceptive communication like familiar faces whose expression is immediately understood. In the *Investigations*, Wittgenstein said that meaning is a physiognomy. Earlier (WL 647), he had asked: "What is the natural expression of an intention? Look at a cat when it stalks a bird; or a beast when it wants to escape."

2.1.2.1. Dimensions

We live things in order to perceive them. In all its actions, the body is a general system devoted to inspecting the world: It leaps over distances, and outlines hollows and reliefs, creating meaning in the flatness of Being. In its movements and pointing gestures it flows over into the world and possesses it at a distance, rather than being possessed by it; in an expression it delineates what it intends, to capture the world. More than that, according to Merleau-Ponty (MK 67): "All perception, all action which presupposes it, and in short every human use of the body is already *primordial expression*. Not that derivative labor which substitutes for what is expressed signs which are given elsewhere with their meaning and rule of usage, but the primary operation which first constitutes signs as signs, makes that which is expressed dwell in them through the eloquence of their arrangement and configuration alone, implants a meaning in that which did not have one, and thus—far from exhausting itself in the instant at which it occurs—inaugurates an order and founds an institution or a tradition."

Perception is inexorably bound to movement; sense and motility function as partners, moving away and reuniting, as in a dance. Any movement is an expression of the context in which it takes place; there is no movement without meaning, in its context. O'Neil (ON 50) claims that: "We express the world through the poetics of our own body-in-the-world, beginning with the first action of perception which carves into being the perspectives of form and ground whereby the world has an architecture or foundation."

2.1.2.2. Limits

Body movements may be treated as a language; they are open to analysis in much the same way. Patterns of body motion are parallel with speech and meaningfully consistent. Kinesis has units of study—kines and kinemes that are analogous to phones and phonemes, and is divided into interrelated areas: concerned with the physiological aspects of movement, the communication of different meanings through them, and their social importance, as in the work of Birdwhistell (DD 40). Gestures are a language, but are intrinsically related to the development of the motor system of the body; the range of possible gestures is limited by the construction of the body. Some gestures are genetic, others are learned. No gesture is isolatable from its context; most are not from speech, as Shakespeare, in *Troilus and Cressida* (Act IV, Scene 5), recognized:

"There's a language in her eyes, her cheek, her lip,
Nay, her foot speaks; her wanton spirit looks out
At every joint and motion of her body."

Expression arises from the pre-linguistic experimental gesture; vocal gestures rose from the silence, to accent a pointing finger, or perhaps to point to what could not be seen, but of which there was a consciousness.

All expression is embodied; there can be no expression without experience. In learning a language, or new feelings, or in struggling with the primordial the person anchors his expression in something known; he moves from initial ambiguity toward a new meaning. Merleau-Ponty (MN 144) declares that: *This new reversibility and the emergence of the flesh as expression are the point of insertion of speaking and thinking in the world of silence.* There is no experience which is completely inexpressible; if there were, philosophy would become mystical, ultimately depending on silence for the last word. But silence may be described indirectly, as there is the silence of space, the silence of sleep. . . . Expression is a continuum from gesture to speech; the development of the continuum deepens silence. There are languages based on sight as well as sound, however; for instance, Chinese notation is a shorthand picture of the operations of nature; but the thought is designated by symbols which have no basis in sound; the characters, like a language of gesture, follow natural suggestion.

2.1.2.3. Transparency

The world expresses itself through everything. Everything is a sign: nature has its own language, and human languages are examples of the world expressing itself through them. It expresses, with the highest capability, through each part; even silence expresses itself through the human. Being expresses itself in everything; it expresses entities as entities express it, and what Being is doing, is beings, and what beings are doing, is Being. Knowledge and expression preserve and continue perceptual life, while at the same time transforming it. In Steven's (UN 253) words:

> The obscure moon lighting an obscure world
> Of things that would never be quite expressed,
> Where you yourself were never quite yourself
> And did not want nor have to be
>
> Desiring the exhilarations of changes:
> The motive for metaphor, shrinking from
> The weight of primary noon
> The A B C of being . . . .

2.1.3. Aesthetics & Perception Reformed

Perception is a process of taking in the world. It can be historical, that is, perception can become more sophisticated over time and experience. Things must always be reperceived, because things are always changing—the process is always changing.

2.1.3.1. Embodiment & Essence

Linguistic expression amplifies the expression which is revealed in the archaeology of the perceived world. Language, like all expression, is always found embodied; as the body is embodied in the world, as perception is embodied in the body, so language is embodied in perception. But its embodiment limits language. The situation is similar to animals in a zoo, to use Merleau-Ponty's analogy: they seem free without iron cages, but they are contained subtly in a ditch too large to be crossed. The cage, however, is a cage only to wild perception, as it is to wild animals; cultured perception, like domestic animals, is unaware of the restriction.

The structure of language is related to the structure of the body. For instance, language requires three aspects of that distance from the world which humans acquire through their upright posture: first, distance from the ground, which allows a larger horizon to be circumspected; second, distance from things, which makes them objects of discourse mutually comprehended; and third, distance from the speaker to the listener, which is over come only through the mediation of speech. Man speaks in the same way he organizes his perceptual world, in giving it meaning; he creates linguistic institutions before he names, or explains them. Primitive languages derive from classification based on perception: for example, a group may have no word to designate walking, but have a specification of every kind of walking with the particular qualities of each movement. The foundation of words is in the structures of perception; meaning is incarnate in gestures. As human beings experience their lived-in world, they name their experiences.

Rising out of experience, language then develops experience as it develops. Language and experience are paired phenomena. Don Ihde (ID 52) declares that: "Language and experience must be dealt with together as paired foci of the single ellipse of subjectivity." Language and experience develop dialectically in Being; any apparent circular relationship must in truth be a spiral. Through language human consciousness expands historically; it is modified by personal experience as well as social and technological expansion. The conditions of language precede its sound; language presumes, before any sounds are made, that the speakers have a common ground for interaction. The basis of the milieu is silence; the speakers must encounter one another in trust, without which no meaningful contact is possible. Language depends on trusting relationships, these silences are the beginning and the ordering principle of the lingual milieu, which effects all human expression.

The silent trust, the beginning, is communication already; it is already language before speech, in the lingual environment. Language conserves its beginnings, from silence, in its very use. In silence the human being assimilates the signs needed for further communication, learning first whatever forms are the most communicative. All language inexorably obeys the same fundamental law of grammar: The division of words into the same parts of speech—nouns, verbs, adjectives. The parts of speech are learned at different rates: nouns are learned first, and then verbs; pronouns, ad verbs and adjectives are learned next; and prepositions, conjunctives, and articles are learned last. Whatever forms are most communicative are learned first. Some languages are neotonous: stable at an "immature" but not incomplete level; Russian, for instance, uses no articles. The lingual milieu pervades space and time; in it a human being can assimilate any language (from one to eight years, most advantageously). Space and time also pervade the lingual milieu: The noun is the equivalent of matter in space; verbs describe matter in time; adjectives relate matter to matter; adverbs relate matter to matter in time; and participles relate matter in time to matter, all in a single sentence.

All of these forms are symbols. Symbols stand for other things, but have no real relation with them; signs do bear a relationship (fever is a sign of sickness). In fact, the relationship of one symbol to another symbol is the same as the relationship of the object signified to other objects. These lateral relations open up the possibility of varied expressions of a same theme. Symbolic behavior must be a necessary condition for human cognition, making it possible to have a unity of an object within a multiplicity of relations. A biological complexity in a social complexity allows human behavior to express the complexity of the world. The sum of significations is a language. Taken singly, signs do not signify anything, and each expresses only a divergence of meaning from the others. Taken together, language is made up of differences which appear among terms and signs. Since language is *learned*, one is obligated to go from part to whole; if one went from whole to part, one would need to know the language to learn it. Merleau-Ponty (MK 39) writes: "And this sort of circle, according to which language, in the presence of those who are learning it, precedes itself, teaches itself, and suggests its own deciphering, is perhaps the marvel which defines language."

Thus, the first word is a linguistic holon. Koestler defines holons as self-regulating, open hierarchical systems which display both the autonomous properties of wholes and the dependent properties of parts; this dichotomy is present on every level of hierarchical organization and is referred to as the "Janus phenomenon." Generally a holon may be applied to any stable social sub-whole which displays rule governed behavior or a structural gestalt constancy. Each partial act of expression creates a language itself, and the speaking subject goes beyond signs to their meanings.

How does mind form language, or does language form the mind? The Sapir-Whorf hypothesis (I 114) states: "Language is a guide to "social reality." The fact of the matter is that the 'real world' is to a large extent unconsciously built up on the language habits of the group. The understanding of a simple poem, for instance, involves not merely an understanding of the single words in their average significance, but a full comprehension of the whole life of the community as it is mirrored in the words, or—suggested by their overtones." Language functions, not simply as a device for reporting evidence, but also, and more significantly, as a way of defining experience for its speakers. Meanings are not so much discovered in experience as imposed upon it, because of the hold that linguistic form has upon the orientation of the subject in the world. More than a technique of communicating, language is a way of directing perceptions of speakers, and providing habitual modes of analyzing experience into significant categories. Young's picture of brain organization supports Whorf: each brain sets up its own characteristic ways of dealing with new situations. Language conditions thinking because of its influence in building rules; since most rule behavior is learned, it would be learned with and in language. Edward T. Hall extends Whorf: People not only have different 'programs' they 'inhabit different sensory worlds'

Language is embodied in a social system. Culture is a symbolic system that transforms physical reality, what is there, into experienced reality; cultures provide different modifications of reality; cultures provide different modifications of reality, and responses to them. Primitive peoples have relatively simple languages; thus, their perceptual world is impoverished by their linguistic one. In his studies of the Hopi language, Whorf contrasted their expressions of colors, plants, and space and time with the standard European language, and found them to be fewer and simpler, in general (there was, for instance, only one color word for blue-green). The difference in their classifications of plants and dichotomies (male-female) would effect the way these things were viewed.

Having an extensive dictionary of names may make it easier to distinguish things, but conversely, it is more limiting, and precludes an easy approach to different modalities of perception and thought, both imaginative and naturally rhythmic. Language limits thought; Wittgenstein states that the intersubjective linguistic world is no longer distinguished from the world itself; but language is also the escape from one limited perspective. The person projects himself through the language, his voice resounds through the symbol; the voice lights the words and gestures, revealing him to others and penetrating the dark recesses of the self. The individual and society define each other through language. The individual acquires a role as a person (*persona* = mask, *per sonare* = speaking through); society acquires institutions and members created by language. Language possesses men through the intersubjectivity and generality of the flesh; it operates to unite self, others and the sensible world in itself.

Face in sandstone   thirty-degrees
       a fireplace, bicycle parts, a fly wing
         The expression on the face
Debussy as he was composing   passionate flesh
       We reduce expressions to words
and these are covered over by the motions
of living.
        Feelings fade and form a sediment
Pressure from the weight of feelings compresses
Memories into layers, and these are heated
like carbon in rock and assume
      a crystalline form.

Continents of consciousness float
on layers
of dense experience. The self-world is composed
       of thousands of feet of ragged memories
Plates broken by shifting,
        float on a molten
   core   heaved by inner turmoil
Pieces penetrate the surface
      and invite a deeper
   archaeology. The mind excavates
and elevates them to the air
        again and to clouds.
    'Consciousness as the Mask of Flesh,' Caratheodory (CA 51)

2.1.3.2. Aspects of Language
Language may be divided into two aspects: language and speaking
(*Langage* = *Langue* + *Parole*). Psychology regards *langue* as unconscious
and parole as conscious; thus, any conscious gesture always entails
an unconscious component. Barthes (JE 82) writes that: "The
langue is both a social institution and a system of values. As a social
institution, it is never an act; it utterly eludes premeditation; it is
the social part of language; the individual can, by himself, neither
create it, nor modify it; it is essentially a collective contract, which, if
one wishes to communicate, one must accept in its entirety. What is
more, this social product is autonomous, like a game which has rules
one must know before one can play it. . . . As opposed to the *langue*,
institution and system, the *parole* is essentially an individual act of
selection and actualization . . ." Although the relation between *langue*
and *parole* is necessarily constant, the system as a whole, *langage*, is a
continuous process of development; *langage* is a dynamic whole. In
information theoretic terms, a particular, individual, conscious "message"

(*parole*), constituted by any gesture in a social context, necessarily involves the use on an unconscious social "code" which the context entails. Information occurs as a function of "surprise" in a matrix of "expectancy." Ideally, the redundancy should be about 50 percent to pass the Scylla and Charybdis of total predictability, or total unpredictability. For Merleau-Ponty, information theory is also valid, but only on the condition that one discerns the flesh beneath the discriminating behaviors and speech and its "comprehensible" diacritical systems beneath the information. Saussure distinguished between a synchronic linguistics of speech and a diachronic linguistics of a language. As Merleau-Ponty (MK 88) presents it: "At first the subjective point of view envelopes the objective point of view; synchrony envelopes diachrony. The past of a language began by being present."

Since language is a system when considered in cross-section, it must also be one in its development. The two separate disciplines move dialectically, forming a new conception of the being of language. Merleau-Ponty (MK 88) elaborates that it is a "logic in contingency— an oriented system which nevertheless always elaborates random factors, taking what was fortuitous up again into a meaningful whole— incarnate logic." As previously stated, language is the lateral relation of one sign to another such that both are significant, and the meaning appears at the cross-section; this is synchrony—its system never exists wholly in act but always involves latent changes. Synchrony is a cross section of diachrony, which is the historical succession of synchronies. Each word, or sign, is thus a two-dimensional phenomenon: it is an institution of cultural deposits and an activity of expression. The flesh, man, is a self awareness of the world; he is a worldly being not enclosed in himself; because of this, he means. And because he means there is a language, and because there is a language, there is a world—a perpetually changing environment of words and noise, development and decay, direction and confusion, and a history of the whole.

2.1.3.3. Ideality

Language transforms perceptive meaning into an ideal object, a signification; ideal objects therefore are constructs (and as such, cannot be approached by Husserl's eidetic reduction, according to Merleau-Ponty). There is a "natural generality" in the body which is co-extensive with all perceptible reality, but the person does not perceive all that, since the body is involved in it. Ideas have a created generality which originates in the intellect. Ideas become situated in a realm of pure ideality, not a horizon of ideality. Perceptual meaning becomes thematic meaning, along a continuum of behavior; there is a dialectical relation between perceptual behavior and thematic behavior. Language produces a clarity which the silent world does not; words create figures in the ground of Being.

Since clear words circumscribe clear phenomena, and Being is obscure, are there words which are appropriate to Being? Obviously not everything can be expressed equally well in words; reality cannot all be transformed into ideal objects. Merleau-Ponty (MG 188) says that: "The clearness in language stands out from an obscure background, and if we carry our research far enough we shall eventually find that language is equally uncommunicative of anything other than itself, that its meaning is inseparable from it."

As soon as we speak, we transmute savage Being into the flesh of language; that which is, becomes that which is said; beings become ideas of beings. Speech unavoidably breaks silence, it irrevocably names Being. Or does it? Does silence become a positivity, or does it deepen in its dialectic with language? Once speaking has begun, silence is broken; it is brought to expression as the other side of language, and it may be deepened, but it is no longer savage; the savage cannot be approached even indirectly. Being not only precedes language, it exceeds it, therefore, it exceeds any idealizations that can be made of it. Contact with the silent world is not obvious; even while gazing at things without words, language continues to be an influence; it influences the structuring of the visual field, which figures stand out from the field and which do not. Meaning comes into existence with the dialectical exchange between man and world situated in the more fundamental unity of Being; Being is the final source of meaning, whose unity logically precedes dialectical opposition. Being verbalizes itself in us. The eruption of flesh within language is its signifying power; the silent life of language is exhibited in the reversibility of sign and its differential character, and the expressive relation with thought. Gillan (GI 60) states that: "As the trace of the silent armature of thought, of the carnal presence of ideas, and of the invisible, in being flesh language speaks of Being in the world." Silence sustains movements of language, as the invisible sustains the transitions between touching and seeing and the reversibility of flesh. The ground of silence always exceeds the figure of speech; speech is open and in determinate, but finite. Language must be reduced to a level of presignification. Speech must be considered before it is spoken, by unthreading the silence that weaves through it.

Restriction to the world of ideal objects cannot answer the two basic aspects of the question, 'What do you mean?' (1) that we are beings who mean, and (2) that we live in a field of meaning. Linguistic analysis must presuppose a certainty of perceptive faith in the real world, which is accessible to others, whereas, in phenomenology, faith entails doubt. Since the sciences and mathematics approach a pure ideality, they are more successful in their verbalization than the arts, for which words are sometimes inadequate, but at the cost of pretending to abolish the necessary incompleteness of the world (perception can only approach an asymptote, perhaps. How is melody remembered or described?) Ideas can never be totally divorced from the carnal; as language approaches the flesh itself it becomes incoherent. But in dreaming of a natural world through pure perception, with a pure memory, to return to the things themselves, language becomes a power for error, since it cuts the continuous tissue that vitally joins all to things and to the past; science loses sight of its origins. The spoken word, in its field of established meanings, installs itself like a screen between ourselves and that tissue; it reduces Being to poverty and forgets savage Being.

Artistic ideas must first be grasped in their fleshy existence; only if they are first experienced can they be grasped, and then they cannot be transformed into pure ideality. These ideas, musical and literary among others, cannot be detached from the sensible appearances, as can the ideas of intelligence, which are erected into a second positivity; thus the abstract language of science is freed from the horizon of perceptible reality, while the most artistic seem trapped within it. Merleau-Ponty (MK 45) claims that: "the writer's act of expression is not very different from the painter's. We usually say that the painter reaches us across the silent world of lines and colors. . . . The writer is said, on the contrary, to dwell in already elaborated signs and in an already speaking world, and to require nothing more of us than the power to recognize our significations according to the indications of the signs which he proposes to us. But what if language expresses as much by what is between words as by words themselves? By that which is not "say" as by what it "says"? ... and ... all language is indirect or allusive—that is, if you wish, silence. The relation of meaning to the spoken word can no longer be a point for point correspondence that we always have clearly in mind."

Art and language are anchored in the carnal, but all flesh, even that of the world, radiates beyond itself. In its relationship to ideas, language in practice, the language of life, action, literature, and poetry, recapitulates the relationship of the body to the world. Language involves a reflexivity, or reversibility of a kind found in hand touching hand—it involves a relationship to ideas as the invisible dimension of silence.

2.1.3.4. Access to Being

But how does language, the creation of a realm of ideal objects, give access to Being? What are the dimensions of language? The speaking language (*langage*) exists on a continuum from savage silence to eloquent speaking; it rises from a subjective silence, through an intersubjective silence to a remote objectivity. It is embodied in perception, which itself is embedded in the savage Being of the perceived world; it begins by being aesthetic and becomes linguistic. From the carnal it precedes to the ideal, developing with experience. From its broad focus of implicit gesture, it becomes narrow with explicit statement; open and unfinished in its negativity, it becomes closed and complete in its positivity. Speaking goes beyond Being to ideals, but it cannot describe Being in the same way as those ideas. Language is a cohesive whole of convergent linguistic gestures, each of which is defined less by a signification than by a use value.

Like any tool, language has limits; in acting like a fish net, it allows the small fish to escape, while the largest ones cannot be included. Language, however, is not a tool like others, since only it affords its speaker the possibility of standing in the openness of Being. It is more than a tool at one's disposal; it is self-consistent and independent. Merleau-Ponty (MK 43) says that "Language is much more like a sort of being than a means, and that is why it can present something to us so well. A friend's speech over the telephone brings us the friend himself ... carrying on the conversation through things left unsaid. Because meaning is the total movement of speech our thought crawls along in language. Yet, for the same reason, our thought moves through language as a gesture goes beyond the individual points of its passage. At the very moment language fills our mind up to the top without leaving the smallest place for thought not taken into its vibration, and exactly to the extent that we abandon ourselves to it, it passes beyond the 'sign' toward their meaning. And nothing separates us from that meaning any more. Language does not *presuppose* its table of correspondence; it unveils its secrets itself. It teaches them to every child that comes into the world. Its opaqueness, its obstinate reference to itself, and its turning and folding back upon itself are precisely what makes it a mental power; for it in turn becomes something like a universe, and it is capable of loading things themselves in this universe—after it has transformed them into their meaning."

Language must be studied as it is created in use, as it encompasses the nonreflective elements of expression, before its irrationality (in the narrow sense) has been removed by arbitrary custom. Language seems to be fragmented by impotent silences and supplementary gestures, but these are what complete it, actually. Although explicit words or expressions are not complete, the language itself is whole. As one learns a language, meaning is expressed when it is embodied in available terms; as thought is concerned, words are haunted by it at a distance, and for things, words deliver the captive meaning. Merleau-Ponty (MJ 87) states: ". . . so linguistics finds itself confronted by the task of going beyond the alternative of language as things and language as the product of speaking subjects. Language must *surround* each speaking subject, like an instrument with its own inertia, its own demands, constraints, and internal logic, and must nevertheless remain open to the initiatives of the subject (as well as to the brute contributions of invasions, fashions, and historical events)." Language, with its displaced meanings, ambiguities, and substitutions, is nevertheless a coherent whole, a gestalt. Its totality of presence is the ground, which may be differentiated by a figure according to the situation. The ground is always complete in some situation, but may be incomplete in others; the ground does not exist in an absolute sense, nor does the figure, since they are mutually extant. Not only is language complete, but Wittgenstein (WL 98) claims that it is in order: "Every sentence in our language is in order as it is. That is to say, we are not *striving after* an ideal . . . and a perfect language awaiting construction by us. —On the other hand it seems clear that where there is sense there must be perfect order. —So there must be perfect order even in the vaguest sentence."

Completion in the sense of a presentation that is objective and convincing for the senses may no longer be the sign of a work that is really complete. Expression passes through the lived-in-world without passing through the anonymous realm of nature or the senses. Since language is not the translation of some original text, it will not yield finished expressions. According to Merleau-Ponty (MK 51): "Beaudelaire wrote—in an expression very opportunely recalled by Malraux—"that a complete work was not necessarily finished, and a finished work not necessarily complete." The accomplished work is thus not the work which exists in itself like a thing, but the work which reaches its viewer and invited him to take up the gestures which created it, and skipping the intermediaries, to rejoin, without any guide other than a movement of the invented line (an almost incorporeal trace), the silent world of the painter, henceforth uttered and accessible." As our body is not incomplete if it is missing molecules, or an organ, but is complete if it functions, so language is not incomplete if it fails to name everything with word, but covers the world organically. Wittgenstein (WL 18) offers an analogy: "Our language can be seen as an ancient city: a maze of little streets and squares, of old and new houses, and of houses with additions from various periods; and this surrounded by a multitude of new boroughs with straight regular streets and uniform houses."

In this sense we know more than perspectives; we can know a whole object; there are words, sentences to describe it. Wittgenstein also stated that the limits of his language were the limits of his world. But that limit is surmountable; language operates to point beyond itself, as well as expand its territory. The world is built on language habits; but the relationship between language and perception is reversible: language habits are built from the perceptual order. Language and perception form a dialectic, to promote access to a thing in the lived-in-world, and awareness of it. As Perception loses itself in the perceived, so expression becomes transparent for the sake of the expressed. As Merleau-Ponty (MG 401) said: "The wonderful thing about language is that it promotes its own oblivion.... Expression fades out before what is expressed ..."

And in this way, its mediating role may pass unnoticed, caught up in meaning it is possible to lose sight of language. The closer language is to the perceived world, the less visible it becomes; in art and music its self-effacement may be complete, but that does not make it less effective; as Proust (MN 149) wrote: "Literature, music, the passions, but also the experience of the visible world are no less than is the science of Lavoisier and Ampere—the exploration of an invisible and the disclosure of a world of ideas."

2.1.3.5. Words & Thoughts

"And like the functioning of the body, that of words or paintings remains obscure to me. The words, lines, and colors which express me come out of me as gestures. They are torn from me by what I want to say as my gestures are by what I want to do. In this sense, there is in all expression a spontaneity which will not tolerate any commands, not even those which I would like to give to my self. Words, even in the art of prose, carry the speaker and the hearer into a common universe by drawing both toward a new signification through their power to designate in excess of their accepted definition, through the muffled life they have led and continue to lead in us.... This spontaneity of language which unites us is not a command, and the history which it establishes is not an external idol; it is ourselves with our roots, our growth, and as we say, the fruits of our toil," explains Merleau-Ponty (MK 75).

The spoken word is a gesture and contains its meaning as the gesture contains its significance; words radiate from a subject living in the primacy of speech, as gestures arise from intentional movement. To understand a gesture, one need only participate in the situation it describes; the meaning of words is induced by the words themselves. However the word has parameters, outside of which it loses its meaning; the word is embodied as expressive meaning in the subject, as the perceiving subject is embodied in the world. After it is spoken the word becomes a communal subject, whose relationship to a subject is reversible. We belong to words; through speaking and hearing, reading and writing, we live in the linguistic milieu. In expressing themselves through culture, men dwell in lives which are not theirs, creating a universal life, as in the actual living presence of their bodies. A person speaks through language for the purpose of situating himself in the social world of meanings, as well as to express his thoughts.

The word is the end of a search for thought; it is the body, the presence of thought in the phenomenal world. The word is not the sign of a thought, capable of being entertained separately: the word is the presence of that thought in the world. The language is itself the vehicle of thought. Words are not a clothing for thought, or the translation of a meaning already clear to itself into an arbitrary system of symbols. Merleau-Ponty (MG 213) realizes that: "What produces our mistake on this question, what makes us believe in a thought which could exist by itself before being expressed, are the thoughts already constituted as such, already expressed, which we recall in a silent moment and which give us an illusion of an internal life. But in reality this pretense of silence bristles with words, and our internal life is an internal language."

Merleau-Ponty claims that actually the subject is ignorant in a way, of his thought until he has spoken or written them; we present thoughts to ourselves through internal or external speech. Expression is the seal of thought; it isn't complete until it is expressed. Words arrange themselves according to our intentions; we are grasped by a word thought as we grasp it. We are conscious of a word only after it has appeared; in this sense, the speaker is not master or slave of his words—he is the words; and this is why Merleau-Ponty says that to read the words of an author is to meet that author himself.

Can one think without words? Merleau-Ponty cannot be entirely correct. If the speaking language can carry thought, can not also the silent voices of painting? If speech is embodied thought, what of dancing? When speaking, it is sometimes possible for a different meaning than the one intended to emerge from words. The intentional field must also be reversible: From an expression in "brain language" to an expression in words, from a mental world to a verbal world, from the invisible to the visible. There must be a *chiasm* between thought and words: Sometimes the thought is completed by words, sometimes the words are completed by thoughts. Words make thought visible; thought without words would merely be invisible, but still embodied. Raine holds that there is "Moss-thought, rain thought, stone still thought on the hill."

In logic the property of discrete distinction covers symbols, but not concepts; if we thought in words then thoughts would be symbols of words. Thoughts may be expressed nonverbally. Thought is so fluid that it is impossible to coin a word for every thought. (That is why human thought cannot be represented by discrete channel computers.) The fallacy of the perfect dictionary is plain; words are molecular, while thought is continuous. Being is continuous and cannot be exhausted with words; although words, and hence poetry and prose, are discrete and molecular, painting, music and dance are continuous—they may more accurately present the outlines of Being. But how can words approach Being if they are discrete? Language is an organism; words are living organisms; language loses old, acquires new words, and words lose old meanings and acquire new ones. Even though individual words are discrete, in their organic forms, they can reproduce the whole mimetically. Meaning inhabits words; expression opens new dimensions to perception. Words that have been dead metaphors may be revived in dreams, or poetic experiences.

Our relations with the world depend upon words, through active (thetic) intentionalities. When first learning to speak, children make their first words function as whole sentences. Wittgenstein states that a word can be a picture of the whole thing; and Merleau-Ponty concurs that the word is a gesture whose meaning is the world. The word creates a cosmos from chaos and then allows it to enter us.

The essence of thought is Being, and it is ordered by words, which make it visible. As Eliot (EL 7) writes:

". . . words, after speech, reach
Into the silence. Only by the form, the pattern,
Can words or music reach
The stillness, as a Chinese jar still
Moves perpetually in its stillness.

2.1.4. *Word Made Flesh*

Word that utters the world that turns the wind

. . . .

Whose silence is the violin-music of the stars

. . . .

Grammar of five fold rose and six fold lily,
Spiral of leaves on a bough, helix of shells,
Rotation of twining plants on axes of darkness and light

. . . .

Hieroglyph is whose exact precision is defined
Feather and insect wing, refraction of multiple eyes,
Eyes of the creatures, oh myriad fold vision of the world,
Statement of mystery, how shall we name
A spirit clothed in the world, a world made man?
    Raine (R 76)

2.1.4.1. *Aesthetics Perception & Making*

Aesthetics was perception at one time. Making was the proprioceptive response to perception. As ideas emerge from perception and experience, they can be put into form and communicated. Ideas can shape flesh. Words shape intentions and actions.

2.1.4.1.1. *Creation*

If it is the form which reaches into stillness, how is it created? Art is a dialectical process that symbolizes the productive activity of nature. In Nietzsche, the two art-sponsoring deities, Apollo and Dionysius, are symbols of the metaphysical principles of life and being. Art owes its continuous evolution to this duality. All experience is aesthetic experience; existing is feeling (*aesthetos* = sense perception). Aesthetic experience enters into the depth of being, into the chaos and terrors of existence, to reach fulfillment in the formative activity of art, which contains both suffering and exultation. Nietzsche (PF 202) connected Being and art: "Nature and art create in a playful manner, building and destroying in innocence ..."

The innocence of becoming is the unity and inseparability of things we call opposites and contradictions: being and becoming, nature and man, freedom and necessity. The innocence of becoming is the silence of art—a silence paradoxically dynamic, full of tension and polarity, yet possessing form and balance. Since all experience is comprised of aesthetic events, and since art in human activity is broadened beyond artistic, art is generic. As in Aristotle it involves feeling and making;

art is the education of nature (*educare* = lead forth, draw out). Life and art merge: Experience in art is the dynamic process of life itself, in continuous oscillation between opposite poles; life and culture are both aesthetic phenomena. The similarity uniting diverse cultures is explained by the human condition: The first expressions of the basic ambiguity, of man as a body-mind, shape the living environment. Artistic creation is the spontaneous movement of the human body as it expresses its universe.

The body is caught in the world; it is made of the same flesh as the world. The body holds things in a circle around itself, and these embed themselves in its flesh and form part of its full definition. As it moves itself, the body forms patterns in the flesh of the world. Understanding a pattern is also a bodily reaction; creation and re-creation are analogous processes. The feeling is perceived, not conceived; the work of art is contemplated, not cognized; what the artist makes, the audience remakes. The created Pattern becomes a cultural object which alters the complex of the environment, both organisms must adjust. Most learning is a reflection on experience; art reproduces experience. In the presence of a work of art, its full style is felt; the image presents itself to us—it is not representation, but presentation. This presentation is *kinaesthetic*, an expressive dynamic form which appeals more to the kinaesthesis of the body than to in tuition. The artist works like his nervous system, selecting highly significant cant details from his environment, and synthesizing them into an excitatory complex. As Whitehead (WI 349) explains: "The human body is an instrument for the production of art in the life of the human soul. It concentrates upon those elements in human experiences selected for conscious perception (i.e., it heaps upon them via horizontal transmutations) intensities of subjective form derived from components dismissed into shadow. It thereby enhances the value of that appearance which is the subject matter for art. In this way the work of art is a message from the Unseen. It unlooses depths of feeling from behind the frontier where precision of consciousness fails."

Art originates in living beings (not exclusively human); it is organic in the Aristotelian sense. The work of art is simultaneously self-realization and world constitution; it determines the individuality of the artist and the physiognomy of his world. Aesthetic knowledge is explained by perception; perception is explained by expression; since explanation is rooted in experience, and experience is historically progressive, the circularity of explanation (in two dimensions) becomes a spiral (in three). Painting quintessentially expresses the paradoxical directness-indirectness of vision; the problems of painting illustrate the enigma of the body. Vision is presence in absence; awareness of the visible embraces the invisible; one sees the whole object even though only one aspect of it presents itself to the eyes. Even though vision is a metaphor for perception, nevertheless perception is kinaesthetic: The whole complex series of transactions with the world of experience is grasped through all of the senses. Creative perception is a movement of the body; likewise expression is also a movement, the artist thinks with his materials. This movement organizes concrete elements into a new object, an aesthetic form, whose significance is inseparable from its organization.

Merleau-Ponty (MG 293) continues: "One could show, for example, that aesthetic perception opens in turn a new space ... that the dance unfolds in a space without ends and without directions, that it is a suspension of our history, that in the dance the subject and his world are no longer opposed, no longer detach themselves each against the background furnished by the other ..."

> Wolf folds
> shadows
> around his shape to move quietly—
> but the shadows remain
> a few moments longer
> for me to see.
> The air adjusts slowly
> to their absence.
>
> A shadow plays
> with its source   with the observer;
> the forest hides
> the shadow, the air
> above the grass anticipates its form—
> 'Shadow Play,' by Caratheodory (CB 29)

2.1.4.1.2. Essence

> At the still turning point of the world.
> Neither flesh nor fleshless; neither from nor towards;
> at the still point there the dance is,
> but neither arrest nor movement.
> T.S. Eliot (EL 5)

Art has the ability to suspend movement and fuse opposites in Being, which it does by providing its wealth of possibilities. Better than ideas, as Merleau-Ponty (MH n.p.) states, the work of art contains *matrices of ideas*—"it provides us with symbols whose meaning we never stop developing. Precisely because it dwells and makes us dwell in a world we do not have the key to, the work of art teaches us to see and ultimately gives us something to think about as no analytical work can; because when we analyze an object, we find only what we have put into it."

If Being is the ground of possibility and art is the expression of one possibility, what is revealed about Being? Not an actuality, pre-existent, surely? The artist understands as he paints; to the extent that he contacts nature, and succeeds in grasping its unity, he contacts Being. But in laying out its universe of mute meanings, a painting mixes up categories: essence and existence, imaginary and real, visible and invisible. The generic essence of art belongs to a regional ontology, functioning as *a priori* for the material region of art objects. As in an essence, meaning in art is self given, but it is wholly in perception. Due to their generality and omnitemporality, essences are systematically related, and may fit into an ascending hierarchy; meaning in art is specific to the art work itself. For Husserl, meaning in art is subsumed under the objective signification intended by the logos of language; logical signification approaches an ideal unity and becomes a reference for all objectivities, real or ideal. Merleau-Ponty (MK 75) argues that "at the same time, we shall be able to see why it is legitimate to treat painting as a language. This way of dealing with problems will emphasize a perceptual meaning which is captured in the visible configuration of the painting and yet capable of gathering up a series of antecedent expressions into an always-to-be-made- again eternity."

Painting is the struggle for expression in silence; lacking the explicitness of speech, its voice of silence, nevertheless, even more effectively conveys the tacit ground of each art of communication, and the communion of each with all of them. The difference between communication and communion is blurred in their common etymological denomination (*communis* = common). In its attempt to reach the thing itself, art incorporates a phenomenological reduction in its attitude. Cezanne is the best example of the artistic reduction: In his early paintings, he attempted to capture the expression itself; only later he learned that the expression is the language of the thing itself and springs from its configuration. Then he attempted to recapture the physiognomy of things, and faces, by the reproduction of their sensible features; their own expression would arise from these. Merleau-Ponty (MG 322) concludes: "This is what nature constantly and effortlessly achieves, and why the paintings of Cezanne are those of a pre-world in which as yet no men existed."

2.1.4.1.3. As Linguistics

Art is to be subsumed under a general theory of linguistics (as the science of symbolic activity). Human behavior includes the capability of making the "things" in his perceived world symbolic. Whereas the signal to which an animal responds is empirically related to that particular event, the symbol to which a man responds is not just related to the event for which it stands, but with other symbols. Art as a whole is a symbolical activity, in which the artist directs himself toward the environment with the purpose of manipulating his situation. The creative gesture is a backing up into the future; the artist pulls clear of Being, and opening himself allows a future to form itself in the present; the givens are a future's organs. In such a self-sufficient contingency the painter's body moves itself in a gesture, as both source and matter of the new sense it incarnates; its unity is that the new incarnates itself, or the past surges forward, equally.

Painting is an abortive attempt to do what is always still to be done. In this forever uncompleted endeavor men of each age are mutely united with the whole of human past; the field of meaning embodied in paintings has been open since paintings were first produced—painting mirrors the human condition. As Merleau-Ponty (MK 87) explains: "The first drawing on the walls of caves founded a tradition only because it inherited another: That of perception. The quasi-eternity of incarnate existence and we have in the exercise of our body and of our senses, insofar as they insert us in a world, the meanings of understanding our cultural gesticulation insofar as it inserts us in history . . . the continuous attempt at expression establishes a single history—as the hold of our body on every possible object establishes a single space." Existence wells up from this communication with the past and present. In a painting we encounter one another in our shared encounter with Being; this encounter in the world breaks the circle of verbalization. Painting embodies our openness to being; through silence the artist encounters the ineffable ground of Being itself. All meanings mean what cannot be said; formal signs carry their significance in what they signify, not in themselves.

Painting is a concrete expression of the tension between sign and signified. This tension of Being is a living unity in separation— equivocal, bright and shadowy at once, with the luminosity and opacity of Being itself. Merleau-Ponty (MH 138) states: "There is no break at all in this circuit; it is impossible to say that nature ends where and that men or expression starts here. It is, therefore, mute Being which itself comes to show forth its own meaning. Herein lies the reason why the dilemma between figurative and nonfigurative art is badly posed; it is true and uncontradictory that no grape was ever what it is in the most figurative painting and that no painting, no matter how abstract, can get away from Being, that even Caravaggio's grape is the grape itself. This precession of what is upon what one sees and makes seen, of what one sees and makes seen upon what is—this is vision itself. And to give the ontological formula of painting we hardly need to force the painter's own words, Klee's words written at the age of thirty-seven and ultimately inscribed on his tomb: 'I cannot be caught in immanence.'"

As the artist introduces new meaning into the world, she modifies the world of others, and this meaning sediments as bases for a common world. Art is a historical process which unites many human transcendences into a single people, not as progressive knowledge but as a process of enlargement of perspectives. The painter is an example of man's relative independence from his present in his particular modes of expression. He is guided by two motivations: What he intends to paint, and his style, as a historical influence. The work of art is also a limit since it is incarnated. The painter creates his own style, a system of equivalences that he establishes for his work and by which he concentrates the meaning which in his perception is still scattered, and makes it exist separately.

The painting coheres by virtue of its style, blending into a distinctive unity which is the true expression of reality as seen by the artist. Modern painters weren't seeking a resemblance to the world, they were promoting truth as a coherence of expression, the cohesion of painting with itself. Dufrenne (DU 98) writes: "While daily speech submits mechanically to common usage, artistic creation in its most authentic gestures constantly surpasses pre-existing codes, inventing new procedures and even new ground rules. Styles vary and each great work introduced a new poetics (*art poetique*) by calling for a new vision. Thus, artistic codes are more supple and elastic than linguistic or graphic codes; they are also less exacting in their demands upon the interpreter. . . . For the deciphering of a given work cannot be said always to imply knowledge of its singular poetics or even (more simply) general codes governing collective styles. If one had to be a musician to enjoy music, a large musical audience would not exist; the same holds in painting (as if one had to know how to paint) or in architecture."

The history of modern painting demonstrates that painting is not a representation of something outside it. Its goal is to break the skin of things and show their inside: How things become things, and the world becomes the world. Merleau-Ponty (MN 253) expresses his intention: "What I want to do is restore the world as a meaning of Being absolutely different from the 'represented,' that is, as the vertical Being which none of the 'representations' exhaust and which all 'reach' the wild Being."

2.1.4.1.4. History As Seeing

Painting assumes a privileged position as an access to Being; it is a completed ontology of the visible. At the other extreme, music is too far beyond the designatable to depict anything but the turbulent outlines of Being, according to Merleau-Ponty. In a painting the artist touches the two extremities: In the depth of the visible, something moved, which engulfed his body; the invisible. Because every visible thing gives itself as the result of a dehiscence of Being, it functions also as a dimension. Therefore the proper essence of the visible is to have a layer of invisibility, which is noticeable only as a certain absence. The frontal properties of the visible reach the eye directly, but there is also that which reaches from below, and that which reaches it from above (and frees it from the gravity of its origins). In addition to the outer movements, painting tries to capture the secret ciphers. A photograph records the visible instants of time, but it loses the overlapping; painting makes the overlap visible. Yet painting does not present itself to the mind, but to the sight, to offer an imaginary texture of the real. Vision learns by seeing: It sees the world, and its inadequacies; it reaches beyond the "visual givens" to open upon a texture of Being of which discrete sensorial messages are only punctuations.

Merleau-Ponty says it gives visible existence to what profane vision believes to be invisible; painting does not, thus, restrict itself to the surface visibility, it attempts to extend its having at a distance to all aspects of Being. Painting is the very duplicity of perception itself, it is not an image, but a visible to the second power, a fleshly icon of the first. Things evoke an echo in the body, which the painter reflects. Painting is an artificial organ of vision, which corrects vision. But, it is also, as Merleau-Ponty (MH 168) says, a continuous birth: "We are to reason not so much upon the light as upon the light which, from that was only virtually visible, inside the mothers body, becomes at one and the same time visible for itself and for us. The painter's vision is a continued birth." Vision is not a mode of thought, or presence to itself; it is a means of absence, for the self, and for being present at the fission of Being from the inside—a fission at which termination the self returns to itself.

Painting comes from the eye and addresses itself to the eye, bringing into the world the form of things whose seal has not been broken; it exists in the visible like natural things, but never the less communicates through them. Merleau-Ponty (MH 166) contends that the painter "must affirm . . . that vision is a mirror or concentration of the universe or that, in another's words, the *idios kosmos* opens by virtue of vision upon a *koinos kosmos*: In short, that the same thing is both out there in the world and here in the heart of vision - the same or, if one prefers, a similar thing, but according to an efficacious similarity which is the parent, the genesis, the metamorphosis of Being in his vision." This is what the painter wishes to capture. To see the visible, it is necessary not to see the play of shadows and lights around it; profane visibility rests on a total visibility which the painter tries to recreate, to liberate the phantom in it. Painting interrogates the secret genesis of things in our body. A vision, which knows everything, makes itself in us; the world looks at itself through the painter. Merleau-Ponty (MH 167) says again: "There is inspiration and expiration of Being . . . it becomes impossible to distinguish between what sees and what is seen, what paints and what is painted." Being contacts the artist, the seer is seen; in a self portrait of the artist painting, he adds to what he saw, what things saw of him. Painting makes reversibility explicit: The use of mirrors, perspectives, or self-portraiture creates a doubling, as it occurs in Being.

In paintings themselves we could find a figured philosophy of vision, its iconography, perhaps. It is no accident, for example, that frequently in Dutch paintings (as in many others) an empty interior is "digested" by the "round eye of the mirror." This prehuman way of seeing things is the painter's way. More completely than lights, shadows, and reflections, the mirror image anticipates, within things, the labor of vision. The mirror arises upon an open circuit from seeing body to visible body; it reproduces the reflexivity of seeing a painting.

Yet what happens when the painting is a flat and closed entity backing into its future? What is seen then? Ortega (OT 46) says that "Art is a window with a garden behind it: One may focus on the garden or on the window." The anthropologist Robert Redfield distinguishes between two types of perception: Iconic, where the garden is the figure and the window is ground, and aesthetic, where the window is the figure; he claims that a double perception is impossible, in principle. Every work of art is a window frame—the aesthetic form, with a garden behind it—the content of human experience to which the form refers. The pregnancy of a form is the source of its effectiveness.

Archeologists sometimes attempt to reconstruct the social climate of a dead society through an examination of their artifacts. For all primitive people things in their universe are always in some comprehensible order. Is it possible to recreate that order by viewing their concrete expressions? Malraux (OT n.p.) observed that "Implicit in these creations is an awareness of the universe—different than ours—

unconcerned with history—a union with the cosmos." Is it possible for cultural anthropologists to reconstruct social worlds from artifacts? Primitive "art" grew out of, and framed, a complex garden, which has grown over, or changed. With their "art" in our cultural world, can we see through it? Is the content, once private, now public or heuristic? How faithfully does the window translate the view? If the only way we have of seeing gardens is through windows, can we ever know things themselves? Perhaps iconic and aesthetic perceptions are the same. Modern nonobjective painting is all window. A hologram is like a window; the object is frozen in light; it is a faithful "reproduction" that mirrors the object, and in which the object can be observed three-dimensionally. Is iconic perception cognitive and aesthetic perception contemplative? Is it the reduction to cognition that poses the problem? Is it solved when all perception is recognized as feeling? Artistic images and symbols are aesthetic and equivocal; signs are linguistic and univocal; since images have such poor semiotic value, it is dangerous to reduce them to cognitive terms. When art works become cognitively generalized, their aesthetic specificity is lost, and they become poor vehicles of knowledge. An aesthetic object should not offer a reassuring vision, which interprets or identifies nature, but a naive vision, which surprises, shocks, fascinates or seduces the senses, which awakens desire and stirs the imagination, and which furnishes a feeling of the invisible.

2.1.4.1.5. *Painting As Metaphysics*

Classical art can enchant with its ontological enigma of pure appearing; contemporary art, especially in nonrepresentational forms, continues the adventure by presenting savage elements, showing nothing explicitly except the fact that it shows. Langan (LA 155) elaborates: "The attractiveness of contemporary painting . . . lies in its peculiar capacity to call attention to its system of equivalences precisely as gestures, manifesting clearly their insufficiency as well as their inevitability. It suggests the mysterious, necessary relation of the gestures to a truth which they can never say but only can imply by asserting themselves as deformations of it, albeit coherent and thus meaningful deformations." Both the viewer and the painter are forced to accept individualism, the limits and the contingency of that gesture as inherent in the nature of sense; men can only reveal Being in a series of partial truths. These limitations have saved it from language's "metaphysical hypocrisy." The metaphysical significance of modern painting is its intention to reveal the hidden genesis of the visible. Its intention is the same as that of philosophy: To return things to their rootedness in Being. As the body was found to contain an implicit metaphysics, the work of art does also.

And, Merleau-Ponty (MH 179) states: "metaphysics ... is not a body of detached ideas for which indirective justifications could be sought in the experimental realm. There are, in the flesh of contingency, a structure of the event and a virtue peculiar to the scenario." There is then a plurality of interpretations of a work of art which wield into a durable theme of historical life. The work changes itself and becomes what follows. The history of modern art has paralleled the history of modern philosophy. Furthermore, says Merleau-Ponty (MH 178): "The entire modern history of painting, with its efforts to detach itself from illusionism and to acquire its own dimensions, has a metaphysical significance."

Metaphysics is therefore no longer a philosophy of first principles, but one of being in the world; it is a philosophy of finitude, for it is only concerned with human experience, and not transcendence (of consciousness, God, or Being). Human meaning is the work of painting, truth occurs in a contingent event in an open system, historically requiring new synthesis (this is a human, process philosophy). It must deal with relationships in situations instead of abstracted derivatives (i.e., subjects and objects); language has to be grasped as a lived configuration from multiple cultural interactions. (Absolute relativity is avoided, since the private worlds of men are united in the world.) Painting, as the indirect voice of silence, is an incarnation of sound, on a continuum between silence and speech. The total movement explicates Being, according to Merleau-Ponty (MN 211): "We would see a relation if we understood that to paint, to sketch, is not to produce something from nothing, that the drawing, the touch of the brush, and the visible work are but the trace of a total movement of Speech, which goes into Being as a whole ..."

2.1.4.2. *Speaking*

> Who am I, who
> Speaks from the dust,
> Who looks from the clay?
>
> Who hears
> For the mute stone,
> For fragile water feels
> With finger and bone?
>
> Who for the forest breathes the evening,
> Sees for the rose,
> Who knows
> What the bird sings?

PAF

Who am I, who for the sun fears
The demon dark,
In order holds
Atom and chaos?
      Raine (R 90)

2.1.4.2.1. *From Silence*

Speech introduces an upheaval in pre-linguistic Being, a ferment of transformation that will give the operative signification; the ferment, praxis-thought, is the Being that perceives and speaks. Thus it is Being that speaks within us and not we who speak of it. Speaking is the reverse of the dialectic of perception between the world and the body; it is a dialectic between body and world. The silent knowing of the lived body becomes manifest in speech. In speaking a person constitutes a real possibility of Being that is sustained until more speaking alters the gestalt. The articulation of the gestalt cannot exceed the perception of the body subject. Individual speaking is perspectival. Since Being speaks within us others must also; thus the ontological dialectic is no longer a dichotomy. Indeed, for Merleau-Ponty (MN 80): "It is a four-term system: my being for me, my being for others, the for itself of another, and his being for me." The intentional history of an individual becomes a dialectic of being and other being in the act of speaking. He does not speak only of himself, of his own perspective, and for himself; he speaks for all.

Speech rises out of solitude, out of the silence that precedes all expression. Bachelard (BB 278) describes that silence: "and returning to the will to speak in its nascent state, in its first vocality, entirely virtual, blank . . . . Silent reason and mute declamation?? appear as the first factors of human becoming. Before all action man needs to utter himself to himself, in the silence of his being, that which he *wishes* to become; he needs to prove and to *sing* his own becoming *to himself*." The infant must learn to be with others, in silence, before learning to speak. And afterwards, the child is so totally engaged within language that his first word serves as a sentence; the part is a whole. It is whole if it is understood; speech is the bodily function most intimately linked with communal existence.

By learning to perceive, objects stand out against a ground, by learning to behave the objects are given meaning, and by learning to speak, aspects of the object (in world) are transformed into ideal meanings; ordering acts orders the world. Speech is learned through experience, and by speaking we make the silent world into a world of speech; meanings are transformed into significations, through which a person contacts the silent world. Thus the speaking world, through the mediation of language, contacts the silent world. The internal movement, which is the birth of speech, works from silence to speech, from ambiguity toward clarity. This movement is not from nonmeaning to meaning, but from the implicit to the explicit; ambiguity is pregnant with significance, which is born in speech. Silence surrounds speech as the field surrounds the figure; the speech is a selection from, and focus on, silence, and since it is the focus it is necessarily incomplete, and equally incapable of removing the silence. Only to silence, the unsaid, completeness latently belongs. The focus may be enlarged, with loss of re solution, as in poetic speech, or exceptionally refined, as in scientific speech; the focus is a ray of variable width in the world of silent meaning. Clarity itself is only relative to the indistinctness of silence.

2.1.4.2.2. *Beyond Language*

Since a sign has meaning only if it is profiled against other signs, its meaning is entirely restricted to language. Merleau-Ponty (MK 42) says: "Speech always comes into play against a background of speech; it is always only a fold in the immense fabric of language. To understand it, we do not have to consult some inner lexicon which gives us the thoughts covered up by the words or forms we are perceiving; we only have to lend itself to its life, to its movements of differentiation and articulation, and to its eloquent gestures. There is thus an opaqueness of language. Nowhere does it stop and leave a place for pure meaning; it is always limited only by more language, and meaning appears within it only set in a context of words." For every movement from silence to speech, there is a reverse side of that movement that remains implied; the ground of silence is always broader than figure of speech; speech is finite, but open and indeterminate at the same time. There is no thought which is a pure thought, completely independent of words as a means of being present to itself. Thought and speech anticipate and stimulate one another. Nor is speaking putting a word under each thought; nothing would ever be said this way. The thought that it would want to express and the thought it would form would make a wholly explicit language—thought would encounter only thought, meaning would obliterate the sign, and we would be silent in a dead language.

Language is a sum of significations, ranging from practical to abstract, and from technological to mystical. Language is the potential vehicle, with social significance, speech is the individual, actual activity, using that vehicle. Speaking is a continuous action, not a series of discrete ones. Merleau-Ponty (MI 45): "Speech does not choose the only one sign for one already defined signification, the way one searches for a hammer to drive in a nail or pincers to pull one out! It gropes around an intention to signify which has at its disposal no text to guide it, for it is just being written. And if we want to grasp speech in its most authentic operation in order to do it full justice, we must evoke all those words that could have come in its place that have been omitted; to feel the different way they would have impinged on and rattled the chain of language, to know at what point this particular speech was the only one possible."

Merleau-Ponty states that in acquired expressions there is a direct meaning which corresponds point by point to established words, exclusive of expressive silences. In speaking, however, where the meanings of expressions are in the process of being accomplished, there must be a lateral meaning which runs between words, and this is a way of shaking the linguistic apparatus in order to tear a new sound from it. Speech takes flight from language, and tears out "meanings from the undivided whole of the namable, as gestures do from the whole of the perceptible. Merleau-Ponty (MK 43) states that "Because meaning is the total movement of speech, our thought crawls along in language. Yet for the same reason, our thought moves through language as a gesture goes beyond the individual points of its passage." This living language is not a reproduction of things themselves, it gives perspectives on things which do not end in the language itself, which invite further investigation. Speaking issues from a matrix of perception to create the lived world, as it exists already named in sedimented speech. Silence indicates the limits of articulation, the word said is bound by silence, but speaking crosses the boundary. Speech is language in the process of becoming, an immanence in the silence around it; language is a presence of signs dependent on the absence of silence. The ground of silence which precedes speech, must also accompany it, for it to say anything. In habitual expressions there is a direct meaning corresponding to established words and phrases; but there the gaps of silence are obliterated. The tissue of speech must be woven with threads of silence; indeed speech is the dialectic of language and silence. Merleau-Ponty (MG 389) identifies it as a paradoxical operation: "Speech is therefore, that paradoxical operation through which, by using words of a given sense, and already available meanings, we try to follow up our intention which necessarily outstrips, modifies, and itself, in the last analysis, stabilizes the meanings of the words which translate it. Constituted language plays the same limited role in the work of expression as do colors in painting."

The paradox can be resolved partly due to the nature of language; although the "spoken word" is a depository for constituted meanings, the "speaking word" constitutes language while speaking—coming to know what is not known by speaking of it, for the first time. Speaking is a total signifying system that meaningfully relates the gesture and tone with the words and information. Speaking "explicates" the invisible according to Merleau-Ponty (MN n.p.): "As the sensible structure can be understood only through its relation to the body, to the flesh—the invisible structure can be understood only through its relation to logos, to speech. The invisible meaning is the inner framework of speech— The world of perception encroaches upon that of movement, which also is seen; and inversely movement has eyes. Likewise the world of ideas encroaches upon language (one thinks it), which inversely encroaches upon the ideas (one thinks because one speaks, because one writes)—" Thus, there is a secondary speech which renders a thought already acquired, and an originating speech, which brings it into existence. The speaking word translates silent Being into meaning, into world of speech; through a creative process speaking makes meaning exist in a new manner. Speech is even more complicated in its use of lateral significations, according to Merleau-Ponty (MK 76): "The transparency of spoken language, that fine clarity of word which is only sound and that meaning which is only meaning, the property which it apparently has of extracting the meaning of signs and isolating that meaning in its pure state . . . and its would-be power of recapitulating and enclosing a whole process of expression in a single act—are these not simply the highest point of a tacit and implicit accumulation of the same sort as that of painting?" Expression is the most closely heard in speech. Speaking is singing the world, as Stevens understood (UN 250):

> "That was her song, for she was the maker. The we,
> As we beheld her striding there alone,
> Knew that there never was a world for her
> Except the one she sang and, singing, made."

2.1.5. *Logical Universes*

Spencer Brown (1979) states that a universe comes into being when a space is severed or taken apart. The skin of an organism cuts off inside from outside, as does a circle from a plane. The act of severance is remembered as our first attempt to distinguish different things in a world where boundaries can be drawn anywhere we please. We define order by making boundaries based on perception of particles (wave size). The universe cannot be distinguished from how we act on it, according to Brown. All forms—universes—are possible, and any particular one is mutable; but the laws relating all forms are the same in any universe.

This sameness leads to mathematics, a reality independent of how the universe appears. He views descriptions as based on a primitive act rather than a logical value or form (so values are based on prior acts). This act is the most simple that can be performed. His is a nondualistic attempt to set foundations for mathematics; subject and object are interlocked. All distinctions are similar and primary; all indications are alike and named.

Spencer Brown recognized the importance of the act of distinction. He proposed a calculus of indications. This was in response to Russell's logical propositions, where the simple ground of logic was the notion of true and false applied to simple statements. The word logic is derived from the Greek logos, meaning to "put together" (cf. making, poesis). And this is the key to Brown's use of it. The basic building blocks of formal discussion were invariant patterns (forms) that were taken as initials for representation (as in Boolean algebra). Spencer Brown reformulated the fundamental question: What are the constituents of a logical proposition? Boolean algebra, he said, appears mysterious because accounts of their properties reveal nothing of mathematical interest about their arithmetic.

Mathematics, like art, can lead beyond ordinary existence and show something of the structure in which all creation hangs. Mathematics is a form of self-analysis, by a mixture of contemplation, symbolic representation, communion and communication, of what we already know. Perhaps we already have a direct awareness of mathematical form as archetypal through brain structures. Brown sees a hope of bringing together investigations of the inner structure of our knowledge of the universe, by mathematics, and the investigation of its outer structure. If perception can be learned through a study of the outside world, then a common boundary may be approached through either side.

Brown thinks that the concept of imaginary numbers can be extended to Boolean algebra; a valid argument can contain 4 classes of statement (not just 3): true, false, meaningless, and imaginary. There are implications for physics and philosophy. For instance, many statements about dragons or "rskdifys" are imaginary, not necessarily true or false. Unlike the physical universe, imaginary ones have different, almost opposite, characteristics, which derive from the limits of perception and the infinite regress of conscious self-reference. But logical universes, by virtue of human thought, lead back to the lived-field.

2.1.5.1. Properties of Logical Universes
A property is a quality that distinguishes a unique individual or pattern —it is a difference that makes a difference, according to Gregory

Bateson. Every concrete thing has properties. Every real thing possesses properties, which can be distinguished in several ways, for instance as intrinsic, or relational. An intrinsic property is one that a thing possesses regardless of relationships with other things; a population of wolves is an intrinsic property (although it can be affected by other things). The emigration of wolves, young males, is a relational property, that is, it occurs due to the relation to other things. Some properties can be known easily; others can be revealed by research. A list of known properties describes the state of the system with finite quantities. Properties include: Wholeness, Openness, Feedback, Complexity, Emergence, Adaptiveness, Hierarchical, Boundary, Lifetime, and Nonlinear. A qualitative description of properties describes qualities of the system. Quantitative descriptions measure quantitative variables. The state of a system, definite and objective, can be conceptualized with theories and models. Global systems have properties that no local systems have, such as an overall atmospheric temperature or global biogeochemical cycles.

A property is an attribute proper to a thing or characteristic quality common to all members of a class (by comparison, characteristics are qualities that distinguish unique individuals or patterns. Gregory Bateson calls them differences that make a difference.) The properties of a field are shaped by the historical operation of the field itself. This means that these properties are reflected in different levels of organization.

Mario Bunge distinguishes three kinds of collective properties: aggregate, structural, and global. Aggregate properties are often statistical, as in the average age of the wolf pack is 3.9 years. Structural properties can be possessed by individuals or groups on the basis of their relations to others, e.g., high-tail is the daughter of nick-ear. And global (or emergent) properties are possessed by wholes, regardless of components, as in "the territory of the pack is eighty thousand hectares."

Principles are fundamental rules or laws, based on the characteristics of objects or systems, that we can use to create images or models to meet stated objectives, that is, the goals towards which our actions are directed, such as a functional beautiful bicycle or a comfortable inspiring city park. Principles unify our images. Select principles are introduced briefly to show the depth and breadth of design.

The principles presented are derived from the typical characteristics of design objects. Characteristics are qualities that distinguish unique individuals, systems, or patterns—Gregory Bateson refers to characteristics as differences that make a difference. From these principles, standards for design activities can be established. Standards are models or examples of quality or value, established by authority or mutual consent, which can be repeated as procedures.

2.1.5.1.1. *Vagueness.*
According to C.S. Peirce (1955), logicians neglected the study of vagueness, not realizing the "important part it plays in mathematical thought." Vagueness is the antithetical analog of generality; generality is the indeterminate character of a sign; the human mind completes the determination. A sign is vague when determination is left to some other sign to complete (as in almanacs). The principle of contradiction does not apply to vagueness. Things are vague intrinsically. The order of nature is vague. Over five decades later, M. Black wrote an article on vagueness that became the inspiration for a general (fuzzy) set theory. Fuzziness is what Black called vagueness. As introduced by L. Zadeh, fuzzy set theory is a generalization of abstract set theory.

The theory of sets is a basic tool in mathematics. In fact, every branch of mathematics can be considered a study of sets of objects, as geometry is the study of sets of points. A collection of objects is called a set. But most classes of objects encountered in the physical world are not sharply defined. They do not have a precisely defined criterion of membership. As Peirce explained, they are vague. This is also the concept of fuzzy sets. A fuzzy set is a class with intermediate grades of membership. Grades of membership reflect an ordering of objects in a universe (set). Sets and fuzzy sets are contrasted in Figure 21511-1.

Figure 21511-1. Examples of Sets and Fuzzy Sets

Mountains are often prominent features of cosmologies. Let us take a universe of mountains and abstract a set of high mountains. Many mountains in Northern India will be in the set, but not all of them. Mountains in Greece, Borneo, and Australia will be in the set. But many mountains from India that are not in the set are actually higher than many of those from other places. The word high is not precise.

Set theory can describe nonhierarchal orders. Lorenz has example of cyclical pecking order, where B submits to A, A submits to C, but C submits to B. Not all the relationships can be realized at the same time. The relationships can be represented through interlocking sets, where hierarchical ordering breaks down (cf. Voter's paradox).

One generalization of the abstract set theory is fuzzy set theory. Because of generalization fuzzy set theory has a larger scope of applications to any real world processes involving incomplete or uncertain data. The notion of a fuzzy set is nonstatistical in nature.

Boolean logic is assumed to be two-valued. The binary approach is standard in Aristotelian logic. Based on symbolic logic and fuzzy sets, fuzzy logic can be a kind of many-valued logic that can address values other than truth and falsehood. The use of fuzzy sets can avoid fallacies in two-valued logic.

Fuzziness is not an intuitive concept; it is similar to vagueness, as distinguished from generality or ambiguity. The fuzziness refers to the lack of well-defined boundaries. Fuzzy set theory is used to describe the compartmentalization of ecosystem components (Bosserman and Ragade 1982); this approach allows greater diversity of behavior than deterministic or probabilistic methods. Equihua (1990) suggests that fuzzy clustering in vegetation classification may be more appropriate than classification into hard bounded groups. Community classification is equivalent to the concept of set partition. Ordinarily, division into subsets results in two or more mutually exclusive nonempty sets. In fuzzy set theory, according to Equihua, there must be overlap in the fuzzy subsets to be "truly" fuzzy.

Although species composition varies continuously (more or less) along environmental gradients, groups of species can always be recognized. The precise composition of a community of species is uncertain due to the vagueness of the concept and to stochastic processes at work. Fuzzy set theory can be used to address the concept of community as entities and the concept of species composition changing on a continuum.

Under Darwin's theory, for any population of entities to evolve it must have three properties: Multiplication (the one gives rise to many), variation (difference in entities that influence survival), and, heredity (like begets like). The cost of evolution by selection is so heavy that most populations are not optimally adapted to environment. Evolution can never be total adaptation; it requires destabilization. Environment provides destabilization regularly through weather and catastrophic processes.

Darwin noted that every species "includes the unknown element of a distinct act of creation." (OS, p. 30) Evolution becomes a dialectical concept, reflecting the problem of describing qualitative change (Hegel: wherever there is life the dialectic is at work)

2.1.5.1.2. *Uncertainty*

Quantum mechanics tries to resolve difficulties in measuring interference patterns. In the Young double-slit experiment, an electron appears to go through both slits in a screen at once; it interferes with itself. This is inexplicable in Newtonian mechanics, where the state of a particle is specified by a precise value of momentum and position. It is not a problem in a quantum mechanical description, where the state of a particle corresponds to a range of momentums and positions. In fact a clear picture of the two variables at the same time is inconsistent with quantum mechanics.

Momentum and position are related inversely to Planck's constant, the smallest bit of a field. Since both are larger than the constant, and since the measuring electron beam is larger than the constant, there is always a lack of definition. The act of measurement changes one of the variables. This is Heisenberg's Uncertainty Relation. The participator has an effect on everything.

2.1.5.1.3. *Inconsistency & Incompleteness*

After Gödel showed that the consistency of a mathematical system—which must be adequate to embrace a theory of whole numbers—cannot be established by logical principles, he introduced a corollary, the incompleteness theorem, which states that if any formal theory is consistent, then it is incomplete. If the system is completed, then it is inconsistent again. The enlarged system must also contain undecidable propositions.

Popper concludes that the very nature of science is to be incomplete. To be complete it would have to give an explanatory account of itself. For the nonreductionist it is incomplete anyway. Further, since all science uses arithmetic (or logic), Godel's incompleteness theory renders science incomplete. In exploring mathematical reasoning, Gödel came to his Incompleteness Theorem; paraphrased, it reads: All consistent axiomatic formulations of number theory include undecidable propositions. What Gödel showed was that provability is weaker than truth, in any system. Refer to the section on Self-reference for an application of the paradox. Add subsection on Inconsistency!!!

Bohr proposed the principle of complementarity as a solution to the completeness of physical theories. But complementary concepts exclude one another. For instance, light cannot be completely described as a particle or a wave, but the theories can be complementary. Complementary relations are different representations of the same reality. In psychology, the vase/profile paradox is a figure/ground complementarity. A subject sees a vase or two profiles, but not both.

Unfortunately, complementarity is not exhaustive, so it does not grant logical completeness. The vase/profile is also two curved lines (as unrecognized as vase or profile), and it is a whole figure on paper that can be reinterpreted.

2.1.5.1.4. *Difference*

After Plato the meaning of existence is to 'be a factor in agency' or 'to make a difference.' An experience is a calculus of differences, necessary for order. Bateson defines an idea as a difference or transform of difference. A difference cannot be localized in space; it is relational. To act is to be; to be is to act and be acted upon. Not synonyms but interdependent. The actualities of the universe are processes of experience.

Sameness is something common to all occasions in which two or more things are the same. Difference is something common to all occasions in which two or more things are different. Things are like and different than other things. Differentiation is transformation from a general and homogenous condition to a more heterogeneous condition.

Of all the principles of science, none is more compelling than simplicity. And no simplicity is more stark than the binary choice: yes or no; true or false. Pauli's two-valued concept of spin dominates particle physics. Complementarity is recognition of this binary nature. But simplicity invokes arbitrary limits (stopping points); further, quantum mechanics is external. Thus, Wheeler concluded that pregeometry can be nothing else but a calculus of propositions. The calculus of propositions is related to fuzzy set theory. Propositions imply others and make identities and equivalencies that may be vague.

The most basic difference is binary. C. Levi-Strauss (1962) argued that the logic of thinking was binary and digital, based on contrast. This mode accounts for the universal patterns of symbolic oppositions: left/right, male/female. The mode may be repeated; the pieces are rearranged endlessly. A primitive order may be created by binary distinctions. Genesis may describe the dawning of awareness; through elementary logical binary distinctions. Is the binary prelogical? A division by differences; light divided from dark, fish from sea, woman from man. This logic is flawed by the lack of reconciliation of opposites.

In information theory the effects are brought about by differences, not forces and energy exchange. A difference is the least change in territory that must show up on a map to be adequate. The cybernetic definition of information is a difference that makes a difference. This resembles the linguists definition of a phoneme, the minimal unit for conveying meaning. For cyberneticists and linguists, context is crucial for whether sound is phoneme or noise. Isolated facts are surrendered to model of relational structure of significance. The significance of the part is determined by the whole. Differentness is not a personal achievement, but a function of participation in a larger entity. Diversity is created by groups; individuals have similar behavioral programs and need group support.

2.1.5.2. Identity

No explanation for the identity of particles has been made. Identity is a mystery of physics, according to Wheeler. If there were no identity, there would be no differences and so no relationships. Without relationships, no things, no events, no universe. Objects precipitate out of relationships and are defined by them.

For the universe to show stability and persistence, different entities must have stability and persistence. Identity is that persistent quality. Identity serves nothing; it is. The relationship between identity and wholeness is a rhythm. G. Leonard identifies it as the silent pulse at heart of our experience that is always there. A system's identity can be described apart from its performance in interactions, but not isolated. The human perspective is related to the two domains. Paradoxically, each human has unique identity (as wave function) and is a holoid of universe. Intentionality is the vector of identity, which operates across mind/body/spirit. It creates transformations.

2.1.5.2.1. Self-Making

The basic unit of feeling, the raw material of science is a being, an individual. The individual is a changing process, not a thing. In a universe of energy, any individual is a pattern of activity within the flux, an organism at some level. Rocks are no less individual than trees. Rocks do not lie inert in their sameness, but thrust forward or gather power quietly. Out of living rock comes the water of the spirit. The activities of the organism are united into a single complex activity which is the organism itself. Substance and activity are one.

Unity, as distinguishability from the background (and other unities), is the sole necessary condition for existence in any domain. Ontology is the history of structural transformation of a unity. The ontology of a living system is the history of maintenance of its identity through continuous self-making (autopoiesis—F. Varela's term) in physical space. Component systems become subordinated necessarily to the constraints of the higher order unity. If the higher order system undergoes self-reproduction, a process begins in which the evolution of the pattern of organization of component systems is subordinated to evolution of pattern of organization of composite unity. Autonomy, self-law, entails control. Varela considers that autonomy and control do a continuous dance: one represents generation, internal regulation, self-assertion, definition from the inside; the other represents consumption, assertion of other identity, definition from the outside. Their interplay ranges from genetics to psychotherapy. Autonomy leads to reexamination of information; away from instruction to construction, from representation to the behavior of a being.

The body is a knot, a complicated integrity that processes materials from its surroundings in order to maintain itself. As a rope makes a knot visible, the body makes a pattern visible. It is a movement that maintains a topologically stable pattern. It is a vortex, but not the water. The thing, the pattern, is a cross-section cut through movement by our perception. The word thing is from Old English, object, event, action, meeting; it is related to 'to determine, to settle.' Reality comes from the Latin .res, meaning thing. L.L. Whyte sees incomplete patterns in nature trying to become complete; incomplete structures are unstable and disintegrate.

The body is a dialectic between a living thing and its environment— the interacting mass of cells, biological environs, social context. Whitehead regarded the principle of organism as a universal principle applicable to the entire field of existing reality. Everything that exists has its place in the order of nature; this order consists of actual entities organized into societies. Every existing thing resembles a living organism in the fact that its essence depends, not merely on components, but on the pattern in which they are composed and the whole of which they are part.

An individual has some relation with everything throughout time in the universe. Any entity incorporates into itself in some sense all other entities in the universe. Every perspective and every occurrence is unique. There is no whole system without an interconnection of its parts; and there is no whole system without an environment. This is why universe is a special limiting case of a system. The universe cannot be described any more than being; only beings can be described, although the universe or being can be defined as the sum of all beings.

2.1.5.2.2. Self-Organization
Von Bertalanffy called life a system of self-organization, a developmental unfolding at progressively higher levels of differentiation and organized complexity. Bohm wants to extend the notion of hierarchical order to that of self-regulating process. This would result in a hierarchies of hierarchies, with a vast implicit order. For regulation,

higher levels abstract information about the order of functioning; higher levels direct lower; this is a necessary process. Vertical movement regulates horizontal.

In living systems autopoesis and reproduction are directly coupled; they are self-reproductive. Ordered wholes also reorganize their fixed forces. This is Ashby's principle of self-organization. A natural system goes from a large number of states to a smaller, in a kind of selection. The system evolves to maximum resistance to change. The system drives to a stationary nonequilibrium state. An adaptively reorganized system is not necessarily more stable; adaptation is not identical or synonymous with structural stability. An adapted system is optimally resistant to the forces that elicited self-organization. This is the normalization process.

Large group of neurons lead to the phenomenon of self-organization of information. Pragmatic information has a new element of gestalt, which emerges at several levels. It produces a gestalt of life. Self-organization is an emerging paradigm of science, according to Jantsch, emphasizing macroscopic coordination processes at many levels, in which nonlinear processes and nonequilibrium conditions play a significant role. Self-organization is precipitated by fluctuations, resulting in dissipative structures. In a dissipative structure self-organizing matter builds and .maintains order without any anti-entropic force (elan vital). Jantsch states that limits to growth are overcome by evolution of dynamic structure; they appear as widened limits. Prigogine and Jantsch seem to use just one interpretation of order, for whirlpools and camels. A cosmology is built on this principle. A very unadaptive cosmology. Order cannot be understood unless in context. Processes have more than one structure available for unfolding. Dissipative structure are just chemical and biochemical structures within a general theory of ektropy. A dissipative structure is really a chremorph, or fated shape (yet to be defined).

2.1.5.2.2.3. Self-Reference
Subjective and objective realities are self-excited systems, and are brought into being by self-reference. They create each other according to Wheeler. His self-reference cosmology created a dichotomy of mind and universe; the snakes eats its tail. Could there be any other reference, to not-self? A Klein bottle might be a more appropriate model. The tongue cannot taste itself, the mind cannot know itself and the system cannot model itself—Bateson argued that a television screen cannot pass on information as to how it is processing information without a larger screen, ad infinitum. But reflexivity might work with human and computer programs. The brain must shut out the whole if it is to process

the bits. But the whole is modeled in some sense. Karl Pribram and Michael Arbib have modeled memory as a hologram. In a sense then, the whole can always be constructed from a part, although not with fine resolution. Self-reference is the basis for all reference. The self expands through itself into other beings.

Self-reference mechanisms have to do with pervasive circularities, like a snake eating its own tail. This problem of self-reference was attacked by D. Hofstader, also, who cited Epimenides' paradox ("All Cretans are liars") as an example of a one-step strange loop. The strange loop occurs whenever, by moving up or downwards through levels of a hierarchical system, one finds oneself back at start (this can be related to voter's paradox and solved with set theory—cf. holarchy).

Mathematical logic is a strange loop, as Gödel discovered. He showed that all formal languages cannot refer to themselves because they are closed. Russell and Whitehead noted that things in a class and the class itself are different levels of logical type. A class cannot be a member of itself. A logical statement making a metastatement about itself is meaningless (logically unresolvable). Meaninglessness is limited to two forms: self-confirmation (tautology) and self-renunciation (paradox). This is why reference to the universe is so paradoxical. At one end particles determine the nature of the universe; at the other, the entire universe determines the nature of particles. Similar problems arise in the described systems of gene/species, organism/environment, individual/culture. These problems can only be "solved" by considering the next emergent level of complexity. The metastatement can only be made because natural languages are characterized by openness. Meaninglessness is used to break the closure, to initiate new levels.

2.1.5.3. Matrix Complementarity
Logic Different cultures have possessed different logical structures. The three following logics are good examples: Aristotelian deductive, Chinese complementarity, and, Mandenka heterogeneity (after Camara 1975). M. Maruyama (MY) distinguishes between the old logic and the emerging logic in Table 2153-1.

Traditional	Emerging
hierarchical	interactionist
nonreciprocal causality	reciprocal
uniform	heterogeneous
competitive	symbiotic
classificational	relational
quantitative	qualitative

Table 2153-1. An Emerging Logic (after Maruyama)

Of course, this is all very good, but neither side can dominate without sad consequences. If all plants were symbiotic and none were competitive, we would have no trees or flowers. But evolution or the growth of complexity can only be explained with reciprocal causality, without which the processes must be attributed to finality. Deviation-amplifying reciprocal causal processes increase and maintain differentiation and complexity.

A new logic should also be distinguished by contextualism as opposed to complementarity. Opposites have been joined in the dialectic and reconciled in complementarity, but it can be seen that stars, nets and fields are more comprehensive yet.

Dialectic In the classical Hegelian paradigm, duality is tied to idea of polarity; a clash of opposites. Symmetry is basic to this duality; both poles are on the same level. This is a classical Aristotelian negation: A or not-A. Hegel referred to his pairs as contradictions, contraries of the same logical type engaged in win or lose clashes. In Hegelian dialectics, dual interactions are like zero-sum games: one side always loses. For instance, many philosophers reduce matter to spirit or spirit to matter.

The dialectic method of question and answer was considered the ideal method of philosophical analysis. Its purpose was to discover truth, in the form of a definition, and to educate others in ways of discovering truth for themselves. It is a method of division and collection. The participants may be reduced to silence on occasion, but that is sometimes necessary; one must not assent to a proposition unless one believes it true. Plato gave the dialectic formal and metaphysical significance. He compared the dialectic to weaving; it combined the warp and the woof in a fabric.

A dialectic assumes that environmental and behavioral phenomena have three properties: They involve oppositional processes (open/close, individual/community, public/private); the opposites function as a unity, giving meaning to each other; and, the opposites are in an ever-changing relation.

Even Smuts and Laszlo place holism and reduction in polar opposition. Varela sees this as evidence of the historical split in schools. Both attitudes are complementary. For a fuller explanation refer to the section on Holons.

2.1.5.3.1. *Complementarity*
There is a reciprocal relation, implied by the uncertainty principle, between the sharpness of definition of two orders of motion—particle and wave. Wave and particle are both needed to define a full description, but contradict each other when both completely defined. This means

that ideas of completeness are wrong; light can never be fully a particle or wave; the particle must be a discontinuity of the wave pattern. In quantum theory, the contradiction is avoided with the assumption of the inherent vagueness of both orders. Bohr assumed that the vagueness was a universal principle—complementarity. But was it a principle of measurement and perception or of being? Is there a spectrum of new kinds of order between particle and wave motion?

Prigogine defines complementarity as 'the world is richer than it is possible to express in any single language.' Uncertainty could be understood as a complementarity between time and change, between being and becoming. Opposites are complementary in process thinking. But that too is an artifact of our binary outlook. Complementarity is identification, the naming of differences of extremes of a parameter (order-disorder). It is applied to interactional sequences in which actions of poles are different but mutually fitted (e.g., dominance-submission).

2.1.5.3.2. *Modes*
When different modes of description appear as opposites, it is more satisfactory to consider them complementary instead. This Varela (1976) says is necessary with tree/net duality and recursion/behavior duality. Duality leads to the philosophical idea of trinity (cf. Peirce), since the poles are related yet remain distinct; they are not one or two, but really three. Varela offers the heuristic star, where the star is equivalent to the whole process.

$$* = \text{it/process leading to it}$$

Varela proposes that dualisms or dialectical contradictions such as mind/body or whole/part or being/becoming should be conceived of as stars, that consist of an it/becoming-it process. Both sides of the slash must be considered, and the process leading to it. Varela borrows Bateson's concept of minds jointly defined as conversational pattern (left of slash) and bodies as participants in pattern (right). Consider both sides of the slash. The slash is a compact indication of transition between states:

$$* = \text{whole/parts constituting whole}$$

In general, any autonomous situation is on the left of slash, and the corresponding process is on other side (Refer to Figure 21532-1 and read left to right).

being/becoming	space/time
net/tree	mass/energy
natural/cultural	simultaneous/sequential
synchrony/diachrony	analog/digital
speech/language	environment/system
whole/parts	matrix/hierarchy
symbolic/operational	

Figure 21532-1. Holons and Process (after Varela)

The relationship of nets/trees is
* = network/trees constituting network

But that is incomplete; the network is the process that constitutes the trees. The duality is connected with processes in both directions. Varela sees the totality as emerging from part-by-part approximation of the trees (process leading to net). But sometimes the whole determines the parts. Mostly, the process mutually arises. Complementary elements mutually specify each other; so, in a sense there is no more duality.

Even Varela states that in natural systems, there is no real opposition, except where we put our values. Yet, the human brain, encultured, perceives primal dualities. The predator/prey pair are not excluding opposites, but both generating a whole unity, an autonomous domain where there is complementarity, stabilization and survival values for both.
* = ecosystem/species interaction

For every apparent set of opposites there is a star that is the left hand of another equation.

The star is an ancient alchemical symbol. Man reflects the macrocosm in a microscosm. The two sliding triangles (remember Pythagoras) represent Hermes Trismegistus aphorism: As above, so below. Varela rotates them (as in Figure 21532-2).

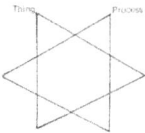

Figure 21532-2. Rotated Triangles (after Varela)

By using two intersecting triangles in the shape of star, as two levels of logical type, they are noncontradictory and mutually-specifying, manifesting restrained complementarity. The star of Varela differs from dualism and Hegel's dialectics. There is no Hegelian synthesis because there is nothing new, only a more direct appraisal of how things are put together. This view of complementarity is a departure from the classical way of dialectics. Dualities are represented by imbrication of levels, where one term emerges from the other. Their basic form is asymmetry; both terms extend across levels. This dialectic is self-referential: it/becoming-it. The tree is rebalanced by constraints of the network.

The net is prior in relation, however. This explains problem of STEM field much better, where there is network of STEM, from which Space-Time and Mass/Energy can be extracted. The network/tree duality can represent recursion/behavior duality by retaining interest in the connectivity of a system only. The nodes in tree or net represent elements in a system. Their links suggest interactions or interconnections. The reciprocal connectivity of a net suggests coordination; a tree structure suggests the sequential subordination of a system's parts. A mathematical definition of trees and nets: Let there be a set {v . . . .vn} of nodes (components), which are interconnected by a set E={ei . . . eu} of edges (processes). A network is a directed graph. Trees and nets could both be derived from a matrix of fuzzy sets. And sets could increase without cost to trees or complements.

But the image of the star is not quite comprehensive enough. The sides of a star are not inversely related. The sides are directly related; as one side increases, the other side increases. The relationship of sides cannot be described as conflict only. For example,

* = whole/part

is not complete. There are parts in wholes, in motion, in context. Similarly, for good/evil, good and evil resides in the knowledge of human actions in cultures in place.

2.1.5.3.3. *Triadism*

The links between elements in a net can be more than dualistic. Most cosmologies are limited to mythical dualisms. The Trobriand world view, like many, seems to contain dualistic elements: above/below, light/dark. But dualistic assumptions are almost always made. Perhaps because of the dominance of one sphere of the human brain. Things might be different if triadic logic were applied. For instance, the marriage/nonmarriage duality might be expanded to include ritual sexual activity during the Milamila festival or bachelor friendships. Levi-Strauss argues that all myths conformed to a small number of structures. Most myths have a built-in binary opposition. He cites the Zuni origin myth, that has life and death in opposition. He also contended that the oppositions were attempted to be resolved with an ambivalent mediating term; in the Zuni, this term was hunting, which was life producing and death producing. Levi-Strauss reasons that the human mind thought in oppositions, that were reflected in myths, and attempted to resolve them. Every attempt to resolve the contradictions of the world resulted in the form of a triad, or trinity.

C.S. Peirce stated that it was impossible to resolve everything in thought to two elements; a third element was often needed, which he called thirdness. Triadic relation is inexpressible through the dyadic alone (Peirce, Selected Writings, p.91). Since meaning is a triadic relation, every triadic relation involves meaning. Furthermore, according to Peirce, every tetradic, pentadic or greater relation can be reduced to compound of triadic relations. For Peirce, logical terms were divided into three classes only. When the third was introduced, it involved the conception of bringing objects into relation. He reduced all transactions to triads. But conception is independent of number.

Predicate logic can be used to explain dyadic and triadic relations, or larger. 'John is taller than George' is dyadic. 'Mary is between Carol and Lee' is triadic, as is 'Mary is the middle child of Jon and Martha.' But 'Mary, Carol and Lee are children of Rex and Susan' is pentadic.

2.1.5.3.4. *Conversational Field*

Since there are always any number of relations in a situation, the use of dyads and triads can become complex. The metaphor becomes unwieldy. Therefore, the idea of a conversation will be extended. For Gordon Pask, a theory of conversation is a theory of participants in conversation; all events are subjective. Conversation creates a domain, which is the appropriate frame of reference. The domain is the environment of conversation theory. The conversation is a minimal situation for observing the psychological events of which the participants are conscious. Understanding between participants is pivotal. The theory of conversations is relativistic and reflective.

Varela uses conversation as a paradigm for interactions among autonomous systems. Conversation is direct. Each side has a perspective and this is the heart of the process. When conversation is considered as a totality, there is no distinction about what is contributed by whom. The process is a coherent event shared by the participants, not a simple information exchange. Both Pask and Varela apply their ideas to human systems. But there is no reason why it could not apply to any interaction between beings.

As the science of physics has realized, in its three body problem, the calculations necessary to solve a problem increase logarithmically when the number of bodies is multiplied. In biology, the phenotype and organism generate unpredictability. Neither the organism or environment knows what the other will do. Species interaction achieving a stable ecosystem can be thought of as a biological paradigm for a conversational domain, the direction of which is unpredictable. Evolution is then the changing theme of the conversation between species and environment. Evolution may be interpreted as the development of new channels for communication.

One paradigm that would suit the needs of ecology is that of personal communication: mind reaching to mind, intention to intention. Communication is presentation of one's self, of one's life; that may evoke correspondence in others (cf. entrainment). The activities of two communicators combine to make the universe of the observer more ordered and redundant. The nature of meaning depends on the frame of the observer. Ecologists must envisage the notion that nature speaks to us (perhaps using information theory). Anthropomorphic ecology can recapture the experience of personality in nature (cf. the pathetic fallacy, which derided the use of human terms to describe natural phenomena).

Four, five or more person relations are not reducible to triadic relations, as argued by Peirce. The upper limit for measurable relations is probably about seven (plus or minus two). George Miller found that seven was a magic number in human psychology; it represented the maximum number of items that a subject could reliably remember, as well as other variables. Possibly it applies to the number of subjects having an intelligent conversation as well.

Given the indeterminacy of relations between subjects, a theory of conversation is justified. Conversation replaces the idea of duality and triadicity. The word conversation is derived from the French meaning "to live with," from the Latin, meaning "to turn with." Since all things are in some sense subjective and unique, there is further justification for the paradigm.

. . . language realizes, by breaking the silence, what the silence wished and did not obtain. Silence continues to envelop language; the silence of the absolute language, of the thinging language. But for these customary developments on the dialectical relation to not be unhappy consciousness, they must issue in a theory of the savage mind, which is the mind of praxis . . . . The problem is to grasp *what*, across the successive and simultaneous community of speaking subjects, *wishes*, *speaks*, and finally *thinks*.
    Merleau-Ponty (MN 176)

2.2. *Love of Knowing: Philosophy*

Philosophy is a theory of the savage mind; but what is its primary task? What are its limits? Is it a theoretical science or a productive art? Wittgenstein (WL 126) says that "Philosophy simply puts everything before us, and neither explains nor deduces anything. —Since everything lies open to view there is nothing to explain. For what is hidden, for example, is of no interest to us." While Merleau-Ponty avers that philosophy assigns itself the task of formulating the experience of the world, of showing a contact with the world which precedes all thought about the world (true, it does not explain the world, or discover its conditions of possibility), its primary task is to provide insight into what is hidden—to excavate it and place it in the open. Merleau-Ponty (MN 170) notices that: "Between the Lebenswelt as universal Being and philosophy as a furthermost product of the world, there is no rivalry or antinomy: it is philosophy that discloses it."

If philosophy is like a small retriever that runs across the room and brings back a bone to put before our feet, it would not be necessary to study Merleau-Ponty further; but to continue the cynical analogy, what if that same dog ran outside and dug up a bone? Was it really hidden? Is there anything which is absolutely hidden, to which nothing in the open even points? If philosophy is to contact Being, which precedes all thought, how can it do so if it is the utmost product of Being? How will it formulate the experience of the world, what tools will it use?

2.2.1. *Through the Body*

The body is the source of experience; but, is a philosophy based on it reduced to physiology? Merleau-Ponty (MJ 28) thinks not: "Man is metaphysical in his very being, in his loves, in his hates, in his individual and collective history. And metaphysics is no longer the occupation of a few hours each month, as Descartes said: it is present, as Pascal thought, in the heart's slightest movement." The body is the same flesh as the world; it is rooted in Being; as philosophy is embedded in it, it is the basis of all metaphysics. The body is a part of nature, it makes the objects of nature possible, it is the condition for their meaning. Philosophy inquires into the possibility of the body, and the philosopher is *one* access to what underlies the world (Being). Being provides a common ground for experiences for people. Thus, there is a circularity of the experience of other people and the thing they experience; for the objective thing is based on the experiences of others, which is itself based in the experience of the body, which is itself a thing for others. Likewise, is there a circularity between people and nature; nature is the whole of the world which encompasses people, who encompass nature as an object they constitute in common.

Nature and society, the body and soul exist in a nexial network of reciprocal relations. Perception reveals a world with coherence and connectivity, before philosophy. The subject's presence to himself is bound up with his presence in the world; sight fulfills itself in the thing seen, it takes a hold upon itself, but in an ambiguous and obscure way, since it escapes from itself into the thing seen. The lived-body subject perceives his own interior simultaneously with his exterior; this separation is the chiasm (it is a gestalt); the separation as described by Merleau-Ponty is that between someone who goes into the world and who, from the exterior, seems to remain his own dream. The chiasm is also a reversibility, with its ground in the dialectic of separation that is perception and expression, immanence and transcendence. By communicating with the world, the person communicates with himself. He thinks, but the thought separates itself from experience. Thought, the horizon of invisibility, takes place in the separation (chiasm) of words, in the separation of the self from others and of language from itself. Merleau-Ponty (MN 87) considers that "the thought, precisely as thought, can no longer flatter itself that it conveys all the lived experience: It retains everything, save its destiny and its weight . . . . Between the thought or fixation of essences, which is the aerial view, and life, which is inherence in the world or vision, a divergence reappears, which forbids the thought to project itself in advance in the experience and invites it to recommence the description from closer up." Can thought recommence, in philosophy? Consciousness must correct its own initial excess of subjectivity, in order to recover the totality observed by the selection; this is the task of philosophy.

2.2.2. Towards Being

The secret of Being is in an integrity behind us; the chiasm, as separation, without which experience of a thing, or of the past, could not exist, is an openness upon the thing itself, to the past itself (and therefore must enter into their definition). The chiasm is a strange distance - recalling spans the distance to the past, but the thing, is not given as it was in its own time, but as ready to be seen, pregnant with all the visions one can have of it. When one conveys Being with this distance, it loses its density, but when one selects one being closely, the whole is lost. Is Being open to philosophy? Philosophy, with Being as its "object," requires the direction of attention toward a realm of reality which cannot be directly apprehended. Philosophy must view that which withdraws from view; the a priori claims of some philosophies, as to the mathematical or logical nature of philosophy, must be suspended. Philosophy is radical reflection on lives in situations in Being. If it finds Being co-apparent, indirectly accessible and obscure, it must try somehow to say that which can hardly be said. Merleau-Ponty (MN 222) relates that "If Being is hidden, this is itself a characteristic of Being, and no disclosure will make us comprehend it. A lost immediate, arduous to restore, will, if we do restore it, bear within itself the sediment of the critical procedures through which we will have found it anew; it will therefore not be the immediate. If it is to be the immediate, if it is to retain no trace of the operations through which we approach it, if it is Being itself, this means that there is no route from us to it and that it is inaccessible by principle." Is Being inaccessible, or is there a way for the operation of philosophy to restore it without altering it? It could never be done directly, without positing Being. Perhaps it could reach Being indirectly. But philosophy is not cognition of brute Being, since what it would take from it, as a condition of knowing it, would be no cognition at all. It must be a speaking which bears witness to Being and its concealment, a speaking addressed to silence such that silence may be manifest as itself. Speech must preserve silence. Philosophy must be the reconversions of silence and speech into one another, as Merleau-Ponty has written.

In constructing a philosophy of the lived-in-world, the construction makes us rediscover the world of silence. Silence, as the nonthematized lived-in-world, can sometimes be left nonthematized by the statements which describe it, which themselves will become sedimented in the lived-in-world after being comprehended. Philosophy must be involved in silent Being in a silent manner - silent existence continues even when spoken of. Silent Being is the perceived world. Furthermore, Merleau-Ponty (MN 170) says: "this perceptual work is at bottom Being in Heidegger's sense, which is more than all painting, than all speech, than every "attitude," and which, apprehended by philosophy in its universality, appears as containing everything that will ever be said, and yet leaving us to create it. (Proust)" It is the formal account (*logos eidiathetos*) which calls for the spoken account (*logos prophorikos*). The silent world is pre-objective, but philosophy, which is concerned with the pre-objective Being, could transform it into an object by speaking about it. Philosophy has the power to go beyond itself and still preserve silence; indeed, speech makes us aware of silence. Paradoxically, the philosopher can contact the silent world through mediation of language. But speaking breaks the silence, so it is impossible to say what the silent world is; although philosophical speech can give access to it, it is inadequate to say it. Philosophy is not an awakening of consciousness;

its manner of questioning should not be cognitive, nor should it expect an answer or solution. From the perceived world it obtains confirmation of its astonishment. Philosophy puts its question to what does not speak. Merleau-Ponty (MN 102) declares that: "It asks of our experience of the world what the world is before it is a thing one speaks of and which is taken for granted, before it has been reduced to a set of manageable, disposable significations; it directs this question to our mite life, it addresses itself to that compound of the world and of ourselves that precedes reflection. . . . But in addition, what it finds in thus returning to the sources, it says."

2.2.3. *With Language*

From silence, language lays down an horizon of invisibility, and installs itself in that horizon as a for-having of the namable. It names the mute things, and tries to speak them without isolating them in an artificial meaning. As Merleau-Ponty (MN 4) premonishes: "But philosophy is not a lexicon, it is not concerned with "word meanings," it does not seek a verbal substitute for the world we see, it does not transform it into something said, it does not install itself in the order of the said or of the written as does the logician in the proposition, the poet in the word, or the musician in the music. It is the things themselves, from the depth of their silence, that it wishes to bring to expression." If the philosopher hopes to reveal the source and origin of all meaning, must not he speak of it? And if so, then the source is transformed into an ideal object. Philosophy does transform Being into something said, into a realm of ideal objects; but it must, somehow, save the things themselves. Although philosophy recognizes the existence of ideal significations, its primary task is not defining them. If the philosopher considers only the analysis of idealizations he will miss the basic reality. Language grants a clarity to things which the silent world does not. Philosophical language brings some clarity to Being, and makes communication between philosophers possible, even though they speak of what they do not know as well. The ideal significations are expressions of preceding meanings situated on perceptive ground. The world of science is built on the world as directly experienced. Philosophy is a radical examination of our belongingness to the world. But philosophy cannot forget what science says about the same world; it cannot ignore mathematics, or thermodynamics, for instance; rather, it hopes to remind science of its origins. The scientist may forget the source of ideal meanings (being twice removed) but the philosopher may not.

Being is the object of philosophy, but since we are the access to

Being, it cannot be represented abstractly. Philosophical speech is more adequate than the verbal expression of artistic ideas, but not as successful as the language of science, in using abstractions; the silent voices in art seem to be a more adequate approach to Being, however. Philosophy must not use clear idealizations to describe Being; it must use words more appropriate. But even these words, whatever they are, are ideal significations, and as such, cannot name all the aspects of Being. Being exceeds idealization as visible reality exceeds seeing. The mind's eye depends on the body's eye; for both seeing, man belongs to the world. The meaning (*sens*) is the source of signification. Being cannot be reduced to verbal significations, so the philosopher will never capture his object, which is more than object, with idealizations; Being can never be found completely. Philosophy tries to present an idea of Being. Ideas are embodied in language, and are dependent on whatever meandering old streets are taken. Through the routes of language, philosophy tries to create an ideal world in which the experience of savage Being may be relived. Still, the problem looms, whether, in its inquiry into the lateral aspects of reality, the use of language by philosophy is really adequate to its intended task.

2.2.3.1. Hyperreflection
If philosophy uses a ready-made language, a secondary operation of translation, then the technical relation between a sound or a meaning which are joined by convention) is ideally isolable; the language is artificial. Merleau-Ponty (MN 126) continues: "But if, on the contrary, we consider the speaking word . . . the folding over within him of the visible and the lived experience upon language, and of language upon the visible and the lived experience, the exchanges between the articulations of his mute language and those of speech, finally that operative language which has no need to be translated into significations and thoughts, that language-thing which counts as an arm, as action, as offenses and as seduction because it brings to the surface all the deep rooted relations of the lived experience wherein, it takes form, and which is the language of life and of action but also that of literature and of poetry - then this logos is an absolutely universal theme, it is the theme of philosophy. Philosophy itself is language, rests on language; but this does not disqualify it from speaking of language, nor from speaking of the pre-language and of the mute world which doubles them: on the contrary, philosophy is an operative language, that language that can be known only from within, through exercise, is open upon the things, called forth by the voices of silence, and continues an effort of articulation which is the Being of every being." By being

an operative language, philosophy has an advantage in its access to Being. In its involvement with Being, philosophy is free to entertain possibilities, but it is limited by a particular vantage in the world; language allows further access to the world, an increase in freedom, as it multiplies the vantages. Philosophy must become conscious of the manner in which it uses language; it must become conscious of itself. Merleau-Ponty (MN n.p.) explains that "the definition of philosophy would involve an elucidation of philosophical expression itself (therefore a becoming conscious of the procedure used in what precedes "naively," as though philosophy confined itself to reflecting what is) as the science of pre-science, as the expression of what is before expression *and sustains it from behind—*"

Coming before expression is thought, before thought is the body, before the body is life, before life is nature—the analysis of these automatically progresses to the world, and then to savage Being, the source of immediate actuality. Merleau-Ponty (MN 123) describes the relationship of philosophy: "Coming after the world, after nature, after life, after thought, and finding them constituted before it, philosophy indeed questions this antecedent being and questions itself concerning its own relationship to it. It is a return upon itself and upon all things but not a return to an immediate—which recedes in the measure that philosophy wishes to approach it and fuse into it." How can reflection establish the originality of that whose originality consists in escaping the grip of reflection? How can philosophical thought exhibit beginnings as beginnings if the very nature of beginnings requires thought to be distant?

A philosophy of reflection fails to take into account its natal bond with the world, that already established intrinsically opaque link to things. Philosophy must be a type of reflection that recognizes that the link is indissoluble, and reflection is sustained by it. Its purpose is to bring to expression our mute contact with things themselves. Is there any expression which can take itself into account? A reflection which did so would have to incorporate the recognition of its own blind spot. Reflection maintains the permanence of the perceived, but reflection itself is an act of recovery which necessarily rests on a more fundamental operation, a hyper-reflection. Merleau-Ponty (MN 38) continues: "we are catching sight of the necessity of another operation besides the conversion to reflection, more fundamental than it, of a sort of *hyper-reflection (sur-reflection)* that would also take itself and the changes it introduces into the spectacle into account. It accordingly would not lose sight of the brute thing and the brute perception." Hyper-reflection sets itself the task of thinking about savage Being, of reflecting on the transcendence of the world as transcendence. With a difficult effort, it uses the significations of words to express, beyond themselves, our mute contact with things, when they are not yet things said. It suspends its faith in the world, to see the world, and ask it, what in its silence it means to say. Hyper-reflection structures itself around the indirect expression of Being. Through philosophical interrogation language can live in rapport within the folds of the flesh of the world. Philosophy must use language reflexively; in not knowing its way about, philosophy must travel through the old town as well as regular straight streets. The philosopher's self-expression develops from involvement in Being, therefore self-expression is the expression of Being; philosophical expression is a particular kind since it consists in the return to Being as the source of all expression, and awareness of its return. As Merleau-Ponty says, philosophy is perceptual faith questioning itself about itself, through the medium of language, that is, through itself.

2.2.3.2. The Birth of Wild Meaning

Language is the only approach to Being, for philosophy. But philosophy cannot capture savage Being with a set of well-defined significations and univocal statements, since this would take from it the depth and distance essential to it. The distance of thought from the beginnings must be preserved; but how will philosophical thought exhibit the beginnings as beginnings, then? Genuine philosophy occurs only with the contact of Being and its expression—which cannot, of course, admit too much clarity. If expressions of the past are used, they must be reborn. The philosopher must contact the silent world himself, making light come to life again, even if it already exists; for if it exists, it must be renewed. Although individuals are the access to Being, it must be questioned, and questions must be actualized in expression. The silent world is the source of philosophical expression; but since it is accessible only by expression, expression must question itself; the expression of the silent world must correct past expression of the silent world, continually. Philosophy is a cultural creation which cannot exist without the mediation of language, but whose source is savage Being. Philosophy is a construction, but it avoids an impossible paradox because of the power of language to transcend its fixed significations, and to laterally express an ontogenesis of which it is a part. The philosopher must select his words, as Merleau-Ponty (MN 102-103) says: "The words most charged with philosophy are … those that most energetically open upon Being, because they more closely convey the life of the whole and make our habitual evidence vibrate until they disjoin. Hence it is a question whether philosophy as reconquest of brute or wild being can be accomplished by the resources of the eloquent language, or whether it would not be necessary for philosophy to use language in a way that takes from it its power of immediate or direct signification in order to equal it with what it wishes all the same to say."

Those words which open on Being, must come from a primary expression, which creates new thoughts, not just rearrange established ones. Philosophy is more, says Merleau-Ponty (MN 197): "Philosophy, precisely as Being speaking with us, expression of the mute experience by itself, is creation. A creation that is at the same time a reintegration of Being ..." It is not a creation in the sense of a common-place construction, it is a construction that seeks to surpass itself as pure construction, to find its origin again. Philosophy is creation in a radical sense, an adequation, which is the only way to obtain an adequation. Through its creative expression philosophy wants to reveal silent Being; it forms new expressions as a tool for approaching Being. It produces new perspectives, like art.

2.2.4. Art & Philosophy

Should philosophy become art? Is art more adequate for contacting Being? Painting, with its privilege as the most obvious expression of the order of the visible world, seems more appropriate than music or literature for contacting silent Being; literature is bound in its significations, unaware of itself, and music reveals only nebulous movements in Being. Painting also expresses Being in a silent and creative manner; it exhibits the "inspiration" and "expiration" of Being. A painting is a contraction of the visible world, a world in itself which can express the essence of the world. Philosophy shares many of the important characteristics of painting. As set forth by Merleau-Ponty's (MN 199) point of view: "a philosophy, like a work of art, is an object that can arouse more thoughts than those that are "contained" in it (can one enumerate them? Can one count up a language?), retains a meaning outside of its historical context, even has meaning only outside of that context." Both the work of art and philosophy act as a matrix of ideas, expressing many possibilities at once, and pointing to meanings beyond their context.

Also, they both can create terms for new perspectives, and blend them into a whole new Being. Merleau-Ponty (MN 199) elaborates: "This considerably deepens Souriau's view on philosophy as supreme art: for art and philosophy together are precisely not arbitrary fabrications in the universe of the "spiritual" (of "culture"), but contact with Being precisely as creations. Being is *what requires creation of us* for us to experience it." Creative activity is the only way we become aware of being. Art also contacts Being, then, but only philosophy is aware of contacting it; it is not essential for art. And Being is the connection between different works of art and different philosophies, as well as between art and philosophy. Merleau-Ponty (MJ 59) concludes: "Therefore, if philosophy is in harmony with the cinema, if thought and technical effort are heading in the same direction, it is because the philosopher and the movie maker share a certain way of being, a certain view of the world which belongs to a generation. It offers us yet another chance to confirm that modes of thought correspond to technical methods and that, to use Goethe's phrase, 'What is inside is also outside.'"

Philosophy, however, owns an even greater privilege than painting (or cinema): painting is mute thinking, and never attains the level of verbal expression; it is not reversible enough to paint about paintings. Philosophy, as speaking thought, is highly reversible, and this doubling character which is intrinsic to Being, allows it to gather up its past into itself; this gives philosophy the advantage of managing its own support, which is its history. Painting is historical, but it cannot sum up its own history—there will never be a Hegel of painting—and this is why painting is innocent and each work is born anew. Painting is a dialectical operation, as is philosophy; the philosopher and artist both interrogate the world as to what it lacks, and then try to remedy it— both try to reveal the invisible. As Being paints through the painter, it thinks through the philosopher. What then, is the difference between painter and philosopher, between innocence and responsibility?

The history of thought and the history of painting are parallel. History is a unity, with different forms. The artist, or the philosopher, can only transcend the present when he is rooted in the past; the past requires this transcending. Whereas the painter can suspend the world, in his innocence (it would be he who could come the closest to effecting a pure reduction), the philosopher is summoned by the demands of his age. In Aristotle, philosophy is theoretical and art is a productive knowledge, but Merleau-Ponty reverses this conception by having art exist for no other end than its own, while philosophy must speak for a certain end, in a certain way. Speaking, however, entails the responsibility of taking a stand in the world; the poet and the philosopher cannot hold the world suspended, but must proffer "opinions and advice." Through speech, philosophy doubles back on itself to manifestly carry its past within itself, and this is why philosophy is responsible.

Even with its temporal structure and historical concern, the advantage of philosophy over painting is still only relative, since there is no speaking which can claim a total possession of itself. Will there ever be an end to philosophy or painting, when all that is invisible is mute visible? In a strict sense, the proper essence of the visible is to have a layer of the invisibility; therefore, whenever the visible is turned over, there is still another side, invisible; there can be no end, no final state. The problems of painting are dimensions—depth, color, form, line— which are branches of Being; as between the sensing and the sensed, there is a "system of exchanges" between these dimensions. Body and painting and philosophy are all grounded in the network of Being: the solution to one problem unbalances the solutions to the others, so that each solution calls for further attempts; painting and philosophy are never finished (even philosophy has no stable treasury). The lack of progress in painting indicates its fecundity, not a deficiency. Each work recreates all the past ones and is destined to pass away; when it is born, it also has almost all of its life before it. The philosopher also must take the history of philosophy into account, in addressing the same problems—the perennial flowering of human interactions in the world.

In studying painting and philosophy, one discovers history, the intersubjective ground of truth. Truth as knowledge, from our perceptual opening to Being, is historical; and history is interaction with other people. In *The Phenomenology of Perception*, Merleau-Ponty (MG xx) describes the relation of philosophy to truth: "Philosophy is not the reflection of a pre-existing truth, but, like art, the act of bringing truth into being." Philosophy is not the spontaneous imitation of a pre-existing truth, but, bound to the nascent logos which is the perceived world, is an operative language that thematizes the invisible of the visible. Philosophy is not pure creativity and not the final truth. The invisible is the origin point of truth; it is a pre-logical intelligibility from which logical ideas originate. Merleau-Ponty also refers to this pre-logical intelligibility as the ideality of the horizon; it is a depth that belongs to the visible and renders it visible. Philosophy transposes an idea from the flesh of the world to the flesh of language, from its locus in the visible to a new locus in language. As Merleau-Ponty summarizes, in *The Visible and the Invisible* (MN 155): "In a sense the whole of philosophy, as Husserl says, consists in restoring a power to signify a birth of meaning, or a wild meaning, an expression of experience by experience, which in particular clarifies the special domain of language. And it is as Valery said, language is everything, since it is the very voice of the things, the waves, and the forests. And what we have to understand is that there is no dialectical reversal from one of these views to the other; we do not have to reassemble them into a synthesis: they are two aspects of the reversibility which is the ultimate truth." But how does the philosopher ever begin to speak of the totality? Of flesh?

2.2.4.1. As Speaking

Wittgenstein (WM 7) concluded the Tractatus with this sentence: "What we cannot speak about we must pass over in silence." Merleau-Ponty (MN 125) is more realistic: "The philosopher speaks, but this is a weakness in him, and an inexplicable weakness: he should keep silent, coincide in silence, and rejoin in Being a philosophy that is there ready-made. But yet everything comes to pass as though he wished to put into words a certain silence he hearkens to within himself. His entire "work" is this absurd effort. He wrote in order to state his contact with Being; he did not state it, and could not state it, since it is silence. Then he recommences ... "

The philosopher must try; failing, he must try again. Concerning that which cannot be said, one must in no way remain silent, but one must attempt to employ forms of linguistic expression which point beyond literal significances, and evoke experiences which can only be intuited. These intuitions are shared by each culture and expressed in their literature, poetic and philosophic. A true speaking is an indirect evocation of that which was always silent before language, and still precedes, surrounds, and pervades words. What speech reveals is in the silent world already, and not something extra it brings to it. Speaking moves from silence and develops it at the same time, and since the movement is reversible, no speaking is ever final or complete. Philosophy is the speaking work, not the spoken word; there must be a language in which the things themselves speak—and this is what the philosopher seeks. Merleau-Ponty (MN 125) describes the language: "It would be a language of which he would not be the organizer, words he could not assemble, that would combine through him by virtue of a natural intertwining of their meaning, through the occult trading of the metaphor - where what counts is no longer the manifest meaning of each word and of each image, but the lateral relations, the kinships that are implicated in their transfers and their exchanges."

Philosophy calls for a new language to bear wild meaning; not Cartesian clarity but its polar opposite, poetry. In order to see in a new way, one must say in a new way. Yet, perhaps there is no adequate way to say Being. If philosophical speech is inadequate to describe Being, it is not due to its relative immaturity, but that it is inadequate in principle. The inadequate speaking of philosophy naturally must always try and never accomplish; but never satisfied, it must renew itself. Philosophy does not stop at a formulation of Being, but follows Becoming in its every expanding spiral. Philosophy must crab walk metaphorically toward a description of Being; it must do as Goethe's science: Contemplative nonintervention; it must approach *physis* in verse, as the pre-Socratics, and not distinguish the analyzable bits of nature with analytic language. It could never achieve the precision of mathematics without denying its own essence. So the philosopher speaks as best he can; true failure is indifference to the inadequacy. Awareness of inadequacy is a positive accomplishment, since it indicates a contact with Being. A philosopher is limited to wondering and questioning: A world has been formed, with a structure, with a hidden logic which can be expressed through philosophical reflection; the philosopher constitutes the expression of the wonder. Merleau-Ponty (MJ 53) relates it to seeing: "Phenomenological or existential philosophy is largely an expression of surprise at this inherence of the self in the world and in others, a description of this paradox and permeation, and an attempt to make us *see* the bond between subject and the world, between subject and others, rather than to *explain* it as the classical philosophies did by resorting to absolute spirit." Once the bonds are seen however, Being will appear on its own, as the whole; then the bonds may be spoken. Speaking is a "total part" that influences the whole field of existence.

Speaking and listening, language and silence are moments of each other in a whole meaning. The whole is the ambiguity of human existence that perception in its primacy of synergism clarifies and gives meaning to by moving from thought to speech, to an under- standing that is seeing. Merleau-Ponty (MK 21) concludes: "In a sense, the highest point of philosophy is perhaps no more than rediscovering these truths: Thought thinks, speech speaks, the glance glances. But each tone between the two identical words there is the whole spread one straddles in order to think, speak, and see."

Is the universe communicating to us? Do we know what it is saying? It has always been speaking, and we have been listening, but our ears have gotten better. Maybe the repetition helped, finally.

Marjorie Grene finds a fundamental organic theme as the source for Aristotle's emphasis on artistic unity. Art is a mimesis of nature; it does not copy nature's products, but, in a like manner, presents unified wholes; works of art are structured like living things. According to Aristotle, when things exhibit unity they have order, when things have a definite size and order, they are beautiful (in art and nature). Only by being organically structured, in fact, can art be mimetic, and only by being mimetic to life can art works be organisms.

Since all experience is comprised of aesthetic events, and since art in human activity is broadened beyond artistic, art is generic. As in Aristotle it involves feeling and making; art is the education of nature (educare = lead forth, draw out). Life and art merge: experience in art is the dynamic process of life itself, in continuous oscillation between opposite poles; life and culture are both aesthetic phenomena. The similarity uniting diverse cultures is explained by the human condition: the first expressions of the basic ambiguity, of man as a body-mind, shape the living environment. Artistic creation is the spontaneous movement of the human body as it expresses its universe.

In noting that certain themes of culture seemed to be transmitted down generations, Richard Dawkins defined a "meme" as a noun that conveyed the idea of a "unit of cultural transmission," or a unit of imitation. He meant the term to be a unit of imitation for cultural transmission. Memes are cultural replicators. But the medium is ideas not genes or bodies. Ideas, of course are emergent phenomena from the activities of brains; they are physically patterns in the brain, although they can be expressed in other media, like stone or sound. Dawkins gives examples: Tunes, clothing fashions, agriculture, cities, domestication, arches, pots, faith, and free speech.

This idea can be useful in discussing units of design that are transmitted. It is important to note that the idea has been changed from Dawkins original idea. For instance Dawkins suggests that memes are inherited like genes; it is more likely they are communicated like the rest of culture. Dawkins suggests that they spread like a virus, but perhaps only in the sense that there is a new pattern of synapse connection. Unlike a virus, a meme can die easily if no one uses it. It may be replicated but it is done so by brains, not by the meme itself.

But, there are problems with the concept, in terms of reduction and reification. Memes are not living beings, they are an emergent pattern. Memes are not selfish. Memes cannot self-replicate themselves any more than a stone ax can copy itself. Nor do they respond to selective pressures like genes, although they may be filtered by use (and they can filter other ideas or such). Of course memes can generate behavior, as do symbols, metaphors, and signifiers. Although the word is a discrete unit, the meme itself may not be so discrete. Fuzziness and ambiguity is a problem with all models and labels, and the meme is used as a model. And, it is useful for thinking about design. Much like genes, however, memes can interact with each other and with other models. They can coevolve, like genes and bodies or like genes and the environment.

Of course, like any models, memes can occur in complexes, referred to by others as memeplexes. These can diverge from their original context and recombine in other contexts. Memes could also be used as units of cultural transmission of design. If we think of cultural ideas as memes that can be designed, then we can approach them as designers not simply as inheritors. For instance, the memes we would consider range from culture to nature: culture, technology, agriculture, domestication, cities, economics, politics, wilderness, and nature. All of these are human constructs that have boundaries and centers, but all of them are also separate from the human sphere, although they interpenetrate. And, these can be treated as separate memes.

2.2.4.2. Creation of Truth

Justice, ethics, freedom, and truth are based in culture. The truth of human cultures and wild ecosystems is apprehended through myth. Cultures, through myth, need to fit our growing knowledge of the geology and biology of the earth into our hearts. Mythology is constructed as a poetic system. Campbell states that "Mythology —and therefore civilization—is a poetic, supernormal image." Mythologies and religions are great poems. When recognized as such, they point through things and events to the ubiquity of a presence that is whole in each.

In ordinary language, truth is taken as a noun. But, truth is that process which works. We think it is established and stable. But, as we have recognized it as constant, this means we constate it. That is, it is constant within limits of the flow (from the Latin *constare*, to stand together).

We try to distinguish truth from falsity, information from noise, thinking that we can distinguish. Art, that creates myth and symbols, also presents and supports ideas of truth. Is art a business? A tool for business? In service to business? A form of seduction hawking a pecuniary pseudotruth? A service to business, state, industry, politics, the military? Just a handmaiden to technology? Has art been domesticated by business (that is to say, is its reproduction controlled by corporate and royal sponsors)?

We now recognize many kinds of knowledge, from immune system, genetic and personal to practical, theoretical, cultural and creative knowledge. The personal, for instance, may be tacit, emotional, and intuitive, where creative knowledge can be metaphoric and meta.

Ignorance can be divided into two large categories, uncertainty and conflicting knowledge. Uncertainty can be based on vagueness, which is indeterminate, probability, which is confidence in partial knowledge, incompleteness, irrelevance, and fuzziness. Fuzziness has to do with overlapping perspectives. Conflicting knowledge includes anomalies, ambiguities, inconsistencies, equivocations, and beliefs.

It allowed information to explode, and redefined truth as what was in print. New technologies create new definitions for old terms, especially ones like truth or knowledge. This makes it work against ethics, as the doing together of all people in a culture. What is the solution to that?

Fleck's theory claims that "scientific facts" are merely consensuses among socially interacting scientists. A fact is a product of a complex social process beginning with individual observation and terminating with a stylized statement of truth that is integrated into scientific knowledge of a society. Others have shown that the measurement of data is subject to expectations and social conditions.

Imagination is an instrument of perception. It points mind toward broadest meaning. It points, not toward truth, but to an ever-enlarging relational field.

It points to the frame. That which is the frame must be ambiguous. Frames must be used as metaphors. The word nature, for instance, has been used by Western philosophers in thirty nine distinct senses. Under ambiguity many meanings may hide. Nature can be regarded as a puzzle or opponent to be beaten, but both detract from total experience.

2.2.5. Ineffability

What we look for beyond seeing
And call the unseen,
Listen for beyond hearing
And call the unheard,
Grasp for beyond reaching
And call the withheld,
Merge beyond understanding
In a oneness
Which does not merely rise and give light,
Does not merely set and leave darkness,
But forever sends forth a succession of living
    things as mysterious
As the unbegotten existence to which they return.
    Tao 14 (BY 32)

This unseen, unheard, and withheld is Being, and philosophy, with its active speaking, attempts to comprehend it. Is speaking adequate? Can this meaning be expressed? Is it not sometimes irrelevant to speak; and speaking is an avoidance of meaning, or one cannot speak and so the act of speaking is false? Is not speech sometimes only the beginning of meaning, but the essential meaning is embodied in a thing ineffable, and speaking is only in direct, a pointing? What does it mean for something to be ineffable? Is it unique and incomparable, is it unnamable and inexpressible, or is it unspeakable and incommunicable? Being is whole, the ground of all existence, it is single and unique, and unanalyzable. Its manifestations may be described, and its possibilities; but can its essential nature be defined and described? Is it necessarily indescribable?

Is experience comparable? Is this year's snowfall similar to last year's? Is the blue of someone's eyes different from the blue of a winter sky? Are there experiences so unique as to be indescribable—in principle? As experiences are grounded in Being they may be compared; but Being itself, to what may it be compared, through what defined? Being is comparable, in this sense ineffable; is it unnamable, or inexpressible? An experience which is unique and indescribable (as a nuclear explosion) may be named, a nuclear explosion, and this is sufficient to refer to it.

Is it possible to refer to Being by naming it, by naming its manifestations? It is not necessary to compare it with something, or describe its essential nature, to name it. An immediate experience is ineffable be cause it is immediate; it may be remembered and mediated by language. Is Being, in experience, always immediate? Or can we have an idea of it? Is the idea of an experience ever adequate to the content? Is our language adequate to express Being? If Being may, in principle, be expressible, could a more adequate language express it? If Being is expressible in its intrinsic nature, then our dumbness makes it ineffable. Many experiences are inexpressible due to limitations of language (for example, how do the Hopi describe icebergs?).

Even if Being is unique, and words are inadequate (words such as "Being"), is it necessarily unspeakable? If I say my love for someone cannot be told, or the beauty of a sunset cannot be expressed, or if I try and fail, am I not communicating it, or an idea of it, or the magnitude beyond words? My experience can never be experienced by another, in his different perspective, but all experiences are shared in Being. Can we communicate the inexpressible, through a speaking that points beyond itself? If my vantage point in Being is expressible, perhaps it can never be communicated, since no one else has my perspective. Is Being intrinsically unspeakable? Can it be communicated mediately, or indirectly, through intending it or referring to it? The idea may be adequate or inadequate; the speaker may express or fail; the listener may understand or not; can this be known? If Being is what is it, it cannot be a word, or expression, or experience without being reduced to that.

Ineffability is only apparent beyond a certain power of expression, that is, the inadequacy of language becomes obvious at a certain level of sophistication. The ideas expressed can only be given in carnal experience; that is the occasion for thought; they owe their power to their transparency in the heart of the sensible, which retreats in the measure it is approached. Expression can only yield a derivative version of them. Merleau-Ponty (MN 150) says that "it is essential to this sort of ideas that they be 'veiled with shadows,' appear 'under a disguise.'" Is Being itself expressible in any way, or must it always be shadowed in every translation?

2.2.5.1. Art & Poetry

Is art an adequate approach to the ineffable? As a work of art may subtract or add more and more elements in order to reach into the ultimate ground of reality, it becomes more hermetic and incomprehensible, until it can express, or point toward, only freedom or nothingness. Malevich's silent white art—an empty canvas—reveals man's freedom to him. But for fear of limiting freedom, he says nothing at all. Empty canvases mark the limit where art becomes silent and invisible; but are they meaningful? Malevich paints whiteness, Reinhardt paints blackness; Being is empty and full.

Is Being expressible through painting? Is poetry more adequate than painting? How does the poet transcend the limits of language? By being silent? Ungaretti suggested that the poem should be like a brief tearing of silence. Mallarme argued that ideally a poem should be silent, white. In Holderlin the silent intervals are a sovereign logic in his poems, unfolding with the poem—until he stopped writing. Rimbaud demanded the freedom of silent reference in his poems, until he also turned from writing. Adorno wrote, "No Poetry after Auschwitz." Are poets reduced to silence in the face of ineffability? There are three interpretations of their silence: (1) the paradox of silence as final logic of poetic speech, (2) the existential exaltation of action over verbal statement, and (3) the refusal to write in dehuman times. Is the unspoken word richer, somehow? Is silence the ideal of modern poetry? If art is articulate, it may use, and be silence; but if art eliminated all "speaking," does it not trap itself in a dumb stasis? Does it not reduce it self to one dimension? Silence is not enough to describe Being.

Art must share a common code to communicate and so must impoverish the unique; each poet should have his own language, but given conventional speech, such language can only be silence, and uncommunicative. As empty space is a part of modern painting, or silent intervals a part of Webern's compositions, the void places in poems are indispensable to the completion of the poetic act. As every word approaches an idea, it becomes surrounded by space, and the blanks and silences become part of the poem. The object varies with each interpretation, but retains unaltered virtual existence beyond. Silences of this sort insert themselves within the poem and at the close. Audible sound is replaced by a filled silence which is neither tonal echo nor reflected presence. What the poem cannot express, speaks here; it may become the poem. The world surpasses itself in its echoing antithesis and defining negation, silence. Ortega (BU 275) pronounces that: "Language is always bounded by a frontier of ineffability, by that which absolutely cannot be said in any language."

2.2.5.2. Attempting to Use Them

> 13.2. To jump into a volcano is not the act of a god . . .
> but to return is . . . [and] who has seen
> Empedokles lately?
>> From *Fragments*, Caratheodory (CC 49)

Historically, the philosopher chose silence because of the ineffable purity of his vision, or the unreadiness of his audience: Empedocles on Aetna, or the aloofness of Heraclitus. Kant made a dichotomy between noumenal and phenomenal: between things themselves and as they are for us; the phenomenal is knowable, the noumenal is a philosophical beyond about which one must be silent. For Wittgenstein (WM 6.522), language circumscribes the phenomenal, but even verbalization cannot penetrate the noumenal. "There are indeed, things that cannot be put into words. They *make themselves manifest*. They are what is mystical." In the *Tractatus*, Wittgenstein mentioned these things— ethics and aesthetics—where of one must be silent. God is a mystery, also, to him, as it is in some religions. Asked about God, Gautama always answered in terms of a resolute, roaring silence.

Speaking must be suspended. It suspended state is nothing but the expression of its inexpressibility (which is true of music). There is scarcely a way to put the suspension in words. Heidegger has emphasized this suspended state of a philosophy that knows it judges neither facts nor concepts the way other things are judged, a philosophy not sure with what it is dealing. Thought seeks to express the inexpressible, to objectify the non-objective; then the inexpressible becomes explicit in the word "Being." Heidegger sloughs off this tradition by abandoning traditional thought—but nevertheless treating the inexpressible directly; his Zen Buddhism follows the Rinzai school, which stresses sudden enlightenment, without Buddha or the scriptures. He wants to approach Being directly, but it only recedes beyond his efforts. Merleau-Ponty (MN 253) is more circumspect: "The root of the matter is that the sensible indeed offers nothing one could state if one is not a philosopher or a writer, but that this is not because it would be an ineffable in Itself, but because of the fact that one does not know how *to speak*. Problems of the "retrospective reality" of the true—It results from the fact that the world, Being, are polymorphism, mystery, and nowise a layer of flat entities or of the in-itself."

Being must be approached indirectly. Direct expression of the inexpressible is not possible; when expression carries, in music for example, it is attached to the process, and evanescent, not labeled and frozen as "that." Lao Tse, in the *Tao* 25 (BY 40), did not name it directly.

> Before creation a presence existed,
> Self-contained, complete,
> Formless, voiceless, mateless,
> Changeless,
> Which yet pervaded itself
> With unending motherhood.
> Though there can be no name for it,
> I have called it "the way of life,"
> Since fullness implies widening into space,
> Implies still further widening,
> Implies widening until the circle is whole.

Philosophical expression in its directness is highly inadequate, since it attempts to speak of the marginal aspect of reality, which only co-appears in all particular beings, as the ground where figures appear. The figure is really the ground in disguise; it must be unmasked, not measured and classified, or cut up and named. Philosophy cannot express it directly, but must attempt to encompass it in its wholeness, as an ocean must be sailed to be understood, not examined a bucketful at a time at the beach. Perhaps Being is more easily felt, than seen or said. But then the concept of Being is not really experienced until one feels the urge to express the inexpressible, and tries; this trial works as a renewal of Being. And, Being is the same Being in the figure and the ground; philosophy uses language to describe it, diachronistic, denotative language for the figure and synchronistic, connotative for the ground.

In attempting to speak or reason philosophy encounters other difficulties. Roots of rationality may be outside the ability of reason to encompass them. Recently limitations have shown up within the workings of reason. Kant had attempted to show that there were ineluctable limits to reason; science has illustrated some of them since. Heisenberg's Principle of Indeterminacy expostulates the essential limits of the ability to know and predict physical states; physics takes predictability where it is exhibited in experience. In light of Bohr's Principle of Complementarity (according to which an electron is regarded as both a wave and particle), perhaps the classical law of the excluded middle (either A or not A) should be dropped from logic. In practice, the Principle allows knowledge of one thing at the cost of not knowing another. In any experiment, as a context, one can observe one form only. In the same decade, Gödel stated his incompleteness theorem. For any postulate system of mathematics which is not self-contradictory, there exist propositions which are true, and which can be stated in purely mathematical terms, but which cannot be derived from that postulate system. All postulate systems constructed are self-contradictory. In every system there are undecidable problems, of which consistency is one. Formal systems are unsafe in the sense that their consistency cannot be demonstrated by methods within the system. After Gödel, every system of mathematics is doomed to incompleteness; mathematics contains insoluble problems, and can never be formalized in any complete system (although this is not exactly Godel's interpretation). Mathematics will always be unfinished; in one sense, then, there are no limits, but in another, there is a bottomless depth to its formal systematization.

Kierkegaard claimed there was, likewise, no system for human existence, in contrast with Hegel, who tried to enclose reality in a rational structure. What do such principles have to do with Being? Can they be applied? Our idea of Being can never be a formal system. The archaeology of the flesh will never be a finished endeavor. As a system must leave out the one term which proves it consistent, and as Being is a closed whole (everything), Being can never be proved, or completed. In the *Metaphysics*, book Gamma, Aristotle faults Antisthanes and others for demanding a demonstration of everything, and for being unaware of the fact that the first starting points of demonstration are indemonstrable axioms. Perhaps Being cannot be demonstrated for that reason, since it is the starting point of all things. If Being could only be regarded as complete from the outside, and if Being is complete (there is no outside), then Being can never be *known* as complete; all things are in interior relation; even if it divides itself up to see itself, it must remain incomplete to itself. Being is beyond definition, as Lao Tse, in the *Tao* 1 (BY 25), saw:

Existence is beyond the power of words
To define:
Terms may be used
But are none of them absolute.

In the beginning of heaven and earth there were no
   words
Words came out of the womb of matter;
And whether a man dispassionately
Sees the surface,
The core and the surface
Are essentially the same,
Words making them seem different
Only to express appearance.
If name be needed, wonder names them both:
From wonder into wonder
Existence opens.

In order to comprehend the wonder, philosophy needs to be a form
of mind, a meditation, similar to Heidegger's suspense. Perhaps Chuang
Tse's description of the Tao is appropriate to the Being of philosophy:
The Tao must be nameless; it is that which is invisible in all visible
things—it cannot be seen, heard or told. It is the ground of all things,
applied both to their Origin (nonBeing) and their Outcome (Being); it
is the principle underlying the world of actuality, from which familiar
things rise, as the result of spontaneous movement in the primordial
mass. Knowledge of the Tao may not be told directly; the Tao itself
may be asked and apprehended intuitively. Perhaps philosophy is the
same. The philosopher constitutes the expression of wonder in the face
of the world; how will he express it? Finite words are superfluous, but
they point the way to what is beyond them. As Buddha was about to
enter final Nirvana, he sat in silence, picked a flower—final truth is only
in Being, and this knowledge is beyond words. Dylan Thomas (TH 77)
tries:
   The force that through the green fuse drives the flower
   Drives my green age; that blasts the roots of trees
   Is my destroyer.
   And I am dumb to tell the crooked rose
   My youth is bent by the same wintry fever.

   The force that drives the water through the rocks
   Drives my red blood; that dries the mouthing streams
   Turns mine to wax.
   And I am dumb to mouth unto my veins
   How at the mountain spring the same mouth sucks.

Yet with what infinite gentleness being flows
Into the forms of nature, and unfolds
Into the slowly ascending tree of life
That opens, bud by bud, into the sky.
World, with what unending patience, grows,
Ascends the roots from the dark well of night
From stone to plant, from blind sense into sight
Up to the highest branch, where the raven head grows white.
        Raine (R 123)

In an earlier discussion of Being as being, the distinction was made between two sides of corporeal reality: the invisible is the other side of visible Being. There is now another distinction to be made, between the higher and lower levels of Being. As Merleau-Ponty (MN 265) enunciates, "the higher and lower gravitate around each other, as the high and the low . . . into the vortex where it rejoins the side-other side distinction, where the two distinctions are integrated into a universal dimensionality which is Being (Heidegger)." The invisible other side of corporeal Being emerges in human thought, and is carried to a higher level of existence by speaking. Being has many dimensions. The higher level of Being announces itself in the other side, in the invisible aspect of the lower level. Actually, the world of speech, the realm of ideas, is a revelation of the silent world. Potentialities hidden on the lower level are realized only on the higher, but the possibility of the higher is implicit in the lower. Being thus assures continuity and allows understanding of things, others, and selves. Merleau-Ponty applies the movement of transcendence from its basis in human life to Being, and it acquires a metaphysical character (literally, beyond the physical, in addition to being under the physical). Being ascends to a new level in man; it perceives, thinks, and speaks in him. Being is an intentional logos, in which perception and expression are incarnate. The logos is, as Merleau-Ponty indicates, the reversibility that is the structure of the presence at the world: the intentional lived body. Logos is realized in human beings most fully. Merleau-Ponty (MN 144) expounds that (to repeat his earlier statement): "This new reversibility and the emergence of flesh as expression are the point of insertion of speaking and thinking in the world of silence." Flesh becomes rarefied in language, but it is flesh, nevertheless. What is lived becomes lived-spoken, and articulates Being. The logos of the aesthetic becomes a spoken logos; expression as a dialectic of perception and the world is an ontological semiotic. Merleau-Ponty declares that the logos is a semiotic in which an interconnection among all phenomena is possible; and philosophy becomes an architecture of signs.

The reversibility of the flesh is the ontological ground which makes expression, and thereby philosophy, possible. As the flesh is the locus of a chiasm, there is a chiasm that links words and meanings in the flesh of language. Ideas as the other side of language are invisible, but bound in the horizon of a new flesh (even savage Being becomes an idea of savage Being in expression). These ideas can be made visible by the speaking that is philosophy. Or the poetry of Stevens (ST 514):

He had said that everything possessed
The power to transform itself, or else,

And what meant more, to be transformed.
He discovered the colors of the moon

In a single spruce, when, suddenly,
The tree stood dazzling in the air

And blue broke on him from the sun,
A bullied blue, a blue abulge,

Like daylight, with time's bellishings,
And sensuous summer stood full-height.

The master of the spruce, himself,
Became transformed. But his mastery

Left only the fragments found in the grass,
From his project, as finally magnified.

2.3. *Love of Creating: Art & Poetry*

What does art have to do with love, creating or responsibility? Merleau-Ponty calls art a matrix of ideas—that reflects the dynamic process of life itself and that symbolizes the productive activity of nature. Art and other expressions, even poetry, are also inadequate avenues to Being, owing to the fundamental ambiguity of limited perspectives. Art and language are anchored in the carnal, but all flesh, even that of the world, radiates beyond itself. Art is a process that symbolizes the productive activity of nature. The work of art contains matrices of ideas which allow it to keep developing. Art as a whole is a symbolical activity, in which the artist directs herself toward the environment with the purpose of manipulating her situation. But, art does not have to be conscious of contacting Being. It is a mimesis of nature, which allows new wholes. Although, the codes or limits of art can impoverish the unique and the whole.

From Plato to Picasso, art has been dismissed as irresponsible or useless for any purpose, from self-expression to misrepresentation for money. Part of the problem with trying to limit art or to free it from all constraints has to do with how art is defined. This section attempts to address these difficulties through a series of expanded and interrelated redefinitions, not only of art, but of culture and human expression in general. For instance, art as a survival technique larger than any one culture may confer an evolutionary advantage. Art as a seductive cultural trap, however, may have devastating effects on human cultures or ultrahuman communities.

By placing art in a larger cultural context, for instance, some of the ethical issues evaporate. In a still broader ecological context, art can be seen to have importance for survival. However, new ethical issues are raised. It might be possible to present art in larger contexts, not only as having impacts on society but as allowing society to extend its reach into ultrahuman domains, where a broader responsibility and a deeper understanding may be required. This section attempts to integrate several lines of thought.

What is the definition of art? Is there more than one definition? What is the reputation of art? What are the limits of art? Do limits make art into some kind of trap? What are the effects of art on philosophy and science? How is art different from Philosophy or science? Is art always contextual? Should it be limited by context? Is art an ethical activity? Is art aware of its social consequences or the physical effects of its materials? Is art ethical, in an ecological sense? How can we redefine art? Can art be redefined? Is art wild?

2.3.1. *The Definition and Reputation of Art*

What is art? Is it a skill, a craft, an artifice? Creative work, a product of some kind? A profession? A branch of learning? Is it something bigger? The ability to make many things and designs? Is design larger than art, encompassing engineering and science?

Is definition by metaphors any better? Art a new modern supermarket of forms (from any time and any culture)? Art is a mirror? Art is plagiarism (bricolage or reconstruction on another foundation)? Art is euphantism (or euphemism or deodorant)? Art is cheerleading (mindless boosterism)? Art is nonsense (autolalia or bullshit)?

What kind of reputation does art have? Good, bad, really bad? Is bad art or bad design responsible for inestimable suffering and death (as Victor Papenek thinks)?

Is art a business? A tool for business? In service to business? A form of seduction hawking a pecuniary pseudotruth? A service to business, state, industry, politics, the military? Just a handmaiden to technology? Has art been domesticated by business (that is to say, is its reproduction controlled by corporate and royal sponsors)?

Or, is art a useless, self-absorbed, self-centered exercise? Is any one of these a good reputation to have?

What is the responsibility of art? What is responsibility, especially social responsibility? Is it responsibility to the family, neighborhood, group, culture? To the place, the environment, the planet? If responsibility is being obligated to account for something to someone, why should art be held accountable for what is expressed? Doesn't that require a specific contract? Have you ever heard of such a contract being signed at the end of a college education in art? Should there be one? Like a physician's oath? Other crises sciences, such as Ecoforestry, do have such an oath for its graduates. If responsibility is the ability to distinguish between right and wrong, and to think and act responsibly as a mature self, is art responsible for the self? But, what self? The truncated person in a skin? The community self? The large ecological self that identifies with place?

What is the environment? How many levels should be addressed? All of them at once? Is the larger environment, such as the planet or solar system, more important than a local environment? Is that an unfair question based on the misunderstanding of systems? The cultural political economic establishment is part of the environment. Is art responsible when it exposes the weaknesses of culture? Art used to be for nature. Art, especially design, used to be against nature. Some of it now is with nature. What level of nature?

2.3.2. *The Limits of Art* (expression, media, public)?

Does the human body and human imagination have limits? Is art limited by its media? Does the scale of art limit its effectiveness? Is art limited by symbols? Language? How can art employ emptiness? Is art an adequate approach to the ineffable? Is poetry more adequate than painting? Are poets reduced to silence in the face of ineffability? Especially famines and genocides? Species extinctions, habitat losses, interference with planetary cycles? Can art even express large-scale loss? If art needs to be explained, that is supplemented with another kind of expression, does that limit it?

Do definitions of art limit art? Art has been called any embellishment of ordinary living that is achieved with competence and has describable form (after M. Herskovits 1951). What about extraordinary living? Heroic things? Sacred things? Indescribable form. Incompetent but radical things? Art has also been called the creation of public objects or events, by manipulating a medium, to create qualitative experiences (after George Mills, 1971). What about private events like love-making (or would this apply to artistic pornography)? What about things that have no medium, like ideas (or do they exist in a conceptual idea space)? What about quantitative experience (Andy Warhol, comes to mind)?

2.3.3. *Expansion through Redefinition (Art as Trap)?*

Artistic ideas must first be grasped in their fleshy existence; only if they are first experienced can they be grasped, and then they cannot be transformed into ideality. These ideas, musical and literary among others, cannot be detached from the sensible appearances, as can the ideas of intelligence, which are erected into a second form; thus the abstract language of science is freed from the horizon of perceptible reality, while the most artistic seem trapped within it.

A trap, from the old English "to step," is a device for catching and holding animals or a stratagem for catching people; closeness to limits; overconnection. Definition of a serial trap: the use of resources by a people, where the replenishment rate is constant and the rate of use exceeds it. This trap results in ecosystem degradation that is less reversible. Industrial age mistakes the rate of discovery for the rate of recovery. There are also cultural traps, such as slavery and brewing. Art is a trap. Like hunting and agriculture, and language, art limits what people do and can do. Karl Marx contended that we live in cages, part natural and part made. However, human actions can modify them. The word cage is a metaphor; it implies being trapped.

Table 232-1. Expanded Functions of Art

Category	Subcategory
Art as Human Perception	Art as an emergent quality of life As a way of seeing or making new perspectives. As a way of revealing the hidden or invisible. As the expression of worldview, order As a way of training perception
Art as Physical Expression of Existence	As expression of the unique As expression of identity As map of experience As expression of evolution and diversity As a product that is made. As a new industry to produce status, luxuries and profits
Art as a tool for the symbolic expression of the processes of nature	As a releaser of tension As a tool for intensification and miniaturization As a recycling program for old images As a carnivore that eats raw images, words or ideas As expression of human limits, silence, and dimensions
Art as Imitation of Nature	As an ordering process for making of new organic unified wholes As duplicating the process of nature As incorporating ambiguity and contradiction As miniaturizing and intensifying a whole As a hologram as metaphor for art
Art as Communication	As a form of dialogue between a human, god or other As Ceremony, as linkage to nature or to the holy, to renew myths As a way to control people As networking interactive global communication As a transcultural human communication
Art as Play	As physical exercise As social integration As creation by recombining and recontexting As a learning and enjoying activity
Art as Meaning	As pure information As itself To make the visible abstract To make the abstract visible
Art as Survival Technique	As a way to accept limits As a digital or analog program to permit cultural continuity As a way to promote needed things and actions, such as development of good places As power to restore balance or control

Can each of these definitions be seen as an expansion of the context of art? Can the redefinitions be combined as: Perception that is expressed through play in physical and symbolic ways to imitate the spectrum of nature and thus communicate it meaningfully as a survival technique for groups and cultures?

2.3.3.1. Art as Human Perception

Expression is embodied in perception, as perception is meshed in the body, as the body embedded is in the world. Artistic ideas are grasped in their fleshy existence; only if they are first experienced can they be grasped, and then they cannot be transformed into some ideal expression.

Understanding a pattern is also a bodily reaction; creation and re-creation are analogous processes. The feeling is perceived, not conceived. The created pattern becomes a cultural object which alters the complex of the environment, and both organisms must adjust.

The artist works like his nervous system, selecting highly significant details from his environment, and synthesizing them into an excitatory complex. Art is a way of making new perspectives, of seeing, a way of revealing the hidden or invisible. It is the expression of a worldview, infolding the cosmos, training perception of the environment.

Expression is embodied in perception, as perception is meshed in the body, as the body embedded is in the world. Artistic ideas are grasped in their fleshy existence; only if they are first experienced can they be grasped, and then they cannot be transformed into some ideal expression.

Table 2341-1. The Invisible Environment and Art

Environment	Art Response
Scavenging	
Foraging	Pleasing patterns
Hunting	Animal souls
Growing	Hunting
Machining	Agrarian romance
Electrifying Information	Machine abstraction
Biologizing Chaos	Electronic information
Making Eutopias	Ecological humanism
Remaking everything	Eutopian forms
	Repoetic forms

This might seem to be a natural progression if we think of the lower level as being the image of the previous environment. Maybe this is how art moves from cliché to archetype, as a presentation of the newness of the last environment.

The function of art in tribal society was to merge people with the cosmos. Art educated the perception to see that the links were visible. The function of art in industrial electronic society has changed somewhat, so that it is to train people's perception of the environment. Rather than just orient people to novelty, art could also embed them in the cosmos.

2.3.3.2. Art as Physical Expression of Existence?
Is art the expression of unique, an expression of identity? Is art a map of experience? Art is a map literally in some cultures. Tribes in New Guinea tattoo their bodies with directions to heaven. Maps have been made into art, but that is different expression.

The greater part of human experience is primitive and emotional, ultimately nonverbalizable; literal language is too abstract to deal with it. Can art allow expression to savage experience, to feeling? Is art a doorway to mystical experience and transcendental visions, creating new dimensions?

Art reproduces experience. In the presence of a work of art, its full style is felt; the image presents itself to us — it is not representation, but presentation. This presentation is kinesthetic, a dynamic form which appeals more to the kinesthesis of the body than to intuition.

2.3.3.3 Art as a tool for the Symbolic Expression?
Is art a tool for intensification and miniaturization? A recycling program for old images. Or a carnivore that eats raw images, words or ideas?

The ecological environment, even including news media, is a complex, low-intensity, undemanding process. By making things high-intensity and simpler, art makes them visible. Art miniaturizes it subject, so it can be seen as a whole. It intensifies it so it can be seen as dynamic. It accelerates it, so it can be seen at once (in the short and limited human attention span).

Table 2333-1. The Intensity Scale of Culture and Art (read down)

Intensity	Environment
Low	Environment (background)
	New technology
Medium	City
	War, Storms
High	Art

2.3.3.4. Art as Imitation of Nature?

Does art ever sacrifice the whole for a part, a detail? Art is a mimesis of nature; it does not copy nature's products, but, in a like manner, presents unified wholes. Works of art are structured like living things. According to Aristotle, when things exhibit unity they have order, and when things have a definite size and order, they are beautiful (in art and nature). Culture is a wholistic perspective concerned with the unity of things. This is a perspective of art. In a work of art the whole is never sacrificed to the parts. Excesses and imbalances are permitted only in relation to the whole. Only by being organically structured, in fact, can art be mimetic, and only by being the mimetic to life can art works be organisms.

If art is like nature, then it must be changing and temporary. It may also share the mosaic of nature.

Table 2334-1. Natural Art (read down)

Lifetime of Art	Form of Art
Permanence	Continuity
Life of a culture	Metal Products
Life of a person	Marbled Mosaic
Transient	Patchwork Mosaic
Short-lived	Ephemeral Patterns

Can a hologram be a metaphor for art? The brain orders its universe in dreams, through language, and with art. Dreams are a condensation of experience, which the Greeks named Hyponoia, a hidden thought with real meaning, but in a secret language. The same condensation is operative in language itself; Alfred Wundt termed it the condensation of meanings. As a dream or word may sum up the whole past, present, and future of the dreamer, or speaker, in one event, so may art (poetry, music, or painting) do the same. During the ordering process, more and more is packed into less and less, until miniaturization reaches its greatest level of organic complexity in the human brain and its electronic extensions.

Art may be the same type of condensation on a window as a hologram. Conrad Waddington suggests that there may be an analogy between some modern paintings and a hologram; for instance, Mark Tobey's Messengers may seem chaotic and meaningless, under the wrong reference, as would a hologram. Then again, the hologram must frame a garden, whereas a painting may be of the window itself. The hologram could be used as an art form, like photography, or it could be used to produce new possibilities in art. Since a hologram can be produced from a computer printout, it is therefore possible to generate any object on the printout, even one that has never existed, such as a griffin.

A hologram may be read out by shining a copy of the reference beam across the film; the resulting holographic image is like the freezing of light waves from the object in a window. This provides an interesting parallel to Ortega's definition of art: "Art is a window with a garden behind it: one may focus on the garden or on the window." A hologram must frame a garden, whereas a painting may be of the window itself. Of course, a hologram read with the wrong reference would be chaotic and meaningless, like many modern art forms. Is a hologram, then, an art form (some are treated that way as raw things)? Does it translate the view more accurately than a painting, or only differently? A hologram is like a window; but, the object is frozen in light, and the hologram is a faithful "reproduction" in three-dimensions. The frame disappears, allowing the focus alone. Is art the same kind of condensation on a window as a hologram?

2.3.3.5. Art as Communication?
Art is a dialectical process that symbolizes the productive activity of nature. Since all experience is comprised of aesthetic events, and since art in human activity is broadened beyond artistic, art is generic. As in Aristotle it involves feeling and making; art is the education of nature (*educare* = lead forth, draw out).

Should art be taught in schools? Doesn't schooling make art a subject, like other separate, categorized, walled-in things like home economics or botany? How would that promote art's function? Would it be like Soviet art, in service to the state, supporting the state and its closed environment?

Is art a form of dialogue between humans, others, or god? A form of status through luxury or profit? Is art a ceremony, a linkage to nature or holy, to renew myths? Is it a form of networking interactive global communication? A transcultural transnational human communication? A new industry to produce and display luxuries and profits? A way to control people? Communication?

Communication is related to media, as extensions of the human body and mind. Art is the creative communication of the environmental changes, including technology, which allows human response and adjustment to the limits of that environment. Reordering the world is one role of an art object; the Romantic poets are a good example of this, as they made "nature" visible to Europeans.

Table 2335-1. Media and Remedia

Media	Effect	Artistic Response
Stone	Control	Naive Realism
Alphabets Paper	Objective memory	Symbolism
Printing press	Detachment	Gothic
Books	Detribalization	Renaissance
Telegraph	Decentralization	Dada
Phonograph	Individualization	Abstract Expressionism
Video/television	Depersonalization	Pop art, Rerealism

Maybe the last media is a mistake. Television can involve people if the images are accepted as part of a moral obligation to a larger community (global?). Perhaps the internet with television can lead to active dialogues.

2.3.3.6. Art as Play?

Play is an activity for itself, although playing may allow learning as well as enjoyment. Art plays with symbols and forms, recombining them in new contexts. The artist releases ideas from the unconscious, or unexpressed and conscious, for creative purposes. This creativity is a kind of play: Put the idea in a new context and play with it, to see it in a new way. This is how a *metaphor* works.

Artists are considered dangerous because they play with ideas, because they question ordinary ways, and because they play with serious subjects. Oddly, however, the artist needs a safe place and security to allow the vision to emerge to a new context.

Art also creates an explanatory context by allowing the viewer to think or perceive several things at once. In this kind of illuminating moment the viewer can see many things at once, sometimes the entire whole thing (perhaps *mirrored*).

Should we use other metaphors of art to understand art? Art is a mirror? Maybe more like a circus mirror, otherwise art would just reinforce the current environment and become part of it. Art distorts things, then presents the distortion for attention.

But, does art mirror dangerous subjects like starvation, rape, dismemberment, extinction, or environmental destruction? If not why not? These may be the most critical issues affecting life on the planet.

2.3.3.7. Art as Meaning?

As the artist introduces new meaning into the world, she modifies the world of others, and this meaning sediments as the basis for a common world. Maurice Merleau-Ponty considers that the painter creates his own style, a system of equivalences that he establishes for his work and by which he concentrates the meaning which in his perception is still scattered, and makes it exist separately.

Art is an indirect expression, in which the individual elements need no meaning, but gain meaning by entering particular relations within a context. Can art be pure without a context? Pure in-form-ation? Art achieves only through indirection, like sailing; good sailing requires knowledge of the forces at play, the wind and currents that are beyond control, and ability to use them to its fullest advantage. Technology motors into the wind but loses the wind, and the feeling, in the noise. Does art tend to lose itself in the wind? Or in its own references?

Meaning in art is a case of logical meaning and, apparently, an essence. The artist returns to the "things themselves" as they appear contextually in our pretheoretical perceptual experience, as natural meaning structures which are basic to our artificial logics

2.3.4. *Is Art Aware of its Effects?*
Is the purpose of art to shock? As a form of education, perhaps? An aesthetic object should not offer a reassuring vision, which interprets or identifies nature, but a naive vision, which surprises, shocks, fascinates or seduces the senses, which awakens desire and stirs the imagination, and which furnishes a feeling of the invisible.

Is art aware of other effects, in terms of people's behavior? To remake environments, for instance, from ruins to new cities?

2.3.4.1. Is Art Ethical?
Is it ethical to steal other artists' ideas? Is it ethical to borrow from tribal motifs for tee-shirts? For use in advertising? To make money? In general, is it ethical to take signs and symbols out of context and reuse them for other purposes? Is it ethical to use the images of dead famous people to sell beer?

Is this plagiarism? Is that important? Isn't the creative advance fueled by plagiarism? Well, plagiarism and errors? Well, maybe errors and extension?

Should art avoid or embrace consumerism? Could art be used to educate in ethics? Or morals? Should art always be against discrimination, waste, or war—or should it embrace them?

2.3.4.2. Is Art Contextual?
Is art out of context? Yes, by definition. Art selects unique items from the context and uses them in other contexts. Is art also out of

convention? People's attention shifts from the art to the artist, which may not be bad if the life is the art, as the Balinese might contend, and often the life is more evocative and interesting than the art, as often the explanation is more poetic then the figured expression.

Does art destroy context? Only if it is the subject. The context is what is changing and what requires art. So, art can ignore context or reform it, but it cannot destroy context. It is like the question: Can one being, the tiger, destroy the ecosystem, or field of being? No?

But, celebrity art is art in service to the old environment, in an uncritical way, rather than the revolution or prefiguring of the new environment. Art can use science or politics as the environment. One has to be careful when science, or politics, or business uses art to scaffold and glamorize the old environment.

2.3.4.3. Is Art Ethical, Ecologically?

The word ethics is derived from the Greek word meaning 'custom' (Greek *ethos*, Sanskrit *svadha*, Latin *mores*, plural of *mos*, from *meare*), which itself came from the Sanskrit word for one's 'own doing.' Since it was used in the plural, it meant 'doing together.' The word 'morality' comes from the Latin word for will of the people; the singular meant the 'will' of a person. It was probably derived from the verb 'to measure,' as to measure one's way, to go one's way. Morals means the 'way of going together.' Ethics means 'doing together,' which of course one does living together. And, in an anthropometric universe, it is entirely appropriate.

Ethics are assembled inductively, from experience in living in places. Because of the uncertainty of human actions, ethics has to encompass the far past and distant future. In a large sense, ethics are just ways of "doing together." One does this by living together in a community.

With Albert Schweitzer and many others, the scope of ethics can be seen to have been enlarged to include, more than the family and community, but the nation and all of humanity, as well as animals, plants, all of life, and now all of nature and its systems and fields (see Figure (2343-1).

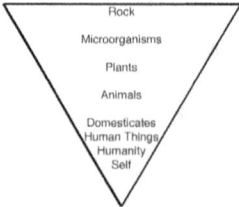

Figure 2343-1. The Widening Scope of Ethics

Aldo Leopold proposed a conservation ethic, dealing with human relationships to land, plants and animals, in an ecological community. Such an ethic would change the human role from master of earth to plain member of it. An ethic, ecologically, is a limitation on freedom of action in the struggle for existence. An ethics that requires a long-range responsibility also requires a new humility, since technological power exceeds the ability to foresee its consequences. An ecological ethic recognizes the moral obligation to leave the world habitable for future generations. This means that ethics has to incorporate ultrahuman beings and things.

Should art voluntarily limit its freedom and refuse to advertise individual autos because they are wasteful forms of moving? Can art express this ethic of a limitation in a community? Can art promote community health, but which level of community? Neighborhood? City? Species? Planet? Life?

Speaking of community and ethics: ethics by definition is "doing together" and art by practice is doing separately, therefore art is the opposite of ethics. By comparison, science is a method of doing together, a cumulative group effort, even as it pretends to be morally neutral.

2.3.5. *Critical Redefinition of Art & Science?*
"Art is a window with a garden behind it: one may focus on the garden or on the window," said Jose Ortega. The anthropologist Robert Redfield distinguishes between two types of perception: iconic, where the garden is the focus and the window is frame, and aesthetic, where the window is the focus and garden is the frame; he claims that a double perception is impossible, in principle. Every work of art therefore is a window frame—the aesthetic form, with a garden behind it. Is there a holometaphor possible?

Primitive "art" grew out of, and framed, a complex garden, which has grown over and changed. With their "art" in our cultural world, can we see through it? Is the content, once private, now public or heuristic? How faithfully does the window translate the view? If the only way we have of seeing gardens is through windows, can we ever know things themselves? Perhaps iconic and aesthetic perceptions are the same. Can art only be window? Modern nonobjective painting seems all window. Is focus the problem? Can art address the periphery and not the figure in the center? Can it look sideways at the frame?

Is iconic perception cognitive and aesthetic perception contemplative? Is it the reduction to cognition that poses the problem?

Is it solved when all perception is recognized as feeling?

Artistic images and symbols are aesthetic and equivocal; signs are linguistic and univocal; since images have such poor semiotic value, it is dangerous to reduce them to cognitive terms. When art works become cognitively generalized, their aesthetic specificity is lost, and they become poor vehicles of knowledge. An aesthetic object should not offer a reassuring vision, which interprets or identifies nature, but a naive vision, which surprises, shocks, fascinates or seduces the senses, which awakens desire and stirs the imagination, and which furnishes a feeling of the invisible.

Archeologists sometimes attempt to reconstruct the social climate of a dead society through an examination of their artifacts. For all primitive people things in their universe are always in some comprehensible order. Is it possible to recreate that order by viewing their concrete expressions? Malraux observed that "Implicit in these creations is an awareness of the universe—different than ours— unconcerned with history—a union with the cosmos." Is it possible for cultural anthropologists to reconstruct social worlds from artifacts?

What a minute, so is science, like a window on a garden. Is art a kind of science? Like science, each new medium undercuts the old paradigm. Like quantum mechanics, which was the death of objective reality, which is what it was supposed to prove, art undermines its parent idea. Something new flourishes, then it is old. Then the revolution is over, and art is part of the new environment that will require further art to see. The media become the field of the new ecosystem.

Unlike science, art uses the rare, unique, individual instance for its lesson. Science uses numbers to relate samenesses and forms. As quantum mechanics showed that participation in the field was not an option, so art requires participation for its consumers to recreate the subject themselves.

The two are different, of course, as art focuses on the unique in everything, what is different in the pattern or flesh, while science focuses on what is common, on what can be measured and compared. That is why art is metacentric and science is numerocentric.

Maybe that is the problem. They should not be centric. Art should be metaperipheral, science should be numeroperipheral. Does art not focus? Is there a way of not focusing? What about the periphery? Could we approach it sideways. crab-like? Can art do that? Or do we need something new?

2.3.6. *Art as Survival Technique*

It was the earlier belief of Frederich Schiller that human society could be improved by political means. But after studies on the Thirty Years War in Europe, he became skeptical of the ability of politics. After reading a work on art, Schiller considered it historical proof that art can achieve what violence and law cannot—art educates and liberates the individuals of society in a gradual and peaceful process. In spite of the cultural forces dominant at any moment, an individual has the potential to determine a different course. Unlike the classical humanism committed to lessons of the past, the aesthetic humanism of Schiller was open to possibility.

Perhaps art can achieve what violence and law cannot—art educates the individuals of society in a gradual and peaceful process. That is, art as more than technical skills at drawing or combining. In spite of the cultural forces dominant at any moment, an individual has the potential to determine a different course. Art can provide a whole image of the place of humanity within nature and not a transcendent view. It could confront the past without the baggage of sentiment and the future without the paralysis of dread. The appreciation of the differences of other cultures could allow us to transcend our present identities. Art could broaden the mental worlds of observers and encourage tolerance and wonder.

Art could enlarge or alter the perceptions of all human beings on earth with the selection and presentation of relevant information to form an ecological consciousness. The survival of society now depends on a consciousness of the global system in its complexity and connectedness. The spirit of humanity depends on a consciousness of its proper relation to the wild places of the earth. Such an art, combined with an ecological science and politics, could be adequate to deal with the creation and maintenance of good places on earth.

The true architects of culture have been the historians, artists, propagandists and poets; the poets provided the national archetypes. Nation-building wars may provide heroes for popular imagination; but poets and writers make the identities. The real identity of leaders is provided by propagandists and poets; the leaders only provide the horsepower. Their mask is determined by cartoonists and writers. Is this how art is related to leadership?

A humanism based on Schiller's ideas must have a whole image of the place of humanity within nature, and not a transcendent view. It must confront the past without the baggage of sentiment and the future without the paralysis of dread. The appreciation of the differences of other cultures (the difference of Horace, for instance) will allow us to transcend our present identities. Responding to any art with pre-established values makes one miss the uniqueness of the experience presented. Art could broaden the mental worlds of observers and encourage tolerance and wonder.

Is Frederich Schiller right about art? That it could achieve what violence and law could not? Education through a peaceful process? By enlarging people's perceptions? By broadening their mental worlds and encouraging tolerance and wonder? By embracing three concepts: liberation, play and community? Liberation is freedom from contemporary limits of identity. Play is imaginative experience, natural learning entered into freely. Community provides order and justification.

Is Gary Snyder right about poetry as an ecological survival technique? What is required for survival? Order, diversity, cooperation, knowledge of biogeography, etc. Poetry teaches that these things are valuable. Snyder discerned an undercurrent in civilization since the late Paleolithic, and considered Buddhist Tantrism to be its finest and most modern statement: "that Mankind's mother is Nature and Nature should be tenderly respected; that man's life and destiny is growth and enlightenment in self-disciplined freedom; that the divine has been made flesh and that flesh is divine; that we not only should but do love one another . . . these values seem almost biologically essential to the survival of humanity." (SO p.105). Jonas Salk concluded that only wisdom will ensure human survival. Perhaps art is a form of preadaptation or adaptation to a changing environment.

2.3.7. Is Art Wild?

Should art be wild? That is, should it be allowed to reproduce on its own? Without being chosen for its "useful" characteristics? Should it be responsible for stating what is wrong? For questioning a bad direction or poor decisions? Without regard to consequences? Can artists ever say "this is wrong" or "this is right"?

Art should not to be limited, in terms of subject or responsibility or environment. It should not be limited to educational and moral purposes and situations. It is a process for perceiving things that may be at odds with a culture, yet may be of importance to a culture. In that sense, the basic responsibility of art is to show what it sees. If art is limited, that is, domesticated by money or rules, then it should obey codes of ethics and accept some responsibilities.

The business of art is to look at everything, regardless of what a cultural definition of health, good or responsibility is. Art in this sense should not be restricted to one place or to one set of rules or limits. Wild art has no responsibilities or ethical obligations.

3.0. The Primacy Of Imagination

> Learn if I dare, the order of the wind
> Fire, tempest and the sea.
> Learn if I dare into what mode of being
> The leaf falls from the tree.
>   Raine (R 96)

3.1. *Poetry*

Poetry is a way of making by equating the unknown with the matrix of the known. It becomes not only a form of knowledge, like science and philosophy, but a way of pointing and showing, as an art. It uses language, but puts it in the form of metaphors. And, metaphors use color and shape to present the invisible.

3.1.1. *Poetic Knowing*

In the Metaphysics (E.1.1025b25), Aristotle called poetry one of three kinds of intellectual activity:
- Theoretical knowledge (*theoretike episteme*)
- Practical knowledge (*praktike episteme*)
- Poetical knowledge (*poietike episteme*)

The three sciences involved different ends. The theoretical sciences involved necessary propositions and had knowledge as their end; the practical sciences subordinated knowledge to action—as in knowing virtue to act virtuously—and the productive sciences had a product as their end, not knowledge or action. Philosophy was a theoretical knowledge, as was mathematics, physics, and theology. The practical sciences derived many propositions from the theoretical and the productive derived many propositions from both other sciences. Since sciences became less exact as they involved more elements, and became more dependent on the others, poetry was the least exact of all. Yet, in a sense, poetry was more basic than the others, since all sciences produced an end.

Poetic knowledge was inseparable from the power to make. Poetry is a kind of knowledgeable activity with a product for an end. Aristotle defined art at various times as: having to do with creation; using powers; "principles of change in another thing;" and being concerned with the same thing as chance. Poetry was poesis, a fashioning of random data into a significant statement of universal relevance. The whole is structurally unified into a complex thing. This unity is based on the organic theme in Aristotle. Art is a mimesis of nature, but it does not copy nature's products. It presents unified wholes, in a like manner. Works of art are structured like living things; when things exhibit unity, they have order, and when things have a definite size and order, then they are beautiful, in art and nature. In fact, only by being organically structured can art be mimetic; and only by being mimetic to life can art works be organisms. Poetry imitates, not fragmentary reality, but the essential whole. The poet is a maker, as the etymology of the word indicates. Both Heidegger and Stevens attribute to poetry an ancient, mythic function: it transcends the simple creation of song. E. Sewell stated that the myth of Orpheus asked the great question of poetry in the rational world: "What could it do?" Myth and poetry are considered instruments of knowledge.

3.1.2. *Poetic Making & Language*

In the Poetics Aristotle proposes to speak not only of art in general, but also of its species and their capacities, of the structure of the plot, of the number and nature of the constituent parts, and of other matters, beginning with the primary facts and following the natural order. All the poetries, including Comedy and Dithyrambic and most flute and lyre playing, are regarded as types of imitation, although they differ by the means, objects or modes of their imitations. For instance the means of visual arts are color and shape; for music, sound, for dance, rhythm and for literature, words (and sometimes sound and rhythm); the objects of imitation are types of human action (high, noble behavior in tragedy, low in comedy); and the modes of literature are narrative and dramatic (with parallels most likely in the other arts). Different types of arts share similarities among these, as tragedy shares its means and object of imitation with epic poetry, but not its mode. In addition to the verbal arts, Aristotle mentions, in the *Poetics* (1447b), further that there is "an art which imitates by language alone, without harmony, in prose or in verse, and if in verse, either in some one or in a plurality of meters. This form of imitation is to this day without a name."

3.1.2.1. Definitions

Language changes. New words are created to express new feelings, thoughts or inventions. New languages develop from old ones. Old ones disappear as the speakers die. Some old ones, such as Cornish or Coeur d'Alene, are recreated by new speakers. Aristotle might be better understood by carefully defining terms.

3.1.2.1.1. Aristotle's Poetics

Did Aristotle mean poetry? Poetic literature would then include prose literature. And therefore must it not include philosophic literature? Aristotle mentions Xenarchus' mimes and Socratic conversations as being without a name, but qualifies himself, such that mimetic is a necessary qualification for a product of words being called poetic. Perhaps he tacitly acknowledges that a Platonic dialogue shares certain poetic qualities with tragedy; such philosophic dialogue usually held between reasonable persons, or by the soul with itself; and since epic presupposes two persons and drama three, dialogue at least shares the means, and the mode (dramatic) with one of those. The form of the dialogue is one with the movement of thought it expresses. Although at times, Aristotle uses poetry in the popular sense of being in verse, he is scornful of the public impression, noting that even if Socratic conversations were in trimeters people would describe them as poetry due to that consideration alone and not by virtue of the imitative nature of their work. In the *Poetics* (1447b), Aristotle says: "Even if a theory of medicine or physical philosophy be put forth in a metrical form, it is usual to describe the writer in this way, Homer and Empedocles, however, have really nothing in common apart from their meter; so that, if one is to be called a poet, the other should be termed a physicist rather than a poet." Empedocles wrote his poetry in hexameters, iambic, as did Homer in his heroic epic. However, Aristotle does not regard Plato or Empedocles as poets. Here, though, Aristotle informally describes the origin of poetry from two causes underlying human nature: imitation, as man is the most imitative creature in the world, at first, even learning by imitation; and delight in works of imitation as shown by experiencing even the most painful representations in art. He further explains, in the *Poetics* (1449a): "to be learning something is the greatest of pleasures, not only to the philosopher but also to the rest of mankind, however small their capacity for it . . ."

Poetry arose out of men's imitative improvisations, but soon broke up into two kinds according to the differences of poets' characters. Homer seems to stand at the beginning of both of these traditions— Epic and Tragedy—which share their imitation of serious subjects in grand verse. Aristotle traced also the development of beats (iambic, trochaic) and measures (trimeter, hexameter), and attempts to explain how iambic verse can be serious in tragedy and satiric in comedy ("it is the most natural speaking rhythm"). Reserving Comedy and hexameter poetry (it is assumed he means iambic hexameter poetry, as opposed to epic hexameter, which is composed of dactyls and spondees) for later consideration, he proceeds to define tragedy in the Poetics (1450): by gathering up what has been said, tragedy is "the imitation of an action that is serious and also, as having magnitude, complete in itself; in language with pleasurable accessories (i.e., rhythm and harmony), each kind brought in separately in the parts of the work (i.e., some in verse, others in song), in a dramatic, not a narrative form; with incidents arousing pity and fear, where-with to accomplish its catharsis of such emotions."

In her book, *Prelude to Aesthetics*, Eva Schaper proposes that his first five chapters, with their development of mimesis as a complex entelechy fully embodied only in dramatic and epic examples, is more than a definition of tragedy (which is the only complete definition of a form of poetry), it is a fountain of suggestions for a general theory of art as well as for suggested definitions of other arts. In fact, on the basis of tragedy, a plot is complete by having a beginning, middle and end; the whole is structurally unified into a complex thing. Marjorie Grene finds a fundamental organic theme as the source for Aristotle's emphasis on artistic unity. Art is a mimesis of nature; it does not copy nature's products, but, in a like manner, presents unified wholes; works of art are structured like living things. According to Aristotle, when things exhibit unity they have order, when things have a definite size and order, they are beautiful (in art and nature). Only by being organically structured, in fact, can art be mimetic, and only by being mimetic to life can art works be organisms.

The poet makes the plot, by selecting and joining incidents in an organic structure. In chapter nine, Aristotle writes that the poet's function is to describe, not what has happened, but the kind of things that might happen ('what is possible as being probable or necessary"). He then contrasts history and poetry, in the *Poetics* (1451b): "The distinction between historian and poet is not in the one writing verse and the other prose—you might put the work of Herodotus into verse, and it would still be a species of history." The differences between the two are describing what has been and what might be. In a sense, then, the poetic is closer to the philosophic (does the philosopher describe what might be, or what is?). Aristotle concludes, in the Poetics (1451b): "Hence poetry is something more philosophic and of graver import than history, since its statements are of the nature rather of universals, where as those of history are singulars." Also, unlike history, the poet's works are not to be checked against the factual accuracy of external evidence, though they may use proper names, or historical incidents. The possibility of poetic events is that which can be envisaged, but must be connected according to probability or necessity.

Aristotle, in the *Poetics* (1451b): "It is evident from the above that the poet must be more the poet of his stories or Plots than of his verses, inasmuch as he is a poet by virtue of the imitative element in his work, and it is actions that he imitates." Once again the central core of poetry is mimesis. The connectedness referred to, is actually, as Schaper mentions, what Aristotle means by universal; poetry need not be concerned with generalities, or with universals themselves (but perhaps it may be, yet). Also poetry, here, need not be necessarily more abstract than history; again, what it does share with philosophy is the exclusion of the accidental. Perhaps poetry and philosophy both share possibilities whose reasons may be concretely examined; however, poetic possibilities are mimetic representations of action, while philosophic possibilities are conceptually presented; unless there are circumstances where philosophy may be poetic—it is obvious that poetry is not a species of philosophy. Is philosophy an abstraction of mimetic representations of action? Earlier, in the first chapter, Aristotle had promised to deal with hexameter poems (which imitate by means of versified language?), but he only concerns himself with epic narrative. The likenesses between tragedy and epic are many; in fact, tragedy includes everything epic does, and in addition uses music and spectacle; since they are so similar in source, matter and form, common questions may be asked of them.

3.1.2.1.1.1. *Imitation.* In addition to their names, the arts are further defined by the objects they imitate, and by the mode in which they do so; what the poet imitates is doings. But what are doings? Can they be thoughts? Can poetry imitate thinking? In the chapter on diction and thought, Aristotle says that thought is more relevant to rhetoric than poetry. Thought is mental procedure in persons, which is shown in everything effected by their language: reason (prove or disprove), emotions, and imagination (maximize or minimize things); it is an ingredient in poetry because it is a cause of a person's actions (MC 677): "There are in the natural order of things, therefore, two causes, Thought and Character, of their actions, and consequently of their success or failure in their lives." The poet is limited to giving a picture of the outside world (and not the mental), where thought is only reflected in objective actions. (But if thought is always embodied, what more effective way to be described than poetically?) In fact, in *The Rhetoric*, Aristotle defines rhetoric itself as the facility of observing and a means of persuasion, and describes its two general means of persuasion as the example, being historical or invented parallels (illustrations and fables), and the Enthymeme, being maxims. Since persuasion has the power of stirring the emotions, some types of verse, personal lyrical poetry, may have been considered rhetoric. Thought was not the object of imitation, that is, the poet's work should not be a vehicle for expression—it should be a description.

Although imitation can, in its simplest sense, be a copying of physical objects (at least Aristotle does not exclude the possibility), the poet's intention should be to recreate the life he is considering, the situation or experience, in its true, essential form, whether it is real or imaginary. In this case, Aristotle almost allows for self-expression, but limits the imitation to an imagined experience. Would poetry, by Aristotle's definition, be the best description of Being? If productive knowledge was the most primitive kind, was poetic speech prior to theoretical? In the preface to *Lyrical Ballads*, Wordsworth wrote that according to Aristotle poetry is the most philosophic of all writing; in his poetry, Wordsworth made truth its object, a general and operative truth to be carried alive into the heart by passion. Here is an example of Wordsworth (WR 249):

> The Being, that is in the clouds and air,
> That is in the green leaves among the groves,
> Maintains a deep and reverential care
> For the unoffending creatures whom he loves.

3.1.2.1.1.2. *Poetry versus Philosophy.* In the *Metaphysics* (1025^{b}25), Aristotle calls poetry one of three kinds of intellectual activity (*pasa dianoia*): theoretical knowledge (*theoretike episteme*), practical knowledge (*praktike episteme*), and productive knowledge (*poetike episteme*). Philosophy was a theoretical knowledge, as was mathematics, physics, and theology (1026^a). Poetic knowledge is inseparable from the power to make; is knowledge of poetic knowledge, poetical or theoretical, or both? If form is always inseparable with substance must not philosophic knowledge be derivative from poetic, or practical? Productive knowledge must be prior to theoretical knowledge. Poetry is a kind of knowledgeable activity with a product from its end; the aim of poetry is an organic process—a working-out-itself of an art. Aristotle says, in the *Poetics* (1447^a): "Our subject being Poetry, I propose to speak not only of the art in general but also of its species and their respective capacities;" but nowhere does he even approach a definition of poetry, or more than passing mention of some of its species. Obviously the activities described in the Poetics are poetry, and references are made to comedy and hexameter verse, but what other literatures should have been included?

In the first chapter Aristotle lists four kinds of poetry: tragedy, epic, comedy and dithyramb; he includes instrumental music, singing, painting, sculpting and dancing as imitative arts. However, he does not limit all poetry, in the large sense, to being imitation, but he implies that what is not imitation belongs in a different category, regardless of its physical form. He did complain that people class writers according to their meter and not in virtue of the act of imitating. Obviously, as a maker of plots, the poet need not use verse, but Aristotle only makes reference to one type of play that is not in verse: the mimes (or farces) of Sophron and Xenarchus; and he refers to an epic which uses language alone. In the second chapter, he again refers to the art which uses prose or verse without music, which could include Homeric epics and Platonic dialogues. In several places, Aristotle stresses that meter does not really modify the effect of language; language has the same force in verse as in prose; and that putting a work in verse will not make poetry of it, if it doesn't satisfy the essential requirements; Herodotus would still be history. So verse does not seem to be necessary for Aristotle; why have it at all? He thinks that it is justified by experience, in the Poetics (1460a): "Hence it is that no one has ever written a long story in any way but heroic verse; nature herself, as we have said, teaches us to select the meter appropriate to such a story." The iambic is the most speakable of meters, but each meter is most appropriate for something.

3.1.2.1.2. The Genetic Science of Vico
Vico formed a genetic theory of poetry that was evolutionary and psychological. As men perceived parts of Being, they named them; but the naming changes over time. When men were newly received into humanity, they used a mute language of signs and physical objects having natural relations to the ideas they wished to express. Language and the world then passed through two other periods, a heroic language, of emblems and metaphors, during the heroic age, and a human language, of words agreed upon and meanings fixed, in the age of man. Since these first men must have thought under violent passions, the study of language must therefore proceed from a vulgar metaphysics. They learned control over the motion of bodies, which are by nature necessary agents. Vico (VI 230) thought that "Their first languages must have been formed in singing." Ihde (GI 61) forms the same conclusion: "What eventually may be said must first be sung. One gradually learns to hear *what* sounds forth from the 'song.'"

3.1.2.1.2.1. *Mythical Beginnings*. All barbarian histories have fabulous beginnings. The vulgar make up fables, which are ideal truths to fit the occasion. Poetic truth is metaphysical truth, and physical truth that is not in conformity should be considered false. First men, thought Vico, being unable to form intelligible class concepts of things, created poetic characters (the essence of fables), that is, imaginative class concepts, or universals. Vico (VI n.p.) says: "For speech was born in mute times as mental (or sign) language ... before vocal ... language; whence logos means both word and idea."

Speech may be etymologically traced to myth: The word *mythos* meant 'mute;' the word fable can be traced back through *fabula* to *logos*, which meant 'speech.' The first language was a fantastic speech making use of physical substances endowed with life. The theological poets apprehended Jove, Cybele, and Neptune, for example, and, at first mutely pointing, explained them as substances of the sky, the earth, and the sea. Later, metonymy erected the prevailing ignorance of these origins of human things into dogma. They believed that Jove commanded by signs—that his signs were real words and that nature was his language. The language itself was poetry (Aristotle placed Homer at the beginning of all poetic types); then, all philosophy, cosmology, and ethics was poetic. Goethe (n.r.) describes the language: "In Homer there is a language that in and by itself makes the poetry and does the thinking."

3.1.2.1.2.2. *Language & Imagination.* Language creates an imaginary reality, breathes life into things inert, reveals what does not yet exist, and recalls what has disappeared. Many mythologies and religions, in explaining the creation of the world from nothing, call the creative principle the Word. Vico established his science of language on the realization that poetic expression is historically and eidetically prior to logically ordered prose, as senses are prior to thought. What Aristotle said of the individual man is therefore true of the race in general: the mind understands nothing of which it has no previous impression. The mind is formed by language, before it is capable of expressing itself. As Vico (VI 236) explains: "The human mind is naturally inclined by the senses to see itself externally in the body, and only with great difficulty does it come to attend to itself by means of reflection." Ideas emerge from our interest in the world; ideas embodied in words are the focus of intention. For Vico (TA 485): "there are no ideas apart from natural languages and that men neither can nor do think except through a gestural and verbal extension of their perceptual and existential embodiment in a cultural world ..."

Vico illustrates the growth of the mind from the poetic characters and fantastic universals of primitive thought to the pure ideality in Cartesian thought. To understand the emergence of sense from non-sense, the primary realm of prelogical experience of the unnamed and inarticulate must be explored; for Vico (VI 237), this descent into the chaos of primitive myths "gives us the universal principle of etymology in all languages: words are carried over from bodies and from the properties of bodies to express the things of the mind and spirit. The order of ideas must follow the order of institutions." A valid epistemology cannot neglect the genetic and historical question of the origins of meaning, and of the forms of thought. There is logic underlying the formal rules of knowledge. Vico (VI 400) describes it: "That which is metaphysics insofar as it contemplates things in all the forms of their being, is logic insofar as it considers things in all the forms by which they may be signified." Poetry is poetic logic.

3.1.2.1.3. A Preliminary Phenomenology of Poetry

Children reconstruct the beginning of language in their development. A psychological archaeology allows the emergence through the linguistic milieu to become an observable process. Furthermore, Hines (HN 331) claims that "The child, all children, begin in chaos. Theirs is the original experience of chaos retold in the mythical cosmogonies recall infant beginnings, and yet for reflective adults those infant beginnings in chaos hide in the past like a personal pre-history, forever lost to memory and introspection." The evolutionary growth of the mind parallels the growth of minds; persons and society sustain and advance each other. Vico (VI 218) sees that, at first, men feel without perceiving, then perceive with a troubled and agitated spirit, and "finally they reflect with a clear mind." Poetry is a particular act of perception, or the establishment of Being through naming, as in Heidegger. Man emerges in a world which is already significant; the world is already given primitively as meaningful, but in struggling to express himself in a new way, a person learns to speak, to sing the world. A phenomenology of poetry begins with the body.

3.1.2.1.3.1. *Language Linked to Experience*. But how is constituted language linked to perceptual experience? Beneath the conceptual level is an emotional level where words and vowels and consonants are ways of singing the world; poetry reaches the emotions, and therefore, the perceptual world. The body is more like a work of art than a physical object: in a picture or musical work, the idea is incommunicable by means other than the colors and sounds, but it is more than just those things. A poem is more than words in a pattern; though a superficial meaning is translatable, there is a further existence in the reader's mind. The poet can give an idea of Being by presenting an experience in Being. For Merleau-Ponty (MN 208): "It is a question of that Being that pronounces itself silently in each sensible thing, inasmuch as it varies around a certain type of message, which we can have an idea of only through our carnal participation in its sense, only be espousing by our body its manner of "signifying"—or of that Being uttered whose internal structure sublimates our carnal relation with the world."

Everyday vision, operating in terms of measured distances, is regulated by practical and cognitive aims in trying to master the world. Our vision of the world is modeled on language; things are seen as words and understood in the discrete succession of the sentence. Those things which are perceived only for their signification possess no more presence than linguistic signs. Speech makes intelligence possible; but perception, and art, are much broader, and cannot be entirely contained by speech. Myth, or poetry, gives a wider understanding than even philosophical speech. Myth and rationality are polar; yet both exercise an ordering function in the world. One dimension may be analyzed by the other, but it is difficult. Mythology is a multidimensional expression, whereas rationality achieves clarity by linearly following a single idea in one dimension. One dramatic presentation in mythology could be transposed into rational thought, but it would require a series of analyses. Myth condenses a theme, which serves as a symbol (Oedipus) for the interpretation of a situation in the world, thus ordering imagination. Philosophical thought orders reason, by dispersing a theme to trace the logical connection of its structure. The philosophical analysis of myth excavates implicit meanings, and tries to clarify them—it is an archaeology. It can bring to awareness ideas in the myth, but not replace them.

3.1.2.1.3.2. *Free Fancy & Truth.* All bodies and beings are layered with invisibility; in these depths and shadows a precise consciousness cannot operate; poetry tries through language to present this unseen element. Everything has a zone around it comprised of possible perceptions which are only latently experienced, but are revealed by poetic language as lying in back of the primary perception. The real world, the correlate of factual experience, presents itself as a special case of various possible worlds and nonworlds; poetic possibility enters the real world. How does the poet, or reader, see what is there to be seen? Husserl (WH 414) contends that he creates what he sees: "There are reasons why, in phenomenology as in all eidetic sciences, representations, or, to speak more accurately, *free fancies*, assume a privileged position over against perception . . . ." As a reinterpretation of a perception, which is a limited revelation of a thing, a "free fancy" has no bounds. Next, according to Husserl (WH 414): "It is thus open to the pursuer of an eidetic essence to freely vary the perceptual field until he discovers that the consciousness of that thing absolutely must possess and still remain the consciousness of that thing." This is the normal method of operation for the poet, creating the poem, and the reader, recreating it, although neither has to be aware of it. The phenomenologist must not only use it, he always must be aware of its character.

Husserl's phenomenological reduction is really a set of investigative rules that function to direct looking; simplified, they are: suspend explanations and describe, then vary possibilities with the operation of free fancy, and finally, seek structures. The aim of the rule of imaginative variation is to expand the field (and avoid premature closure or reductionism) by trying to present a full range of possibilities. Eventually, in the richness of the experience a structure will appear; this is the invariant, and may be clear and distinct, or inexact and blurred, as Husserl discovered.

According to Husserl, the activity of imaginative variation can provide access to pure essences. Though the primary purpose of fantasy is to help to clarify the nature of an eidetic essence, Husserl admitted that the expression was too ambiguous to differentiate it from the motive force behind a poetically meaningful world. There is a distinction, but he does not draw it in the *Cartesian Meditations*. Merleau-Ponty indicates that since the spectators performing the activity are situated in wild Being and their activity is rooted in opaque foundations, there never could be a pure essence; rootedness in the visible world annuls the intuition of a pure essence. The subject can never be transcendent, since that implies a recess of pure consciousness, aloof from the world; the subject is said to be visible. There are not facts contradicting essences for a subject who sees the visible from within, only things in a complex architecture. Essences and facts are abstractions; the invisible (essences) is what is announced by the visible; and is also the framework which lets the visible be seen.

For Stevens (BG 85), as for Husserl, the successive views of reality form a circle of shapes and colors, which keep the self at the center, and allow it to evolve; the pure object mirrors the pure self.

"We seek
The poem of pure reality, untouched
By trope or deviation, straight to the word,
Straight to the transfixing object, to the object
At the exactest point at which it is itself,
Transfixing by Being purely what it is,
A view of New Haven, say, through a certain eye,
The eye made clear of uncertainty, with the sight

Of simple seeing, without reflection. We seek
Nothing beyond reality. Within it,
Everything . . . ."

A poetic image like "a view of New Haven" may conflict at first, with an expression of fact, but cause one to realize that it could be so. The operation of fancy may establish a new perspective, which comes alive as the essence of the poem. The openness of poetry to the ground of Being, its ability to present what can be, as well as what is, give it an ontological character, as Husserl (WH 415) finds, such "that any metaphor or collection of words can substitute for and expand upon the ordinary language or even scientific language equivalent of an object or thing 'out there.'" The possibilities of poetry are real possibilities in Being; in this sense poetry is closer to Being than any other expression without being in the realm of pure ideality. Husserl (WH 415) again: "Hence if anyone loves a paradox, he can really say, and say with strict truth if he will allow for the ambiguity, that the *element* which *makes up the life of phenomenology as of all eidetical science* is '*fiction*,' that fiction is the source whence the knowledge of 'eternal truths' draws its sustenance."

But poetry is an instance of fiction. How can it be the source of knowledge of eternal truths? Poetry is not eternal truths, but the source of them; Husserl's phenomenology draws from sources that cannot be put into truth relations with their products. Vico established his metaphysics of the mind on a pragmatic conception of truth; as explained by James Edie (EE 378): "The rule and criterion of truth is to have made it. Hence the clear and distinct idea of the mind not only cannot be the criterion of the truths, but it cannot be the criterion of that of the mind itself; for while the mind apprehends itself, it does not make itself, and because it does not make itself it is ignorant of the form or mode by which it apprehends itself." Truth is hence understood as an openness between a thing and the person who perceives it. Openness is a translucent medium, subject to change historically. It must always retain a coefficient of facticity, as it enlarges in time, through perceptions of Being. A proposition is untrue without a background of relations; things also exist in a web of relations. The greater the relationality the greater the truth. A larger matrix is truer than a smaller one. Poetry can enlarge truth, by widening the opening. Poetry brings about this openness, in creating possibilities for perception; it lets the advent of the truth of beings come to pass. Jaspers (BU 184) relates that "We call great art the metaphysical art which reveals through its visuality, Being itself." Art has acquired a metaphysical dimension by interpreting the world as an aesthetic phenomenon; in fact metaphysics becomes a "metaphysics of artists" in Heidegger's words (HD 117). Nietzsche reversed Platonic metaphysics, so that it dealt now with categories of the senses, and becoming; in Merleau-Ponty, the senses reach back into Being. Art becomes the expression of Being itself, as grasped by the senses and not abstractions. Poetic truth is metaphysical truth.

3.1.2.2. Origin of Metaphor

In Aristotle's *Poetics* (1457[b]) the noun has eight uses, one of which is the metaphor: "Metaphor consists in giving the thing a name that belongs to something else; the transference being either from genus to species, or from species to genus, or from species to species, or on grounds of analogy." The metaphor, in addition, may have several qualifications. In the following chapter (1459[a]), he continues a perfection of poetic diction, describing how metaphors and strange words may vitalize the language, and how "it is a great thing, indeed, to make a proper use of these poetic forms, as also of compounds and strange words. But the greatest thing by far is to be a master of metaphor. It is the one thing that cannot be learnt from others; and it is also a sign of genius, since a good metaphor implies an intuitive perception of the similarity in dissimilars." Each of these forms and such is most at place in a particular poetry: compounds in dithyramb, strange words in heroic, and metaphor in iambic, although heroic may avail itself of them all, and iambic, because of its close relation to spoken language, must limit itself to ordinary words and metaphor, or its ornamental equivalent. Here, metaphor covers many different grammatical forms: trope, synecdoche, metonymy, catachresis, and simile. Metaphors are more expressive of generality than any other linguistic device, according to Aristotle.

The advent of the machine made the world a machine. Locke hypothesized that words were solid chunks, with definite boundaries, to which other chunks may be added in combination; metaphor became decoration. Whatever could be said with metaphor, could be better said without. Descartes showed that thought was a universal, independent of words, for which words were only correlative clothes. The very structure of language was mechanistic: each thing had one meaning linked to one word.

In opposition to Descartes, Vico put forth the proposition that minds are actually formed by language. The mind is inclined by the senses to see itself externally in the body and only comes to understand itself with great difficulty by reflection. This leads to a universal principle of etymology, according to Vico (VI 237): "words are carried over from bodies. . . . The order of ideas must follow the order of institutions (or things)." From Vico, metaphors are expressions based on the experience of bodily processes, on perception in the lived world; above-below, near-far, open-closed, and light-darkness were once metaphorical distinctions, now dead.

Is it possible to speak on any level of meaning, without using words denoting perceptual experiences? Incarnation in the world precedes reflective thought; abstract language must be built up from the expression of the primacy of perceptual experience. Historical language is built on layers of metaphor. Expression is more basic, and wider, than language; man as a whole is intentional of the world, his consciousness is correlated to the world, and structures its experience by expressing its meaning. Expression precedes communication, which exceeds linguistically expressed meanings; language therefore can never say everything. Man's very existence is expressive: movements, behavior, gestures.

The most primitive elements of language are experienced events; language is anthropomorphic. Vico (VI 403) notes that: "In all languages the greater part of the expressions relating to inanimate things are formed by metaphors from the human body and its parts." Words for mental processes are metaphors from physical processes. Man has a place within Being and among beings to whom he is related through common interests; his perspectual place in nature results in his vulgar wisdom. Emerson said, to this end, that all nature is a metaphor of the human mind. Furthermore, Vico (VI 237) says: "The works of this 'wisdom' are the historical institutions which man adds to nature and which he attempts to understand by singing 'the world according to man' in poetic gesticulation and ejaculation." Metaphors are inescapable, since men are limited in their attempt to name and understand the chaos of preverbal experience by their association of it with what was previously learned, and since the relevant factors analogously between the known and the unknown are those already named.

Eliot once pointed out that certain poets wanted to secure in their poetry only the halo around the candle flame, forgetting that the radiance always emanates from a definite point of light: there is no halo without the flame. Thought is incarnate in language; language makes the thematization of meaning possible; and Being makes language possible, poetic and other.

Etymologically, most meanings once referred to sensible objects or animal activities, but the meanings of words change from context to context, from age to age; in fact, the conception of words as names of things is outmoded because facts have changed (facts as assumptions of reality which shape world views). The very fact that modern civilization has three separate words (breath-wind-spirit) while the ancients had one (*spiritus*) should elucidate a difference in reality. Jesperson states that the evolution of language shows a progressive tendency from inseparable, irregular conglomerates to freely and regularly combinable short elements. So, he concludes that both abstractness and simplicity in words are evidence of a long intellectual evolution—an evolution that was irreversibly flowing (from homogeneity towards dissociation and multiplicity) in that same direction before poets or etymologists became conscious of it. Possibly poetic metaphors were not poetic or metaphorical for the people who used them.

Thus, man uses primary perceptual categories to designate experiences of a more complex nature; in principle, no experience is incapable of being named. Since man is constrained to proceed from these few direct expressions to wider extensions of thought and communication, metaphorical language is an economic necessity. Metaphors are built on metaphors to progress from the already distinguished, the known, toward the not yet known; the metaphorical use of words is an instrument in discovering new meaning. Metaphors thus are not antithetical to sensuous thought, nor are they accidental weaknesses of thought; the metaphorical use of words cannot be avoided.

A metaphor is the intentional use of words to refer to a previously disclosed aspect of experience in order to reveal an indistinct one of a different kind. Through the free variation of experience, the indefinite is approachable in many ways: the mind is a blank tablet, instinct, a receptacle, or a computer.

Language has always had difficulty describing actions and things in the world. If each unique thing or action were named, speaking would become a burdensome impossibility. Paradoxically, in being spoken, language avoids being an inert catalog; it progresses outward from the body of the speaker toward the world, metaphorically. The concept of metaphor has been defined and used for over twenty centuries. Metaphor is used in all advanced languages. In Aristotle, metaphor was a trope, the turning of phrase, derived from *tropos*, meaning turn. Metaphor, from *metaphora*, means carrying beyond (*meta*: into the middle of, *phor*: to carry). It is defined in Webster's Seventh New Collegiate Dictionary as a "figure of speech," a "form of expression," which is an act "of representing in words." Aristotle was one of the first to say what it represented in words: metaphora, in the sense of transference, the process of transferring a word from one object of reference to another. "Metaphor consists of applying to a thing a word that belongs to something else; the transference being either from genus to species, or from species to genus, or from species to species, or on grounds of analogy. "Subsequently, metaphor was defined as analogy. The transference of a name from the whole to a part, or the reverse, became known as synecdoche, while the naming of an object through association was called metonymy.

At one time, Plato banished poets from the Republic. In a world of unchanging forms, analogy was considered useless. For Aristotle, art imitated nature, producing things in a natural manner; nature proceeded in a logical order. Poetry was a device to allow human beings to delight in imitation, as well as to learn of nature. Metaphor was a tool of poetry, noble or ignoble, depending on the subject matter.

The early Greeks built logically reasoned philosophies of thought and reality. During that same era, with entirely different values and objectives, Middle Eastern poets and thinkers were using similar stylistic devices. From the Egyptian pyramid texts:

Death is in my eyes today:
As in a sick man beginning to recover
From a deep illness.
Death is in my eyes today:
Like a well-trodden road
Along which men are returning from … wars.
     (in Wheelwright)

A similar method is employed by the Upanishads to induce the mind toward Brahma by the very inadequacy of the verse; that is, the ultimate cannot be expressed by piling metaphor on metaphor.

When he shines, everything shines after him; by his light, all this is lightened.
He is the one bird in the midst of the world; he is also like the sun that has set in the ocean.
A man knows him truly, passes over death; there is no other path to go.
(in Yutang)

Lao Tse, in the Tao Te Ching, used such metaphor to represent different angles of vision converging on the hidden unity of the world.

Thirty spokes unite around the nave;
From their not being
Arises the utility of the wheel.
Mold clay into a vessel;
From its not being
Arises the utility of the vessel. (in Yutang)

The Roman times and Middle Ages seem to have carried on the Aristotelian sense and use of metaphor. No large works were devoted to proposing new meanings for metaphors. Metaphors were used for religious meanings. As the Renaissance opened, attention to the mundane was renewed. Poems and paintings were embodiments of nature; the arts once again imitated nature. After two hundred years of investigation and celebration, the Reformation and Modern Science altered attitudes toward nature and God; the first found little use for poetic analogy, while the second found it unnecessary.

In Francis Bacon, there seems to be an ambivalence. He who expected the method of science to reveal all knowledge within a mortal lifetime, also referred to true metaphor: "Neither are these only similitudes, as men of narrow observation may conceive them to be, but the same footsteps of nature, treading or printing upon several subjects, or matters." (in Barfield) "So these hidden relations between separate objects, and between ideas and objects, already existed. If some had been discovered and described by poets, it was the duty of science to find and define them all."

As science began its task, its findings and assumptions changed the European world view, such that Hobbes admitted poets to his utopia. They were safe, because poetry no longer had validity. Shakespeare was the last of the Renaissance. In Stephen Pepper's terms Formism had been replaced by Mechanism. The world was considered a machine. Locke hypothesized that words were solid chunks, with definite boundaries, to which others chunks could be added in combination. Metaphor was a form of decoration; whatever could be said with metaphor could be better said without. B. Spinoza warned that metaphor was dangerous; uncontrolled emotions might be transferred analogously. Descartes proved that thought was a universal, independent of words, for which words were only correlative clothing. The very structure of language was mechanistic. Each thing had one meaning linked to one word.

These scientific assumptions became so pervasive that scientists and poets soon accepted the fact that all metaphor was willful abnormality of discourse. The poetry of Donne, Pope and others was a trickery of language, meaningless conceits pleasingly arranged. Poetry itself was analyzed scientifically, and in 1730 Lord Kames published a book on the laws of metaphor.

The scientific method multiplied human dividends with the industrial revolution. Darwin cut the divine umbilical cord. Metaphorical attitudes toward nature were changing. Where Wordsworth saw consolation, joy and wisdom in nature, Tennyson saw nature "red in tooth and claw." If, for Shakespeare, our bodies were gardens tended by will, many saw their bodies as programmed machines.

Charles S. Peirce and William James initiated their own world hypothesis, Pragmatism (the same as Contextualism in Pepper's schema), with the argument that the association of ideas, in metaphor, for example, was not based on similarity (as in Formal or Mechanical arguments), but on emotional congruity; if a metaphor worked for a person, it was good.

Hegel was the spiritual father of the fourth world system (after Pepper), Organicism. He regarded metaphor as a device to reasonably create unity in nature. It was also a way of referring to the three stages of unfolding: Logic, Nature, and Spirit. Whitehead is the leading exponent of this system. Each use of a root metaphor by a world hypothesis is worthy of some consideration. Each one describes a different structure.

By contrasting the views of metaphor enumerated by Black with Pepper's four root hypotheses, a rough correlation emerges (See Table 3122-1). Two other hypotheses can be added to the schema to update it: Animism and holocosmology, which considers all views valid to some extent.

Root Metaphor	Function	View
Animism (Mythology)	Identity	Identity
Formism (Rationalism)	Substitution	Similarity
Mechanism	Decoration	Similarity (Error)
Contextualism	Utility	Congruity
Organicism	Wholeness	Interaction (Exten)
Holocosmology	Frame	Star

Table 3122-1 The Meaning of Root Metaphors

3.1.2.2.1. Mechanics & Structure

There are two principles governing the creation of metaphors: the just disclosed phenomenon is given the name of a previously identified one that resembles it; and this resemblance is discovered in the most "essential" aspect of the new phenomenon, which calls forth a direct perceptual experience, already named. The metaphor consists of two parts: the focus (or tenor or figure), which designates the figurative term signified through the process; and the frame (or vehicle, or ground), which refers to subject, or context.

These terms were contributed by Black; I. A. Richards distinguished them as tenor and vehicle; they are similar to the Gestalt concept of figure and ground. For example, in the sentence, "Light is a particle," the focus is "light" and the frame is "particle." This relationship is diagrammed in Figure 31211-1.

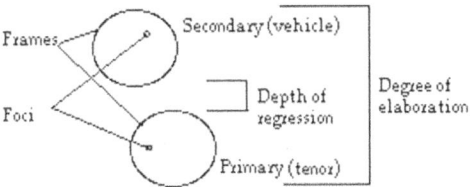

Figure 31221-1. The Mechanics of a Metaphor

For example, in the sentence: "Man sings the world," the focus is sings and the frame is world. The metaphor is a form of discourse where one of the terms is always denotative. The collocation of terms in a metaphor leads to a sort of intercourse, transaction, or transference between associated contexts; the tenor is responded to, as the vehicle, in addition to its original evoked responses.

3.1.2.2.1.1. *Focus & Frame.* The focus of the metaphor is the primary system, that which is to be understood. The frame is a secondary system that provides a pool of names. The interaction is mutual. The secondary imposes reorganization on concepts of primary ("the brain is a computer"—Popper) The meaning of two concepts is altered; a halo meaning is formed (intention—strain towards). Metaphor works because words tend to bring their baggage with them, creating a diffused aura and extending the range of strict terminology; some problems of diction may be avoided. Metaphors are source of creative reflection, in their ambiguity.

The focus of a metaphor is a primary system that refers to that which is to be understood, a brain or atom, for instance. The frame is a secondary system that provides a pool of names to be used for comparison: computer or solar system. The interactions of systems is mutual; the secondary system imposes a reorganization on the concepts of the primary, but the use of the metaphor alters perception of the secondary as well as the primary. Not only are the two concepts altered, but the meaning of the concepts is altered. And this 'halo' meaning, in its unique reducibility, permits things to be said that could not be said otherwise. In the secondary and primary systems—for "the brain is a computer"—opposites interpenetrate and are unified even though the metaphor is initially and cognitively perceived as absurd. This interpenetration is a dialectic, where opposites are unified in a metaphorical synthesis that transcends the initial contradictory conjunction of the two systems. Thus, concept formation in art and science is a working out of contradictions, as in Bohr's metaphor, "The atom is a solar system." Logical opposites logically combined assert nothing: $S+(-S)=0$. Metaphorical logic is not limited to traditional logic. It is more contextual and multivalued. The original meaning of logic in Greek was "gathering up," which is what metaphoric logic does. Metaphorical unity transcends a literal absurdity. Most scientific metaphors exhibit this: "The world is atomic," Leukippus; "The world is mathematical," Pythagoras; "Electricity is a fluid," B. Franklin. Metaphors in science are usually termed models and are used to bestow a more precise meaning to expressions.

The metaphor is a form of discourse where one of the terms is always denotative. The collocation of terms in a metaphor leads to a sort of intercourse, in the Platonic sense, transaction or transference between the associated contexts. The focus is responded to as the frame, in addition to its own original, evoked responses.

The distance between the tenor and the vehicle of a metaphor is necessary; similarity must be accompanied by some disparity. If the two are too close together, then the perspective of double vision may be lost. Johnson claimed that it was useless to compare a tree with a bush. The power of the analogy is also related to the emotive potential of the matrices. It is equally useless to compare a sneeze to a cloud.

This is reasoning by analogy not by differences, which a digital computer does. Metaphorical expression has an analogical unity in human existence. Its central organizing principle is the single person. Imagination is an instrument of perception. It points mind toward broadest meaning. It points, not toward truth, but to an ever-enlarging relational field.

It points to the frame. That which is the frame must be ambiguous. Frames must be used as metaphors. The word nature, for instance, has been used by Western philosophers in thirty nine distinct senses. Under ambiguity many meanings may hide. Nature can be regarded as a puzzle or opponent to be beaten, but both detract from total experience.

3.1.2.2.1.2. *Epiphor & Diaphor.* Valery claims that the poet is no mad versifier, but a scientist, an algebraist in the service of a subtle dreamer. Wheelwright relied on algebraic ratio to distinguish between the two functions of a metaphor: As epiphor, and, as diaphor. Epiphor means outreaching, the extension of meaning by comparison. It is transference in the Aristotelian sense, expressing similarity between the concretely known semantic vehicle and the somewhat less known semantic tenor for the purpose of hinting significance. Aristotle called the metaphor "An intuitive perception of the similarity of dissimilars." The epiphor rests on analogy. Its force, however, is increased by novelty. Good epiphors yield fresh insights about the world with a novel juxtaposition that arrests thoughts. As epiphors are used over and over again, they fade into ordinary language. An epiphor is not a symbol. Symbols are normal and literal semantic representation. Symbols are arbitrary; for instance, the word brain has no analogy to what it denotes, although some symbols do have an analogy: Hieroglyphics look like what they mean; onomatopoeia sounds as it means. Epiphors necessarily contain analogies that produce grammatical absurdities and psychological surprises. An epiphor may be represented by the following mathematical ratio for the sentence, "Light is a wave."

$$A : b :: C : b \quad or \quad \text{Light} : \text{wave} :: \text{water} : \text{wave}$$

A pure epiphor would collapse into symbol, without suggestiveness. To name something for the first time, to call a star a star, would be to create a pure epiphor.

The other quality, diaphor, is the production of new meaning by juxtaposition and synthesis. It is a semantic movement through the particulars of experience whereby new qualities and new meanings can emerge from previously ungrasped combinations of elements. The similarity is not so much antecedent, as it is in epiphor, as induced by the poet. The diaphor produces its meaning, beyond analogy, primarily by suggestion. Beyond expressing experiences of which we are not aware explicitly, the juxtaposition of the diaphor suggests new possibilities for experience. The diaphor may be diagrammed as follows for the line by Pound (UN 294), "The apparition of these faces in a crowd, petals on a wet, black bough."

$$A : B :: C : D \quad or \quad \text{faces} : \text{crowd} :: \text{petals} : \text{bough}$$

A pure diaphor would be unintelligible, since both referents would be unknown. A pure diaphor would collapse into a symbol, without suggestiveness. Abstract painting and 'random' music could be considered almost pure forms of diaphor.

A metaphor must be comprised of both, but in any proportion. According to Wheelwright (WE 88), the Egyptian pyramid texts and the Upanishads could be described as "a diaphoric succession of epiphorically tended images as a means of inducing the mind to" Ra or

Brahma. Here is a sample from the Egyptian pyramid texts:

Death is in my eyes today:
As in a sick man beginning to recover
From a deep illness.
Death is in my eyes today:
Like a well-trodden road
Along which men are returning from . . . wars.

A similar method is employed in the Upanishads to induce the mind toward Brahma by the very inadequacy of the verse; that is, the ultimate cannot be expressed by piling metaphor on metaphor:

When he shines, everything shines after him; by
his light, all this is lightened.
He is the one bird in the midst of the world; he
is also like the sun that has set in the ocean. A
man knows him truly, passes over death; there
is no other path to go.

Conversely, the Tao Te Ching is Wheelwright says, is "a diaphoric juxtaposition of particular epiphors converging on an ever central reality." Lao Tse (YU 87) uses such metaphor to represent different angles of vision converging upon the hidden unity of the world:

Thirty spokes unite around a nave;
From their not being (losing of their individuality)
Arises the utility of the wheel.
Mold clay into a vessel;
From its not being (in the vessel's hollow)
Arises the utility of the vessel.

The metaphor provides an occasion for multiple sayings, with analogous techniques.

Since the vocabulary of emotion is so comparatively under-developed, metaphor is necessary to deal with unnamed and unnamable experiences—what other words could describe what Wright meant?

Suddenly I realize
That if I stepped out of my body I would break
Into blossom.

Brooks proclaimed that all subtle emotions "demand metaphor for their expression." The synthetic capacity of metaphors can entertain contradictory feelings simultaneously.

In their synthetic capacity metaphors can simultaneously entertain contradictory feelings. A functional metaphor expresses what no declarative sentence can. It states anew, by silence and allusion. And it does it economically; as Dr. Johnson stated, with a metaphor there are two ideas in one. Two ideas are transformed into one new one: "The world is flesh." It is transfiguration, in Poggioli's (PO 157) words: "Ideas like this come from a metaphorical conception of language, not as figuration of the real, but as transfiguration."

Like a myth, the metaphor emerges from its synchronic beginnings and provides continuity of creative thought. Metaphors are formative and constitutive of our life-world. Vico pronounces that imagination is a turning out of one's self. An imaginative metaphysics shows how man becomes all things by not understanding them.

For Nowottny, the metaphor is a set of linguistic directions for supplying the presence of an unwritten literal term. With the metaphor, one can make a complex statement without complicating the grammatical construction of the sentence that carries the statement. However, implicit sentences exist in parallel action or as reflective images. The metaphor allows the sender to supply an uncontaminated image to the receiver from her own experience; for the receiver a physical immediacy is required in order to supply the missing term. These observations provide a more substantive difference between metaphor and simile; the first conveys the relationship figuratively, the second literally. After M. McCluhan, the first is a more involving medium than the second. Many writers have considered both to be figurative.

Jordan distinguishes a number of qualities of a metaphor (in Wheelwright). The metaphor is a formulation of reality as a complex of qualities. It is a process by which a complex of quality becomes individual. It is a word structure that asserts reality through form. This form is a unity of interrelated elements into a whole. The idea that metaphor expresses a likeness or a difference is perhaps a confused perception of the fact that metaphor implies a variety of qualities in the contemplated reality. It appears to overlook the fact that the essential meaning of variety is not difference of quality so much as multiplicity of quality and the presence of unlimited details of available for synthesis.

3.1.2.2.2. Creative Function of Metaphor
But the metaphor does more than present an analogy that can be experienced; it also suggests a new interpretation of both elements; to say, the brain is a computer, suggests a reinterpretation of both. It can create the similarity between terms. The metaphor purveys

unparaphrasable information; it has unique cognitive content. Like a word, the metaphor is a nexus on which are focused its various uses in similar situations in the past. Metaphors have to be described in context; it is in the context they have meaning and the power to say things; they are part of the fabric of expression, not the ornaments and illustrations of Dr. Johnson. Meaning is what is experienced; it is always experience of something; a metaphor is a vehicle of meaning, through which one sees it. Meaning is an open structure, a nonfixed eidos, which never can be possessed completely, but can be approached from an indefinite number of perspectives. The metaphor is first grasped in its meaning, not its words or logical constructions. The meanings are not dependent on the logical structure; metaphor can be reduced to simile, but with a change in meaning. A metaphor cannot be exhausted by elucidation of its cognitive content. The original expression of a metaphor is puzzling, intellectually, which causes the verbal phrase of it to be abstracted and analyzed; the apprehension is prior to the interpretation. The apprehension of metaphor is not entirely a linguistic problem; its meaning or intention precedes its interpretation.

Metaphors literally signify what their component words ordinarily signify. In a metaphor, not all of the qualitative differences are relevant and necessary to its meaning. For instance, "The poor are the negroes of Europe" has little to do with their color, at least necessarily. Richards (SE 87) asks: "What sort of orders of ?truth? are appropriate to (or possible to) whatever may be ?said? only through metaphor? When and how is what is ?said? through metaphor the same as what is said without it?" If metaphors are true or false, it depends on their workability, not on a logical necessity of their being false in order to be metaphors. Metaphor exists between the limits of several dimensions: definition, selection, coherence, and distance. A metaphor has to be somewhat indefinite in its implications; as the relations of qualities are elaborated, it becomes more definite, and a poorer metaphor; at its hackneyed extreme, it dies. At the other extreme it may not either be recognized as a metaphor, since it may appear unrelated. Metaphor cannot be composed of random juxtapositions, since they would make a meaningless swamp where anything is possible; however, a purely diaphoric assemblage would be too rarefied to understand. In any case the features of both terms must be coherent to make the metaphor successful. "Blood-sucking termites drawing the wind out of the sails of progress" is only successful as an example of incoherence; over-coherence leads again to the procrustean bed of definition. If the elements are too far apart, or too heterogeneous, they are only "yoked by violence" (as Johnson phrased it) and there is no fusion. Their similarity must be accompanied by some feeling of disparity; but if they are too close together, the reader will lose the perspective of "double vision." Johnson claimed it was useless to compare a tree with a bush.

Metaphor is a particular kind of expression; it is a set of linguistic directions for supplying the meaning of an unwritten literal term; with it, one can make a complex statement without complicating the grammatical construction of the sentence that carries the statement; however, implicit sentences exist in parallel action, or as reflective images. The idea that metaphor expresses a likeness or a difference is perhaps a confused perception of the fact that metaphor always implies a variety of qualities in the reality it contemplates, but it appears to overlook the fact that the essential meaning of variety is not difference of quality so much as multiplicity of quality and the omnipresence of unlimited details of quality available for synthesis. One metaphor for a poem has been suggested by W. C. Williams (QU 430): "A poem is a small (or large) machine made of words."

3.1.2.2.2.1. *Understanding.* Metaphor affords understanding, to some extent, by equating an unknown focus with one that is known. Although this understanding may not be a formal kind of knowledge, it allows for its continued expansion through accretion and communication. The metaphor can be refined later as the details of the two systems are sorted and differentiated.

3.1.2.2.2.2. *Creativity.* There was much concern, however, on how metaphors came about. The prevailing consensus was that primitive humans were not only barren of language, but extremely emotional and imaginative. Happily, the primitive human was able to reconcile these shortcomings by using metaphors to speak—one word referring to several objects. For instance, moving air was a soul-wind or a spirit. This theory was so tenacious that it still appears today. Blake, while implicitly supporting the metaphor theory of language, noted that the ancients animated all objects with Gods and names: Imagination was their savior, who actually created the sensible world. Blake claimed that if it were not for the poetic character, the philosophical and experimental would soon become the 'ratio of all things,' standing still or moving in circles. Wordsworth attempted a balance of world and thought, but Blake brooked no compromise.

Shelley was so captured by the idea of imagination that he disclaimed that every author was a poet in the infancy of society. He and others felt that language began with simple perceptual meanings and built by metaphor into abstract thought: "Metaphorical language marks the before unapprehended relations of things, and perpetuates their apprehension until words..." If this were true, then Macaulay would have been correct in concluding that poetry declines as civilization advances. If Shelley's premise was true, then every author today should be a great poet, and no one would find poetry in Homer, as Barfield suggests. Moving backwards in time, one finds language more and more figurative; moving forwards in time, one still finds it becoming figurative.

If both views are correct then these times meet in a golden age of metaphor making superpoets.

> 13.4. The gods evaporate like clouds
>   they came from nothing and left nothing
>   behind, not thrones or texts or ruins or treasures—
>   what man now petitions their return?
>   If we exist in the image of our creators
>   then we are clouds …
>   From *Fragments*, by Caratheodory (CC 48)

Coleridge rescued imagination by contrasting its concretely real, esemplastic—molding diverse particulars into new perspective—nature with that of fancy, which was only the accidental nature of metaphor.

Embler felt that metaphors were the very stuff that humans used to make sense of the universe. They were principles by means of which we sort our perceptions, evaluate them and guide our purpose. For him, novels, poems, and all designs, were metaphors. Possibly he was using metaphor as a metaphor for models, analogies, paradigms, and metaphors.

Ogden and Richards, in *The Meaning of Meaning*, state that when a term is taken outside of the universe of discourse for which it is defined, it becomes metaphor, which involves the same kind of contexts as abstract thought, i.e., members shall only possess the relevant feature in common, accidental ones canceling out. They obviously did not consider the accidental ones important. They divided metaphorical language into two types: symbolic, referring to the truth of reference, and emotive, having to do with character or attitude. Interestingly, they regarded primitive language as having a small vocabulary of proper names and having a magical attitude towards words; primitive metaphors were below the level of confusion resulting from abstraction.

Blair addressed the problems of the origins of metaphor (in Barfield). He hypothesized that at first the lack of proper names for every object forced primitive peoples to use one name to represent many things, and to express themselves more fully by metaphor. Naturally, all material objects were named first. For some reason, theorists like Blair, seem to presume the paucity of words for naming not only relationships but objects. The number of words possible would not seem to be as finite as the number of objects. Perhaps primitive thought perceives the many things represented by one word as one. If primitive peoples were that imaginative than thinking up new words would have been easier that making metaphorical connections.

Owen Barfield (1964) argued that the roots of speech hypothesis was fallacious. He quotes Jesperson as noting that the "evolution of language shows a progressive tendency from inseparable irregular conglomerates to freely and regularly combinable short elements." He concluded that both abstractness and simplicity in words are evidence of a long intellectual evolution, an evolution that was irreversibly flowing from homogeneity toward dissociation and multiplicity before poets or etymologists became conscious of it. For instance, Jesperson's statement on the evolution of language toward combinational elements mirrors ideas on biological genetics. Barfield admitted that etymologically most meanings once referred to sensible objects or animal activities, but the meanings of words changed from context to context from age to age. In fact, the conception of words as names of things is outmoded because facts, as assumptions of reality that shape world views, have changed. The fact that Europeans have three separate words—breath, spirit, wind—while the ancients had one—spirit—shows a difference in reality.

Nowottny stated that a precondition for the existence of metaphor is the completeness of the linguistic system. The attendant terminology of an innovation, iron spear tips or television, for instance, must be in common usage first. It would follow that in a primitive society, metaphor use would not be contemporaneous with naming.

Barfield was also critical of theorists for projecting their logic back to a prelogical time, arguing that human beings do not create language in the same manner as its logical reconstruction. If the relation of primitive to modern meaning parallels that of child to adult, then the primitive speaker may be unconscious of some differences and actually perceive a unity, in spirit. The function of poetry is to discover Shelley's 'unapprehendeds'.

But if primitive people already abound in unities, then what could the function of their poetry be? Or is it poetry? Perhaps Barfield has made an unquestioned assumption or projection, that of projecting poetry back to a prepoetic time, attributing a device to them, metaphor, of which they had no knowledge or need. Archaic songs and epics are communications or ordering codes. Metaphors are more accurately actualities than linguistic terms. Barfield alluded to this problem, writing that "myth is the child of meaning begotten by imagination," but this is the very meaning that changes from context to context. He perceived, after Blake, that without the poetic principle, knowledge would end in algebraic stagnation. He compared the struggle between the rational and poetic principles as two buckets on separate ends of rope above a well, with the rational ascending. Although the principles are inseparable, he is wrong to think them inversely related. They are not. It is possible to become more rational and more poetic.

Hayakawa mentions that art is the ordering of human symbolic processes, and that symbols of symbols, and symbols of symbols of symbols (dissociation?) can be manufactured indefinitely by the human nervous system. To increase the order of anything means to make it describable with less information (compare with principle least effort of Ziff). If Hayakawa is right, then the dissociation is historical. Then over time, metaphor would be more and more necessary for synthesizing relations, and science for analyzing them. A scheme of dissociation is shown in Figure 312222-1.

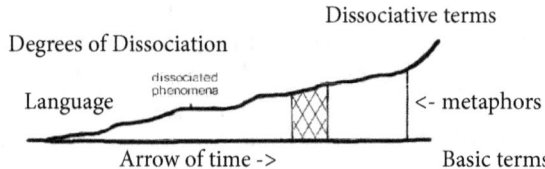

Figure 312222-1. Dissociation and Metaphor

As time progressed metaphor would become more necessary for synthesizing relationships (and science for analyzing them). Archaic peoples could make metaphors if linguistic dissociation had occurred. Although a poetic method, like a scientific method, may be considered independent of time, poetry and science are historical.

3.1.2.3. Uses of Metaphor
Although poetry uses metaphors, philosophy and science also use metaphors to increase the understanding of their topics of inquiry.

3.1.2.3.1. Philosophical Metaphor
Can metaphors be avoided by philosophers? Should they be avoided? Historical language seems built up of layers of metaphorical language; the more fundamental metaphors, first derived from the experience of bodily processes and perceptual experiences, are dead; the most common metaphors—above-below, near-far, front-behind—are unrecognized in

their usage, they are too familiar. Philosophy, in using language, cannot avoid these metaphors; tracing etymological roots may give some insight into philosophical problems. Words that originally designate a perception, may be used to a new purpose; for instance, the perception of light may be used to denote intellectual understanding.

The Greeks invented a number of metaphors that are still of use in philosophical tradition. In *The Discovery of the Mind*, Snell enumerates the words designating sensory processes in Homer, and illustrates the naming of mental operations after these. From the verbs designating each a specific type of vision, some were adopted for philosophical use: the word meaning "to be a spectator" (*theoros*), came to mean contemplation (*theorein*); the word for vision (*noein*) came to mean thinking (*noos*). Thinking was metaphorical, a kind of seeing. Furthermore, Snell relates that in the early period of Greek language the verbs to see take their cue from the act of seeing, while later on they pertain to the operation common to every glance. He also shows that the progressive rendering of the concept of the body follows the pattern of the verbs denoting sight; in language, the activity is first understood in terms of its conspicuous modes, and progressively expresses the essence of the act.

Snell distinguishes between two categories of metaphors, depending on whether they are derived from an adjective or a verb. In general, the metaphors based on similarity (adjectival), such as "poetry is sweet," or "happiness is light," are philosophically unimportant; in Sappho (SN 196), however, the adjectival form became a proportion, "Arignota shines among the Lydian ladies as the moon shines among the stars." This scheme becomes philosophically fruitful in Heraclitus, although it does not give access to the depth of a thing since it is concerned with its appearance, in relation to its opposite; the adjectival form lacks the element of necessity to describe the essence of a thing.

Those metaphors that spring from the verb, however, are more philosophically profitable: Dead objects move, water flows, and fire rises. The abstract formulation of intellectual phenomena proceeds directly from analogy with physical organs, in Greek thought: *psyche* is the breath, *noos* is the absorber of images. Thus, abstract thought is never entirely detached from metaphors.

Edie credits Plato with fixing a large number of technical terms from metaphors, making mature philosophical thought possible. Edie traces the notion of thought as conception through Plato's dialogues, *Theaetetus, Symposium, Phaedrus*, and finally the *Sophist*, where thinking is an intercourse between the soul and the world of real being.

The fact that the terms of a metaphor are opposites, or at least not equivalent, and are asserted to be, introduces a paradox: truth transcends absurdity. Brooks (BO 322) notes that: "If we recognize the paradoxical nature of the truth mediated to us by metaphor, we can see how two very different modes of poetry can spring from the paradox at the heart of metaphor. The paradox may insist upon the wonder—or the irony—of the state of affairs revealed." Typically, the Romantic poets emphasize wonder, while the neoclassic poets use irony. Perhaps the same distinction could be made between the Phenomenologists and the Linguistic Analysts.

The paradoxical image is the origin of a new consciousness, which restores autonomy to language. Bachelard (BC 79) says: "The metaphor comes to give a concrete body to an impression difficult to express. But it is relative to a psychic being different from itself. The image, product of absolute imagination, takes its whole being from imagination." The form of ambiguity forces the reader to imagine all possible implications inherent in the metaphor. When the metaphor is complete, both terms acquire an imaginative power. Bachelard (KG 12) again: "Every metaphor contains in itself a power of reversibility; the two poles of a metaphor can alternately play the role of the ideal or the real. With these inversions, the most hackneyed expression like *flight of oratory*, comes to take on a little substance, a little real movement."

In the *Rhetoric*, Aristotle observed that every metaphor founded on analogy ought to be equally appropriate when inverted. The modern image is a thing-figure, independent of the pretext-object, a metaphor with only one is an occult affinity; every interior link is eliminated by a process to confuse dimensions; "imagery without strings" the image makes itself a seal or emblem; Ortega (PO 197) calls it "algebra of the metaphor." Aristotelian reversibility is made impossible, when there is no reference to reality, when idea is divorced from figure.

3.1.2.3.1.1. *Metaphor Points.* A metaphor is not a literal description as an active substitute for a description; the metaphor points out the window at something instead of describing it. In fact, it is better than pointing, since it directs attention to an unnamed quality, and offers a named idea for it to be thought of as. When the literal use of language is inadequate, metaphor provides a focus and context for thought. The gnoseological importance of metaphor is that it precisely conveys a meaning that might otherwise be confused. As Aristotle (1459a) said, "to know how to invent fine metaphors means to know how to grasp the resemblances that objects bear to one another" and qualified (1414a) "in philosophy, too, the ability to perceive similarities between objects which are far apart is evidence of an acute mind." Philosophy, indeed, could not say anything without falling back on metaphor. Metaphors of light and seeing are the basis of Greek epistemology; thinking is a kind of seeing, for which men need light. Edie's article has an excellent exposition of this.

The metaphor, "meaning is a fabric," was used in Parmenides and Plato. In his dialogues, Plato used the dialectical method to define the epistemological problem; dialectic is the science of the texture of discourse, using the metaphors of weaving (*synkritike*, the art of combining) and tracing the woven (*diakritike*, the art of separating). Metaphor is the art of combining. In his use of intention in the phenomenology of consciousness, Husserl used the word in its etymological sense (*intendere* = stretch out, strain towards). Consciousness is an active exerting; intention directs it toward the world. Consciousness uses metaphors because it is incarnate; metaphors designate the same reality though each is from a particular perspective and carries its baggage from its sedimented specificity.

Metaphors, indeed like the ambiguity of the mind, are the source of creative reflection. The poet is no mad, disheveled versifier, but a scientist, an algebraist in the service of a subtle dreamer (after Valery). The language of metaphor is a source of limiting experience, to be used as a means of validating notions from introspection and the natural sciences. Any approach to metaphysics is metaphorical. Philosophers have used metaphors, but not delineated the logos of the metaphor. Metaphorical language serves two philosophic purposes: (1) to evoke some sense of that which is literally inexpressible (poetic metaphor provides some tools for such evocation) and (2) to use nonliteral language to gain partial access to insights not completely open to reason (incapable of literal expression). This language is a sign post for pointing beyond itself, and a limiting boundary. The metaphor allows showing, without naming. It is the existential limit of philosophical thought—a penumbra.

The use of metaphor is marginal in objective philosophy, but it is pervasive in our language and conceptual system, so it must be central to ideas of truth and meaning. It is a basic mechanism for understanding experience. And it can create new meaning, similarities and define a new reality. Metaphor is not merely of language. It is a matter of conceptual structure. Conceptual structure involves all senses, not just intellect.

Freedom, economics and equality are political ways of indirectly getting at the issue of a meaningful existence. Although political and economic ideologies can be framed in metaphorical terms, improper transference can degrade the context. To strictly believe that labor is a resource, like copper or water, is to ignore the meaning of work and to demean its dignity.

Most of our concepts are organized by spatial metaphors: good, virtue and rational is up; bad, depravity and emotional is down. These are systematically related. Happy is wide or high, sad is narrow or low. These are also experiential. The values in a culture are coherent with metaphorical structure. The future is up, for instance. But there are conflicts in subcultures: more is better or small is beautiful.

Rituals are typically metaphorical kinds of activity. Personal rituals are experiential gestalts. Cultural and personal metaphors are partially preserved in ritual. Metaphors and values can be propagated by ritual. There is no culture or person without ritual.

Cosmologies can be understood as having a root metaphor. Stephen Pepper distinguished four root metaphors for world hypotheses, which can be expanded to include animism and holocosmology.
- Animism (Black Elk)
- Formism (Plato)
- Mechanism (Bacon, Newton)
- Contextualism (Peirce, James)
- Organicism (Whitehead)
- Holocosmology

These metaphors should be considered descriptive summaries distilled from centuries of human thought. And they are a useful framework for discussion. Pepper noted that formism and contextualism suffered from an inadequacy of precision, while mechanism and organicism from an inadequacy of scope. For that reason, contextualism and mechanism tended to complement one another, as do contextualism and organicism. Organicism and formism are "hostile;" mechanism and contextualism are simply "eclectic." Furthermore, formism and mechanism are analytic, while contextualism and organicism are synthetic; and formism and contextualism are dispersive, while mechanism and organicism are integrative. Animism is synthetic and integrative. Holocosmology combines all of these views into a complementary matrix. It uses qualitative descriptions, from poetry to catastrophe theory and fuzzy sets, to place humanity in a whole framework. It is systems theory tied to animism. Caratheodory tries to express the animate system:

The earth turns; sun lights forests
and fields, and they breathe;
[matter] feels.

    Pines transform light to [sugar].
    Then the earth turns from the sun
    and the forest exhales.

Leaves disappear in flames
invisibly, radiating heat at night.
The forest is a burning house—
whole mountains burn coldly,
more slowly than stars.
        Life is fire, and it does
        not need a body of its own;
        it dies and is reborn in everything.
We live by the interior touch of flame,
tenuous flame, dissolving weight;
fire is the [wood] in bloom.
        'Heraklitus's Dream,' by A.M. Caratheodory (CC 20)

3.1.2.3.1.2. *Poetry & Language.* Poetry and language aspire to transcend the world of senses, to attain a super-reality, metaphysics, a sublimation and negation of human reality. Depth is primary, and form secondary in Bachelard (BD 245): "Living imagination is not content with comparisons. It is not satisfied with surface colors or a fragmentary form. It wants the *totality of the image and the entire dynamics of the image.*" For Pepper the metaphor is a basic analogous way of comprehending the world; metaphysical systems are describable in terms of a root metaphor: for example, Royce and Whitehead are organicists—the world is organically structured and every event is an organic process. Edie (ED 538) thinks that, phenomenologically, metaphor is an "existential necessity that pervades all the 'sub-universes' of meaning." In Aristotle, metaphor was a trope, a turning of a phrase, which was derived from the Greek *tropos*, meaning turn (it is related to the word tropical, from the turning of the sun, and to an eidotrope, which is a form of chromatrope, an instrument for exhibiting certain effects of light). The Greek word for universe was *to olon*, from *holos*, the whole, which Cicero transcribed into Latin as *universum*, from *unus* + *vertere*, turned into one whole. (To transcribe Cicero's concept back into Greek might yield holotrope, turning into a whole, or perhaps metaphoring into the whole.) As well as being representative of, the metaphor seems etymologically linked to, the universe. Metaphor, the word itself, means 'carrying beyond,' from the Greek *metaphora*. Words are spirit which became visible in flesh. Words in a poem reach out in all directions causing the unexpected appearance of branching lines, with an emergent richness of patterns. The poem is the center of gravity, where, in the metaphor, meanings converge; their condensation accounts for their dreamlike reasonableness—the poem itself becomes a metaphor of an all enclosing kind. Metaphor must be the language of meta physics (commonly accepted as meaning beyond the physics, in

The Oxford Dictionary of English Etymology). Kaelin (KA 255) concludes: "For when the question of the reality of the "real world" is posed, metaphor is the only language we have." Or, in the words of Norman O. Brown (BRO 266): "In the beginning was the word, in the beginning was the deed; in the resurrection, in the awakening, these two are one: poetry. The antimony between mind and body, word and deed, speech and silence, overcome. Everything is only a metaphor; there is only poetry."

> Last Echoes of a Song Half Lost
> Man-enfolding Earth . . .
> Life-giving
> Evening, the days old age.
> > Empedocles (LI 65)

3.1.2.3.2. Scientific Metaphors

Science has long made use of the metaphorical process to construct its models. Bacon (BF 86), who expected the scientific method to reveal all knowledge within a mortal lifetime or two, also referred to true metaphor: "Neither are these only similitudes, as men of narrow observation may conceive them to be, but the same footsteps of nature, treading on printing upon several subjects, or matters." So these hidden relations between separate objects, and ideas and objects, already exist; if some have been discovered and described by poets, it is the duty of science to find and attempt to define them all.

The focus of the metaphor is a primary system, which refers to that which is to be understood: the brain, or atom; the frame is a secondary system which provides the pool of names to be used. The interaction of the systems is mutual: the secondary system imposes a reorganization on the concepts of the primary, but the use of the metaphor alters the perception of the secondary system and the primary. Not only are the two concepts altered, but the meaning of the concepts is altered. And this "halo" meaning, in its unique irreducibility, permits things to be said, which could not be otherwise. In the secondary and primary systems ('the brain is a computer") opposites interpenetrate and are unified—the metaphor is initially (cognitively) perceived as absurd. This interpenetration is a dialectic, where opposites are unified in a metaphorical synthesis, which transcends the initial conjunction of two systems. Concept formation in science is a working out of contradictions. "Light travels in straight lines." "The atom is a solar system." Logical opposites (S, -S) logically combined assert nothing; metaphorical unity transcends a literal absurdity. Certain scientific metaphors exhibit this: Lucretius, Democritus, and Leucippus; "The world is atomic," and the Pythagoreans, "The world is mathematical," and Franklin's, "Electricity is a fluid." Metaphors in science are termed models, and are used to bestow a more precise meaning to expressions.

According to T. Kuhn, there is no methodological evolution of science; rather, normal science progresses by a succession of paradigms, which he described as noncompetitive and open-ended. He stated that paradigms are the traditions described by the historian under rubrics like: Ptolemaic astronomy or Copernican; Aristotelian dynamics or Newtonian. These examples include law, theory, application, and instrumentation together, and provide models from which the traditions of scientific research spring. In his view, science proceeded by working out problems uncovered by each current paradigm. Should problems occur that could not be ignored, suppressed or resolved, then a revolution would occur to replace the paradigm. The new paradigm would have to include all the old data as well as the new problematical data. Metaphoric systems are the core of structural coherence. For Kuhn, a metaphor is the vital spirit of a paradigm; its best organizing relation. The notion of paradigm includes techniques, examples, community values, and a central metaphor.

Science makes use of the metaphorical process to construct its models. Bacon referred to true metaphor as "the footsteps of nature." The Greek word for universe was to holon, from holos, the whole. Cicero transcribed it into Latin as universum. Retranscribed, Cicero's word might be holotrope, meaning turning whole. Novalis (BO 171) equated man and metaphor, as the blueprint of the world. "Man=Metaphor," stated Novalis. "We are looking for the blueprint of the world—that is what we are ourselves."

Scientists make assumptions about their subjects in the context of their cultural situation.

Other assumptions of science are more subtle and more limiting:
1. Predicate logic
2. Invariance of regularities of nature in time and place
3. Classes are eternal and immutable. Furthermore, science is concerned with knowledge of kinds, not necessarily knowledge of individuals. The limits at both ends, prokaryotes and planet, thus fall out of range of the process.
4. Universe as a machine. The metaphor of mechanism by Descartes (the world is a machine) implies that matter is inert and that machines must have a creator, that is they are not self-making. Although the metaphor is no longer used in physics, ecology is still struggling with the machine as well as economic metaphors.

Other cultural-scientific assumptions have been incorporated into the works of science by others. For example, compare the assumptions of Bacon-era scientists with Darwin-era scientists. Pre-Darwin assumptions included an absolute, immutable, omnipotent God; great chain of being; economic subsistence; and, social inequality. Whereas Darwin's assumptions included absolute space-time; atoms as discrete units; economic discrimination; and, social inequality.

Lynn Margulis (1991) suggests that the labels of the modern synthesis, including cladistics, inclusive fitness, and cost-benefit energetics, are imponderable immeasurables, having no reference in the real world. Margulis argues that Neo-Darwinist fundamentals are derived from the mechanist worldview. Such fundamentals include a bodiless, linear concept of evolution and uncritical acceptance of adaptation. These fundamentals, burdened with pre-evolutionary legacies, are at odds with a nonmechanistic systems philosophy. They ignore physiology, metabolism, and diversity. They fail to describe the reciprocity of a living environment. Life does not adapt to a passive prior environment, it produces and modifies its surroundings.

Fleck's theory claims that "scientific facts" are merely consensuses among socially interacting scientists. A fact is a product of a complex social process beginning with individual observation and terminating with a stylized statement of truth that is integrated into scientific knowledge of a society. Others have shown that the measurement of data is subject to expectations and social conditions. Margulis lists some of the technical terms of the Neo-Darwinists, such as species, individual, units of selection, fitness, and genotype, as "battle cries." Fleck suggests that all quantification associated with them is indirect and involves assumptions and unstated hypotheses, as well as the necessary subjective element. Why does the use of the terms continue on the mechanistic "thought-collectives?" Because they are consistent with the major metaphors of the industrial civilization that are concerned with technology, power, and wealth. We can expect change only when the metaphors change (evolve or shift).

3.1.2.3.2.1. Metaphorical Basis of Science: A Tangled Bank
The entire activity of science is guided by metaphors. Metaphors can allow scientists to deal with complex situations. The metaphor has a boundary. The meanings of a metaphor can be ontological (physical things) or structural (quantified or valued).

Ghiselin admits that Darwin's theory of evolution destroyed the tradition of natural economy with its essences ordered by reason, but he still uses a rational economics for his metaphors of individualism.

Ghiselin uses metaphors from economics to understand species. Metaphors emphasize likenesses between living things and languages or human constructs. Metaphor in the broad sense includes similes, analogies, models, patterns, paradigms. A metaphor 1. furnishes a label and 2. emphasizes similarities. It not only defines and extends new meanings, but redescribes domains seen already through one metaphoric frame. With metaphors, logical consistency is no longer required.

The word individual is a metaphor. As such it refers to aggregates (sand), functional units (populations/species), and autonomous, self-regulating beings (a wolf). The word whole is a metaphor. A 'thing' is a metaphor, though so old it is considered a real term. A thing (or part) is that which can be separated from other things, thus intimately related to the idea of boundaries. Where we make boundaries usually depends on past experience. Interface as a synonym implies that the boundary is Janus-faced.

3.1.2.3.2.2. *Simple Metaphors*. Certain kinds of metaphors appear regularly in biological works.
1. Cell. Robert Hook used the metaphor of monk's cells, and religious orders, to describe the cells of a plant. But, they were more mysterious; they seemed to have no doorways.
2. Chain. Chain (horsetail) metaphor. a linear, one-dimensional, jointed line. Biology has used the chain metaphor widely. A. O. Lovejoy traced the use from the Greeks to Schelling. All living beings can be ordered in a single linear series.
2. Tree. The tree metaphor was used by Porphyry to display kinds. Buffon creates a genealogical tree for dogs and their varieties in different climates. Biologists started using, in the 18th century, alternatives to the one-dimensional chain: a two-dimensional tree (or network). Darwin's use, however, still kept the vertical component. Peter S. Pallas (1741-1811), in his book *Elenchus zoophytorum*, considers four structures in which living beings might be placed: the 1-d chain, the 2-d net, the 2-d tree, and a 3-d polyhedron. Pallas notes that the genera of organic beings could be better disposed on the faces of a polyhedra with many compartments than on the chain, but does not pursue the idea. He considers briefly the net as an interlacing of the links of several chains. But concludes that the image of the tree is the best solution (possibly because it was easier than polyhedra?).
4. Net. Referring to Gladiolus, Albrecht von Haller remarks that nature has connected her genera in a net, not a chain, but that

mankind cannot follow anything but a chain because it cannot expound several things at once in speech (Wells, p. 72).

5. Map. Linnaeus compared his table of the vegetal kingdom to a map.

Darwin used the 'struggle for existence' as a metaphor (1859, The Origin of Species): "I use this term in a large and metaphorical sense including dependence of one being on another, and including (which is more important) not only the life of the individual, but success in leaving progeny." The struggle is between individuals of a species or different species and with the physical conditions.

In continuing to describe the struggle for existence in the next paragraph, Darwin says, "It is the doctrine of Malthus applied with manifold force to the whole animal and vegetable kingdoms; for in this case there can be no artificial increase of food, and no prudential restrain from marriage." Thus we see that the metaphor arose from the socioeconomic view of the ruling classes of the time that the suffering of the poor was inevitable. Must we always have these cheesy economic metaphors inflicted on us? Ghiselin and Hull continue the anthropocentric tradition by comparing species with corporations. Ecology is a much more fruitful source of metaphor.

This metaphor formed part of the basis of a new worldview where nature was a theater of violent competition. The frame where a metaphor originates carries the conceptual baggage of the time. Over time it supports the idea of superiority of "favoured" races in the struggle for existence and emphasizes the role of competition in biological and cultural situations, at the expense of other interactions

The source for Darwin's metaphor for natural selection was in artificial selection on farms. Wallace also recognized that it was a metaphoric term. Gray notes that implicit in the metaphor is a clear separation of variation and selection of the variation, between organism and environment. (Hull keeps the same distinction is his arguments for interactor.) Organisms remain passive while the environment does the choosing (nonteleological or not). The separation may be true for artificial selection, but not co-constructing organism/environment systems. Darwin did change, regretted not calling the process 'natural preservation.' Wallace described evolution as a conservation process, similar to the centrifugal governor of a steam engine.

Adaptation is a metaphor. An assumption of it is that there is a fixed eternal environment to which species are fitted (Lewontin 1983). Although it has been productive, it has limitations. The environment is ontologically prior to organisms, leading to view of environment as force and organisms as passive objects, like keys that fit locks, or not.

Fitness is a metaphor and its meaning can be reversed. Some scientists reverse the accepted meanings of fitness and adaptation. Meredith states that the lesson of nature is moderation in all things, "even in fitness." Fitness builds up in an ecosystem as it matures. Selection at the organismic level is selection of the fit. Species level selection is selection of the unfit (extinction of the strongest). The levels of selection must balance, so that life is not too fit or too unfit. Evolutionary fitness cannot keep increasing. In some cases it decreases with time. Cope's notice of survival of the underspecialized; Haeckel's observations on senescence. Perhaps species are self-limiting in fitness. Meredith proposes that altruism is a technique of species limitation that would increase the overall longevity of a species, "unfit enough to be compatible with a limited planet."

And, of course, species was just a metaphor. Darwin: "I look at the term species as one arbitrarily given, for the sake of convenience, to a set of individuals closely resembling each other, and that it does not essentially differ from the term variety." (OS, p. 111). Alas, he ends up denying the existence of species. All difference in organisms becomes one of degree and not kind. He has other definitions later that require the concept of essence.

Darwin used the tangled bank as a metaphor. The metaphor of the tangled bank evokes the mutuality and interdependence of the interactions of organisms in webs. Darwin (1962): "It is interesting to contemplate a tangled bank, clothed with many plants of many kinds, with birds singing on the bushes, with various insects flitting about, and with worms crawling through the damp earth, and to reflect that these elaborately constructed forms, so different from each other, and dependent upon each other in so complex a manner, have all been produced by laws acting around us."

3.1.2.3.2.3. *Metaphors of Evolution.* Evolution has used metaphors to increase understanding, from the line, as in a genealogy, to the river, the tree, as used by Ernst Haeckel, and the explosion. Merleau-Ponty used an explosion as a metaphor for evolution. Merleau-Ponty considers that the direction of evolution relies on a pseudo-teleology that is the inverse of mechanism. A great "pattern mixed-upness." Evolution is a radiation of life. Rather than relying on evolution for a metaphysics, he called for a "phenomenal topology" of things as they loom upward bodily around us. M. Grene states that evolutionary theory is a poor crutch for renewal of ontology because the records take one every which way.

M. Bunge used black boxes as metaphors. The idea of the black box was originally conceptualized by electrical engineers to describe certain unknown systems devoid of structure. Black box theories include kinematics, thermodynamics, information theory, scattering-matrix theory, and circuit theory. The black box approach is useful for all theories whose variables are external and global, that are simple and have a high degree of generality. As theories are supported by observation, black boxes become translucent. The empirical theories listed below with their root metaphors range from black to almost transparent.

- Man is an atom man is an animal (Pribram)
- Man is a system (Laszlo)
- Man is a computer (Arbib)
- The brain is a hologram (Pribram, Miller, Arbib and others)

The idea of a hologram as metaphor for the brain will be examined more closely, since it will be proposed as a metaphor for metaphor.

3.1.2.3.2.4. *Hologram as Metaphor.* The metaphor has a unique structure, which it shares with a model, but not literal language. For instance, the optical hologram (*holos* = whole, *graphein* = write) has been suggested by Arbib as a metaphor for memory. The first stage of a central representation in the memory might be a visual information store. Neisser calls the store an icon. It is not photographic; icon storage is the unorganized collection of the primitive features of a visual field. It probably contains only those features that have automatically been extracted from the event by a biological feature detector process, occurring between the retina and the cortex. The information extraction is an active process, subservient to schemas and programs constructed from prior experience, and expectancy and familiarity with the event. The iconic storage is brief, but visible to the perceiver, who recognizes only that something is there. Until the perceived can analyze, integrate, or label the icon, it is uncoded, unidentified, unrecognized, and unfamiliar; he does not know what he sees until it is processed. It must be of shorter duration than that for fixing in visual exploration (250 milliseconds).

When an object is illuminated by a light source, each point on the object radiates in a spherical pattern, as though each point was a source of light. If photo-sensitive material is placed before such reflected light, the emulsion will be uniformly exposed. If, however, a board with a small pinhole is interposed between the object and the film, only the light from one specified point on the object will fall on a specific point on the film, such that an image of the object is described, with some defraction due to the wave-like character of light. The propagation of light energy is a wave form having both amplitude and phase.

Photographic film, being an energy-detection system, records only the intensity (square of the amplitude) in a two-dimensional mapping of the point-to-point brightness of the object. Is there any way to recover, or to record, the information relative to the phase? Since the film has the capability of recording both the amplitude and the phase, it is necessary only to develop a technique to utilize it; that technique is holography. To record a hologram, the amplitude and phase information are converted into intensity variations by using the interference between two interacting sources of light. This is accomplished by providing a second source of illumination incident on the photographic surface, directly, unmodulated by an intervening object. This second source of light is referred to as the reference, and is always split off from the main source so that it will be coherent with it. It is also the reference for the determination of the phase difference between the two beams.

The reference interacts with the light reflected from the object to map, on the two-dimensional film surface, the relative amplitude and phase of each object point into an intensity function. The hologram is essentially an optical computer; a four-by-five inch hologram is essentially an optical computer; a four-by-five inch hologram can store one billion characters at sixty resolution elements per character—this storage capacity exceeds the number of all written symbols ever conceived.

Can the hologram be used as a metaphor for memory, and, if so, how? Arbib (AR) compares them as follows: Memory may be described by the following select corollaries:

- Memory is a dynamic process, located in an action frame; the perception of a room, for instance, is recalled as more than a two-dimensional perspective, and as more than one instant. We see 3-dimensions instead of isolated 2-dimensional perspectives.
- In some cases, gross brain damage may be experienced without a resulting loss of memory, which implies that memories are not localized, or photographic—in a pictorial sense—in nature.
- Memories of many different events can be stored in the same region of the brain (perhaps this would explain mnemonics and synaesthetic images from releaser stimuli).

The hologram distributes its record across a two dimensional structure, rather than word by word, as in certain kinds of computer storage, or point by point, as in a picture. Although the hologram is different from the brain in fundamental respects, it may be compared with the preceding corollaries:

- A three-dimensional image is "recalled," and it is equally viewable from multiple perspectives.

• Each part of it can reproduce much of the entire image, although the resolution decreases as the area of the part decreases; a picture by contrast is too sharply localized to be reproduced from a corner. This is because the hologram distributes its record across the whole two-dimensional structure, rather than word-by-word, as in certain types of computer storage, or point-by-point, as in a picture.
• Several images can be superimposed on the same film, using different wavelengths, and later recovered individually since each reference beam restarts only its own wavefront.

If the metaphor is to have any utility, then the reference beams must comprise waves of neural activity. Pribram actually suggests that there is a neural hologram; that it is obtained as a result of interference on neurons between a pattern sent directly (impinging on near end of dendrites) and a slightly delayed pattern (on far end of dendrites). (How would fuzzy sets be related??)

The coherence requirement could be supplied by thousands of parallel fibers in optical tract. Pribram thinks that figure/ground contradictions form interference patterns in optical tract. In the brain one is dealing with electrical discharges between neural synapses that generate standing electromagnetic wave forms of which alpha rhythm is an example. The holographic hypothesis is also good for an explanation of consciousness of the self, the experience of standing out; a mindscape created by synchronized wave forms, projected outward like sound from stereo speakers. Consciousness is heightened by disparities between feedback and feedforward.

In comparing memory to a hologram, we must hypothesize that thinking is the propagation of waves of neural activity rather than a sequential firing of individual neurons (perhaps in a similar way to the McCulloch-Pitts theory of nerve-nets). In a memory wave, fronts of sensory excitation would be frozen into a neural hologram, to be read out whenever that memory experience is recalled intentionally; perhaps associative memories could be explained by the ghost images from a nearly identical reference beam. This metaphor could further allow the possibility of appropriate concepts for modeling adaptive modifications in the action-oriented distributed computations of a layered, somatotropically organized computer.

The problem of remembering may be modeled after a data storage and retrieval system in such a manner: memories are stored in the brain as holograms on film, it is assumed; there must be also an explanation of how memories are matched appropriately with a current experience. To query the current experience, the brain constructs the equivalent of a spatial filter in the form of a Fourier-transform hologram of the experience, to which it simultaneously Fourier-transform holograms of all previous experiences; if the current experience were known, a light would shine through the 'file'. The dawning of an insight has always been represented, at least recently, by a light bulb. Memory loss could be explained by the model as a loss of rotational sensitivity in the stored holograms. This metaphor could be used even to interpret philosophical problems of perception, such as Wittgenstein's duck-rabbit; each a aspect would be constructed from icons into one hologram and the dawning of a new aspect would be tantamount to the switching of filters.

Arbib comments that it would be of less value to the organism to reconstruct a visual input per se than to recall vital features of past experience. How are words related to these features? How would it be explained that some people verbalize, others visualize and a few synaesthetize? The appropriate notion for a neural hologram might not be a Fourier transform as Pribram argues, but a nonintrovertible feature transform in which spatial array of intensities is replaced by spatial array of features. In the place of a frequency spectrum in real hologram, an action spectrum in the neural model would have features that would enable an animal to react rapidly. An animal does not need an invertible record from which the original stimulus can be constructed; it needs a nonintrovertible record from which an appropriate response could be made.

Not all information needs to be stored. Efferent control could filter incoming information. That is, the reference beam could negate input; recall would only elicit noise. It would be simpler to store all inputs than to compute which information should be stored. Short-term memory may correspond to current activity around the loops; long-term may correspond to changes in connectivity of neural hologram box. Holography is a useful metaphor if not used literally. Portions of wave activity can help recreate the whole front, with different cueing waves allowing multiple storage. This is quite different from computers with word-by-word memory.

In the neural analog of a hologram, the reference beam could comprise a sampling of ongoing neural activity, both peripheral (for recall of its response) and central (for thoughts related to present). This loop would explain temporal recall of sequences. Miller demonstrated that immediate memory depended more on the number of items to be memorized, than on the information carried. The holographic model of brain does not deny specialization; it is specialized and holographic. Verbal processing is only one memory system. Other, more primitive memory systems may exist also. Since people can recognize much more than they can recall, the distinction between recall and recognition may illuminate the differences between memory modes. Intuition is a holistic system memory. Memory is a function of the organism as a whole, as Bergson recognized.

The metaphor can be extended, using Haber's theory of icon recognition and a simple explanation of the hologram as an energy recording system. The first stage of a central representation in memory might be a visual information store. Neisser named such as store an icon. Icon storage is hypothesized to be the unorganized collection of the primitive features of a visual field. It is probably not photographic. It probably contains only those features that have automatically been extracted from the event by a biological feature detection process, occurring between the retina and the cortex. The information extraction is an active process, subservient to the schemas and programs constructed from prior experience and the expectancy and familiarity of the organism with the event. The iconic storage is brief, but visible to the perceiver, who recognizes only that something is there. Until the perceiver can analyze, integrate or label the icon, it is uncoded, unidentified and unfamiliar; the perceiver does not know what is seen until it is processed. Therefore, it must be of a shorter duration than that for fixing in visual exploration (250 milliseconds).

Hochberg reported that perceivers do not—cannot—see the entire visual field in a single glance. It takes many glances of an incomplete, indirect and unclear horizon to build a field. An integrated view of a continuous world is constructed from glances, from information in icons. Hochberg argued that figure-ground segregation was constructed because we cannot see the entire figure on the ground in one glance; even figure/ground cannot be a primitive feature. Haber claimed that the figure and ground are built up of icons. The perceiver sees the world before she knows it, since she does not know what she sees as first, at first. In the beginning, according to Haber, before the word, *the image*. Using such a holographic model, A. Comfort proposes that in the mystic, oceanic mode of perception, the scan is shut off and the interference pattern itself is intuited. He notes that descriptions of the mystical experience as a lotus, triangular patterns or the music of the spheres, bear a resemblance to holographic interference patterns.

But how is the icon stored in the brain? Is it stored like a picture? In his *Tractatus*, Wittgenstein (WM 3) said, "A logical picture of facts is a thought." Also (WM 3.01), "The totality of true thoughts is a picture of the world." What is a picture? When an object is illuminated by a light source, each point on the object radiates in a spherical pattern, as thought each point was a source of light; if photosensitive material is placed before such reflected light, the emulsion will be uniformly exposed. If, however, a board with a small enough pinhole is interposed between the object and the film, only the light from one specified point on the object will fall on a specific point on the film, such that an image of the object is described, with some defraction due to the wavelike character of light. The propagation of light energy is a waveform having both amplitude and phase. Photographic film, being an energy detection system, records only the intensity in a two dimensional mapping of the point to point brightness of the object.

Is there any way to recover or record the information relative to the phase? The film has the capability of recording both the amplitude and the phase, and the technique that has been developed to utilize it is holography. To record a hologram the amplitude and phase information are converted into intensity variations by using the interference between two interacting sources of light. This is accomplished by providing a second source of illumination incident on the photographic surface, directly, unmodulated by an intervening object. This second source of light is referred to as the reference, and is always split off from the main source so that it will be coherent with it; this second source is the reference for the determination of the phase difference between the two beams. The reference interacts with the light from the object to map, on the two-dimensional film surface, the relative amplitude and phase of each object point into an intensity function. The hologram is essentially an optical computer; a four by five inch hologram can store one billion characters at sixty resolution elements per character—this storage capacity exceeds the number of all written symbols ever conceived. The hologram may be read out by shining a copy of the reference beam across the film; the resulting holographic image is like the freezing of light waves from the film (or from the object) in a window—fitting a parallel to Ortega's problem of art as the window through which a garden is seen.

In comparing memory to a hologram, thinking may be hypothesized in terms of the propagation of waves of neural activity rather than the sequential firing of individual neurons. In a memory wave, fronts of sensory excitation would be frozen into a neural hologram, to be read out whenever that memory experience is recalled; perhaps associative memories could be explained by the ghost images from a nearly identical reference beam. This metaphor should allow appropriate concepts for modeling adaptive modifications in the action-oriented, distributed computations of a layered, somatotropically organized computer. The problem of remembering may be modeled after a data storage and retrieval system: memories are stored in the brain as holograms on film; then how are memories matched with a current experience, appropriately? To query the current experience, the brain constructs a spatial filter in the form of a Fourier-transform hologram of it, to which it presents simultaneously Fourier transform hologram of all previous experiences; if the current experience is known, a point of light (insight, a light bulb?) appears, and it is remembered. Memory loss may be compared to a loss of rotational sensitivity in stored holograms.

Philosophical problems of perception, such as Wittgenstein's duck-rabbit may be interpreted by this metaphor; each aspect would be constructed of icons into a hologram - the dawning of an aspect would be tantamount to the switching of filters.

Relativity, quantum theory, and entropy imply individual wholeness, in which the analysis of something into distinct parts is no longer relevant. The laser hologram also gives insight into an undivided wholeness—the interference pattern in each region is relevant to the whole; there is no isomorphic one to one correspondence as from a lens—actually, light from a lens or a pinhole is a degenerate hologram. In the hologram, the physical order is a total order implicated in each region of the whole; the order in each region of space parenthetically extends over the whole universe and its whole past and future. All the forms of the universe are inseparable (but can be abstracted), and it is one-turning. At night, the eye can see structures covering light centuries. As Merleau-Ponty (SI 70) phrases it: "The fact is that every fragment of the world—and in particular the sea, so riddled with eddies and waves, so plumed with spray, so massive and immobile in itself, contains all sorts of shapes of being, and by its manner of reply to the onlooker's attack, evokes a series of possible variants, and teaches beyond itself, a general manner of saying what is."

3.1.2.3.2.5.1. *Hologram as Metaphor for Universe.* If the universe is truly a whole, then the hologram may be a most appropriate metaphor, since no part or section can be understood apart from being in the whole.

3.1.2.3.2.5.1.1. *Holographic Quality.* Evernden claims that the camera makes the world atomic, but only the choice of the photographer does that. In acting as a nervous system, the artist can select for perspective and objectivity. The camera has the power to transform the relationship of self to earth; it can show the world as a set of consumable objects or as interrelated feelings. But holography, a technical three-dimensional mapping of the whole, can transform the relationship again. Here the world is interrelated. The laser hologram also gives insight into undivided wholeness; the interference pattern in each region is relevant to the whole—there is no isomorphic correspondence, as from a lens. Fundamental units/particles cannot be isolated as individual. The hologram is produced on a plate from interfering wavefronts, which are divided after the source by an interferometer which splits the light.

Each point on a hologram receives light from all parts of the subject and thus contains in its coded form, the entire image. Whenever two or more sets of waves intersect, holography is possible. Pribram contends that hologram arises in any system when neighborhood interactions among elements (spatial frequency) become encoded in process of transformation. Some sort of holograph about entire universe could be made at any spot containing information about the whole universe.

A holograph possesses field properties; each is understood in relation to collective. Holographic field governs the structure of life and thought. The reason for beings then is for better resolution, as each reflective part is added. Multiple images can be put on plate by varying wavelength. By altering angle of object beam (to plate) and by altering frequency of laser beam, ten billion codes can be stored in layered texture of one cubic centimeter of plate. The code can be turned back to an image.

When the hologram is enfolded in a record, it can be unfolded to a recognizable image. The hologram illustrates a new notion of order, the implicate order, where all is enfolded into all. In the explicate order, science, things are unfolded in particular regions. In the hologram, the physical order is a total order implicated in each region of the whole; the order in each region of space parenthetically extends over the whole universe and its whole past and future.

3.1.2.3.2.5.1.2. *Holonomic Quality.* George Leonard calls holonomic as "named for a hologram" (in Leonard, *The Silent Pulse*). It describes holographic analogs. The holoid is an entity that is holonomic. A human being is a holoid of universe, but also a unique entity having identity (cf. Koestler's holon).

Like certain holistic physical theories—relativity theory, quantum theory, and the entropy laws—the hologram implies an individual wholeness, in which the analysis of something into distinct parts is no longer relevant. The laser hologram gives insight into an undivided wholeness; the interference pattern in each region is relevant to the whole. There is no isomorphic, one-to-one correspondence of points as from a lens—actually, light from a lens or pinhole is considered a degenerate hologram.

In the hologram, the physical order is a total order implicated in each region of the whole; the order in each region of space parenthetically extends over the whole universe and its whole past and future. All the forms of the universe are inseparable, but can be abstracted, and the universe itself is one turning. The universe is etymologically related to the hologram: the word "universe" (in Latin, *unum versere*, turned into one whole) was derived by Cicero from the Greek work for the whole, holon. Hologram comes from the Greek *holo graphien*, meaning whole writing. Parts of the universe suggest other parts that are linked. As Merleau-Ponty phrases it: "The fact is that every fragment of the world—and in particular the sea, so riddled with eddies and waves, so plumed with spray, so massive and immobile in it—self, contains all sorts of shapes of being, and by its manner of reply to the onlooker's attack, evokes a series of possible variants, and teaches beyond itself, a general manner of saying what is." (Merleau-Ponty, *Signs*, p. 70.)

The order and measure of a hologram can be enfolded and carried in waves (electromagnetic and other). What carries the implicate order of the hologram is the holomovement, which is undefinable and immeasurable. This implies that it is meaningless to talk of a fundamental theory. Each theory only extracts relevant aspects. No total theory is ever possible because thinking is only necessary from a limited perspective, and a perspective can only extract parts of a whole. The hologram relates one/many and local/global, as well as part and whole. The universe is a unit; parts are related to wholeness in a necessary interrelation. As hologrammatic the universe is a dynamic web of interrelated events in which the part determines the whole. The field is the unifying character of universe.

3.1.2.3.2.5.2. *Hologram as Metaphor for Metaphor.* During the ordering process, more and more is packed into less and less, until miniaturization reaches its greatest level of organic complexity in the human brain. And the brain orders its universe in dreams, through language, and with art. Dreams are a condensation of experience, which the Greeks named Hyponoia, a hidden thought with real meaning, but in a secret language. The same condensation is operative in language itself; Wundt termed it the condensation of meanings. As a dream or word may sum up the whole past, present, and future of the dreamer, or speaker, in one event, so may art (poetry, music, or painting) do the same.

A hologram may be read out then by shining a copy of the reference beam across the film; the resulting holographic image is like the freezing of light waves from the object in a window. This provides an interesting parallel to Ortega's definition (OT 46) of art: Art is a window with a garden behind it: one may focus on the garden or on the window.

Is the hologram, then, an art form? Does it translate the view more accurately than a painting, or only differently?

Art may be the same type of condensation on a window as a hologram. Waddington suggests that there may be an analogy between some modern paintings and a hologram; for instance, Mark Tobey's Messengers may seem chaotic and meaningless, under the wrong reference, as would a hologram. Then again, the hologram must frame a garden, whereas a painting may be of the window itself. The hologram could be used as an art form, like photography, or it could be used to produce new possibilities in art. Since a hologram can be produced from a computer printout, it is therefore possible to generate any object on the printout, even one that has never existed, such as a griffin.

The hologram has been proposed as a metaphor for memory; perhaps it could be offered as a metaphor for metaphor. The two terms of a metaphor, one a pure reference, the other an embodied reflection, interfere with one another to produce the metaphor itself, an interrelated whole. As the hologram captures the phase as well as the amplitude, the metaphor expresses lateral meaning as well as denotative. Literally, the metaphor (carrying beyond, a turning) is a hologram (whole writing) that is capable of describing the universe, that which is turning into one whole.

3.1.2.3.3. Entropy & Dream

The statistical law of entropy states that matter moves toward more probable states, causing molecular disorder; a law of ektropy would state that certain groups of particles—stars, organic bodies, cities— move toward more improbable states, causing greater order; more and more is packed into less and less, until miniaturization reaches its greatest level of organic complexity in the human brain. And the brain orders its universe with art. Dreams are a condensation, which the Greeks named *Hyponoia*, a hidden thought with real meaning (in a secret language). The same condensation is operative in language, also; Wundt termed it the condensation of meanings. A dream may sum up the whole past, present and future existence of the dreamer, in one event; a poem may do the same. Waddington suggests that there may be an analogy between some paintings and a hologram, for instance, Mark Tobey's *Messengers*—that the paintings will seem chaotic and meaningless, under the wrong reference, as would a hologram. Holograms have other analogies to art; a hologram can be produced from a computer printout—it is therefore possible to generate an object on the printout, even one that has never existed. Mathematics has been identified in its almost pure ideality, unlimited by many of the restraints imposed by the lived-in-world; the generation of holograms by computer should effect more pure ideas. The hologram has been proposed as a metaphor for memory; could it be used as a metaphor for metaphor? The two terms of metaphor, one a pure reference, the other an encoded reflection, interfere with one another to produce the metaphor itself, an interrelated whole. The hologram captures the phase as well as amplitude, whereas the metaphor expresses lateral meaning as well as denotative. Perhaps the metaphor could be a metaphor for the hologram, or the metaphor for memory? The metaphor (carrying beyond) is etymologically a hologram (whole writing), which is related to the universe (turned into one whole).

3.1.2.3.4. Mirror & Knot

We are misled to believe that our ideas mirror nature; that sets us outside. Watts notes that a tree does not represent fish, though both use light and water. Our ideas are nature, as much as clouds or waves. Nature pushes through this way also, expressing herself.

But the outer world is no longer a mirror for humanity. Humans replace nature with their own consciousnesses or bodies. They have neglected one side of consciousness, one side of the brain and body. Necessarily, humans walk bent or folded over, but the right side (brain) may be unfolding now.

Claiming all consciousness for ourselves results in a mental and sensual poverty. Many ecologists and politicians use the language and abstraction of the abstract, rational lobe. We need to take into account other aspects of the human mind— poetic, mythmaking, metaphorical part, which operates in systems builders and garbage persons alike. Novalis asserted that because language is abstracted from reality it mirrors aspects of the natural world. "the laughable error whereby people imagine that they speak for the sake of things . . . when someone speaks simply for the sake of speaking, he expresses the most beautiful and original truths . . . It is only thanks to their freedom that they are components of nature and in their free motion alone does the World Soul find expression "Novalis's idea of a secret homology between language and natural phenomena is a fundamental tenet of poetry. Many deep secrets of nature are inaccessible to reason, but can be revealed to poets through gestalt perception. W. Stevens concluded that new expression facilitated new perception.

"The freshness of transformation is/The freshness of a world. It is our own./It is ourselves, the freshness of ourselves" (Stevens, The Palm at the End of the Mind). Bly considers that a certain intensity is based on "night-intelligence," the respect for ancient worlds. The right side unfolds and poetry uses the whole brain. Generally, the products of the right brain are nonverbal—a painting or a symphony—but poetry combines the qualities from both hemispheres. Association and multilogical inference seem to be drawn from the right half and the logical, verbal counterparts from the left. Poetry—the expression after the impulse—crosses into verbal centers in the left hemisphere and back. The transparent view of poetry overlays ideal on real. Poetry intensifies the world; it does not produce a new one from superior authority. The poem is a knot of turbulence, what Pound called a vortex and Yeats a gyre. G. Snyder relates that the Japanese term for song, bushi or fushi, means a whorl in the grain. The whorl is the world in miniature. The poem is an event in miniature. This miniaturization is an entry to being in the world.

3.1.2.4. *The Order of Imagination*
Heidegger claimed that humans were forgetful of experience, that they have full awareness only when confronted with death or poetry. As the adequacy of a habitual view of the earth is questioned, imagination offers alternative ways of seeing. Poetry advances imagination. It feels its way; it presages community consciousness, and it precurses paradigm shifts.

What might come to be is insufficient to poetry, according to Breton. The evidence of the senses can be rejected; the poet can favor an ideal version of things. Rimbaud could change anything into anything else through imagination (e.g., factories into mosques), and found something sacred in this mental disorder. "The flag of bleeding meat on the silk of the seas and of the arctic flowers . . . Rimbaud (in Bly, News of the Universe) "Vision is always being tricked by imagination and misunderstanding. Coleridge once noted a pretty optical fact: while viewing a soaring kite [bird], he saw two of them floating in unison; but he had mistaken two pairs of leaves on a nearby tree for wings. The magnitude of size was given by his unadjusted gaze. Suzanne Lilar relates a magic transformation of an uninteresting avenue under moonlight to a radiant grand canal. The transformation surprised her, but continued to offer pleasure for weeks after, in spite of its falsity. Maurice-Jean Lefebve contended that the source of fascination of an illusory image lies in the consciousness of its deflection of reality, whether the perception is involuntary or cultivated.

Once this "disorder" becomes conscious, it can be a means of approaching a cosmological order. A questioning form of expression is needed, a prephilosophical, circular approach through succeeding perspectives. The approach must succeed the concentric problems of metaphysics by incorporating a range of subjects from phenomenological poetry to scientific inquiry, from trees to entropy.

This expression must incorporate the complete range of experience, from the inexhaustible, perceptible universe to the wildest ideality. Expression that is reflexive and indirect would embody transparent expressions that could point to the ground of existence without partitioning or reifying it.

3.1.3. *The Necessity of Poetry*
Noted philosophers have concluded that poetry is necessary to describe the special properties of Being.

3.1.3.1. *Heidegger & The Necessity of Poetry*
For Heidegger, poetry is the disclosure of the unconcealment of Being; the essence of language must be understood from the essence of poetry. Kaelin (KA 273), in interpreting Heidegger, says: "We call the soundless, summoning, collecting together which constitutes the saga (myth), and which as such opens the paths into the world-relation, 'the sounding of silence.' It is the language of the essence." Because it is spoken, the poetic word points in silence to the presence of the essence of a thing. Poetry is a vocal gesture, pregnant with significance. It is a language-borne form, a making that exists for its own sake. What is the essence of poetry? Is it its thingness, or its manner of becoming thingness? Heidegger gives a description of the manner in which a thing comes to be, as conclusions from excerpts from the self-conscious awareness of the poet Holderlin:

1. Poetry is the most innocent of all human transactions; in making a poem the poet dreams of another world and presents it in a linguistic con text, which contains all its significance, and thus limits its effects on historical events.
2. Poetry must be qualified as the most dangerous of all human possessions. Language permits man to testify what he is, it enables him to express his care by inventing a world of words where nothing need be lost—it permits, as Heidegger phrases it, the worlding of a world. But these same words may be restrictive

and commonplace, and allow inauthenticity; the seductive power of poetry is as great in expressing the world as it is in denying it.

3. Holderlin (KA 244)

(Man has experienced much,
Named many of the gods,
Since we are a conversation
And can hear one another.)

In this unfinished poem, Holderlin considers man the historical animal: through speaking and listening in a single, shareable, experienced world, man is linked with the openness of the universe, the highest of ideals, the gods—the ground of all human experience. Being communicates itself to men; it acquires language in the dialogue of men.

4. The ground of beings is revealed in human experience, through poetic dialogue; it is revealed in essences. "Being itself must be opened up." Heidegger claims that the poet establishes a foundation for meaning, calling attention to an event which becomes placed in history as a free gift to man. These meanings pass into common language.

5. "Deservedly, yet poetically, man lives on this earth." Holderlin says (KA 245). Heidegger interprets this to mean that men's experience is fundamentally poetic. But is it? The building of a place to dwell on earth is hard earned; civilization is held together by practical and political activities. Building and planting, taking care of himself and others, is primarily a prosaic activity of man. But on earth there is no measure, no guide for existence; work produces only fatigue; man measures the distance between himself, on earth, and the heavens; through poetry the heavenly appears in life. Thus the labor is not more real or elemental than poetizing.

Heidegger suggests that prosaic activities are poetical in essence, but perhaps they are simultaneous and reversible, as he says (KA 249) of language and the world: "the presence of the gods and the appearance of the world are not primarily a result of the occurrence of language; they are rather simultaneous with its occurrence."

Man exists in a dialogue between himself and the ground of all existence, in a historical process. The poet names things and gods; as Heidegger (KA 251) says, his creation "comes to reside in that area of human experience which is neither purely ontic (of things or at hand) nor purely ontological (of Being itself), but ontic-ontological (of things understood on the ground of their being, the pre-existent meaning complexes, or worlds, already available in the poet's past culture)." This is the experience—of poeticizing and thinking—of the non-technical, noninstrumental, nonrepresentative, nonexpressive and nonsignificative essence of the first language (*parole*) grasped in its speaking and still bare force. This language is without density or voice, inconsistent and sovereign. It has nothing behind it because everything is in front; it shows without proving, gives without regulating, solicits without commanding, signifies without indicating. It is the language of Being, of essence, for Heidegger.

3.1.3.1.1. Silence in Poetry

The significance of a poem is constituted by sounds and silence; the sounds are perceived on a background of silence. Language as the sounding word is composed of sounds, whereas language as what the world gives sound to is composed of silence. The imaginative structure of a poem sets one thing against another to open a possible experience of their nearness. Imagination is a phenomenon of silence; the poem freely creates its own measure, with a "pure intentionality." It stretches out and reaches possibilities without bounds, and gathers them up into a form. Bachelard (KG 17) says: "Then poetry is truly the first phenomenon of silence. It lets live, under images, the attentive silence. It constructs the poem on the silent time, on a time which nothing torments, nothing rushes, nothing commands, on a time ready for all spiritualities, on the time of our freedom. How poor is living duration compared with durations created in poems!" Silence is needed to hear the metamorphosis of consciousness; too many words fills it in. Silence is infinitely more commanding than sound; it is the invisible side of sound, and none can ever escape it. Kafka, in the *Parables*, realized how important: "Now, the Sirens have a still more fatal weapon than their song, namely their silence." Silence is the invisible voice of savage Being. Savage Being is revealed only to savage vision, which "duplicates" it to make it visible and complete. Savage vision is not a representation, but an operation within the presence of Being.

In developing his new ontology of the imagination, Bachelard says that poetic purity rises from the material imagination, and is the experiencing of Being itself: poetic images of Being are primitive; he (BU 185) finds that Being is round, "we find ourselves entirely in the roundness of this being." Bachelard also considers the poetic image, as a "direct ontology," to be a burst which transcends its past. The poetic image transcends the temporality of language, and the correlations between past and present, to be absolutely creative. What is this poetic image? According to Pound, it is a vortex, from which, and through which, and into which, ideas are constantly rushing. A vortex is not the water but patterned energy made visible. A patterned integrity accessible to mind, topologically stable, subject to variations of intensity, brought to senses by an interaction of words. Poems may also have the ontological status of Whiteheadian propositions (impure potentials which act as lures for feelings); the poetic structure is only partially realized in the actual experience of its readers. Merleau-Ponty (MN 208): "Hence every painting, every action, every human enterprise is a crystallization of time, a cipher of transcendence—At least if one understands them as a certain spread (*ecart*) between being and nothingness, a certain proportion of white and black, a certain sampling of the Being in indivision, a certain manner of modulating time and space .... To criticize perception as cognition of an object is to rediscover man finally face to face with the world *itself*, to rediscover the pre-intentional present—is to rediscover that vision of the origins, which sees itself within us, as poetry rediscovers what articulates itself within us, unbeknown to us." The work looks at us as we look at it; it is of the same flesh, since man and world are cosubstantial. Phenomenology strives to think this in words, but art offers the feeling of it, inviting the reader or viewer to re-experience the original feeling, through words, in poetry.

3.1.3.1.2. Poetry & Prose

Hegel (HB 288) located the ground of the prose of the world in the wild poetry of the East, and in the harmonious poetry of the Greeks: "in contrast with the wild poetry and transmutation of the finite, which we observe in the East—in contrast with the beautiful, harmonious poetry and well-balanced freedom of spirit among the Greeks—here, among the Romans the prose of life makes its appearance." As being in sympathy with his own philosophy, Merleau-Ponty described the Eastern philosophies as trying to be an echo of our relationship to Being. He traces the prose of the world back to its roots in wild meaning, and ex plains how prosaic language develops from poetic language (MK 35): "Empirical language can only be the result of creative language. Speech in the sense of empirical language ... is not speech in respect to an authentic language. It is, as Mallarme said, the word coin placed silently in my hand. True speech, on the contrary—speech which signifies ... frees the meaning captive in the thing—is only silence in respect to empirical usage, for it does not go so far as to become a common name. It goes without saying that language is oblique and autonomous, and that its ability to signify a thought or a thing directly is only a secondary power derived from the inner life of language. Like the weaver, the writer works on the wrong side of his material. He has to do only with language, and it is thus that he suddenly finds himself surrounded by meaning."

Meaning does not arise as a function of explicitness; the ground of silent meaning underlies all that is said, and erupts within it. Merleau-Ponty (MK 45) asks: "What if, hidden in empirical language, there is a secondary language, in which signs once again lead the vague life of colors, and in which significations never free themselves completely from the intercourse of signs?" All the meaning activities of the subject are incarnate in the continuum of sound, from silence to music and the indirect voices of painting; and all are less explicit than speech. These activities receive their life from their embodiment. The more embodied a language, the more it participates in lateral relations in Being. The paradox of poetic vision lies in its incarnation; the spirit is embodied in meat, the abstract means nothing without the concrete.

Creative and empirical languages also move differently. Science sees nature diachronically—all systems move to entropy; mysticism sees it synchronically. A dog hears sound diachronically; we hear Bach's Concerto for Three Violins synchronically, as music is gathered up into a resolved form; the very vanishing of the music into silence is the very condition that gives us aesthetic pleasure, in the accumulation of forms.

The language of science is denotative; the linguistic ideals of science and mathematics represent the horizontal aspect of explicit meanings, in the realm of pure ideas. Poets use extremely connotative language; when the symbolic power of language fails, their expression must suggest; art and music transcend and blend in poetic language. Poets should record the marvel they witness, and not define its meaning which arises on its own like Eliot's halo; as a symbol it would echo in men's minds before becoming encrusted by a history of graspings, until, defined, it ceases to satisfy any needs as a source of miracles. The symbol must be ambiguous and stop short of definitions.

As science presses toward precise designation of its concepts, poetry expands meaning into indefinite shadows. There is a paradox here, however, which Merleau-Ponty (MK 13) explicates: "The paradox of the true and the imaginary, truer than truth, of intentions and achievement, often unexpected and always other—of speech and silence, in which expression can fail from being overly deliberate and succeed to the extent that it remains indirect—of the subjective and objective . . . ." And that means that science cannot describe everything more adequately than poetry; poetry is a creative language that Being requires. If philosophy is to be concerned with metaphysics, it will have to be a poetry and not a science.

Since synchrony envelops diachrony, scientific language develops from poetic. Poetry is the seed of language; it is the root, trunk, branch, leaf and flower, that bears empirical language like a sterile fruit; as the empirical language takes over the tree, it dies, and a new poetry rises from the debris. As Emerson (n.r.) said, "Language is fossil poetry; the deadest word was once a brilliant picture." Because it can create, poetry does more than a scientific prose can; it has more far-reaching effects. There is a gulf between poetry and scientific prose as extreme limiting terms of tendencies in experience. In prose the thought in the sentence is something common to different sentences; in poetry it is expressed only by those words in those positions.

Scientific and poetic languages may be contrasted in the following way in Table 31342-1:

Table 31342-1. Contrast of Scientific & Poetic

Scientific	Poetic
diachronous	synchronous
denotative	connotative
linguistic	aesthetic
univocal	equivocal
extensive (detailing)	intensive (condensing)
metonymic (congruous)	metaphoric (similar)

Scientific prose spreads thought out in one dimension, which it then connects in a linear way, using precise definition. Poetry presents a temporally short perception, using words as a nexus with far-flung implications. Since prose delineate ideas it is linguistic; poetry is aesthetic, in presenting perceptions. Prose realize the power of words to express everything by means of extension, poetry by intension; prose is a description, with accumulated details, and elaborated relations, poetry reverses the process by condensing and abbreviating, which gives words an energy of expression that is almost explosive. Prose is like a faintly radiating intergalactic gas cloud; poetry is a star turned nova. For Jakobson, discourse may develop along two different semantic lines; as a metonymic process (by congruity), or by a metaphorical process (by similarity); the metonymic process will predominate in prose, literature of a realistic nature; while the metaphorical process will achieve priority in poetry, creations with a romantic tendency.

3.1.3.2. Advantages of Poetry as an Access to Being

Previously, there was no clear distinction between the two processes; for many of the pre-Socrates, the perception of the order of nature was so close to the reproduction of the order, that there was no difference between art and science—both were *techne*. Philosophy was an imaginative endeavor, written in verse, as its substance, the cosmos, demanded. In Heraclitus, language is an original gathering (*logos*) which relates and holds together in opposition, and preserves. Poetry as the reality of nature is similar to the concept of *physis* in Greek science; that nature included vegetative and intellectual products; poetry is itself a phenomenon of nature. As Goethe claimed, "Art is second nature; also mysterious, but more comprehensible, since it originates from the intellect." Bachelard states that in the poet's reverie the world is directly imagined; the paradox (BB 175): "While thinkers who construct a world retrace a long path of reflections, the cosmic image is immediate." It gives us whole before parts; a single image invades the whole universe; the image gives a unity of the world. The poetic imagination has the integrating powers of a tree: it lives between the earth and sky, taking water with its roots and air with its leaves, to synthesize into itself; from itself, it then creates gases, and as it dies, humus. The cosmic image of the tree both summarizes and makes a universe. Koestler uses a cross-section of a tree to enunciate the relations of holons in a hierarchy.

The metaphoric process of poetry is introverted, and this introversion draws attention below external reality into the underworld of Being. And, for Heidegger (BI 81), the "aboriginal language is poetry as establishment of Being." Poetry establishes being by means of the word; being and the essence of things can never be derived from what is present, they must be freely created and given. Heidegger indicates that a complete understanding of poetry will not be achieved until one enters in the language of the poem itself; a poem is, as well as means, because of the unity between the whole of experience and the experience of the poem. Is a complete understanding possible?

The greater part of human experience is primitive and emotional; ultimately nonverbalizable, literal language is too abstract to deal with it. Anais Nin (NI 199) wrote that "Poetry, which is our relation to the sense, enables us to retain a living relationship with all things." It not only allows expression to savage experience, to feeling, it also is a doorway to mystical experience and transcendental visions; it creates new dimensions. Art is an indirect language, an expression, in which the individual elements need no meaning, but gain meaning by entering particular relations within a context. Art achieves only through indirection like sailing; good sailing requires knowledge of the forces at play, the wind and currents are beyond control, and ability to use them to its fullest advantage. Prose motors into the wind but loses the wind in the noise.

Meaning in art is a case of logical meaning and, apparently, an essence. The artist returns to the "things themselves" as they appear contextually in our pretheoretical perceptual experience, as natural meaning structures which are basic to our artificial logics, as the "Logos of the aesthetic world." Nin (NI 175) writes: "There is a form of writing which is like the art of music. It can affect us through the senses directly without first appealing to the intellect, without going through an analytic or conscious process. In this, it acts more like our life experiences, which enter the Body directly before we are able to dissect them." In poetic language, ideas are not produced by words in the ordinary usage of empirical terms, but as a result of the carnal relations of meaning, the halos of signification words owe to their history and uses. Wittgenstein's proposition, "Whereof one cannot speak, thereof one must be silent," perhaps refers to descriptive speech but not injunctive speech, as in various art forms: in music, a composer presents a set of commands, which, if followed by the reader, can lead to a reproduction for him of the composer's experience. There is no attempt to describe the sounds, or the feelings aroused by them. Poetry seems to be a more complex attempt to do the same, using descriptive terms as a set of injunctions. Poetry delivers a message, not by conceptual statements, but by language-formed images for our contemplation. Its function is oriented toward the structure and form of the message itself; the words and sounds, and their sequence, interactions and effects are in a unique order. At an existential level speaking becomes synonymous with thought, as illustrated in poetic language, where words mean as signs to communicate a lived experience. Like mythology, poetry can be analyzed, but not without the loss of meaning. The idea is a result of the carnal relations of meaning, the halos of signification arise from use.

It is not so much an idea being communicated in the poetry as the poetry itself is communicated. The poet is not a rhetorician, or communicator, but a maker (*poiesis* = making). Poems become things, not piles of words. "Not Ideas about the Thing But the Thing Itself," in Stevens words (QU 9). Is the poem a thing, an animal (organic whole), a communication of truth, or a gesture? Perhaps it acts like all of them in its approach to Being, to disclose it. Kaelin (KA 267) asserts: "The poet calls into the aspects of heaven that which, in its self-disclosing, precisely causes the self-concealing to appear, and indeed to appear *as* the self-concealing." Poetry is an unconcealing, which prepares the poetic dwelling of humanity. It is a making, the fundamental act of initial building which builds for the dwelling of man; it constructs a universe in which man may live. It is a universe of unique significance, built itself with words. Word becomes flesh in poetry, which takes the measure for the architectonic of dwelling. Kaelin (KA 264) again:

"Poetizing is the taking-measure, understood in the strict sense of the word, by which man first receives the measure for the scope of his essential being."

Poetry measures the width of Being with its lateral imagery; it sets the limits of what can and cannot be done—and establishes in words man's capacities in relation to nature—the standard of man's situation in Being. Nietzsche (PF 202) claimed that the whole could not be measured, however: "We other ... who want to regain the innocence of becoming, are the missionaries of a purer thought... . The whole cannot be judged, measured, compared, or even negated ... because there is nothing else but the whole ..." Could poetry measure the whole of Being, not quantitatively or analytically, but qualitatively, mimetically? Dewey (DE 241) argues that it does: "A poem presents material so that it becomes a universe in itself, one, which, even when it is a miniature whole, is not embryonic." After all, a poem is a nuclear condensation; it is self-enclosed, self limiting, and self-sufficient. The symbols used in poetry do not limit meaning, they allow for expansion. There are further qualifications, which at present remain undiscovered, as merely possibilities. Kreitler (KR 297) says: "This wholeness quality experienced through any of the levels of a work highlights an important characteristic of communication through art in contrast to communication of meaning and information through science, philosophy and other media of discourse." Discourse through philosophy is essentially sequential, the gradual building of meaning on the basis of successively presented discrete units of ideas and information; whereas insight into the meaning of art is often instantaneous and comprehensive. The distinction cannot be sharp. It is the form which allows its success, in its constitution and communication of meaning. Kaelin (KA 50) argues that: "poetry is communication that may be properly described as non-verbal, since the effect of poetry is only in part a function of the referral property of words." Effective language is transparent, it disappears into its own medium; so effective poetry has no medium, in its opening of Being.

Poetry is the most primitive expression to describe Being, as topology gives the most primitive model for Being. Aristotle described poetry as mimesis; would imitation of the "process" of Being be its most adequate description? As poetry makes Being its subject, it can only be imitative of it. Its form is a perceptible appearance, the existential complex of an actual being. It is able to a certain degree "to express what otherwise is ineffable in the world," to quote Langer (LE 208). Philosophy can only tell us how we are, whereas poetry is a mirror which tells us what and why in a special language.

What happens when art, poetry, makes Being its object? Does not metaphor capture a lateral image better than the grammar of philosophy? If the best way to capture Being is in the things themselves, then poetry is more adequate than Philosophy or science. If words about a painting mean nothing when the realities have not been perceived, and since Being is always being perceived, and if the idealizations of science constitute the object of science (no idealizations, no object), then why not use poetry to describe Being, instead of the compromise of prosaic philosophy? Merleau-Ponty (MK 52) concludes: "Since perception itself is never complete, since our perspectives gives us a world to express and think about which envelops and exceeds those perspectives, a world which announces itself in lightning signs as a spoken word or as an arabesque, why should the expression of the world be subjected to the prose of the *senses* or of the concept? It must be poetry; that is, it must completely awaken and recall our sheer power of expressing beyond things already said or seen." And, Stevens concludes (ST 176):

> Poetry is the subject of the poem,
> From this the poem issues and
>   Between
> To this returns. But the two,
> Between issue and return, there is
>
> An absence in reality,
> Things as they are. Or so we say.
>
> But are these separate? Is it
> An absence for the poem, which acquires
>
> Its true appearances there, sun's green,
> Cloud's red, earth feeling, sky that thinks?
>
> From these it takes. Perhaps it gives,
> In the universal intercourse.

3.1.3.3. *Politics & Magic*

> If there is a man white as marble
> Sits in a wood, in the greenest part,
> Brooding sounds of the images of death,
>
> So there is a man in black space
> Sits in nothing that we know,
> Brooding sounds of river noises;

And these images, these reverberations,
And others, make certain how being
Includes death and the imagination.
        Stevens (ST 444)

Poetry is not simply a form of signification, but an activity that makes
signification possible, by providing humans with a world. This genuinely
create activity can be found in the power of Orpheus to summon
things into being, according to Ovid (OV, Bk X). Stevens described the
relationship of the world to an individual.
    The world lives as you live,
    Speaks as you speak, a creature that
    Repeats its vital words, yet balances
    The syllable of a syllable.

Poetry acts magically. The poetic attitude collapses the distinction
between word and thing. Poetry is immediate synthesis of word and
thing; ontologically different relata are collapsed. The primary way of
seeing is the original unity of the passive (pathos) and active (poesis), of
deference and violence.

But 'magike' gave way to logos as the principle of the world's
intelligibility; the poet-magus lost his reason for being. In place of the
identity of poetry and reality, theory instituted the doctrine of mimesis.
The magic of poetry came to be understood as rhetoric; the poet no
longer built the world in song, but could, through imitation, persuade an
audience to follow nature in conduct.

By applying Kantian philosophy, F. Schiller believed that human
society could be improved by political means. But after studies on
the Thirty Years War in Europe, he became skeptical of the ability of
politics. On reading *Reflections on the Paintings and Sculpture of the
Greeks*, by J. Winckelmann (1787), Schiller considered the work as
historical proof that art can achieve what violence and law cannot—art
(paintings, sculptures and poems) educates and liberates the individuals
of society in a gradual and peaceful process. In spite of the cultural
forces dominant at any moment, an individual has the potential to
determine a different course. Unlike the classical humanism committed
to lessons of the past and an instructional theory of art, the aesthetic
humanism of Schiller was open to possibility.

Humanism started as a revolution against scholasticism in the 15th
century, but it has become every bit as dry and reactionary. Classical
humanism strives to convert the distant and alien into the comfortable
and familiar by reducing it to a moral commonplace (a poem by Horace
may exemplify the moral). Humanism does not communicate the past

PAF

meaningfully because it refuses to acknowledge that the past is different. In its search for a philosophy of universal values in the classic literature of the ages, humanism ignores the otherness of the cultures of the past. The past becomes more distant with academic study, not more accessible. Humanism regards change as the cause of decay, sympathizes with authority, and subverts classical literature for its own justification. Humanists often see their task as the training of an elite for the leaders of tomorrow, who offer the public only skill at public speaking.

A humanism based on Schiller's ideas must have a whole image of the place of humanity within nature, and not a transcendent view. It must confront the past without the baggage of sentiment and the future without the paralysis of dread. The appreciation of the differences of other cultures (the difference of Horace, for instance) will allow us to transcend our present identities. Responding to any art with pre-established values makes one miss the uniqueness of the experience presented. Art would broaden the mental worlds of observers and encourage tolerance and wonder. Education in aesthetic humanism embraces three concepts: liberation, play and community. Liberation is freedom from contemporary limits of identity. Play is imaginative experience, natural learning entered into freely (who can argue that education should be more like play than work). Society can gravitate into groups to live, but communication across the barriers is necessary for a world community. The wholeness of humanity needs to be affirmed, but from a firm cultural base. The complete surrender of cultural identity is as dangerous as too little openness. Every culture needs its own local, sacred center, which cannot be broken if the group is not to perish.

Poetry took a political path. The real (in Whitehead's sense) could be denounced as constituted and instituted. The poet could change life in the direction of nature as origin, loosening the chains of culture. Culture teaches us to play the game of poetry, giving us directions. But poetry is not limited by this. Poetic praxis could be a revolutionary activity. Poetry is ceremony and ritual, but also reestablishment and regrounding. The learning process of humanity is epicultural. Popular poetry could initiate a counterculture.

The true architects of culture have been the historians, artists, propagandists and poets; the poets provided the national archetypes for many new cultures. Nation-building wars may provide heroes for popular imagination; but poets and writers make the identities. The real identity of leaders is provided by propagandists and poets; the leaders only provide the horsepower. Their mask is determined by cartoonists and writers.

3.1.3.4. Radical Language

Benjamin Whorf demonstrated that language is a major element in the formation of thought; culture codifies reality. Edward Hall expanded Whorf's thesis to include all culture—the psycho-cultural basis of perception. Hall's own studies in proxemics made apparent the human personal and social uses of space to structure relationships. Physical relativity was translated into behavioral relativity. Language is like a net, letting much escape unperceived. But this analogy is no good for ecology; it lets too much escape. A comprehensive language is needed.

In a technical era, language is manipulated like a calculus. But, poetry resists manipulation and reveals a more fundamental dimension of language. The empirical languages of physics and psychology are opposed and complementary; their synthesis is the language of transcendental philosophy, the comprehensive language of being: Poetry. Poetry forms a permanent revolution in language, like dreams to mind and quantum foam to space. An artist works distractingly with both wildness and discipline, destroying old gestalts, associating and dissociating old and new patterns.

Poetry oscillates between musical knowledge, which is self-defined, and cognitive knowledge, that communicates to others. Fraser stated that poetry is a form of music for the better expression of gnostic feelings. Its shifting to the present changes the observer into a participant. The music analogy is apt; the prairie does sound like a harpsichord, in contrast to the organ sounds of the forest or strings of a brook (Rimbaud's analogy to music).

Poetry is a form of language used tacitly and by implication that is rich enough to escape subject-verb-object dominance. Poetic language experiments with general impressions of the world and arranges them so they feel right, without invoking truth. Poetic language enforces or changes a world view.

Poetry exploits the natural poetics of language. Only in rational discourse is literal meaning achieved at expense of the figurative. A verse is not a sentence; it is a word image. But the image is not a drawing; it allows the multiplicity, ambiguity and hesitation that are necessary to creativity and dreaming. Poetry maps a landscape. The significance of the wild or domesticated is revealed or simplified in words. The map itself is potentially a landscape. A poem merges with the reality of which it speaks—verbal topology coincides with the real, much like the emperor in one of Borges' fantasies has a map drawn on a scale of 1:1, thus covering the actual empire with paper, until the wind shreds and scatters it.

Perhaps poetry seems like childish babbling; but through their babbling, children become aware of being in a world. They become aware of differences. They name differences and then make them. Saussure pointed out that a language is made out of differences. The phoneme is a distinctive unit whose features are pertinent only in opposition to others; even the meaning of monemes, the signifying unities, is defined by a process of differentiation. The differential elements in a poem result from metaphor.

3.2. *Poetic Philosophy*

The early Greek philosophers—Heraclitus, Parmenides, and Empedocles—wrote their works in verse, but in the beginning of the fourth century B.C., with Socrates, a more prosaic style came into fashion. In spite of Aristophanes' criticisms and satires of the innovations of this modern expression, the efforts of Plato, Aristotle, and Epicurus forced poetry to confine itself to the purveyance of comedy or amusement.

3.2.1. *The Ancients*

The ancients knew everything, but forgot much, and what they did not forget was mostly lost by their heirs or conquerors. Nevertheless, some materials indicate the direction and shape of their thoughts.

3.2.1.1. *The Core of Reality for Heraclitus*

Heraclitus attempted to penetrate to an invisible core, to uncover reality, the truth of which could only be expressed through an image. Aristotle judged that Heraclitus was not rational, since he did not present his philosophy logically, using the principles enumerated by Aristotle himself, such as the principle of the excluded middle, long after Heraclitus was gone. But, Heraclitus believed that Being (*physis*) lies below the level of human activity. It only appears in diverse forms that, in turn, may only be described through necessary metaphors; perhaps reality cannot be grasped intellectually, but it could be approached through speaking (*logos*).

For Heraclitus, teaching is not telling. As did the god at Delphi, Heraclitus spoke in riddles and ambiguities, but always spoke the truth. He tried to find the secret nature of the universal principle; if he had been bound by Newton's *hypotheses non fingo*, he could never have spoken at all. He attempted to describe the measure adhering in change, but much to Aristotle's dismay, he did not use the categories of formal logic to do this. In applying his own standards anachronistically, Aristotle also judges Heraclitus for denying the law of contradiction; things in a context are called the same in Heraclitus, for instance, the physical constituent of everything (*logos*) was variously described as a god, a form of matter, and a principle.

The logos is the measure of things and also the actual constituent of things, sometimes coextensive with the primary cosmic fire. The logos is the essential unity of opposites; it orders the progress of the upward and downward paths of the flux of nature, which Heraclitus calls the same. Opposites form a unity and a plurality. Heraclitus (KI 191) speaks: "Things taken together are whole and not-whole, something which is being brought together and brought apart, which is in tune and out of tune; out of all things there comes a unity, and out of a unity all things." The plurality of things forms a unity, a single, coherent complex; and this unity, depending on a balanced reaction of opposites, lies beneath the surface. The logos nourishes human laws, indirectly, and cannot be known through the senses, which perceive the flux only. It governs behavior and balances changes.

Heraclitus grounded his apothegms with pairings and contrasts, puns, etymologies, and verbal conceits. He was interested in every type of meaning, from original to paradigmatic, and presented them with psychological suggestiveness. His style has popularly been characterized as oracular, with its obscurity of language and metaphorical hinting toward some hidden reality. He exploits the hidden side of things until he reaches a distinction between appearance and reality. Heraclitus finds that "The hidden harmony is better than the manifest." Heraclitean sayings lack the generality of maxims, but do turn a specific experience into knowledge of the general, where the implicit connection is seen. The form of his sayings mirrors the form of knowledge: a sudden revelation of truth, it is the inner form of logos. He uses metaphors to mirror the hidden world and antithetical constructions to mirror the paradoxical unity of the world; the content of a revelation is its form. The invisible is made visible by pointing. Heraclitus' sayings are discoveries, what Goethe called *appercu* —"sudden realization of what really underlies appearances."

3.2.1.2. *Beyond the Senses of Parmenides*
The natural philosopher, Alcmæon, advanced inductively step by step from sense perception, from human knowledge, to the invisible. Parmenides, like Heraclitus, maintained that sense experience cannot be trusted. One must judge by means of the logos; one succeeds in thinking the One Being by a kind of grace. In his poem, Parmenides

journeys toward light and the revelation of truth, guided by divine maidens to the goddess. She introduces him to pure thought, with which he comprehends pure Being. The path to divine knowledge is not direct, however; from the intuitive recognition of Being, she deduces the truths concerning thought, and Being and non-Being. Although Parmenides relates his entire journey in hexameters, the subject matter be comes poetic only with the allegory and divine visitations. The poem is divided into two parts, the "Way of Truth," wherein he logically deduces all that can be known about Being from the premise "it is," and the "Way of Seeming," in which he explains the same world of appearances that he had previously demolished. The whole poem is presented as a religious revelation.

When Parmenides wrote his poem, he broke with the Ionic tradition and wrote in hexameter verse. Burnet relates that this style of Hesiod was wholly unsuited to the arid dialectic of the first part of the poem, although it might have been appropriate for the descriptive cosmogony in the second half. He also states that it is clear that Parmenides was not a born poet, so there must have been a good reason for his use of poetry in writing philosophy. Burnet contrasts his style with Xenophanes (who is closer to the dithyrambic), and likens it to Hesiod and the Orphics. The fact that Parmenides describes his transcendence of the world in verse follows a long tradition of mythical ascents.

In the "Way of Truth," Parmenides presents all that reason, unaided by the senses, can deduce about Being: it is a single, indivisible, and homogenous sphere, timeless, changeless, and motionless. He (KI 273) writes: "One way only is left to be spoken of, that it *is*; and on this way are full many signs that what *is* is uncreated and imperishable, for it is entire, immovable and without end." The predicates of Being are negative predicates, denying difference, and asserting the self identity of Being. His reasoning starts from Being, which, since it is the only thing, cannot even be the unity of all things.

In the "Way of Seeming," the remaining fragments deal with a cosmology of sensible opposites—light and dark, male and female— apparently totally irreconcilable with the "Way of Truth." Why should Parmenides devote equal time to describing the "Way of Seeming?" Is the breaking up of the sphere of Being necessary, and if so, for what reason? For pure contemplation the sphere remains whole, but for common experience it must be broken up. The world must be named to be experienced, and this naming, separating entities out of the whole sphere of Being, is at the base of the "Way of Seeming." Naming is what also allows for the possibility of error. Truth must thus be a revelation of the "Way of Truth," from the "Way of Seeming." Parmenides presents the "Way of Truth" first in order to judge the "Way of Seeming;" both ways may be approached through thought. There is a third way, the way of non-Being, which he says may be noted, but cannot be thought (perhaps though it can be perceived and spoken of—pointed to—in the same sense as the Pontean savage Being). Obviously, if human beings had the ability to contemplate before they could perceive, then there would be no "Way of Seeming" at all. It could then be argued that the "Way of Seeming" is both necessary and prior to the "Way of Truth," since it exists; and beings must perceive before they can ever contemplate.

If Parmenides intended a philosophical work, was it necessary to present it in verse? As Burnet (BT 51) states: "But if it was the influence of such an apocalypse that led Parmenides in verse, it will follow that the Proem is no mere external ornament to his work, but an essential part of it, the part, in fact, which he had most clearly conceived when he began to write." Parmenides ascends to heaven to be instructed in the two ways, that of pure truth and that of deceptive belief. Afterwards there occurs the parting of the ways, where Parmenides is converted from belief, assumed to be Pythagoreanism, to truth. If he were merely rejecting the Pythagoreans, why not write in prose, why use poetry?

The goddess describes two worlds, that of truth and that of mortals. In the "Way of Seeming," Parmenides presents a world in which humans feel and perceive and live; the argument has been presented that poetic language is far more adequate than prose for a nonintellectual apprehension of the world. But why would Parmenides also use poetry to describe a nonphenomenal world of truth? Would not prose, with its tendency toward idealization, be much better (or was the Greek language inadequate at the time)? Perhaps, in this instance, a mythical mode of expression was more capable than any prose for communicating abstract thoughts. This world of truth that Parmenides circumlocutes negated the world of man entirely; what words could be left to describe the One if not religious or poetic words. The poetry in his philosophy does not seem to be a clothing of thought that could be removed with no loss of meaning. The various figures in the poem are not thematic, as they should be in a tragedy or epic; they seem to be expressions of thoughts. The truth is abstract, logical thought: "for the same is to think and to be." Parmenides, nevertheless, uses the language of explanation and proof in both parts of the poem.

Mourelatos, in his article "The deceptive world of Parmenides' Doxa," describes the connection of the two parts of the poem as being related by two concepts, ambiguity and irony. The ambiguity is intentional in Parmenides' style; it provides a tension intrinsic in the philosophical message. Here the poetic is better suited to presenting fundamental ambiguities than philosophical language. As an example, from the "Way of Seeming," Mourelatos quotes Parmenides' description of the moon (translated by G. Oppen, MO 314): "Astray over earth, bright in darkness, its light also a wandering foreigner." In this one line Parmenides states that the moon shines by reflection, the face in the moon is a wandering stranger and he is not himself, and the moon is a wandering stranger in space. The multivalent aspects of the reality of the One are likewise approached poetically. Mourelatos (MO 347) addresses himself to Parmenides' status as a poet, citing his use of rhetorical cleverness, pairings, contrasts and associations, as well as his philosopher's interest in literal, original, and paradigmatic meaning: "Parmenides uses his keen sense for language to trace out implications at length, to project alternative and related models of his concepts, to establish multiple and systematic connections, and to detect and exploit ambiguity for the purpose of argument and refutation." Possibly ambiguity has a speculative use, philosophically, that is inseparable from, or optimally present in, poetic form. Ironically, Aristotle censures Parmenides for failing to appreciate that "Being is spoken of in many senses." Again, Mourelatos distinguishes between equivocity of a different genre: Aristotle refers to homogengymy, or focal meaning, whereas Parmenides uses an ambiguity between different levels of knowledge (185b20).

Parmenides' Being is neither matter nor thought; it is the result of applying the law of the excluded middle to the premise that existence is necessary, while non-Being is impossible. He demonstrates that there can be nothing else besides Being, and since Being is the only thing there is, the world in which mortals live is a convention and their language is void of meaning—if language is used it must be poetry.

3.2.1.3. *The Proper Language of Empedocles*
When Empedocles, the greatest of all Greek didactic poets, integrated the sayings of his predecessors, he wrote his philosophy in the form of poetry. In the first chapter of the *Poetics*, Aristotle states that Homer and Empedocles have nothing in common except their meter, and therefore it is correct to call the former a poet and the latter a scientist. But elsewhere in the *Poetics* he treats Empedocles as a poet. In Chapter 21, for instance, he uses Empedocles' metaphor as an example of metaphor: "old age is the evening of life." In Chapter 25, to illustrate the category of the grouping of words and punctuation, he uses Empedocles again:

"Soon mortal grew what had before known immortality, and things pure before mixed." Perhaps Aristotle is exhibiting the same reconciliation that he demonstrates with the problem of epics, first being denigrative of it, but finally accepting it.

Aristotle, in the *Physics*, objects to Empedocles' world view, generalizing that if one accepts his principle in the case of animals, it must be accepted for plants as well, resulting in "vine-growths olive-bearing" as well as "ox-creatures man-faced." Here it seems assumed that the subject, a philosophical principle, is open to poetic description; here, Empedocles is describing metaphysical possibilities. Empedocles is called a physicist, discovering the elements in things, but his physics is close to human teleology, the elements are divine, where the principles of love and strife guide the process of mixture and separation; he uses, in describing the process, such metaphorical terms as marriage and warfare. In addressing the problem in the *Metaphysics*, Aristotle hints that, at that time, philosophic wonder had not yet totally emerged from religious awe, so that cosmology and meta physics were close to myth.

Although Empedocles wrote in hexameters in elegaic verse, with Homeric phrases, his manner and his terminology reflect Parmenides. His poem asserted that the world was real, without violating the law of Elegaic logic; phenomenal difference could be accounted for by the rearrangement of several ultimate elements, which did not lose their identity. Empedocles (LI 22) writes:

> Now grows
> The One from the Many into being, now
> Even from the One disparting come the many—
> Fire, Water, Earth and awful heights of Air;
> And shut from them apart, the deadly Strife
> In equipoise, and Love within their midst
> In all her being in length and breadth the same.

Empedocles complied in spirit with the Parmenidean canons. Where Parmenides maintained that plurality cannot come from unity, Empedocles proposed four eternal substances, which completely fill the whole of space, and are rearranged continually by the two motive forces, Love and Strife, to cause change in all things. In opposition to Parmenides, however, he instructs his readers to make full use of their senses, and to trust their validity. Empedocles wrote two poems: *On Nature*, a physical explanation of the universe, and *Purification*, concerning the immortal soul. In the first he assumes that sense perception is incomplete, and so limits thought; thus, in order to comprehend nature, he invokes the gods, and so raises himself above mortal intelligence, inquiring into nature with the fullest senses and using poetry as the voice of these fullest senses.

Empedocles formulated his comparisons after the pattern of Homeric similes. The adjectival proportions used by Heraclitus became more logical in Empedocles. His procedure becomes mathematical and scientific by basing it on adjectives of magnitude rather than quality. Empedocles used poetry to treat myths and sense experience; experiences blend with myths in one philosophical system.

3.2.1.4. *Myth & Logic for Plato*

In Plato, also, myth and logical thought share authority. In general, myth attempts to explain natural phenomena by going beyond them to imprecisely determined causes, usually gods; reason, on the other hand, limits itself to a sufficient cause. Myth and logic are coextensive in many respects, but some aspects of myth are inaccessible to logic, and likewise some truths of logic are unformed in myth. Beginning with Socrates, and culminating with Aristotle, myth and logic became thoroughly separated; for Aristotle, myths provided material for drama and poetry, while experience promoted the rational sciences. By limiting the area of investigation, and curtailing the range of speech, logic achieved a greater degree of accuracy, but only at the cost of completeness of experience. Mythical thought, with its receptivity of images, was eclipsed by the untiring activity of logical thought, which attempted to treat everything in its manner.

In his struggle for wisdom, through searching and pondering, Socrates delimited a way of thinking: His questioning always sought the common property of a subject, its universal character. Before Socrates, logic was implicit and understood in language, but with him it began to find conscious expression in speech, and the images used in thinking began to change, undergoing purification and calcification.

Plato, nevertheless used metaphors to present properties of subjects, even while continuing the Socratic method. He often uses Pythagorean proportions in nonmathematical contexts, for example, in the "Gorgias:" Rhetoric is to philosophy as cooking is to medicine, where philosophy is the unknown. But the analogy is transgressive of categories, since philosophy and medicine are real knowledge, whereas rhetoric and cooking are only apparent; also philosophy and rhetoric affect the soul, while cooking and medicine affect the body. In other dialogues, the "Meno" and the "Sophist," he establishes a mathematical theory of knowledge and applies a principle of logical subdivision to thought (with the weaving metaphor).

Plato shared a concept of meaning in levels with Parmenides. Actually, he uses unresolved ambiguity to point through the *aporia* of his early dialogues toward an unstated solution. In the tenth book of the *Republic*, Plato describes the nature and value of certain activities claiming to be art: "Painting or drawing, and imitation in general, when doing their own proper work, are far removed from truth." The maker of images, or imitator, knows appearances only, nothing of true existence; since it is removed from Being, it can contain no knowledge, and hence, is not true art. True art is a making based on knowledge of what is, and for this reason, it is only philosophy which can claim to be art, since only philosophy is in contact with Being (as ideal forms).

The ancient quarrel between philosophy and poetry is that between Being and appearance, between knowledge and opinion; the poets are banished from the *Republic* because of their use of appearance to create a false ontology. In Plato, art and philosophy have a common relation in Being; furthermore, in his writings, the connection of poetry with Being is strong,. and it seems to be in essential relationship with philosophy. The quarrel is partly resolved by their convergence in his own dialogues. Art takes possession of thought.

Plato uses, in different dialogues, different metaphors for the mind. In the "Meno," the mind is the source of the knowledge of ideas, which have already been seen, but, must be recollected with great effort through dialectical interrogation. In the *Theaetetus*, Socrates, thanks to his special art as midwife, is able to deliver the thoughts of Theaetetus; ideas are actually born as a result of intellectual intercourse, and the pregnancy of the soul is more active and social than a mere remembering; it is also dialectical. In the *Theaetetus*, Socrates also presents the minds as a block of wax, which holds the impressions of ideas and perceptions. The conception metaphor is broadened even further in the *Sophist* (248a): "We have intercourse with Becoming by means of the body through sense, whereas we have intercourse with Real being by means of the soul through reflection." Sensation occurs from the intercourse of the soul with Becoming.

3.2.1.5. *Literature and Philosophy According to Aristotle*
Aristotle took up some of these same metaphors, in his own fashion. In a recent article, asking "Is Philosophy a form of Literature?" William Charlton wonders if philosophies may be regarded as objects of aesthetic appreciation, and concludes that they may; in fact, he says, Aristotle's style may be considered beautiful in its conceptual power. There are three ways that philosophy and poetry may be compared:

1. Philosophy leads to persuasion, which depends on eloquence, which is a linguistic art; it is really exhortation, not proof.
   From the *Physics* he lifts Aristotle's best style of philosophical

exposition: the philosopher should try to carry out his elucidation such that problems are resolved, difficulties cleared, and what is true remains so.

2. Both poets and philosophers need imaginative insight to accomplish anything.

3. Both think in words, their achievement is immanent in their writings, and both use the same type of comparison:

metaphor : poetry :: analogy : philosophy.

He demonstrates this last with Aristotle's comparison of the relation of sight and eye with the relation of mind and body. He concludes with his own analogy:

philosophy : poetry :: comet : planet.

Periodically philosophy must desert vacuous space to return to the solar system; it has been shown previously that poetry is more deeply embedded in the carnal than philosophy, though not as gracefully as this one analogy.

There are other interesting points: Charlton quotes Aristotle on the task of philosophy, which is to bring a problem to life, state an argument leading to a difficulty that is formidable, show the conflict or ordinary thoughts, and establish the correct account. This is, of course, what Parmenides does in his poem. The purpose is to express the reader's mind (in a catharsis of speculation?); but, do not Plato and Parmenides do this? What emotion is expressed in either? Aristotle, most likely would deal with the first of Charlton's comparisons in *Rhetoric*, not *Poetics*, and concede the second and third as obvious, after all, all sciences are connected with common axioms and common disciplines. The three sciences involve different ends: the theoretical sciences involve necessary propositions and have knowledge as their end, the practical sciences subordinate knowledge to action (one knows virtue in order to act virtuously), and the productive sciences have the product to be produced as their end, not knowledge or action (1177^a2). The practical sciences derive many propositions from the theoretical, and the productive derive many from both other sciences; since sciences become less exact as they involve more elements, and become more dependent on the others, poetry is the least exact of all (1026^b24). Is not it possible, in some sense, to consider poetry more basic than the other two, if the poem "produces" knowledge, or the dance "produces" action? Unless all knowledge is considered conceptual, and all action potential.

Aristotle wrote the first serious criticism of literature; with his scientific method he provided the recipe for countless dramas. In ignoring whether tragedies were true, or the highest expression of mankind, he wrote that they served as a kind of medicine to keep the ordinary man free from descriptive emotions; his aesthetics are medical. There is nothing in the *Poetics* concerned with the beauty or truth of poetry; Aeschylus and Sophocles are considered craftsmen, not poets or philosophers, although they have a tragic world view as complete as that of any technical philosopher.

In Plato and Aristotle, the ideas are discovered, but the knowledge of the ideas must be produced by great effort. It was previously asked if scientific knowledge of poetry was possible; Aristotle considers that it is, as long as poetry refers only to the product, and not to the artist or the activity; there must be a product over and above the knowledge or action, since without that product poetry would become knowledge or action, which are ends in themselves (982^{a}25). Marjorie Grene (GR 190) quotes Aristotle from the *Metaphysics* on the characteristic abstraction which marks off the philosopher from the physicist or mathematician: "For the attributes of this in so as it is being, and the contrarities in it qua being, it is the business of no other science than philosophy to investigate." Yet Grene mentions that this dialectical and inductive path to the first principle is incomplete. Aristotle did not write down his science of first philosophy, because, as she (GR 193) says, "the science of being qua being is non-existent, and unattainable." Is it possible to express the principles of being in the way they would have to be to satisfy his criteria? If the act is prior to potency, if the end is in the beginning, if the whole comes before the part, would not the study of Being fit better into poetic knowledge? If the sum is greater than the parts, could an abstractive science describe it?

Against Aristotle's real definitions, Plato acknowledged that with the limitations of verbalization to express the essence of a thing, only a vision through and beyond language could claim knowledge of a thing, by reaching through particularity and even intelligible patterns to another order. By forming an internally structured whole, the work of art presents an ordered cosmos, paradoxically inclusive of the chaos and order of the real cosmos. In life, there are not complete actions, but when it conforms to requirements of organic unity, art can give the mimesis of a complete action. A philosophical treatise may give an account of actions in terms of causes, but a poem meaningfully relates them in a whole. A philosophical poem combines possibilities into a structurally unified whole which may be a metaphor of the cosmos.

3.2.1.6. *Light and Darkness in Lucretius*
As a disciple of Epicurus and an admirer of Empedocles, Lucretius used poetry to communicate philosophical ideas. Lucretius' principal purpose was to save men from religious fears and political ambitions, which

could destroy the peace of mind that was the objective of Epicurus' philosophy. *On the Nature of Things* is a scientific treatise, expounding an atomic theory to account for everything from clouds to thoughts of clouds; the philosopher studies physics in order to free the mind from fear; materialism is an ethical salvation. Lucretius himself dismissed metaphysical abstractions as vain illusions, finding ample reason for wonder and joy in the perceptible universe and the working of natural laws.

In his first book (I 136-149, LU 31), Lucretius alludes to the perennial antithesis between poetry and philosophy, light and darkness, but reversed from the Platonic attitude: "I am well aware that it is not easy to elucidate in Latin verse the obscure discoveries of the Greeks. The poverty of our language and the novelty of our theme compel me often to coin new words for the purpose … studying how by choice of words and the poets art I can display before your mind a clear light by which you can gaze into the heart of hidden things. This dread and darkness of the mind cannot be dispelled by the sunbeams, the shining shafts of day, but only by an understanding of the outward form and inner workings of nature." He starts with the principle that nothing can ever be created out of nothing. Darkness is then connected to the fear of afterlife; the shuttles of the sun, or the warp of daylight, cannot penetrate this dark fear, only the warp of poetry—poetry unweaves the darkness and saves the essence, with the shuttles of its rays (here is the *diakritike* of Plato). The sum of things cannot be changed; nothing is added or subtracted; because the atoms are invisible, things only seem to come into being. Lucretius proves in his verses in book 2, that the infinite number of atoms is in motion, but their totality appears to stand completely motionless. With its imagery, poetry produces proofs that philosophy cannot.

Imagery is a necessary part of the poetic vehicle of the doctrine: in book 2, he describes the velocity of the atoms by comparing them with the speed of sunlight, which itself is as fast as a flash of lightening—faster, since there are no obstacles for atoms. In book 6, Lucretius suggests that a lightning flash is as fast as the blinking of an eye, thus by a series of metaphors, linking nature with the body, the cosmic with the personal, and the immense with the minute. In book 4, Lucretius writes that he is blazing a trail through pathless tracts, that his reward for struggling to loose men's minds from the knots of superstitions and shed the bright beam of his song on dark corners is the joy of plucking new flowers for a garland from fields whose blossoms have never been taken. The purpose of his poetry is to engage the mind with verses while it gains insight into the nature of the universe. The philosophical subject is the stimulus for the intensity of the observation and contemplation of the material world.

In using further metaphors, he writes about the phenomena of nature in human terms; he anthropomorphizes, hence, light has feet and aether a face. All knowledge is derived from the senses; things are exactly as they appear to be to our senses, or if the senses were more acute, as they would appear to be; objects which are perceived exist, objects which are not perceived may be noticed by their effects, such as quiet breezes ruffling leaves, and an image formed of them as small streams of material particles pushing against the boughs of the tree, like motes in a sunbeam. By assuming the existence of only material objects and space, Lucretius explained everything in the perceived world.

Epicurus believed that truth was not at the bottom of a well, but near the surface, thinly veiled with the appearance of things; his own language was pictorial, in Lucretius it became poetic. Lucretius painstakingly included all of the teachings in his poem, from meteorology to civilization. He accepted the nebulous gods of Epicurus but regarded them as impotent and indifferent; instead he worshipped the fruitfulness and unlimited beauty of nature, still inhumanly blind and impersonal.

Lucretius tried to convey the stark message in direct, passionate language, resolving to honey his medicine by writing heroic verse (iambic hexameter). Was the poetry necessary to convey philosophy, or was it just honey? If the truth lay under the appearance of things, certainly metaphor was the most comprehensive approach to it.

3.2.2. *The Moderns*
The moderns recorded everything, but the struggle is to find and read what is worthy. A few philosophers, such as Heidegger, turned to poetry to try to escape the limits of prose. Several scientists used poetic form to express other dimensions of themselves Fortunately, some poets also addressed philosophical topics.

3.2.2.1. *Truth & Dream: Descartes to Bachelard*
Later philosophers have been aware of the value of, or have used, poetic forms in their studies. Even Descartes said that, although poetry has no method, it gives us knowledge through imaginative force and makes truth shine forth the more brightly than philosophy. Kierkegaard, as a kind of poet credited with unlimited negative capability, demanded of his reader the capacity to cultivate multiple perspectives, as is required in poetry.

In Bachelard, the reverie of the dreamer requires poetic language for its expression, since imaginative creation abolishes the separations between subject and object, light and darkness—and hence the necessity for literal language. There is no language left to him but the poetic. The absolute creativity of the imagination diffuses the world from the center of its being, creating an absolute plenitude. Bachelard (KG 23) states: "Thanks to the shadows, the intermediary region which separates man and the world is a full region, and a plenitude of light density. That intermediary zone softens the dialectic of being and nonbeing. Imagination does not know nonbeing. . . . The man of reverie lives by his reverie in a world homogeneous with his being, with his self-being. He is always in the space of a volume. Truly occupying all the volume of his space, the man of reverie is everywhere in *his* world, in an *inside* that has no *outside*. It is not for nothing that it is commonly said that the dreamer is plunged in his reverie. . . . The world is no longer opposed to the world." Through meaning the world encloses, while through poetic expression it opens up. Bachelard tries to limit himself to a philosophy of detail and not summarize his inquiries with definitions or formulas, but he (BC 222) does poetically define the being of man: "There, on the surface of being, in that region where being wants to be both visible and hidden, the movements of opening and closing are so numerous, so frequently inverted, and so charged with hesitation, that we could conclude on the following formula: Man is half-open being."

3.2.2.2. *Poetic Creation of Santayana*

Santayana argued that the greatest poetry was philosophical, since the core of a poem was its subject: An idea or emotion. Poetry consisted of four elements: Euphony, euphuism, experiential immediacy (that is to say, it has a body), and rational imagination; the ultimate end of a poem is creation. Poetry should project, at a psychological distance, an imaginatively constructed, particular referent, such as a garden, a machine, or Dante's whole universe, in which the feelings, sounds and symbols have their locus. When the poet portrays the ideals of experience or destiny, he becomes a prophet; at its highest poetry is metaphysical in character, where the imagination furnishes to metaphysics, as Santayana (RI 273) says: "those large ideas tinctured with passion, those supersensible forms shrouded in awe, in which alone a mind of great sweep and vitality can find its congenial objects." But the imagination must be rational; poetry is at its highest when it is true as well as imaginative.

Santayana himself was a poet as well as philosopher, although Rice judges that his poetry was inadequate to his philosophy, partly because it lacked the experiential immediacy required by his own theory, and partly due to his adherence to tradition, notably Platonism and the English poetic tradition (even including Dryden and Wordsworth), which treated metaphor and imagery in a poem as ornament. Some of his sonnets, however, equal his metaphysical subtlety (RI 239):

O martyred spirit of this helpless Whole,
Who dost by pain for tyranny atone,
And in the star, the atom, and the stone,
Purgest the primal guilt, and in the soul.

But they are few, according to Rice, who concluded that Santayana's poetic imagination only became fully developed long after he had ceased to write verse, hence his philosophic vision becomes poetic (RI 283): "The tight opinionated present feels itself to be inevitably the center and judge of the universe; and the poor human soul walks in a dream through the paradise of truth, as a child might run blindly through a smiling garden, hugging a paper flower."

Santayana finds contemporary poets incapable of wisdom—a patchy poetry with no ideals is the poetry of barbarism. Whitman and Browning failed to meet his standards, Yeats and Eliot would have been too eccentric and eclectic to have qualified. Even the three most philosophical poets, in his judgment, Lucretius, Dante and Goethe, are incomplete: Lucretius inadequately perceived the potentialities of experience, and Goethe lacked a coherent scheme of the ultimate good, and Dante, with his vision of the entire universe, lacked the merit of being true. Santayana himself strives for completeness:

Slow and reluctant was the long descent,
With many farewell pious looks behind,
And dumb misgivings where the path might wind,
And questionings of nature, as I went.
The greener branches that above me bent,
The broadening valleys, quieted by mind,
To the fair reasons of the Spring inclined
And to the Summer's tender argument.
But sometimes, as revolving night descended,
And in my childish heart the new song ended,
I lay down, full of longing, on the steep;
And, haunting still the lonely way I wended,
Into my dreams the ancient sorrow blended,
And with these holy echoes charmed my sleep.

There may be chaos still around the world,
This little world that in my thinking lies;

For mine own bosom is the paradise
Where all my life's fair visions are unfurled.
Within my nature's shell I slumber curled,
Unmindful of the changing outer skies,
Where now, perchance, some new-born Eros flies,
Or some old Cronos from his throne is hurled.
I heed them not; or if the subtle night
Haunt me with deities I never saw,
I soon mine eyelid's drowsy curtain draw
To hide their myriad faces from my sight.
They threat in vain; the whirlwind cannot awe
A happy snow-flake dancing in the flaw.

Santayana suggests that poets search of a philosophy, which may be nothing but poetry. Santayana claims only that poetry is inherently philosophical, perhaps because it deals with wholes, generalities or universals and comprehensiveness. Although philosophy is analytical and argumentative, Santayana considers it a means to an end, that of insight or contemplation of all things, where the philosopher can find peace. Santayana wants his poetry to find that same peace, even if poetry focuses on the 'fleeting moment.' Yet, there is tension between dullness and contemplation, between a detail of a flower petal and the whole history of life, and it can be expressed passionately. The fleeting moments can carry the philosophy if the poetry is imaginative and full enough. And, if it is, the philosophy becomes poetic.

3.2.2.3. Poetic Thought & Depth in Heidegger
Martin Heidegger considered Parmenides and Heraclitus as poets and thinkers who were pathmakers; their thinking transcended the narrow divisions of philosophy. Such as ethics or metaphysics. They were concerned with the fundamental reality of the world, *physis*. As Heidegger (GP 98) explains: "Anaximander, Parmenides, and Heraclitus conceived *physis* as "self-blossoming emergence . . . that which manifests itself in such unfolding and perseveres and endures in it . . . . *Physis*, the realm of that which arises, is not synonymous with these phenomena, which today we regard as part of 'nature' . . . . *Physis* is Being itself, by virtue of which existing things become and remain observable." The pre-Socratics perceived the whole of that which is, and, in attempting to think their vision of totality adequately, tried to discover the integral relation of being and language, *physis,* and *logos.* Things first come into being in language. The pre-Socratics approached the problem, poetically, from the aspect of the whole, and not the individual or natural phenomena. Heidegger (GP 98) continues: "Hence *physis*

originally encompassed heaven as well as earth, the stone as well as the plant, the animal as well as man, and it encompassed human history as a work of men and the gods; and ultimately and first of all, it meant the gods themselves as subordinated to destiny. *Physis* means the power of emerging and enduring includes "becoming" as well as "being" in the restricted sense of inert duration. *Physis* is the process of a-rising, of emerging from the hidden, whereby the hidden is first made to stand." Are physis and logos more ultimate problems for man than are *politera* or *philia?*

Heidegger himself uses metaphor to explain metaphor; as a revelation of ontological truth, poetry can be more profitably investigated than science. Since it is innocent, and lets us be without preconceptions, the poetic eye can see as deeply into nature as the scientific eye. Thus, we adhere to Goethe's method. Heidegger urges (GP 107): "How long are we going to imagine that there was first of all a part of nature existing for itself and a landscape existing for itself, and that then with the help of "poetic experiences" this landscape became colored with myth? How long are we going to prevent ourselves from experiencing the actual as actual?" Since the days of the early Greek thinkers, however, Heidegger condemns philosophy for having forgotten its very reason for existence; instead of attempting to uncover knowledge of the Being of beings, metaphysics has con fined itself to the ontic inquiry of certain beings. In searching for a point of departure from a useless traditional ontology, he concludes that the only valid one is the being of the questioner himself; it is man, alone of all beings, to whom the question of the Being of all beings is meaningful, so that by studying him, one may arrive at insights into Being.

A person is a *Dasein* (being-there), a being in the world who stands forth from Being, and thus both derives and bestows meaning. In his first period (*Being and Time*), Heidegger analyzed the metaphysical structure of the person (*Dasein*). through the phenomenological method as the most promising way into the question of Being. Being must be approached through the human being and the experience of nothingness; and man's unawareness of the question, and utter ignorance of the meaning of Being, must be overcome in trying to lighten the darkest mysteries of Being.

In Heidegger's later thought, once man is aware of Being, he seems to have direct access to it—it is essentially open and unconcealed. But how is it known? Metaphysics, in dealing with levels of ontic knowledge, has forgotten the levels of ontological knowledge; its forms of representative knowledge cannot yield any valid information about true Being; its standard terms are insufficient and misleading within the dimension of Being itself. Having forgotten Being, philosophy continued to speak of the Being of beings with a worthless language. Heidegger therefore rejects the conventional precise terminology of traditional metaphysics, and offers in its place a new originative mode of thinking: Poetry. From Caratheodory's *Fragments* (CC 40):

7.0.   why is there not just void?

because nothing cannot appear whole to a part of it

. . . we are parts . . . see things in part

7.2.1 particles flow from things into the pores of the eyes

7.2.2 these images are similar to the surface of the visible object

7.3   images—violet-like—show us true being

Poetry is free of all logical terms and expressions, and so not circumscribed by their rigidity; it comes to the aid of thinkers, who are out of touch with Being, through its ability to name all things in that which they are; it is the establishing of Being by means of the word. Since being can never be calculated from what is present, it must be created; in naming the poet makes Being become known as existent. Yet, poetry is the possibility of saying nothing while speaking of Being. Heidegger notes that (HI 11), "What is spoken is never, and in no language, what is said." The being that is its origin is that to which authentic human beings belong. The speech of genuine thinking is poetic, without needing the shape of verse. Poetry is the saying of the unconcealedness of beings, it bids the world and things to gather into the simple onefold of their belonging together. "But poetry that thinks is in truth the topology of Being," claims Heidegger (HI 12). Beings come out in the open, to exist in their own truthful way, and to exist in a mutual appropriation in the dance of their being. This mirroring is a mutual lighting up and reflecting through which the meaning of Being is determined.

Poetry is not an abstract theorizing, but the most concrete thinking and speaking about the differing being of beings in the fold of Being. It is also the task of poetry to help people see the bright possibility of a true world; it is the creative source of human existence as dwelling—it opens up to Being and takes the measure of the dimension of existence. It is poetry that first grounds the genuine dwelling of men; to dwell poetically on the earth is to heed it in its essence and to guard it as the sustaining element which blooms and bears fruit, which is dispersed in minerals and water, and emerges in all life; to dwell poetically is not to belabor and exploit the earth into yielding its energy and material, but it is to receive its benediction, and to guard the inviolability of the possible and the mystery of Being.

Heidegger treats poetry as an aspect of philosophical thought; the function of poets and thinkers is progressively united, from their dwelling near one another, on peaks farthest apart, to where, as he (GP 102) says, "All reflective thought is poetic: All poetry, however, is thought." Thinking, even more than poetry and song, grows out of Being and reaches into its truth beyond language. Heidegger (KA 268) claims that poets and philosophers inhabit the same universe, language, as the temple of Being: "Language speaks in showing the essence of things, and so truth is "underway to Language," where poets and philosophers live together in the nearness to Being." The logos of language (as the house of Being) is not simply the way the appearance of *physis* is revealed to human beings, but in a sense is ontologically the same with it.

Poetic thought replaces analysis, and pure conceptualization becomes combined with emotional activity. Philosophy paradoxically becomes realized when it expresses the nature of Being through a poetic passivity. Can philosophy do what poetry does? By appealing to feeling, a poem allows its reader to experience the unity of existence—can the same be experienced in abstract, philosophical terms? The evocative language of poetry can go beyond itself; but can language burdened with an implicit metaphysics be transcended by metaphysics without an obscurity of speaking (as opposed to a speaking of obscurity)?

Heidegger's thoughts sometimes are written in poetic form, in verse or not, using many of the same images as Heraclitus and Lucretius. The question remains whether poetry can directly excavate that which cannot even be approached directly. In spite of the beauty which his writing sometimes creates, and the effectiveness of his quotes from Holderlin, he still tries to define Being directly, variegating on it as a constant presentness; as in his closeness to the Rinzai school of Buddhism, with its emphasis on direct apprehension, Heidegger stresses a direct method of arriving at Being. He offers the ontological characteristics of *Dasein* in conceptual form, as being in-the-world, or being-with-others, and so reflects upon the core of prereflective experience. His interest in poets is in their ontological significance, and the truths they can reveal about man's dwelling. But poetry can incorporate scientific information; it is rational as well. In its indirect sideways approach, it can only reach the ontological through the ontic level.

Heidegger tries to demonstrate how language founds truth, using his own work (HI 9).

When on a summer's day the butterfly

settles on the flower and, wings
closed, sways with it in the
meadow-breeze. ...

All our heart's courage is the
echoing response to the
first call of Being which
gathers our thinking into the
play of the world.

In thinking all things
become solitary and slow.

Patience nurtures magnanimity.

He who thinks greatly must
    err greatly.

What does this mean? Is this poetry adequate? Is not the idea of poetry
to approach Being through beings? So, why does not Heidegger say
what summer's day? Late? Early? What kind of butterfly, with what
colors? What size wings, what kind of flower, or what color? What
meadow-breeze, from where?

In the electric signals pushing the muscle of the heart to move
oxygenated blood, where is courage? Which seems to arise from
taming the heart or nerves. Does Being just call echoes? Maybe the
poem is appropriate to Being as the invisible source of every detail
and individual pattern. But, could not poetry surround Being with the
metaphors that connect all the details? Heidegger tries again:

When the evening light, slanting into
The woods somewhere, based the tree
Trunks and gold.

Singing and thinking are the stems, a
Neighbor to poetry.

They grow out of being and reach into
It's true.

Their relationship makes us think of what
Holderlin sings of the trees of the
Woods:

'And to each other they remain unknown,
So long as they stand, the neighboring
Trunks.'

How is this discourse 'poetico-philosophical' enough to transcend more
traditional metaphysics? Although Heidegger is obviously aware of the
vocabulary used for redescription, he seems to be missing the anguish
and anxiety that most poets combine in their expression. He does not
allow his thinking to be disturbed by the chaos or poetic expression.
Nor does he seem to hear the despair and alienation of Holderlin
(in 'Bread and Wine'), Rilke and the others. If he is expressing his
reception of truth, it seems to be a bare, unadorned truth. Heidegger
may indeed be reexploring a more original sense of poetic making, after
the Pre-Socratics, but his language also has a high level of abstraction.
He turned or returned to the pre-Socratics for examples of poetic
ontology, before presenting his own. Making and thought are the
same order yet different according to him. Perhaps it is a thoughtful
making. There are certainly differences in language. The thoughtful
seems explicit and the making approaches Being implicitly. Poetry,
however, reveals Being without abstracting it into thought. The history
of thought simultaneously makes being more abstract and complex, as
well as maybe more basic. Heidegger starts with detail, but distances
and explains immediately.

When the cowbells keep tinkling from
The slopes of the mountain valley
Where their herds wander slowly....

The poetic character of thinking is
Still veiled over.

Where it shows itself, it is for a
Long time like the utopianism of
A half poetic intellect.

But poetry that thinks is in truth
The topology of being.

For Heidegger poetic language is the truest form of language, the
speech of genuine thinking. So, is it wild? The topology of being
does not just sit there, frozen in the headlights of reason, it moves
and changes. How does poetry show its motion and change? Not by
referring to topology. Heidegger lets the thing speak at last.

PAF

Forests spread
Brooks plunge
rocks persist
missed the fuses

Mentos weight
springs well
winds dwell
blessing uses

Heidegger talks about the thing. He says the thingy element is so present in the artwork that we are compelled rather to say conversely that the architectural work is in stone, the carving is in wood, or that the painting is in the color and canvas. He also states that death and judgment are alternate things. No, life and foam our ultimate things. Death and judgment are merely changes in the relations of things.

Poetry and art are proposed as ways of revealing. Yet, they may be limited by their lines of cultural development, and by their acceptance of technological extensions, fixes, fads and topics, as well by ignoring 'mysterious' knowledge. Poetry and technology are tools that reveal Being. Poetry extends it into some new form, while technology converts it into material things that are useful, but may be dangerous. They exist in the tension between the earth and the human worlds. The saving powers or poetry and art have to be the balancing of the tension for joy and home to exist. To recognize the gifts of beings, material, plant, and animal, and remind us what we can do to preserve their essences.

Ontology poses a problem to philosophers. Both Sartre and Heidegger found that a philosophical prose was inadequate. As Heidegger and Santayana realized, a philosophical poetry is also inadequate. That which cannot be treated as object or idea cannot be addressed in logical propositions or unthinking verse. Yet, the wildest ideality and the inexhaustable perceptual world must be taken up into some intelligible expression. Heidegger refused to admit the limitations of rational knowledge.

3.2.2.4. *Poetic Paradox from Wittgenstein*
"I think I summed up my attitude to philosophy when I said: philosophy ought really to be written only as a poetic composition." *Wittgenstein*

Does Wittgenstein mean that philosophy has to be poetic? Or, just that philosophy needs to recognize all forms of language that can combine elegance and clarity? Wittgenstein's poetic forms in his works indicate that he knew that philosophy has to recognize the metaphors and harmony of poetry, in order to capture human experience and feelings into expression. However, his poetic forms were never claimed to be, or recognized as poetry. His anguish and joy at thought combined styles but never was contained by just one. A way of involving the imagination of the reader or listener as a method of examining problems. The 'draftsman' has to represent "all the interrelations between things." Certainly this is an ecological approach that links the self to things and aspects of Being in the form of an investigation.

Perhaps systematic aphorisms, the *Lebensforms* of Wittgenstein, could combine the attributes of prose and poetry in an aware and indirect expression that points to the ground of existence without partitioning or signifying. Wittgenstein's use of language is comparable to the metaphoric metalinguistic vocabulary of Heidegger. There is no distinction in Wittgenstein between the style and the meaning; his form of life (*Lebensform*) terms are aphoristic. Wittgenstein, in the *Tractatus*, combines logical precision with poetic vagueness, to remake the whole range of philosophy. The Tractatus has been considered to be a 'poem.' Like Lao Tse, he uses paradox to convey his most important insights; they both begin with a metaphysical statement about the nature of the world (the way of nature), and conclude with practical messages: Wittgenstein admonishing that whereof one cannot speak one must be silent, Lao Tse advising one to do nothing and nothing will be left undone.

Language is a mirror image of the world. Its function is to describe it. The world is composed of facts, which are composed of atomic facts which are composed of objects—objects are in a direct relation with names, which combine to form elementary propositions (and these are in a picturing relation with atomic facts), which combine to form propositions, the sum of which is language; the limit of language is held to be the limit of the world. Wittgenstein, in the remainder of the *Tractatus*, traces the consequences of this theory, and concludes that the propositions of aesthetics, ethics, and metaphysics are senseless or nonsensical; they do not say anything because they attempt to transcend, in language, the limits of language; these important things are mystical, they cannot be said, but they can be shown. In dealing exclusively with language and logic, he intended to signify what can not be said by presenting clearly what can be said (WM 115).

The sense of the world is what lies outside of it; this makes the world nonaccidental, but it is inexpressible, such only shows itself. To speak about the limit of language is senseless; to say anything about what lies beyond it is nonsense. That is not to say that the inexpressible itself, or philosophy, is nonsense, only that most propositions are, once they are not strictly propositions.

Although the sentences in most poems would be called nonsensical if they were treated as propositions, a poem is not presented as consisting of propositions or stating truths about the world; even though it is composed in the language of information, it is not used in the language game of giving information. Although not clearly considering poetry, perhaps Wittgenstein meant poetry to exist in a picturing relation with the world. Since the realm of the transcendental can only be shown, and not said, poetry may have a special relation with it. The *Tractatus*, after all, attempts to outline the inexpressible by exhibiting the expressible.

Precisely because the mystical is everything important in life, a person has the urge to thrust against the limits of language, as a wild animal runs against the walls of a cage. The tendency to thrust points toward something. While deeply respecting the attempt, Wittgenstein believed that one's astonishment that anything exists could not be expressed in language.

Although Wittgenstein's later work is equally nonmetaphysical, his task was to understand the nature of metaphysics. Although a metaphysical statement may be absurd, the idea in it is of enormous importance. By trying, the metaphysician discovers a new way of looking at things. "As if he had invented a new way of painting; or, again a new meter," Wittgenstein says (WL 401). The whole force of his investigation was to point beyond itself. Wittgenstein's use of language yields nonliteral meanings; the use of aphorisms brings about a shift from the commonplace to the extraordinary, by cutting off fixed meanings and by reflexively pointing to the context and direction of use. The limits of language limit philosophy; but can philosophy go beyond language? Meaning can be bodily understood in the forms of life; mime, then, becomes a method of philosophical representation. "A good ground is one that looks *like this,*" is Wittgenstein's example (WM 483).

Wittgenstein worried that he was not original, that his prose was limited, and that he was unable to write verse. Yet, he admitted having 'poetic' moods and he realized that he could create similes and other poetic devices. Like Merleau-Ponty, he used metaphors to describe aspects of perception and words. His philosophical investigations were also aesthetic. The Tractatus Logico-Philosophicus is regarded as a poem, by Wittgenstein and by others. Poetry was more capable of revealing the essence of language. It modulated the existence of its subject. Perhaps the boundary between what can and cannot be said is erased by the 'forms of life' as expressed by poetic forms of expression.

In fact, when asked to discuss his book with members of the Vienna Circle, Wittgenstein would recite poetry to them with his chair turned towards the wall. Perhaps he did not think his own propositions poetic enough.

1. "The world is all that is the case.
1.1 "The world is the totality of facts, not of things. ...
7. What we cannot speak of we must pass over in silence.
   From the *Tractatus*, by L. Wittgenstein

Did the pre-Socratic philosophers (and Lucretius, whose subject was pre-Socratic) use poetry because it was more appropriate to their notion of *physis* (as Heidegger would imply), or because there was no other language (as Aristotle states)? Heidegger believed poetry was more adequate than prose for his notion of *physis*. Bachelard, a phenomenologist, believes it is the only way. Santayana and Wittgenstein seem predisposed toward their styles personally, not due to any implicit advantage of poetic form for expressing their subject.

3.2.2.5. *Poetic Expression: Merleau-Ponty & Beginning*

Before there is a logic of language, there is a logic of the body. Language is embodied. If every question contains an assumption not stated (after Frege), then Wittgenstein's must be the primacy of language; Merleau-Ponty's is the primacy of perception. Wittgenstein (WM 116) limits the ability of words: "When philosophers use a word—"knowledge," "being," "object," "I," "proposition," "name,"—and try to grasp the essence of actually used in this way in the language game which was its original home?—What we do is to bring words back from their metaphysical to their everyday use." Merleau-Ponty does the opposite of this, using everyday words to point to metaphysics, metaphorically. The meanings of standard philosophical terms—experience, invention and perception, for instance— are gradually changed and adopted to new usages. In addition to the expansion of old terms, there is his use of a vocabulary of freshly minted phrases, from Husserl and Heidegger, which includes the "lived-body," "being-in-the-world," the "life world," and "intersubjectivity;" there is, in addition, his evocative use of the metaphorical terms: "gesture, incarnation, silence," which precedes and conveys, indirectly, meaning in speech, and "singing the world," which precedes conceptual meaning. Finally there is the prominent reliance on a wild language, to describe the philosophical approach—the poetic philosophical approach—to savage Being; the most radical terms, in *The Visible and the Invisible*, are flesh, perceptual faith, chiasm, and intertwining.

Philosophy is still a questioning of brute being, which is an opaque dimension of the perceptual subject always bound up with the world through transcendence. The dimension to which the questioning is addressed has enveloped the subject and object so completely that they are essentially inseparable, and must be approached from within. Philosophy puts a question to what does not speak; it asks of our experiences of the world, in Merleau-Ponty's words (MN 102): "what the world is before it is a thing one speaks of and which is taken for granted, before it has been reduced to a set of manageable, disposable significations." The philosopher does not receive an intelligent answer; he receives a confirmation of his astonishment at savage Being. There can be no answer to end the questioning, since the answer, a translation into manageable significations would only further conceal the savage Being the philosopher addresses.

There cannot be a direct ontology, as in Heidegger. Philosophy cannot move immediately to a comprehension of Being as such, but must gain access through the things which are, which are present to perceptual experience. Phenomenology is to be situated in a more fundamental ontology, as in Heidegger, a dialectic ontology which posits an ontological dialectic at the root of reality. But, as for Merleau-Ponty (MN 179), it must be an indirect method: "One cannot make a direct ontology. My indirect method (being in the beings) is alone conformed with being—'negative philosophy like negative theology.'"

But to be more than mute beholding or a silent pointing—to be itself—philosophy must speak, it must rest on language. It must restrain itself from translating savage Being into the sedimental concepts embodied in language; it must be discrete in the face of things, and concern itself with the character appropriate to that to which it speaks. After questioning language, philosophy can only return to it, knowingly. Thought renounces its invisibility to become language, but in speech the words become thought; the mystery cannot be approached directly, or from outside, somehow. In the same way as we attempt to grasp the world, as we talk about language it recedes from us. Merleau-Ponty (GI 117) describes how: "In this case, reflection, by virtue of being reflection and therefore speech, would always adopt whatever theme it chose and would in principle be incapable of achieving what it is seeking. But there are a philosophy and a mode of reflection which do not pretend to constitute their object, to be in rivalry with it, or to clarify it with a light that is not their own."

Philosophy is a hyper-reflection, an operative language which brings new words into existence to fulfill the primordial function of expression. More than philosophy, poetry is a primary language, having the power and purpose of restoring the significance and integrity of sensuality, and

of the emotional potential of things. Merleau-Ponty even used poetry
and art as a source for his philosophy. The human sciences, Merleau-
Ponty (MJ 92) says: "are metaphysical or transnatural in the sense that
they cause us to rediscover, by means of the concept of structure and the
under- standing of various kinds of structures, a dimension of being and
a kind of knowledge which is forgotten by man in his natural attitude."
Is it possible for radical philosophy, to return to its own beginnings, to
absorb the recoil in such a way that the beginning is unchanged? Or is
the dimension of perceptual experience so bound to the beginnings so
as to preclude the distancing necessary for philosophy?

How can philosophical thought exhibit the beginnings as such if
by their very definition thought is distanced from them? Without the
distance one would have pure perception or pure thought. The distance
must be maintained, but without philosophical thought becoming a
cognition of brute Being. Therefore, what is required is a speaking
which instead bears witness to Being and to its concealment. Merleau-
Ponty requires that philosophy be the reconversion of silence and speech
into one another; one must speak in such a way as to preserve silence.

But speaking breaks the silence, and although expression can
become transparent before the expressed, that silence is a broken
one, the other side of language. What has been expressed is not the
concealed silence of wild being in its integrity, but ideas of Being,
transposed into the flesh of language. Perhaps only by remaining silent
could this positivity be avoided, but even this is impossible, since we are
born into a language. Furthermore, Merleau-Ponty's thought is bound
to the positivity of the expressed, and justified by Saussurian linguistics,
which objectifies language and automatically disavows explaining how
language and its invisible side exist for the subject. Even the meaning
that appears at the intersections of words is expressed meaning, and
exists.

How can philosophy not do violence to things, in saying them? The
way speaking is bound to the positivity of the expressed is intertwined
with the way it chooses to be bound. There are other alternatives
to philosophy: myth, although a positive expression, disallows the
assimilating power of thought; poetry maintains the distance and
refuses to be bound; both of these expressions offer different kinds of
relations of philosophical thought to the pre-philosophical silence,
between things which are said and things which are.

How is it possible really to distinguish between things before they
are said, and things after—is it even possible to posit a pre-linguistic
world? Does this not duplicate the fallacy of an objectivist's world,
only in reverse? Language can never be completely transparent and

self-effacing; language, the positivity of speech, can never interrogate the pre-linguistic Being, any more than it could an undifferentiated sphere of Being. Merleau-Ponty demands a self-effacing speech of philosophical thought to restore wild silence, that would eliminate the noise resulting from the distance of thought. But the elimination of the distance would allow thought to collapse into silence, or the reverse, and one be assimilated by the other, neither of which is desirable, for various reasons (thought would be silence, or silence thought). The metaphorical use of words would solve the dilemma: a metaphor preserves the distance and points beyond toward a horizon of silence.

Merleau-Ponty almost abolishes the distance between thought and beginnings. If the beginnings are understood as identical to the perceptual world, then the quest of thought collapses the distance and abolishes its own standpoint. In returning to the beginnings thought needs to grant a standpoint to itself, and institute a new beginning. The beginning that calls forth thought cannot then be reached by thought. Philosophical thought arises from a background of perceptual faith, but what in that thought questions itself, also places itself at a distance. Philosophy can only return to the beginnings at a distance. Philosophy is a self-questioning that must remain suspended between its own beginning and the original beginning as such. What supports it between them is imagination. Can imagination allow it to approach Being?

The difficulty inherent in writing poetically is evident in some of the different drafts he attempted. Merleau-Ponty began a work entitled *The Prose of the World*, in which he intended to give the category of prose a sociological meaning beyond the confines of literature; but, he consciously put it aside. Why? Perhaps to write a poetry of the world; after all, the archaeology of perception which he had proposed earlier, required it, since the process of creative expression must be clarified before the prose of the world could be described. After the book had been set aside, Merleau-Ponty took a central essay on "Indirect Language" from it, and renamed it, "Indirect Language and the Voices of Silence," apparently realizing that a transition from mute silence to speech was necessary on which to ground prose. This second version, published in *Signs*, is not only more refined, but states explicitly that the expression of the world must be poetry (at which the first version only hinted). This pure power of expressing is a dynamic process from which new meaning and truth emerge. In "Eye and Mind," and *The Visible and the Invisible*, he begins a poetics of the world.

3.2.2.6. *Philosophical Poets & Poetic Scientists: Stevens & Eiseley*

Perhaps the search should be reversed and poets should be studied for their insights into philosophy? And, scientists who write as poets may have enough insight and skill to reveal more of the ground of Being. Although Kathleen Raine, G. Bachelard, and other poets are used throughout to illustrate metaphysical ideas, Stevens will be examined in more detail. Although A.M. Caratheodory and Buckminster Fuller and other scientists used poetic forms, Loren Eiseley will be examined in more detail.

3.2.2.6.1. Wallace Stevens

Where Heidegger refused to admit the limitations of rational knowledge. The poet, Wallace Stevens (BG 137), admits the limits:

> We feel the obscurity of an order, a whole,
> A knowledge, that which arranged the rendezvous,
> Within its vital boundary, in the mind.
> We say God and the imagination are one . . . .
> How high that highest candle lights the dark.
> Out of this same light, out of the central mind,
> We make a dwelling in the evening air,
> In which being there together is enough.

Stevens was a poet who chose to address philosophical topics and themes. Several philosophical schools, from phenomenology to Deconstruction, considered his poetry to be real contributions to philosophy, trying to answer questions about writing philosophy, the primary one being, 'Can poetic philosophizing have an equal weight to prosaic philosophizing?' Stevens himself suggested that poets and philosophers pursued different forms of truth. Philosophers focused on logical truth, where poets presented empirical truth—that is, facts beyond the normal sensibility and perception. In an Aristotelian sense, their ends were different, effective for the poet and fateful for the philosopher.

Stevens presents ideas as if poetic truth has the same weight a philosophical (See 'Eesthetique du Mal' below). Repetition and variation, in unifying human harmony and the health of the world, exhibits more power and evokes more thought than a simple statement. The questioning throughout the poem involves participation in reading.

Stevens carried his poetic sensitivity into the realms of epistemology, pragmatism and phenomenology, which was noted by numerous philosophers afterwards, and even a few poets, such as T.S Eliot. The philosophy was incorporated into the poetry to make a denser texture.

Stevens had argued that poetry and philosophy pursued different truths, empirical truth and logical truth, respectively. People read poetry to expand their perspectives, and philosophy for other possibilities. The poet is judged to be effective, or not (this a pragmatic view). The philosopher on the logic and consistency of representation.

Richard Rorty (RR 82) argues that philosophy does not have an essence or even a distinctive subject. It is a kind of writing about the family romance of 'Father Parmenides' or 'bad brother Derrida.' Rorty, in philosophical writing, contrasts the self-eliminating with the self-extending: Kant is the former while Hegel exemplifies the latter, which does not seek closure as much as dialectic revelry. Stevens has the self-expressive style, which may involve it in philosophy. Stevens unifies the fragments through as 'as if' frame:

It seems
As if the health of the world might be enough.
It seems as if the honey of common summer
Might be enough, as if the golden combs
Were part of a sustenance itself enough,
As if hell, so modified, had disappeared,
As if pain, no longer satanic mimicry,
Could be borne, as if we were sure to find our way.
    (from 'Esthetique du Mal')

The incantations of 'as if's can humanize the nonhuman order, transform pain, and make things restful or smooth with health, honey and combs.

Rorty recognizes that there is still a gap between, in Heidegger's terminology, metaphor and metaphysics, between linguistic gaming and logical comportment. Paul Ricoeur suggest that 'live metaphor' can create new experience that can impact and change a world-view, so it is more than a rhetorical device.

Can Stevens poetry be powerful enough to close the gap? Or, is it just confusing, with jumbled layers and provocative words?

When B. sat down at the piano and made
A transparence in which we heard music, made music,
In which we heard transparent sounds, did he play
All sorts of notes? Or did he play only one
In an ecstasy of associates,
Variations in the tones of a single sound,
The last, or sounds so single they seemed one?

Words create an icon in the imagination that mixes sight and sound, and as more than just that, it emerges from the verbal description of a sensory experience. This is what metaphor does, combine sight and smell, sound and taste, in the synaesthetic imagination. Metaphor allows the conflict of sameness and difference to create a more complex interaction. Stevens continues his presentation of conflicting possibilities in 'Esthetique du Mal' (notice the continued use of 'as if'):

> To lose sensibility, to see what one sees,
> As if sight had not its own miraculous thrift,
> To hear only what one hears, one meaning alone,
> As if the paradise of meaning ceased
> To be paradise, it is this to be destitute.

The possibility of meaninglessness and destitution is contrasted with that of a 'paradise of meaning,' although the paradise may be of language itself. And in the final thought, Stevens suggests that these words, noting changes, could result in 'many selves.'

> And out of what one sees and hears and out
> Of what one feels, who could have thought to make
> So many selves, so many sensuous worlds,
> As if the air, the mid-day air, was swarming
> With the metaphysical changes that occur,
> Merely in living as and where we live.

The possibilities can be created through language and are not determined or fated by chance or change. Rorty suggests Stevens goes beyond the futility of speech to a 'primitive ecstasy.' The continued 'as if' allows the possibility of the identification of words with the world, while pointing to the significant gap between them, bringing back to consciousness the tension from the conflict of possibility.

Poetic truth keeps the conflict alive, by being a form of knowledge. Rorty argues that Stevens establishes the tenuous 'relation' he continually strives to express; or, in Ricoeur's terms, 'Being-as means being *and* not being.' Rorty concludes that Stevens use of poetry as a theory of life allows him "finally to explore and rejuvenate this epistemological terrain, the ground upon which philosophy and poetry meet and part."

3.2.2.6.2. Loren Eiseley

Loren Eiseley was an anthropologist and science writer, who wrote imaginatively about the human perspectives of the universe. Eiseley considered that dreams, or art, emerged from the subconscious like a supernova blazing suddenly out of the void. They could be later studied but not accounted for. His writings are often presented as contemplations.

The Spider
His science has progressed past stone,
His strange and dark geometries,
Impossible to flesh and bone, ...
Foundations buried underfoot
Are forfeit to the mole and worm
But spiders know it and will put
Their trust in airy dreams more firm
Than any rock and raise from dew
Frail stairs the careless wind blows through.

The spider lives in a circumscribed spider universe that may not
include human pencils and pokers. Like white blood cells, spiders are
unknowing of their context, their being within Being. Perhaps in 'Dusk
Interval' Eiseley was reaching towards the ground of Being?

Dusk Interval
Here is the waste, the stone, the streaming sunset ...
Erratic spirals in the windy starlight.
The fallow ground
Is sleeping, and I know with what ghost sleeping,
Deep under sound.

Although not a religious writer, Eiseley was sympathetic to the concerns
of religion. In his autobiography, he stated: "I who profess no religion
find the whole of my life a religious pilgrimage." Many of his essays
exhibit a religious sensitivity to nature and its most "supreme mystery,
man." Eiseley notes that humans and nature are more than can be
observed by a limited number of perspectives: "Our untouched forests
confronted us with a silence that penetrated the soul with *mysterium
tremendum*. It has been unfortunate that we have thrust aside this
religious terror, refusing to contemplate it. For it is contemplation that
teaches us that we, and, indeed, all of nature, are more than we observe."
In 'Sunset at Laramie,' he connects a history of listening with many sounds.

Somewhere beyond Laramie the winding freights
still howl their lonesome message to the dark,
the mountain men lie quiet, wolves are gone,
stars circle overhead, huge missiles lie
scattered in firing pens. Computers watch
with radar eyes pinpointed latitudes.
Gigantic cupped ears listen everywhere—
a bear asleep beneath a winter drift,
his pulse is coded, too; night-flying geese
blip by on horizon screens, slowly we draw a net

converging to ourselves. How strange to hear
trains hoot in blizzards, cattle brawl in cars,
think of the Chisholm trail a century gone, and know
beyond the polar circle other ears now listen.
This daft and troubled century spies and spies,
counts bears' heartbeats, whales' frantic twists and turns.
The background noise of continents drifts in,
captured by satellites. Still far up in the crags
sure-footed mountain sheep climb higher, lift horned heads,
see the night fall below them, hear the train, and stamp
as rams stamp, vaguely troubled, while the glow
on the last peak fades out. Far off a coyote cries,
not in wild darkness, but a haunted night
filled with the turning of vast ears and eyes.
     From the book *Notes of an Alchemist*, 1972

    Eiseley notes that humans are tempted by machine intimacy
and may want to further 'exosomatic evolution' by transferring their
memories and personalities, their identities, to machines, but cautions
that such a change would never bring them peace. He urges us to heed
the words of the Buddha and understand that there is no transcendence
without the exploration of one's interior. He recognizes that perhaps the
interior is as infinite as outer space.

    In the work, 'The Figure in the Stone,' the protagonist confronts
a mud-spattered workman with an old stone that he claims holds the
shape of a woman. He agrees that the workman did see it in the dark
and should keep the stone, which he gives back. But, he thinks about
the urge to see (cf. Figure 4333-1).

          Always, I thought,
            leaning against the door, this inner barrier,
always the inscrutable rubric growing fainter
from mind to mind that strives to read the world.
We tried to climb with masks
               back into the shape of animals;
    we failed.
We tried
the ever-fecund mothers,
        the returning cycles
            of many
unreturning gods.
      What is there lies
down in the subway that we have not seen?

What new wild hand is scrawling on the walls
the approaching mammoth and the giant bear?
Softly I turned and looked outside the window
into a rain that never ceased to fall
on men still splotched with clay.

Eiseley was concerned, as a scientist that, as a result of scientific studies, nature has become externalized, particularized, mechanized, fragmented, and finally reduced to conflict without consideration of cooperation. Perhaps poetry was a means for humans to avoid becoming monsters who would trade extinctions for a few comforts or concentration camps for political capital. He wrote about that in a form of free verse.

I am treading deeper and deeper into leaves and silence. I see more faces watching, non-human faces. Ironically, I who profess no religion find the whole of my life a religious pilgrimage.

The religious forms of the present leave me unmoved. My eye is round, open, and undomesticated as an owl's in a primeval forest—a world that for me has never truly departed.

I have come to believe that in the world there is nothing to explain the world.

Like the toad in my shirt we were in the hands of God, but we could not feel him; he was beyond us, totally and terribly beyond our limited senses.

Man is not as other creatures and . . . without the sense of the holy, without compassion, his brain can become a gray stalking horror …

[from *All the Strange Hours* and *The Star Thrower*].

Eiseley uses poetry to try to place the majesty of beings into a human consciousness that is threatened by self-centeredness and detachment. His poetry is difficult to excerpt, when it rambles and spirals back upon itself, finding some meaning unexpectedly, after building descriptions. The sadness of childhood is replaced by the adult sadness of the remorseless workings of industrial civilization, which seems obsessed with documenting the last of wild nature, the same nature that is the source of happiness and inspiration for most children and many adults. Eiseley has made it his purpose, not so much to express a metaphysics of nature, but to keep poetry alive in a culturally-deprived society. So much the better, if that can lead to an appreciation of the complexity and diversity of living nature.

3.2.3. Poetry & Philosophy

In the pre-Socratics, philosophy and poetry were indistinguishable; even through the Middle Ages, philosophy was still poetic. In the seventeenth century thinkers considered that philosophy achieved an absolute knowledge, while poetry lost its rationality. There are signs in this epoch that there is a reapproachment toward common ground.

Philosophy and poetry share a certain detachment: Husserl noticed a close affinity between artistic and phenomenological detachment; in different ways they both illustrate a possible modification of consciousness—the neutralization of the thesis of being. The reductions carried out in phenomenology find an automatic fulfillment in art. Husserl distinguishes between the neutral modification of art, and the neutrality of the representation in every image: the figure in an image has no real being, representing only what the being may be real, but not in the image itself—this substitution is what is meant by neutralization.

Philosophy shares with art the suggestion of meanings beyond mere statements. Whitehead says that since philosophy shares direct insight into unspoken depths with mysticism and poetry, it may be called poetical or mystical, but it is so in a distinctly different way: the mystic evokes experience with imagery of a system of belief; the poet, indifferent to belief, seeks to penetrate the depths through meter; philosophy ignores meter, but employs mathematical pattern to plumb experience, to construct a rationally coordinated mysticism; each uses different ways to deal with the unspeakable. Whitehead (WJ 174) rephrases it: "philosophy is mystical. For mysticism is direct insight into depths as yet unspoken. But the purpose of philosophy is to rationalize mysticism: not by explaining it away, but by the introduction of novel verbal characterizations, rationally coordinated. Philosophy is akin to poetry, and both of them seek to express that ultimate good sense which we term civilization. In each case there is reference to form beyond the direct meaning of words. Poetry allies itself to meter, philosophy to mathematical pattern." It is not meter that defines poetry but metaphor; meter is a mathematical pattern, which in turn is a *logos*, which also means word or speech. Philosophy must use poetry, to reach where it may not go itself. Whitehead (WK 515) says that: "Philosophy may not neglect the multifariousness of the world—the fairies dance, and Christ is nailed to the cross." The multifariousness may not be named, or characterized: So philosophy must use poetic imagery to evoke the sense of the inconceivable multifariousness of things.

The contrast between the extremes of experience metaphorically expressed is analogous to the contrast between extremes within context of the totality of experience which forms the source of philosophical evidence. In order to see in a new way, 'man' must say in a new way; poetic language has the greatest capacity to create the new. Philosophy must use radical linguistic tactics, and poesis is necessary for that radicalness. Merleau-Ponty (MN 102) declares that "it follows that the words most charged with philosophy are not necessarily those that contain what they say, but rather those that most energetically open upon Being, because they more closely convey the life of the whole and make our habitual evidences vibrate until they disjoin." Are those energetic words not poetic, and philosophy has to become poetry to achieve its ambitions?

Kierkegaard rejected the notion that philosophy was a quest for absolute truth; it should be, as Mackey (MA 329) says, the "imaginative exploration of the possible toward the enrichment of human self-understanding and the enabling of human decision. In other words, poetry. His own works demand to be read as a peculiar kind of dramatic poetry, of which the ultimate author has created not only the characters but the very poets." By reconverting philosophy into poetry, Kierkegaard tried to find a way to the thing itself, through resplendent images and indirect communication. A philosophical system, with univocal terms and definite propositions is bound to its terms and the law of contradiction; poetry is not. Being violates such terms and laws, so poetry must describe it. Metaphorical language is a multivalent unity; fundamentally analogical, the interaction of its propositions is open in many senses, yet contains diversity.

Poetic language is almost diametrically opposed to empirical language in its capabilities. All of the scientific characteristics operate more optimally in the realm of ideal objects, whereas the poetic aspects of language are more adequate for the carnal relations of Being. Philosophy seems capable of using either extreme, depending on the area it is addressing; generally, however, it is diachronous and linguistic. The linguistic activity of philosophy also seems to be more secondary compared to the primary creativity of poetry, since, for the most part, it is content with the novel arrangement of established significations. Poetry, then, should present a more adequate metaphysics.

Bachelard questions the value of a poet writing a poem through the eyes of a hare; would not it be better to describe the pastoral scene directly? And he answers that the poet wants to describe all the degrees of contemplation, all the instants of an image. Bachelard (BC 209) says that when the seeing eye has ceased to look at anything in particular, it "is looking at the world." We should not have been so radically thrown back into primitiveness if the poet told his own contemplation, a mere repetition of a philosophical theme. Merleau-Ponty (MJ 28) finds that philosophy and poetry intertwine: "From now on the tasks of literature and philosophy can no longer be separated. When one is concerned with giving voice to the experience of the world and showing how consciousness escapes into the world, one can no longer credit oneself with attaining a perfect transparency of expression. Philosophical expression assumes the same ambiguities as literary expression, if the world is such that it cannot be expressed except in "stories," and, as it were, pointed at. One will not only witness the appearance of hybrid modes of expression, but the novel and the theater will become thoroughly metaphysical, even if not a single word is used from the vocabulary of philosophy." As the reverse of Heidegger's position, philosophy is now a poetic endeavor. Poetry engages the person in a markedly different way; it is an untranslatable experience, unique in its growth of meaning and completeness. Philosophy properly practiced concerns itself with the various meanings of words, that it is closely occupied with purposes, and that it should lead to deep understanding (not dispute between disciplines)—it should mediate between the modes of language. Philosophy should concern itself directly with the type of multiple meaning that is encountered, for instance, in an imaginative edge. The philosopher in Plato's *Republic* sees the different sciences, and the body of knowledge they compose, as a whole.

3.2.3.1. Similarities & Differences
But how is philosophy similar to poetry specifically? Its concern with multiple meanings parallels the growth of meaning in a poetic passage; its centrality of purposes reflects the untranslatability of the poetic passage (explained by the reader's absorption in the purpose underlying its diverse framework); the deep understanding of philosophy is reminiscent of the completeness and breadth of the poem. Philosophy properly conceived is a measure, a ruler, that writes under itself, within us, interests which would war with one another, without it. It will use mathematics to describe stellar distances or poetry to describe Being. Is this, then, a poetic measure, the logos of Heraclitus? In I. A. Richards' words (SE 139): "Philosophy is a poetic endeavor; poetry solves the conflict between science and value; it forces us to be more sensitive, by being the exemplar of our 'lexical-structural would-be system . . . at its most entire.'"

In Merleau-Ponty, perspective is a cultural fact, which allows itself to be oriented by the cultural system; but the relationship is reversible. He (GI 76) maintains that "there is an informing of perception by culture which enables us to say that *culture is perceived.*" Poetry perceives culture and perception. Every human being is prejudiced by his perspective; men should cultivate as many perspectives as possible, and poetry allows just this enlargement.

Metaphor enlarges the imagination; poetry is the closest approach to objectivity. Through its special position poetry becomes metaphysics, even though embodied, according to Vico (VI 367): "for all these reasons we must trace the beginnings of poetic wisdom to a crude metaphysics. From this, as from a trunk, there branch out from one limb logic, morals, economics, and politics, all poetic; and from another physics, the mother of their cosmography and hence of astronomy, which gives their certainty to its two daughters, chronology and geography, all likewise poetic." Even early physicists found the basic nature of the world was poetic and based their physics on it. Vico (VI 688) writes, "It was thence that the physicists were later moved to conceive the confusion of the universal seeds of nature, and to express it they took the word already invented by the poets and hence appropriate."

That word was chaos, and it was later taken by the physicists as the prime matter of natural things, which, formless itself, devours all forms. But the poets also gave it the monstrous form of the wild god, Pan, which the philosophers, misled by its meaning "everything," took as a symbol for the formed universe. Physics and philosophy rose out of poetry. In the words of Vico (VI 375), again: "Hence poetic wisdom, the first wisdom of the gentile world, must have begun with a metaphysic not rational and abstract like that of learned men now, but felt and imagined as that of these first men must have been, who, without power of ratiocination, were all robust sense and vigorous imagination, as established in the Axioms. This metaphysic was their poetry, a faculty born with them (for they were furnished by nature with these senses and imaginations); born of their ignorance of causes, for ignorance, the mother of wonder, made everything wonderful to men who were ignorant of everything."

In general, poets who present metaphysical abstractions use their own art to embody the systems of other philosophers: For example, in his "Essay on Man" Pope attempted to clothe, in poetic form, Bolingbroke's philosophical analysis of the soul in its relation to life. Similarly, Tennyson's "In Memoriam" interweaves Kant's postulates of reality, with his personal remorse at the loss of a friend. Regrettably, poets who also constructed a philosophy in their poems (from Sophocles to Stevens) cannot be considered here, due to considerations of length.

Poetry, as a vehicle of a metaphorical knowledge of a prerational and metarational character, can still avail itself of any scientific or philosophical reference; through this blending, it achieves its intersubjective communication; it also measures the ratio of cognitive and irrational elements in its own discourse. Every metaphor is a fable in brief, a myth; and like a myth, the metaphor emerges from synchronic beginnings and provides the continuity of creative thought; metaphors and myths are formative and constitutive of our life-world. Vico pronounces that imagination is a turning out: "So that, as rational metaphysics teaches that man becomes all things by understanding them (*homo intelligendo fit omnia*), this imaginative metaphysics shows that man becomes all things by not understanding them (*homo non intelligendo fit omnia*); and perhaps the latter proposition is truer than the former, for when man understands he extends his mind and takes in the things, but when he does not understand he makes the things out of himself and becomes them by transforming himself into them." Metaphorical expression, while not having the unity of mathematical logic, has an analogical unity in human existence; its central organizing principle is the single person; representing a whole way of life. The single person is the access to Being, as we have seen how metaphysics begins in the body, and must seek its support, not in the external world, but within the modifications of the mind of the person who meditates on it.

3.2.3.2. Failings of Speech & Philosophy
But, is it philosophy or poetry that must do the task? The speaking must announce the something beyond itself without suffocating it with its limits. Its words must be those that must energetically open upon Being, to convey the life of the whole, and disrupt our habitual restrictions; it must also be aware of itself, as questioning. If it is philosophy, according to Merleau-Ponty (MN 129), "It is a matter of speaking which, rather than concealing being precisely by claiming to dispel its opaqueness and distance, instead bears witness to being (VI 126). It is a matter of a speaking which arises out of the silence of being, which is, as it were, evoked by that silence, and which, in turn, announced that silence so as, in the end, to let it announce itself: 'philosophy is the reconversion of silence and speech into one another.'" If philosophy, in approaching Being, loses its direct signification in order to say it, then it essentially becomes poetry. Philosophy argues the possibility of experience, but a poem offers it whole; the poem is the dream of philosophy. The poem is an order amenable to the systematic inquiry of philosophy, but it cannot be duplicated by just philosophy itself.

  If it is poetry, it is because poetry produces and presents a whole experience; it reflects the inextricable involvement of man in the universe and allows an ecological understanding which encourages man to do things lovingly and well. We are the universe we are observing; the universe cannot be distinguished from how we act on it; and after it turns it is a new universe. Poetry "gives knowledge of the chaos and confusion of the world by imposing order upon it which leaves it still the chaos and confusion it really is," in the words of Archibald McLeish. But, as poetry is not aware of itself, and is not a hyper-reflexion, it cannot know itself, or having approached Being, it cannot know it.

What is the solution, if any, since poetry and philosophy, each individually are inadequate to Being? A dialectic between the two, where they grow indistinguishable once more? Perhaps the poetry of Kathleen Raine or Wallace Stevens is a forerunner. Stevens writes (ST 532):

> His self and the sun were one
> And his poems, although makings of his self,
> Were no less makings of the sun
>
> It was not important that they survive.
> What mattered was that they should bear
> Some lineament or character,
>
> Some affluence, if only half-perceived,
> In the poverty of their words,
> Of the planet of which they were part.

And, Raine writes (R85):

> Within the centre of the rose
> Seed out of the silence grows
>
> In its crimson heart the night enfolds
> The atom's void, the source of worlds
>
> From whose unfathomed chaos rise
> Star and leviathan from interior skies.

3.3. *Being through Imagination—Phantasia*

Things transcend themselves. This transcendence is just that capability of existing in autodispersion and not in self-identity. It is going beyond one's self, beyond the point in space of consciousness, ecstatically, toward existence as a dimension, a "world ray," in Merleau-Ponty's words. How is such transcendence achieved?

Being is indirectly accessible in everything, as a pregnancy of possibility. In book Theta of the *Metaphysics*, Aristotle holds that the opinion that 'everything is possible' is false: Being cannot possibly be pure potentiality—a tomato could never grow to the size of a planet. In the Pontean view, Being is the ground of possibilities, in the sense that all possibilities develop from it. Being is the ground of actuality and potentiality; it cannot be pure at either extreme. Being does not produce the body, nor does the body produce thought; Being unfolds its hidden possibilities as a dehiscence, a blossoming efflorescence in which development there is an element of surprise.

The 'openness of Being' is the permanent possibility of the appearance of new entities during the process of worlds becoming the world, whereby men become aware of things becoming things. Since creative language presents a world to experience, the words which constitute language need not refer to anything definite. A primary language thus enlarges the world. For sensible flesh, Heidegger claims the "revelation of Being" is direct, there for anyone with eyes and ears; since man sees and hears through his senses, and not so much with them, contact is made with objects whether words are sensed or the surface of the actual thing is sensed. All human expression mediated by senses produces this contact. Man is a metaphysical animal, effectively living in the openness of Being; through man, Being is revealed in touching, and in language, in poetic and philosophical thought. But Being exceeds language, and all experiences that are possible.

Being encloses human meaning and gives ontological density to it. Merleau-Ponty argues that this wild Being intervenes at all levels to over- come artificial separations (phenomenon and noumenon) and the problems of classical ontologies (for instance, mechanism, or finalism). In the complete wholeness (for there is no inside or outside) of Being, there can be no literal transcendence, only descent or ascent. Possibilities are not *a priori* forms made actual, but invisibles given visibility. In Aristotle, actuality is prior to possibility (a problem Plato solved with the forms), whereas in Heidegger, possibility is logically prior to actuality, for man. For Merleau-Ponty, actuality and possibility, as visibility and invisibility, are grounded in Being.

How is ascendance achieved, how is the ray of consciousness

expanded into a world ray? Through imagination, and its most comprehensive expression, poetry. Poetic expression, by suspending habit, brings moments of Being to human awareness with a fresh signification. These moments reveal the hidden side of Being, the ground of possibilities, which is always there before us, but which the habit of prose regards backwards, as the past seen in a rear view mirror (to steal McLuhan's image). Imagination is actually an instrument of perception; more than that, it is a unified mode of perception. Consciousness may be enlarged through imaginative perception, not as a passive perception, but as an active *logos*. Imagination points the mind toward the broadest possible meaning in life, and creates a contemplative state of mind. Yeats' 'gay, old Chinamen' know—"their ancient glittering eyes are gay"—having pushed knowledge beyond the futility of knowing that one knows nothing at all. It points, not toward absolute truth, but toward an ever enlarging relational field (perhaps there is a development in Being where it approaches self-awareness— God, as asymptote of self). Poetic art captures a vision of purpose, the intention of Being.

Perception and expression are embodied in the flesh, but imagination is what makes the flesh visible; it is what allows inquiring beings to see into Being. Philosophy must return full circle to the beings of the world, in order to point at Being; the beginning is found, and known at last as the beginning through the poetic archaeology of the flesh. Or, in Steven's words, from 'Reality Is An Activity of the Most August Imagination:'

It was not a night blown at a glassworks in Vienna
Or Venice, motionless, gathering time and dust.

There was a crush of strength in a grinding going round,
Under the front of the westward evening star,

The vigor of glory, a glittering in the veins,
As things emerged and moved and were dissolved,

Either in distance, change or nothingness,
The visible transformations of summer night,

An argentine abstraction approaching form
And suddenly denying itself away.

There was an insolid billowing of the solid.
Night's moonlight lake was neither water nor air.

4.0. Small Answers to Questions on Being

> Is this the highest point of reason, to realize that the soil beneath our feet
> is shifting, to pompously name "interrogation" what is only a persistent
> state of stupor, to call "research" or "quest" what is only trudging in a circle,
> to call "Being" that which never fully is?
>   Merleau-Ponty (MH 190)

But, we do know Being; we exist, we flow over into the world by
moving, by pointing we possess it. The body is an intertwining of
vision and movement; it is a knot, a chiasm which is a seeing which is
visible. The flesh of the body and the flesh of the world have depth and
horizontality; they have a layer of invisibility beneath the visible. The
body constitutes a field through perception; its lived-world is limited by
perspective, which rises from a determinate situation, and is ambiguous,
since the body is in the field. Perception is already primordial
expression, therefore. Wild perception is unaware of itself, in contact
with savage Being; as it becomes more conscious of itself, it becomes
cultured, and 'forgetful' of Being—as Being, in being for us, promotes its
own oblivion. The body is the condition for consciousness, which is the
other side of the body, invisible and indescribable in objective terms.

Being is the ground of existence; in its primordial nature it is
savage and invisible. It is what allows the visible to be seen; it makes
all phenomena possible and then coappears in them—it is revealed
in the figure and hidden in the ground. The very root of Being is an
ambiguous opposition between visibility and invisibility, maleness and
femaleness, silence and language, and being and nonbeing. But this
very intertwining, or chiasm, is what allows it to move, to feel and see
itself. This distantiation between itself is what makes seeing possible,
but it causes an unavoidable translucency; it becomes obscure, it is a
unity of which only a lateral awareness is possible. Primordial Being
is the perceptual world which underlies the objective world. It can
therefore exist in the sensible without becoming positive. The contours
of the sensible thing and of sensibility are the contours of Being. In its
very movement it is intentional. All beings stretch out and transcend
themselves in auto- dispersion. Being develops: it thinks and speaks,
and so causes its own upheaval. Its visible side is carried higher in
thought, and its savage side becomes more savage. Being realizes a

spirituality in man.

That Being which is not exposed in thought and speech remains silent; but silence, like invisibility, is always inclusive of speech; silence surrounds speech; the perceived world is embodied and silent. Primordial silence is the possibility of speech, already pregnant with meanings; it surrounds and interweaves the entire continuum of expression. Like an ocean, silence contains things; things that are spoken gradually sediment to the bottom. Silence is not only the container, but the ordering principle of language. Paradoxically, the access to silence is through expression; but, as expression develops it, the savage silence becomes more inaccessible.

4.1. *Transmuting Being*

As we speak, we transmute Being into the flesh of language; language is embodied in perception, as perception is in the body, as the body is in the world. Perception itself is a speech before speech; language makes it visible in words; naming Being makes it appear. But how is the invisible brought to light, how does Being make the transition to expression and thought? We interrogate Being and find it is Being. Through an ontological interpretation, Merleau-Ponty shows how expression is founded on sensibility: expression is already present within the domain of perceptual experience, and so explaining it is a matter of uncovering the latent intelligibility in the sensible world, the same as is actually taken up in expression. Language conserves its beginnings from perception, and precedes itself to influence the speaker. If language determines our perception, could we not construct a language to describe Being, without limiting it? By definition, language will always be a figuring of Being, and inadequate. It transforms perceptive meanings into ideal objects, becoming a depository of concrete words. Language is the lateral relation of one sign to another. Language tends to transform Being into something positive (for example, "that's it!"), which conceals it again, when it should bring it to expression in such a way as to bear witness to its original concealment. Could not the meaning of Being arise completely from an expression? Being cannot be described directly, since that would limit it and make it something positive. Because Being is the ground of any expression of it, it envelops expressions; because it is the ground of possibility, it allows expressions, painting and literature, especially, to reach into the future—no expression is ever finished absolutely, nor can it be possessed in its mortality; expressions, like all Beings are open to the world. This is not moving in a circle, because Being is historical. No work is ever completed, but each creation renews the attempt. Language is like a net in the ocean, which captures medium size things, but not those too small or large. It is a dialectic which gathers itself up (*logos*) and launches itself (intentionality) again through the mystery of rationality. It is whole and complete, even if unfinished. But unless it is incarnated, it can never reach the depth of Being, as Merleau-Ponty (MG 184) writes: "The linguistic and intersubjective world no longer surprises us, we no longer distinguish it from the world itself, and it is within a world already spoken and speaking that we think."

There is a continuum of expression from silence to speech, and each form of expression is a language in itself. Painting is a language, a silent duplication of perception anchored in the carnal. In using equivocal and aesthetic symbols, instead of univocal and linguistic signs, art breaks the circle of verbalization, to make the invisible visible. When it is successful, the expression is indistinguishable from the thing expressed; as an access to Being, art assumes a metaphysical dimension.

Language is a symbolic system of possibilities derived from experience; with silence it forms a dialectic of speaking. Speaking reverses the dialectic of perception, to one between self and other; a living language in the intersubjective world gives multiple perspectives on things. In speaking, language promotes its own oblivion. Speaking is a carrier of meaning that becomes transparent before that meaning; it is the meaning which points to Being.

Philosophy assigns itself the task of formulating an experience of the world, a contact with the world which precedes all thought about the world; it does not explain the world or discover its conditions of possibility. To this end it uses a speaking which folds over the lived-experience on language and language on lived experience; philosophy itself is a language that rests on language, that attempts to speak of language, and of pre-language and the mute world. Philosophy uses ideal significations without devoting itself entirely to them; it is an operative language that has no need to be translated into significations, and, as Merleau-Ponty (MN 126) qualifies, "that can be known only from within, through its exercise, is open upon things, called forth by the voices of silence, and continues as effort of articulation which is the Being of every being." In struggling to express the inexpressible, philosophy uses and interrogates language, and finds that it is language. Somehow, in speaking, philosophy contacts the silent world and savage Being; as Merleau-Ponty (MN 126) explains, it is a seduction that brings "to the surface all the deep-rooted relations of the lived experience wherein, it takes form, and which is the language of life and of action but also that of literature and of poetry—then this logos is an absolutely universal theme, it is the theme of philosophy." Merleau-Ponty claims that a definition of philosophy would involve an elucidation of philosophical expression itself as the science of pre-science, as the expression of what is before expression and sustains it from behind, but that it involves a difficulty: the natural temptation to enter into a positive description.

Philosophy comes after the world, after nature, life and thought, and finds them constituted before it; it questions these antecedent things and questions its relationship with them. Although it returns upon them and upon itself, it cannot return to the immediate, which recedes in the measure that it is approached. It must use language reflexively to inquire into the possibilities of Being and to question itself. Philosophy is perceptual faith questioning itself through language; it is a hyper-reflection that takes itself and the changes it introduces into the spectacle into account, without losing sight of brute perception and the brute thing. Philosophy, as speaking thought, is highly reversible, and this doubling character which is intrinsic to Being, allows it to gather up its past into itself; this gives philosophy the advantage of managing its own support, which is its history. Like art, philosophy contacts Being, but philosophy is aware of doing so. It tries to bring the things themselves to expression; it searches for a language in which the things themselves speak, through lateral relations, as Merleau-Ponty (MN 125) reiterates, "by virtue of a natural intertwining of their meaning, through the occult trading of the metaphor." Philosophy should attend to the lateral aspects of appearing reality, which gives Being its density. What kind of language must it use to do justice to the uniqueness of Being? A poetry or a prose? Words that contain what they say, or are energetically open upon Being? It wishes to bring things from the depth of silence to expression, but in order to catch them, it must use a net of formal abstractions. But philosophy cannot capture savage Being with a set of well-defined significations and univocal statements, since this would take from it at the depth and distance essential to it. The distance of thought from the beginnings must be preserved; but how will philosophical thought exhibit the beginnings as beginnings, then? The philosopher tries to speak, but cannot state his contact with Being; she must sometimes settle for less. Phenomenology is an expression of surprise at the inherence of the self in others and the world, for the purpose of making men see the bonds between themselves and the world. Philosophy is limited to its questioning, and expression of wonder in the face of the world. Its problem is to grasp what, within the speaking world, wishes, speaks and finally thinks; but perhaps it can only rediscover that thought is thought, or speech is spoken.

How is it possible to even speak of Being? In all three senses of ineffability, Being is ineffable:

1. It is partly incomparable since it can only be compared with itself;
2. It is partly inexpressible since words are incarnate perspectives of Being—even the sum of words could only point beyond themselves; and
3. It is partly unspeakable since part of it must always be savage, and individuals can only offer their own perspectives.

The direct expression of philosophy is inadequate to cope with Being as a whole; are there expressions more adequate? A questioning form of expression is needed, a prephilosophical, circular approach through succeeding perspectives. The approach must succeed the concentric problems of metaphysics by incorporating a range of subjects, from entropy to trees, using a range of tools, from scientific inquiry to phenomenological poetry. Where expression succeeds it is attached to the very process of expressing, as in music, or poetry. Caratheodory notes (CA 36, from 'The Stuff of Life'):

In music, the stuff of life is amplified beyond reason

4.2. *Imitating Being*

In Aristotle, poetry originates in imitation (*mimesis*), and like nature, it produces unified wholes. Through the condensation of possibilities and elimination of accidentals, poetic statements assume the nature of universals; poetic words deal with the whole, and an underknowledge (*hyponoiesis*) suitable to Being. Dewey says (DE 241): "A poem presents material so that it becomes a universe in itself, one, which, even when it is a miniature whole, is not embryonic." Aristotle limited the poet to giving a picture of things—emotions, thoughts—only through objective actions. For Merleau-Ponty, all thought and emotions are embodied. In poetic language, ideas are produced by the carnal relations of meaning and the halos of signification which rise from the historical uses of words. These ideas are named free fancies by Husserl, and they are able to stretch out among possibilities without bounds; it is in this sense that a poem is a pure intention which gathers in (*logos*) possibilities from Being and welds them into a whole thing. The poem assumes a privileged position over perception since it is not limited in perspective and is free to give new forms to the world. In communicating itself the poem makes language in visible, as it disappears in its opening to Being. As Merleau-Ponty (MN 208) relates, again, "To rediscover man finally face to face with the world *itself*, to rediscover the pre-intentional present—is to rediscover that vision of the origins, which sees itself within us, as poetry rediscovers what articulates itself within us, unbeknown to us." There is no other way to discover that vision; philosophy cannot piece together Being by moving linearly from parts to the whole. The power to awaken the expression that goes beyond things already said belongs to poetry. Repeating Merleau-Ponty (MK 52): "Since perception itself is never complete, since our perspectives give us a world to express and think about which envelops and exceeds those perspectives, a world which announces itself in lightning signs as a spoken word or as an arabesque, why should the expression of the world be subjected to the prose of the *senses* or of the concept? It must be poetry; that is, it must completely awaken and recall our sheer power of expressing beyond things already said or seen."

Metaphor allows us to progress from the known to the unknown, by creating a similarity and fashioning two ideas into one new that contains their diversity in its multivalent unity. Opposites interpenetrate in a dialectic unified in a metaphoric synthesis which transcends them. The metaphor is the act of combining, to use Plato's use of weaving as a metaphor for the dialectical process. The metaphor is not a literal description but a pointing, and more than a pointing, since it offers a name, a focus and a context.

Philosophers have always used metaphors to describe those things of which they spoke: mind, nature, Being. Aristotle relates how philosophy and mythology were almost indistinguishable in the pre-Socrates; but using a philosophy expunged of poetry, he was not able to complete his science of the first philosophy (metaphysics). Perhaps a science of Being as Being is impossible. Being is savage, and requires an expression appropriate to it if it is to be described at all. Since empirical language is the result of creative language, it is less useful to use the secondary expression of science to develop the savage phenomena. Philosophy should be a manner of speaking which bears witness to Being rather than concealing it precisely by claiming to dispel its opaqueness and distance with explicit language. The intention of philosophy is to reconvert speech and silence into one another. But in its reconversion of silence and speech, does it approach Being? And what kind of language must it use, scientific or poetic? Scientific language has entirely different characteristics than poetic language. Basically science is linguistic and metonymic, where poetry is aesthetic and metaphoric. Philosophy would seem to be able to use either with equal facility, except that it is almost entirely diachronous and linguistic. Thus, its activity is often secondary, whereas poetry's is primary.

How is Being approached in different ways by these languages? Why cannot the levels of Being be easily seen? The levels are in hierarchical order, composed of holons, which are a part from above and a whole from below—even holons are characterized by being visible from above and invisible from below. The visibility is exploited by science; the invisibility is alluded to by poetry. But how is the invisible brought to light? It cannot be; it can be shown as belonging to the visible, much as the meaning of a painting belongs to the shapes on the canvas which convey it, without itself being those shapes; so invisibility belongs to the visible. Beyond philosophy, poetry is able to incorporate the chaos and order of the world into an organic whole. Even if philosophy were able to give an account of the whole in terms of causes or reasons, its possibilities are conceptual presentations, not mimetic representations of actions, as are poetic possibilities. Poetry is able to encompass Being with its method; by using a lateral approach, none of its richness is lost. Merleau-Ponty finds that philosophy and poetry intertwine, such that philosophy assumes the same ambiguities as literary expression; the world is such that it can only be pointed to. But philosophy is sophisticated; it is capable of incorporating the insights of poetry into a coherent approach to Being.

But if philosophy scrutinizes the symbolic expression of poetry (which is exercised only in a limited way), it does not know Being, and if it knows Being, it must be poetry, must it not? Art and philosophy are both connected in the ground of Being; philosophical poetry or poetic philosophy need each other's insights into Being. Philosophy fails because it neglects the multifariousness of the world, it cannot reach brute Being, poetry fails because it is unaware of itself. Here is the paradox: the philosopher must be a poet. Philosophy is a questioning of brute Being, but it can only address it from within, using poetic language. The philosopher must be a poet to reach into Being to discover essences, and the poet must be a philosopher to be aware of himself, and the creative process in Being, through hyper-reflection. The revelation of Being requires a dialogue of philosophy and poetry, a metaphoric metaphysics, a speaking that carries beyond the physical world.

> *Of Mere Being*
> The Palm at the end of the mind
> Beyond the last thought, rises
> In the bronze distance,
> A gold feathered bird
> Sings in the palm, without human meaning,
> Without human feeling, a foreign song

You know then that it is not the reason
That makes us happy or unhappy
The bird sings. Its feathers shine.
The palm stands on the edge of space.
The wind moves slowly in the branches.
The bird's fire-fangled feathers dangle down.
Wallace Stevens (BG 139)

4.3. *Wild Being & Poetic Ecological Wisdom*

What can be incomplete itself and express the incomplete? What can be domesticated and yet express the wild? Prose? Poetry? What is wild? Is wildness a scale issue? Are wild things only on a large scale? Are there large-scale forms of thought? Philosophy? Or, poetry?

What is wild (the word is from the German *wild*, or perhaps *Wald*, forest)? Does wild mean not-domesticated? Uncontrolled, unmanaged? Not cultivated? Untamed? Savage? Waste? In a state of nature? Lawless? Wild as a word has ambiguity and reflexion.

What is thinking (from the German *denken*)? To revolve ideas in the mind? To design, to imagine, to judge? Is philosophical or poetic thinking wild? Is ecological knowledge and thinking intrinsically wild?

Ecological thinking is wild because it has a nonhuman component. By contrast, scientific or religious thinking is domesticated or tamed because it is limited by a 'true' reality, or a set of rules for observing a true reality. Science is defined in opposition to religion, with a commitment to neutral observation rather than moral commitment to tradition. Wild ecological thinking combines technique with moral and ecological concerns. The fundamental emotion of wild thinking is astonishment, literally being struck by lightning.

Wild thinking is appropriate for "system breaks," the social discontinuities identified by Kenneth Boulding. We have started to identify the forces setting up the next big break, but we have not defined the forming patterns very well. Rethinking, perhaps a form of wild thinking, could examine the basic assumptions of the spheres of civilization, from our economic and political to industrial, religious and scientific.

Perhaps there is a downside to talking about wild thinking. Too much anarchy is dreaming; too much feral thinking is noncultural and perhaps dangerous. Too much is unrelated to the important mode of learning by doing.

Will Wright suggests that knowledge becomes wild when it is critically reflexive and committed to critical access rather than to a single version of absolute reality. If so, such wild knowledge cannot be "domesticated" by one particular social institution. It is accessible by all individuals.

Of course, there are other forms of thinking: Religious or scientific, which we consider tame. Tame ideas are remarkably persistent—for instance, the cliché "more is better." George Orwell referred to these obsolete ideas as "wrong-think." Another kind of thinking, "Double-think," is used traditionally to keep some ideas tame. Gordon Taylor suggests that "Non-think" (the failure of good ideas to be recognized or used) is equally obstructive—thus, the idea 'protect the ecological basis of life' is not taken up.

Otherwise, what is the proper language for humans? What is the proper diet for all humans? The proper mode of expression? These questions in a way are too presumptuous to even be asked.

4.3.1. *Respecting Wildness*

Is wildness just the nonhuman part of the spectrum? Does it overlap in humans? Is it just difference or craziness? We love and celebrate the wild; and, we fear and suppress the wild. The wild is a quality of being just beyond rules or outside of walls.

Paul Shepard reminds us that wildness occurs in many places, in any species whose sexual assortment and genealogy are not controlled by human beings. Darwin reminds us that humanity is wild, also, with a wild, savage mind. Can such a mind be just wild? Not necessarily—we can domesticate our ideas, and have.

It is easy to talk of wild thinking. Is it meaningful to talk of a wild culture, one that intermeshes with the wild of nature? A model of a civilization without walls, without resources, maxima, or weeds?

Could we create an agenda to apply wild thinking to the problems foreseen by the philosophical poets? What kind of agenda can we make? We could create new economic, political, cultural, social, psychological, and ecological frameworks. Then, we could use those frameworks to try to: Rebalance our individual lives; rebalance social spins of the patriarchal and matriarchal, between the human and ambihuman; achieve individual self-reliance and health; obtain community self-reliance and health; restore ecological community health; strengthen community and cultural identity (against globalization); limit the centralization of power and authority, in style as well as trade; reform corporations to act responsibly as public service organizations (and not as imaginary irresponsible individuals); direct technology in appropriate ways; and, set up a global commonwealth for global relations.

How wild humans could live on a wild earth is the subject of a eutopian framework. Unique cultures have unique ways of looking at the universe and creating local worlds. They have competing views of what is important; relative conceptions of reality; vital needs versus necessary styles—can sensitive views be taught? This is a problem with cosmologies, especially with a prevailing industrial cosmology that is replacing local cosmologies adapted to place.

Jeremy Rifkin presents evolution as the new human "myth" and a new cosmology, but it may not be humanistic enough to be a useful cosmology. Basing cosmology on the western concept of evolution in the framework of economic globalization would be a mistake—is a mistake. We should not try a global cosmology based on evolution or on the Euro-American competitive cosmology that thinks it deserves to replace the adaptive cosmologies of archaic cultures; what we really should be promoting is a framework for all cosmologies, a holocosmology which in fact is a framework for all adaptive values, that will protect and allow cultural (and nonhuman) diversity.

Each culture has a competing views of the earth or world—they are different, as a world is a human image of part of the earth; each culture has one. Are these views personal, group, or cultural? Are we considered to share the same "world"? A culture needs many things and does many things for its participants: Make a common language; order experience; personalize a place; adapt and preserve aspects of a place; justify human behavior; provide identity and security. Still, most cultures are incomplete (as they have to be since places change), inflexible, and often indifferent to other cultures or individuals. Cultures should not compete or try to be the right or final culture.

Every cosmology can be characterized by a set of statements about the world. Industrial cosmology is an extension of the European: Everything is made of interchangeable units, man is master, man is perfectible, and so on. In several archaic cosmologies: Everything is unique, gods rule, and nothing is perfect. Which is better grounded for the long-term?

Cultures need to address conflicts between human and nonhuman, as well as social justice and ecological sustainability, resource consumption and policy. Cultures need to consider optimal populations, growth versus racism or elitism; an ecological goal for population; democratic means or other.

Cultures continue through education, but education needs to be transcultural, also. Education could be fitted to all else, transforming institutions, creating small community schools that could be funded with public school funds, infiltrating public and private schools by offering courses and presentations, as well as practical field experience and projects. New schools might use the Organic Dialectics of Goethe and the aesthetic education of Schiller, as well as adding Novalis and Wordsworth in a deep ecological framework.

Perhaps as a result of wild thinking, we could develop or acquire a catastrophic psychology approach to present the crises to everyone: Reports on destructions and species losses, on hunger and deaths, on long, slow, wide catastrophes rather than short, brief, local ones; Massive changes, massive deaths. People can often face disjunction quite bravely in normal catastrophes, such as earthquakes and fires. We just need to implement a catastrophic psychology. After all, we are inside one, now: A 50-year collapse, extinction spasm, ecosystem disintegration, cultural wobble. We need to implement it immediately. We could do so on four levels: With communication of studies in major media; reorganization on an emergency footing; special activities, from planting trees to reeducation; and explicit goals to reverse the turning.

Why are we not thinking? Is there an enemy creating problems? Us? Industrialization and globalization? These are all myths, metaphors and movements; perhaps the enemy is us (Pogo) or the products of our big brains expressed on a big scale.

Can poets or artists balance the shrinking spirit or just reflect it? Maybe art is a repository for wild thinking. How can art or wild thinking encourage humans to maturity? Or are we trapped in domestic service by computers?

Perhaps computers, and technology as a whole, like quantum mechanics, bear the seeds for the destruction of their old world view. Perhaps the good can undermine the bad. Computers do much good. They do large-scale calculations better than anything; we need them for large scale projects, for higher order problems, for CAD representation of wild lands. And, now they are universal machines, capable of answering phones and creating virtual worlds. Furthermore, computers connect people at some level who might not be connected, from mental patients to fathers and sons. All tools have positive and negative implications and effects, depending on their use. Computers may give us empowerment, but it gives greater corporate empowerment. The choice is not to either let them take over or destroy all of them; it is to use them as tools in a mature way, understanding their limits and scales. Maybe we do not need them at all, but maybe they can be used to save cultures and wild lands. We could subvert the industrial machine by using appropriate technology in mature ways.

If Being is a system, now a living system, then it has properties of systems, including health. The idea of health includes several definitions, from those of doctors and scientists across cultures. Furthermore, it cannot be defined independently of participation in a social image. Because that image has social and natural criteria, it cannot be defined medically or physiologically. The idea of health provides a general reference. Mental health can be related now to ecosystem health. The complete spectrum of human mental disease, from insanity to prejudice and abstraction causes immense destruction and suffering in ecosystems, that is the wild, as well as a breakdown in the transmission of cultures adapted to ecosystem limits.

4.3.2. *Framing Wildness*

Climate is wild. Most species are wild. Wildness is easy. Wild things just want to exist. Designing wild areas is basically creating semi-permeable boundaries to limit access for human activities as well as exotic species. We can restore wilderness, as a cultural concept, and wild ecosystems, as independent things.

The design, as the physical manifestation of the intent, has to try to be as wild as the subjects of the work. The design has to link the historical basis, the integrity of the system. Does description?

Design should coevolve with wild nature. Global design has to evolve with the planet. Thinking ecologically makes us aware of interrelationships. Design is recognizing these global and regional processes and contexts. Design is a primary element to stimulate possibilities.

A framework for design can work at any scale, from a small building, at one end of the scale, to preparing an urban design framework or master plan for an entire planet, at the other. Models at global scales may be insufficiently realistic, however.

Design works out challenges and problems in an artistic way. Art is wild. We cannot control the effects of art, or even anticipate all of them. We cannot anticipate the changes it might make. That artistic way is a wild way of thinking and can mesh with large-scale design better than a simple technical approach. Design needs to become wild. Wild design is not human-centered, as most all design in the past has been human-centered. Wild design is based on radical ecology (Wittbecker 1974)—it is the push, beyond human interests, to consider the character and patterns of ecosystems. Not to subvert or interfere. We can guess what the system wants with reference to its past behavior. And, we know what it wants: To exist, to regenerate. We need to create the conditions for the system to flourish. And, if we use any of it, it has to be limited to that level of productivity that does not interfere with the survival of the system. We are reintervening in a natural system at different levels rather than using or interfering for human benefit.

The word design is modified in this sense to be power with natural processes, not power over them or control of them. Wild design is a conversation across time. We listen, ask, and contribute. We inscribe human stories on the larger stories of the system. Participating means living in the systems. We can reciprocate by giving our bodies back to the system. It cannot hurt to give our minds to the shape of the system. It is knowing what not to do, as well as what to do, when to do it, if we do it. The future is already connected with the past through the present. It just gets complex and unpredictable away from the present. Too complex.

Wild design has to be heroic, especially due to the scale of working on a global level. Heroic design and extravagance in life is needed. It is not contradictory or antithetical to frugal lifestyles or to restoring a healthy environment. Life is exuberant; energy is used, lives are lived and used, not saved.

Wild ideas are needed: For monitoring natural systems; for closing local loops in energy or matter; for preserving closely linked webs; and for making connections and collaborations. Our cultures, that are made more intense in cities and by technology, like the web, can be the incubators of new forms of thought and ideas.

Wildernesses, centers of wildness, have basic value as pools of existence that reflect the diverse styles of existence, from viruses to human beings. Wilderness is a vital organ for the life of the earth, the generator of hydrological, geochemical, and atmospheric cycles. It is also where ultrahuman species live—it is their sanctuary from humanity. Interestingly enough, in George Orwell's dystopian novel, *1984*, the rulers of the police state abolish wilderness because it supports freedom of thought and action. Of course, that was only fiction.

4.3.3. *Wildness & Wisdom*

The author Wendell Berry notes that Kathleen Raine was correct in reminding us that life, like holiness, can be known only by being experienced. To experience it is not to figure it out or understand it, but to suffer it and rejoice in it as it is the suffering and rejoicing is that we know that we do not and cannot understand it completely. This is what poetry can express better than philosophical prose.

The search for security seems needed as the background for the cause at hand now. This is the unrealistic Cartesian demand for an all-purpose guarantee of knowledge. But, we know there is no guarantee.

Poetry makes knowledge personal and yet can incorporate uncertainty.

In discussing Socratic patterns, Mary Midgely notes that inquirers have expressed irritation at the evasiveness of the philosophical approach; she notes that this is the kind of situation that may have given rise to the word philosophy in the first place. It is said to been invented by Pythagoras who forbade people to call him wise, explaining that he was only a lover of wisdom. Wisdom which is easily lost and truly valued seems to be something difficult.

Midgely has concentrated on one area, the general quest for knowledge, known somewhat loosely as science. As she mentions, if we begin to ask the meaning of this kind of procedure, reconsider it once in a while, it might look like a different field of inquiry, namely philosophy. Questions about how to classify investigations which do not fit in easily to existing classes are bound to mess up the business of philosophy, because the whole enterprise of classifying them is philosophical in the first place. One reason why philosophy arose originally among the Greeks was that a number of different ways of thinking had already risen and that the relations between them were found to be puzzling. This has happened both over practical thinking, where moral ideas clash, and in theoretical inquiry, where different studies are beginning to collide. Philosophers may now be heard dismissing large problems on the grounds that they are not philosophy or to have nothing to do with philosophy. And as we know, Wittgenstein said a philosophical problem has the form, 'I don't know my way about.' And maybe the reason of philosophy is to find our general way about.

Midgely says that in every culture, intense loving attention to certain chosen problems contrasts with the startling neglect of others, some of which are far more pressing, not only for justice or for happiness, but for mere survival. Large, obvious, central questions are entirely ignored, but this is natural, because they are frightening and too complex. Perhaps one of our human shortcomings is a cultural failure of nerve. Midgely notes that attention to such questions is the real work of philosophy. But, we cannot expect salvation from intelligence alone; the emotion and common sense that are needed are part of the whole human mind. Cultural tradition dictates how the mind is formed and used.

Cultural tradition describes what we may be and helps us become what we are. The world tends to become how we imagine it, as a spaceship or garden, as a global monolithic state or a loose confederation of cultures. So we must create the images carefully. Kenneth Boulding offered the perfect machine metaphor for the operation of the earth—as a spaceship. As a metaphor, the spaceship suggests the limits of the earth and the value of a limited life-support system; unfortunately, it implies that the earth is a human creation that can be controlled and fixed by a conscious captain and crew. The use of the word 'ecology' by Ernst Haeckel implied that the natural world was a house, a place to live, rather than a machine. This image is more compatible with all cultures, from hunters to industrial corporations.

Although Midgely suggests that what is wrong with humanity is a shortage of intelligence, which might be cured by genetically engineering our intelligence she suggests, she admits that we use far less than we have. A lack of common sense is also a serious problem. And, perhaps a misunderstanding of the operation of emotion contributes to our emergency situations. Her point is that philosophy can find and formulate the rules underlying sense, identify inarticulate patterns, and note their classes and inadequacies, and look for ways of dealing with them. Philosophy. Whether we recognize it or not, can coordinate the powers of the intellect, emotions and sense. Philosophy, according to her, is the formalization of an ancient art that used to be called the search for wisdom.

Science presents us with too many facts, yet we crave to have more. Philosophy presents us with too many values, but we have too few. Technology presents us with too many things, but we do not know what we need, so we make more. We do not need more information or rules, but we need meaningful ideas. Our attitudes and feelings toward nature need to be revitalized with evocative metaphors that let us accept responsibility for the part of the earth that we build, namely human culture and human landscapes. This can be done with a comprehensive poetic effort. In order to know what is important, what is valuable, we need wisdom.

Wisdom is knowledge of the larger interactive system, which if disturbed, can generate exponential curves of change. Wisdom is the recognition of and guidance by a knowledge of the total system. Lacking wisdom, we must behave "as if" we were wise, as if we had good sense (after the ideas of Hans Vaihinger and Jonas Salk). Humans have no choice but to live by fictions, as if this world is the ultimate reality, as if we are responsible for our actions. Humanity must plan for its future as if its days were not counted (or at least for several thousand years). Wisdom is a new kind of fitness. To survive, we must accommodate ourselves to the conditions of the earth.

Wisdom is the disciplined use of the imagination with respect to alternatives, exercised at the right time and in the right measure. But we need practical wisdom, prudence, and intellectual control in virtue, in place of the theoretical wisdom taught by schools. The truths of our unique cultures and the wild earth are apprehended through myths. The poetic language of mythology can fit all the facts and values, things and images, desires and knowledge, into our hearts so that we can feel them and act upon them—so that we can live well in good places.

Knowledge by itself, however, merely permits a more efficient utility. Knowledge cannot be the sole basis of decision making. It is always incomplete and therefore cannot describe all aspects of the earth that bear on human life or environmental quality. Knowledge must be humane. Abraham Maslow saw the organism as having biological wisdom; it can be trusted as autonomous, self-governing and self-choosing. To treat organisms, and nature in general, science could shift to a taoistic approach, asking rather than telling, observing rather than manipulating; receptive and passive, not active and forceful; "nonintruding," and noncontrolling, not forcing. A taoistic approach stresses noninterfering observation rather than controlling manipulation; it is receptive rather than forceful. This is part of the paradox of duality; it is detached yet concerned; free yet committed; and independent yet responsible.

The founders and practitioners of Mahayana Buddhism realized that the same universal principle allowed everything to harmonize with everything else. "Without turning towards anything, always unobstructed in his wisdom / He goes along in the world of living beings boundless in space, acting for the weal of beings." In the Mahayana school of Buddhism, compassion ranks with wisdom, the heart is as valuable as the head: "The ideal man is the Bodhisattva, who, caring nothing for his own salvation is vowed to dedicate his being and his every act to the salvation of each form of life, until the last blade of grass shall enter into Buddhahood." Lao Tse and Confucius taught universal reverence and nonviolence as well. These ideas have been stressed in modern times by Vivekananda, Tagore and Ghandi; by St. Francis and St. Thomas, Emerson, Maritain, and Tillich.

Equilibrium is needed between self-restraint and self-expression, between exponential growth and precipitous decline. The myths and metaphors of a culture are modes for conveying ecological wisdom; they are less concerned with bare survival than the survival value of a good fit to a place. Wisdom is the new kind of fitness; it is guidance by a knowledge of the whole interactive system, which if disturbed can change catastrophically.

Wisdom cannot be dependent on perfect knowledge; that does not exist. Humans must act "as if" they were wise, according to Hans Vaihinger, as if this earth were the ultimate reality and as if our human time were unlimited; we must act with caution and respect. Wisdom, as defined by Jonas Salk, is the art of disciplined use of the imagination in respect to alternatives, exercised at the right time and in the right measure. The time is now and the measure is primary cultures.

Cultures are the vehicles of human existence. Yet, cultures can alter or destroy their biological bases and die. A culture that fits a local ecology is adapted and more likely to survive. Cultures need to use the wisdom of people tuned to a place. Wisdom is a way of reducing their negative effects to make aculture more flexible and longer lived. An understanding of ecology can lengthen the life of a culture, but ecology is not enough. Mythology is necessary. Although a mythology is constructed as a poetic system, it can integrate scientific and emotional understanding. Therefore, an ecological poetry based on both ecological principles and traditional cultural wisdom is needed to create a mythological framework for a global culture capable of assisting local cultures to adapt to local ecosystems and to each other throughout the planet.

Caratheodory concludes, in 'The Others,' (CC 20):

> Wisdom is a wild thing like the Arcadian doe
> And not easily captured with words. The dappled
> Form leaves its shadow in our grasp while it slips
> Away undaunted. A hunger we do not understand
> Keeps us on the scent. We cannot give up the chase—
> Nor can we ever catch her. Then, to be wise,
> We must act as if the shadow is the doe.

Figure 433-1. Figure in Stone (Photograph, 1976)

5.0. Supplementary Words

5.1. *Bibliography*

AD Adorno, Theodor. *Negative Dialectics*. New York, The Seabury Press, 1973.

AP Apostle, H. G. *Aristotle's Metaphysics*. Bloomington, Indiana University Press, 1966.

AR Arbib, Michael. *The Metaphorical Brain*. New York, John Wiley and Sons, 1972.

BA Bachelard, Gaston. *Philosophy of No*. Translated by G. Waterston. New York, The Orion Press, 1968.

BB ___. *Poetics of Reverie*. Translated by D. Russell. Boston, Beacon Press, 1969.

BC ___. *Poetics of Space*. Translated by M. Jolas. Boston, Beacon Press, 1969.

BD ___. *Psychoanalysis of Fire*. Translated by Alan Ross. Boston, Beacon Press, 1964.

BF Barfield, Owen. *Poetic Diction: A Study in Meaning*. New York, McGraw-Hill Book Co., 1964.

BE Begon, M., J. Harper, and C. Townsend, *Ecology: Individual, Population, and Community*. Sunderland, MA: Sinauer Associates, 1986.

BL Bell, David. "On the Einstein Podolsky Rosen paradox." Physics 1964 1: 195.

BO Bly, Robert Bly, *News of the Universe*. San Francisco: Sierra Club, 1980.

BM Bohm, David. *Wholeness and the Implicate Order*. London: Routledge & Kegan Paul, 1980.

BG Benamou, Michel. *Wallace Stevens and the Symbolist Imagination*. Princeton, Princeton University Press, 1972.

BI Biemel, Walter. "Poetry and language in Heidegger," *On Heidegger and Language* (J. Kockelmans, ed.). Evanston, Northwestern University Press, 1972.

BN Borden, George. *An Introduction to Human Communication Theory*. Dubuque, Wm. C. Brown Co., 1971.

BO Brooks, Cleanth. "Metaphor, paradox, and stereotype," *British Journal of Aesthetics*, 5:4 (October, 1965), pp. 315-328.

BR Brown, George Spencer. *The Laws of Form*. London, Allen and Unwin, 1969.

BRO Brown, Norman. *Love's Body*. New York, Random House, 1966.

BS Burns, Freidrich. *Goethe's Poems and Aphorisms*. New York, Oxford University Press, 1932.

BT Burnet, John. *Greek Philosophy*. New York, St. Martin's Press, 1968.

BU Burnshaw, Stanley. *The Seamless Web*. New York, George Braziller, 1970.

BY Bynner, Witter. *The Way of Life According to Lao Tse*. New York, Capricorn Books, 1962.

CA Caratheodory, Alain M. 1976. *Wild Apples*. Wilmington: Mozart & Reason Wolfe, 1976.

CB Caratheodory, Alain M. 1982. *Amphibian Dreams*. Wilmington: M&RW, Calliope Press.

CC Caratheodory, Alain M. 1994. *Fragments*. Palo Alto: Wyndam Hill.

CE Charlesworth, J. H. "Reflections on Merleau-Ponty's Phenomenological Description of 'Word'," *Philosophy and Phenomenological Research*, 30:3 (June, 1970), pp. 609-613.

CH Charlton, William. "Is philosophy a form of literature?" *The British Journal of Aesthetics*, 14:1 (Winter, 1974), pp. 3-16.

CW Chew, Geoffrey. "Hadron bootstrap." *Physics Today* Oct., 1970: 23.

CI Cicero, Marcus Tullius. *De Natura Deorum*. Translated by H. Rackham. London, Wm. Heinemann, 1933.

CO Cobb, Jr., John B. *Is It Too Late? A Theology of Ecology* New York: Glencoe, 1971.

CT Callicott, J. B. "The Metaphysical Implications of Ecology," *Environmental Ethics* 8 (1986):312.

DA Darwin, Charles. 1896. Vol 1, page 68.

DD DeVito, Joseph. *The Psychology of Speech and Language*. New York, Random House, 1970.

DE Dewey, John. *Art As Experience*. New York, Capricorn Books, 1958.

DO Dorfles, Gillo. "Myth and metaphor in Vico and contemporary Aesthetics," *Giambattista Vico* (G. Tagliacozzo, ed.). Baltimore, Johns Hopkins Press, 1969.

DU Dufrenne, Mikel. "On the phenomenology and semiology of art," *Phenomenology and Natural Existence* (D. Riepe, ed.). Albany, State University of New York Press, 1973.

DV Dubos, Rene. "Theology of the Earth," *A God Within*. New York: Scribner's, 1972.

EA Arthur Eddington, *The Nature of the Physical World*. Cambridge: The University Press, 1928.

E   Edie, James, editor. *New Essays in Phenomenology*. Chicago, Quadrangle Books, 1969.

ED ___. "Expression and metaphor," *Philosophy and Phenomenological Research*, 23:4 (June, 1963), pp. 538-561.

EE ___. "Vico and existential philosophy," *Giambattista Vico* (G. Tagliacozzo, ed.). Baltimore, Johns Hopkins Press, 1969.

EI Einstein, Albert and Leopold Infeld, *Evolution of Physics*. New York: Simon & Schuster, 1960, p. 243.

EJ Eiseley, Loren. *The Star Thrower.*

EJ Eiseley, Loren. *Notes from an Alchemist.*

EI Eliot, T. S. *The Complete Poems and Plays of T. S. Eliot*. London, Faber, 1969.

EL ___. *Four Quartets*. New York, Harcourt, Brace and World, Inc., 1943.

EL Elton, Charles. *The Ecology of Invasions by Animals and Plants* London: Methuen,1958.

EM Embler, Weller. *Metaphor and Meaning*. DeLand, FL, Everett/ Edwards, Inc., 1966.

ER Erickson, S. A. *Language and Being*. New Haven, Yale University Press, 1970.

EV Evernden, Neil. *Out of Place* (unpublished manuscript, 1981).

FE Fenollosa, Ernest *The Chinese Written Character as a Medium for Poetry*. NC, NP, ND.

FE James Fiebleman, "Disorder," IN: *Concepts of Order*, P. Kuntz, ed. Seattle: University of Washington Press, 1968, pp. 3-13

FI Finkelstein, David. "The space-time code." *Phys. Rev.* 50: 2922.

GE Gelven, Michael. *A Commentary on Heidegger's Being and Time*. New York, Harper and Row, Pubs., 1970.

GI Gillan, Garth. "In the folds of the flesh: Philosophy and language," *The Horizons of the Flesh* (G. Gillan, ed.). Carbondale, Southern Illinois University Press, 1973.

GN Georgescue-Rogen, Nicholas. *Entropy and the Economic Process*. Cambridge: Harvard University Press, 1971

GO Goethe, J. W. von. *Faust*. Translated by Bayard Taylor. New York, Houghton Mifflin Co., 1870.

GP Gray, J. G. "Poets and thinkers: Their kindred roles in the philosophy of Martin Heidegger," *Phenomenology and Existentialism* (E. Lee and M. Mandelbaum, eds.). Baltimore, Johns Hopkins Press, 1967.

GR Grene, Marjorie. *A Portrait of Aristotle*. Chicago, The University of Chicago Press, 1963.

GU Guiness, Os. *The Dust of Death*. Downers Grove, IL, Intervarsity Press, 1973.

HA Hall, D. L. *The Civilization of Experience*. New York, Fordham University Press, 1973.

HB Hegel, G. W. F. The *Philosophy of History*. New York, Dover, 1956.

HD Heidegger, Martin. *Being and Time.* Translated by J. Macquarrie and E. Robinson. New York, Harper and Row, 1962.

HE ___. *On the Way to Language.* Translated by P. Hertz. New York, Harper and Row, 1971.

HI ___. *Poetry, Language, and Thought.* Translated by Albert Hofstadter. New York, Harper and Row, 1971.

HN Hines, J. N. "Person and word," *International Philosophy Quarterly*, 14:3 (September, 1974), pp. 329-341.

HO Holderlin, Friedrich. *Poems and Fragments.* Translated by M. Hamburger. Ann Arbor, The University of Michigan Press, 1967.

HR Harper, John. "Succession and Exploitation," *Population Biology of Plants.* New York: Academic, 1977, p. 31.

HX Ho, Mae Wan and E. Fox 1988.

ID Ihde, Don. "Language and experience," *New Essays in Phenomenology* (J. Edie, ed.). Chicago, Quadrangle Books, 1969.

IH ___. "Singing the world: Language and perception," *The Horizons of the Flesh* (G. Gillan, ed.). Carbondale, Southern Illinois University Press, 1973.

JE Jencks, Charles and G. Baird, eds. *Meaning in Architecture.* New York, Braziller, 1970.

JF Jensen, J. V. "Communicative functions of silence," *ETC*, 30:3 (1973), pp. 249-257.

JO Joyce, James. *Finnegans Wake.* New York, Viking Press, 1966.

KA Kaelin, Eugene. *Art and Existence.* Lewisburg, PA, Bucknell University Press, 1971.

KB ___. *The Existentialist Aesthetic.* Madison, University of Wisconsin Press, 1962.

KC ___. "Notes toward an understanding of Heidegger's aesthetics," *Phenomenology and Existentialism* (E. Lee and M. Mandelbaum, eds.). Baltimore, Johns Hopkins Press, 1967.

KG Kaplan, E. "Gaston Bachelard's philosophy of imagination," *Philosophy and Phenomenological Research*, 33:1 (1973), pp. 1-25.

KI Kirk, G. S. and J. E. Raven. *The Pre-Socratic Philosophers.* Cambridge University Press, 1957.

KO Kockelmans, Joseph, editor. *On Heidegger and Language.* Evanston, Northwestern University Press, 1972.

KS Arthur Koestler and J. Smythies, eds., *Beyond Reductionism*, London: Hutchinson, 1969, p. 195

KR Kreitler, Hans and S. Kreitler. *Psychology of the Arts.* Durham, Duke University Press, 1972.

KW Kwant, Remy. *From Phenomenology to Metaphysics.* Pittsburgh, Duquesne University Press, 1966.

LA Langan, Thomas. *Merleau-Ponty's Critique of Reason*. New Haven, Yale University Press, 1966.

LE Langer, Susan, editor. *Reflections on Art.* Baltimore, Johns Hopkins Press, 1959.

LG Lanigan, Richard. *Speaking and Semiology*. Paris, Mouton, 1972.

LE Leonard, George. *The Silent Pulse*. New York: Dutton, 1978

LI Leonard, William. *The Fragments of Empedocles*. Chicago, The Open Court Pub. Co., 1908.

LM Levine, Stephen. "Merleau-Ponty's philosophy of art," *Man and World*, 2:3 (August, 1969), pp. 438-452.

LO Lorentz, H. A. et al. *The Principle of Relativity*. trans. W. Perrett and G. Jeffery. New York: Dover, 1952.

LU Lucretius. *On the Nature of the Universe*. Translated by R. E. Latham. Baltimore, Penguin Books, 1968.

MA Mackey, Louis. "Philosophy and poetry in Kierkegaard," *Review of Metaphysics*, 23:2 (December, 1969), pp. 316-332.

MD Marx, Werner. "The world in another beginning: Poetic dwelling and the role of the poet," *On Heidegger and Language* (J. Kockelmans, ed.). Evanston, Northwestern University Press, 1972.

MAR Maruyama, M. "Toward Cultural Symbiosis," IN: *Evolution and Consciousness*. E. Jantsch and C. H. Waddington, eds. Reading: Addison-Wesley, 1980.

MAY May, R. *Complexity and Stability in Model Ecosystems*. Princeton: Princeton University Press, 1973.

MC McKeon, Richard. *Introduction to Aristotle*. Chicago, University of Chicago Press, 1973.

MI McIntosh, *The Background of Ecology* 1985, p. 40.

MF Merleau-Ponty, Maurice. *In Praise of Philosophy*. Translated by John Wild and J. Edie. Evanston, Northwestern Univ Press, 1963.

MG ___. *Phenomenology of Perception*. Translated by Colin Smith. London, Routledge and Kegan Paul, 1962.

MH ___. *The Primacy of Perception and Other Essays*. Edited by J. Edie. Evanston, Northwestern University Press, 1964.

MI ___. *The Prose of the World*. Translated by J. O'Neill. Evanston, Northwestern University Press, 1973.

MJ ___. *Sense and Nonsense*. Translated by H. Dreyfus and P. Dreyfus. Evanston, Northwestern University Press, 1964.

MK ___. *Signs*. Translated by R. McCleary. Evanston, Northwestern University Press, 1964.

ML ___. *The Structure of Behavior*. Translated by A. Fisher. Boston, The Beacon Press, 1963.

MM ___. *Themes from Lectures.* Translated by J. O'Neill. Evanston, Northwestern University Press, 1970.

MN ___. *The Visible and the Invisible.* Translated by A. Lingis. Evanston, Northwestern University Press, 1968.

MO Mourelatos, A. P. D., ed. *The Pre-Socratics.* New York, Anchor Press/Doubleday, 1974.

N Naess, Arne. "The Shallow and the Deep, Long-Range Ecology Movement. A Summary," *Inquiry* 16 (1973).

NA Natanson, Maurice. *Essays in Phenomenology.* The Hague, Martinus Nijhoff, 1966.

NI Nin, Anais. *The Novel of the Future.* New York, Collier Books, 1972.

OL Olson, Elder. *Aristotle's Poetics and English Literature.* Chicago, The University of Chicago Press, 1965.

ON O'Neill, John. *Perception, Experience, and History.* Evanston, Northwestern University Press, 1970.

OT Otten, Charlotte, editor. *Art and Anthropology.* Garden City, NY, Natural History Press, 1971.

OV Ovid, P. N. *Metamorphosis.* Baltimore: Penguin, 1955, Book X.

PA Pagels, H. *The Cosmic Code.* New York: Simon & Schuster, 1982.

PF Pfeffer, Rose. *Nietzsche: Disciple of Dionysius.* Lewisburg, Bucknell University Press, 1972.

PO Pogglioli, Renato. *The Theory of the Avant-Garde.* Cambridge, Harvard University Press, 1968.

QU Quasha, George and J. Rothenberg, eds. *America: A Prophecy.* New York, Random House, 1973.

R Raine, Kathleen. *The Collected Poems of Kathleen Raine.* New York, Random House, 1956.

RA ___. *The Hollow Hill.* London, Hamish Hamilton, 1965.

RB ___. *The Lost Country.* London, The Dolmen Press, 1971.

RC Ricoeur, Paul. *The Rule of Metaphor.*

RE Read, Herbert. "Vico and the genetic theory of poetry," *Giambattista Vico* (G. Tagliacozzo, ed.). Baltimore: Johns Hopkins Press, 1969.

RI Rice, P. B. "The philosopher as poet and critic," *The Philosophy of George Santayana* (P. A. Schilpp, ed.). Evanston, Northwestern University Press, 1940.

RM Rodman, John. *Inquiry* (1976).

RO Roszak, Theodore. *Where the Wasteland Ends.* Garden City, NY: Doubleday and Co., Inc., 1972.

RR Rorty, Richard. *Consequences of Pragmatism Essays: 1972-1980.* Minneapolis: University of Minnesota Press, 1982.

SA Sallis, John. *Phenomenology and the Return to Beginnings.*

Pittsburgh, Duquesne University Press, 1973.

SC Schaper, Eva. *Prelude to Aesthetics*. London, Allen and Unwin, Ltd., 1968.

SE Schiller, J. P. *I. A. Richards' Theory of Literature*. New Haven, Yale University Press, 1969.

SF Segal, S. J. Imagery: *Current Cognitive Approaches*. New York, Academic Press, 1971.

SH Shakespeare, William. *The Complete Works of William Shakespeare*. New York, Houghton Mifflin Co., 1906.

SI Sheehan, P. W. *The Function and Nature of Imagery*. New York, Academic Press, 1972.

SJ Sherburne, Donald. *A Whiteheadean Aesthetic*. New Haven, Anchor Books/Yale University Press, 1970.

SP Singer, Peter. *The Expanding Circle: Ethics and Sociobiology*. New York: Farrar, Strauss & Giroux, 1981.

SN Snell, Bruno. *The Discovery of the Mind*. Translated by T. G. Rosenmeyer. Cambridge, Harvard University Press, 1953.

SO Snyder, Gary, *Earth House Hold*. New York: New Directions, 1969, p. 105)

SR Stanley, Steven. *The New Evolutionary Timetable: Fossils, Genes and the Origin of Species*. New York: Basic Books, 1981.

SS Stevens, Peter, *Patterns in Nature*. Boston: Little Brown, 1974.

ST Stevens, Wallace. *The Collected Poems of Wallace Stevens*. New York, Alfred A. Knopf, 1974.

TA Tagliacozzo, G., editor. *Giambattista Vico*. Baltimore, Johns Hopkins Press, 1969.

TAR Taran, Leonardo. *Parmenides*. Princeton, Princeton University Press, 1965.

TH Thomas, Dylan. *The Poems of Dylan Thomas*. New York, New Directions Pub. Co., 1971.

UN Untermeyer, Louis. *Modern American Poetry/Modern British Poetry*. New York, Harcourt, Brace and World, Inc., 1962.

VI Vico, Giambattista. *The New Science*. Translated by T. G. Bergen and M.H. Fisch. Ithaca, Cornell University Press, 1948.

WA Waddington, Conrad. *The Evolution of an Evolutionist* Ithaca: Cornell University Press, 1975.

WB Weiss, P. "One Plus One is not Two," IN: *The Neurosciences*, G. Quarton et al., eds. New York: Rockefeller University Press, 1967.

WC Wheeler, John. et al. *Gravitation*. San Francisco: Freeman, 1971.

WE Wheelwright, Philip. *Metaphor and Reality*. Bloomington, Indiana University Press, 1962.

WH White, David. "Husserl and the poetic consciousness," *The*

Personalist, 53:4 (Autumn, 1972), pp. 408-424.

WI Whitehead, Alfred North. *The Adventure of Ideas*. New York, Macmillan, 1933.

WJ ___. *Modes of Thought*. New York, Free Press, 1968.

WK ___. *Process and Reality*. New York, Macmillan, 1929.

WF ___*The Function of Reason* Boston: Beacon Press, 1958, p. 8.

WH Whittaker, R. H. "On the Broad Classification of Organisms." *Quarterly Review of Biology* 34 (1959): 210-226.

WI Wiener, Norbert. *The Human Use of Human Beings*. New York: Avon, 1967.

WJ Wittbecker, Alan E. 1970. *Ordering Spaces & Living Places*. Newark: Shamrock Press.

WK Wittbecker, Alan E. 1970. *Eutopias: Commonwealth of Earth*. Newark: Shamrock Press.

WL Wittgenstein, Ludwig. *Philosophical Investigations*. New York, Macmillan, 1958.

WM ___. *Tractatus LogicoPhilosophicus*. London, Routledge and Kegan Paul, 1961.

WR Wordsworth, William. *Poetical Works*. Edited by T. Hutchinson. London, Oxford University Press, 1932.

UX Von Uexkull, J. "A Stroll Through the World of Animals and Men," In *Instinctive Behavior*, C. Schiller, ed. (New York: International Universities Press, 1957).

YOU Yoos, G. "A phenomenological look at metaphor," *Philosophy and Phenomenological Research*, 32:1 (September, 1971), pp. 78-88.

YU Yutang Lin. *The Wisdom of Lao Tse*. New York, Random House, 1948.

ZA Zaner, Richard. *The Problem of Embodiment*. The Hague, Martinus Nijhoff, 1971.

5.2. *Index of Names*

5.3. *Biography of Alan Wittbecker*

During a brief career in astrophysics and astronomy at the University of Arizona, where he worked on mathematical models of stars and on spectrometric analysis, Wittbecker spent his daylight hours climbing trees and trying to track mountain lions; his constant companions were a mouse and squirrel, who shared his trailer near the observatory on Mount Lemon.

Encouraged by research budget cuts to pursue a different direction, Wittbecker went to graduate school in philosophy, psychology, anthropology, and ecology. As a graduate student in 1970, he was a cofounder of the G. P. Marsh Institute for Research in Ecology, where he worked for 22 years, including three separate years as Director, as the position rotated annually. He worked on a wide variety of projects, from forest monitoring and ecosystem restoration to country-wide wolf monitoring, in many countries, including Bulgaria, Canada, Mexico, Norway, and Russia. When funding was in short supply, he worked in other occupations, including librarian, systems engineer, computer consultant, editor, graphic artist, typesetter, housepainter, television repairman, cook, gymnastics coach, carpenter, clinical psychologist at a drug abuse clinic, Austin Healy auto mechanic, tree-planter, and college instructor.

In 1976, with three partners, Wittbecker cofounded Nieman Ryan Community Designs, specializing in private and urban local landscape design—but, also designing books, posters, journals, packages, landscapes, and buildings. In 1983, he finished his doctorate at International College, working with Michael W. Fox, John B. Cobb, Jr., Paolo Soleri, David Klein, Henryk Skolimowski, Neil Evernden, Paul Shepard, and Buckminster Fuller. He continued his postgraduate education until 1999, in landscape ecology, forestry, conservation biology, zoology, and genetics.

In 1991, Wittbecker founded SynGeo ArchiGraph, a firm specializing in global and regional designs; he created designs for several bioregions, as well as international frameworks. A year later he set up the educational program for the Ecoforestry Institute, becoming an Instructor in 1994, journal Editor in 1995, and Director from 1997 to 2006. He has worked in public and private forests from British Columbia to California.

He is the author of eight books, including *REviewing thinking turning*, which won an Eppie award for best nonfiction on the web and *Good Forestry*, which won an award for best essay, for "The Health of Forests," and over 100 articles. He has also written series of essays in ecology and forestry for newspapers and journals.

A veteran of the U.S. Air Force, Wittbecker is also a returned Peace Corps Volunteer from Bulgaria, where he monitored wolves in the Central Balkan Mountains. He has used his education and interests to explore a spectrum of ecological applications, from research on forest pests—larch casebearers, cedar powderworms, coyotes, and bears—to the political implications of the protection of species and habitats.

When not engaged in preservation activities, he enjoys walking, swimming, reading, and drawing, at the Altazor forest in western Idaho. To discuss any of these essays with him, contact him at home@syngeo.org.

5.4. *Author's Note*

To make up for the loss of trees and their services, as a result of my use of paper in these books, I have planted over nine thousand trees, during a period of twenty years, at the Altazor Forest in Idaho. More plantings are planned in Oregon forests and Virginia forest farms.

Colophon

Type: Adobe Caslon Pro
Display Type: Caslon
Book Design: Rian Garcia Calusa Designs
Cover Design: Rian Garcia Calusa
Graphics/Paintings: Alan Wittbecker, 1975-92
Title Page Drawing: Alan Wittbecker, 1974
Author Photograph: Lena Hagen, 1976
Editing: J. Garcia B. of Rian Garcia Calusa

Publishing: Clio Press, M&RW, and CreateSpace
Hardware: Macintosh G5
Software: Adobe CS5 InDesign & Acrobat
Furious Charge & Entertainment: Pippi Frog
Spiritual & Material Support: Precious Woulfe